FICTION   Egleton, Clive.
EGLETON
          Cry havoc.

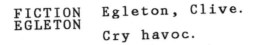

DATE			

Cry Havoc

Cry Havoc

CLIVE EGLETON

 St. Martin's Minotaur ♔ New York

www.minotaurbooks.com

Library of Congress Cataloging-in-Publication Data

Egleton, Clive.
    Cry havoc / Clive Egleton.—1st St. Martin's Minotaur ed.
       p. cm.
    ISBN 0-312-30943-0
    1. Ashton, Peter (Fictitious character)—Fiction. 2. Intelligence officers—Fiction. 3. Europe, Eastern—Fiction. 4. England—Fiction. I. Title.
PR6055.G55C795 2003
823'.914—dc21   2002191964

First published in Great Britain by Hodder and Stoughton
A division of Hodder Headline

First St. Martin's Minotaur Edition: August 2003

10 9 8 7 6 5 4 3 2 1

This book is for Colin and Christine Stephens

Cry Havoc

Chapter 1

Landon shoved both hands deeper into the pockets of his topcoat and hunched up against the cold. Even for early February it was a miserable day with a slate-coloured sky promising more than just the occasional flurry of snow that accompanied a biting east wind. Funerals were a gut-wrenching business for the next of kin at the best of times; how much worse it must be for Mary Orchard, faced with this awful weather, was difficult to imagine. Landon told himself that if a few more people had attended the funeral service itself, he wouldn't be here now, standing by the graveside. The fact was, he had had very little to do with Bill Orchard. True, they had worked for the same 'Firm' but Orchard had been the Assistant Director in charge of the Asian Department, whereas until very recently, he had been a lowly Grade II intelligence officer on the South American Desk.

As for the widow, Landon had met her for the first time a fortnight ago yesterday, on Wednesday, 22 January. He and Roy Kelso, the Assistant Director who ran the Admin Wing, had gone down to Wrotham ostensibly to advise Mary Orchard that she would receive fifty per cent of the pension her late husband had accrued up to the date of his death. In reality their task had been to impress upon her that on no account should she tell the coroner that Bill had spent the better part of twenty-five years in the Secret Intelligence Service. The SIS had always had an aversion to any kind of publicity, let alone the distinctly unfavourable coverage

Orchard was bound to attract if the media learned of his connection with the service.

Sometime during the night of 20/21 January, Orchard had slipped out of bed, put on a dressing gown, and without disturbing his wife, gone downstairs and let himself out of the house. In his bare feet he had walked across the gravel drive and entered the detached garage, locking the door behind him. He had then cut a ten-foot length from the garden hose and shoved one end in the exhaust pipe, holding it in place with a number of cleaning rags. The rear offside window had been lowered approximately an inch to accommodate the other end of the hose and the gap sealed with adhesive tape in order to make the interior airtight. That accomplished, Orchard had got into the Audi, switched on the ignition and started the engine.

He had left no farewell note. His colleagues couldn't think of a single reason why he should have wanted to commit suicide; neither could Mary Orchard. He appeared to have had no financial worries and he had certainly not been under any kind of stress at the workplace. The only time colleagues could remember seeing him upset was roughly fifteen months ago when his four-year-old, top-of-the-range Audi had been stolen from the parking area outside Wrotham and Borough Green station. A few days later the police had found the car in a field three miles from Maidstone. The Audi had been totally trashed. All four wheels had been stolen, the main beams, side- and taillight assemblies had been smashed, the seats slashed with a knife and the paintwork burned with sulphuric acid.

The subsequent discovery that the radiator had been drained and the engine left running, coupled with the estimate submitted by the garage had persuaded the insurance company that the car was beyond economical repair. They had therefore given Orchard a cheque for the residual value of the car based on its age, which had left him several thousand out of pocket when it came to buying a replacement, a fact he had bitterly resented. However, Orchard had not been the sort of man to harbour a grudge, and within a fortnight or so the imagined sharp practice of the insurance company had ceased to rankle. The new Audi had become his pride and joy and Landon had heard it said that the car meant more to him than his wife. Landon thought it strange that Orchard should have used his car as his means of self-destruction. It was like an act of wanton vandalism.

The interment over, the mourners automatically formed up to murmur condolences to the widow. Drawn by the herd instinct, London moved round the open grave and tagged on to the end of the line, his brain working overtime to think of something to say that didn't sound trite. He needn't have bothered; before he could say a word, Mary Orchard stretched out her hands and seized both of his.

'Thank you so much for coming, Mr Landon,' she said in a firm voice. 'It was very good of you.'

'Please . . . it was nothing,' Landon said, and was ashamed of himself for mentally bitching about the funeral.

'You will come back to the house, won't you?'

'Yes, of course I will.'

It was the last thing Landon wanted to do but he couldn't think of an excuse to decline the invitation that wouldn't sound contrived. In a curious way he also felt responsible for Roy Kelso's behaviour when they'd called on Mary Orchard less than forty-eight hours after her husband had killed himself. Kelso might be a very competent administrator but his manner had been tactless, pompous and downright overbearing, especially when he'd counselled her about the inquest. 'It's your duty to lie to the coroner about Bill's career,' Kelso had told her bluntly.

'I take it you're all right for transport?'

Landon turned to face the elegant-looking woman standing

next to Mary Orchard. 'Yes, I am,' he said. 'My car's parked outside the cemetery.'

The woman nodded, placed a hand under Mary's elbow and steered her towards the gates. 'Time we were going,' she said in a tone that brooked no argument.

Landon followed the two women at a discreet distance. They were, he noted, roughly the same height – approximately five feet seven in their high-heeled boots, which made them some eight inches shorter than himself. There was a vague family likeness about them and he wondered if they were sisters. According to the records maintained by the Security Vetting and Technical Services Division at Vauxhall Cross, Mary Orchard had been born on 27 April 1950. The elegant sister was a lot slimmer and for this reason alone, he judged her to be the younger of the two by some years.

The Orchards lived in a house called Downdale, situated in splendid isolation at the foot of the escarpment outside Wrotham. Standing well back from the road on an acre of land, the five-bedroom house with detached garage had been built in the 1920s when it had probably cost under three thousand. At today's inflated prices Landon guessed the property would fetch upwards of a million. The garden featured an ornamental pond, evergreen shrubs and a lawn that sloped downwards to meet the gravel drive. By the time Landon arrived, just moments after Mary Orchard and her sister, most of the available space had been taken up by half a dozen cars parked at irregular intervals. It took him all of five minutes to squeeze his Ford Escort in the narrow gap between a BMW 8-series and a Bentley Continental R.

Landon draped his topcoat over the hall table and walked on through to the drawing room, drawn there by a low buzz of conversation. Mary Orchard and her sister were holding court in the front of the French windows at the far end of the room, but they were the only faces he recognised. After taking a glass of red wine from the tray of drinks on offer, Landon gravitated towards the nearest group of strangers and waited for an opportunity to say a few words to Mary before leaving. He was about to introduce himself when out of the corner of his eye he saw the elegant sister moving purposefully in his direction. He half turned to face her and stood there rooted to the spot, like a rabbit transfixed by the headlights of an oncoming vehicle. There was a professional smile on her lips that was not reflected in her eyes.

'I'm Eleanor Gadsby, Mary's elder sister,' she said coolly, and drew him away from the others. 'I know all about you, Mr Landon and the people you work for.'

Her tone suggested she had a very large chip on her shoulder and was about to give him a piece of her mind. 'What exactly are you inferring, Ms Gadsby?' he asked quietly.

IMPLYING

'You mean you don't know?'

'I'm afraid not,' Landon said, and managed an apologetic smile.

'My mistake. I was forgetting you're only the office boy, or is it middle management?'

'Could we get to the point?' Landon asked as politely as he could under provocation.

'The point is your superiors killed my brother-in-law.'

'You're saying the coroner got it wrong?'

'My sister is a light sleeper. She would have heard Billy get out of bed if she hadn't been drugged.'

'Your sister never even hinted there had been foul play to Mr Kelso or me when we saw her.'

'Foul play – what a quaint expression.' A mocking smile made a brief appearance and was superseded by a glacial expression. 'Mary didn't say anything because she was afraid.'

Afraid? Mary Orchard? That wasn't how Landon remembered their meeting on Wednesday, 22 January. Her husband had been dead a little over twenty-four hours but you would never have known that. She had been totally in control of her emotions and Landon had come away wondering if she had shed so much as a tear for Bill Orchard.

'You don't believe me, do you, Mr Landon?'

'Let's talk about the drug and how it was administered. Did somebody inject it or did Mary imbibe the substance unknowingly? Then again, maybe your brother-in-law put something into the good-night cup of hot chocolate or whatever it is she has before going to bed. I mean, why couldn't Bill have taken steps to ensure his wife didn't wake up?'

'You've forgotten there was no suicide note.'

'It's not mandatory. Lots of people top themselves without bothering to explain why.'

'When was the last time you saw Billy?'

Landon couldn't remember offhand and had to work backwards from the day he'd heard the news of Orchard's suicide.

'It must have been Thursday, the sixteenth of January,' he said presently.

'Did he seem depressed to you?'

'I can't say, I'm not in his department, and we didn't have much to do with one another.'

'You merely passed each other in the corridor from time to time and you gave him a little nod? Was that the extent of your relationship with my brother-in-law?'

'It was a bit more than that,' Landon said uncomfortably.

'But you never saw Billy looking worried? Or agitated? Or showing any other signs that he was finding the job too much for him and was feeling stressed?'

Landon didn't say anything. As far as he was concerned Eleanor Gadsby was talking about a stranger. Around Vauxhall Cross, Orchard had been seen as a very laid-back character. Nothing had seemed to ruffle him, which wasn't altogether surprising since the Asian Department was regarded as a bit of a doddle. Except for the long-running dispute between India and Pakistan over Kashmir, and the bloody guerrilla war being waged by the Tamil Tigers in Sri Lanka, Asia didn't contain any of the world's hot spots, and UK interests were not threatened. The staff worked normal office hours and Bill Orchard was invariably amongst the first to leave the building.

'I can see you have a closed mind,' Eleanor said, her voice still low. 'Call me when it has opened a fraction. Gadstar Promotions, Bruton Place, off Berkeley Square. You'll find our number in the phone book.'

'What do you promote?'

'Everything and everybody at a price.'

'Well, that let's me out,' Landon said cheerfully. 'I couldn't possibly afford you.'

'There could come a time when you might have to, Mr Landon.' Somehow she made it sound like a veiled threat.

Landon glanced at his wristwatch, saw that it was ten after four and decided he had done his bit. He'd also had enough of Ms Gadsby, with her snide observations and her inference that the SIS had murdered Bill Orchard – or 'Billy' as she insisted on calling him. Orchard had committed suicide and, if Mary was anything like her older sister, he could understand why the man had decided to end it all.

'I ought to be going,' Landon murmured.

Eleanor put out her hand to detain him a moment longer. 'Before you do,' she said, 'tell me one thing. Were you aware that apart from Mary the last person to see Billy alive was Jill Sheridan? She was here the night he was killed.'

'How very interesting. Now, if you will excuse me . . .'

Landon edged his way towards the French windows, waited for an opportunity to say goodbye to Mary Orchard, then collected his topcoat from the hall table and left the house. Manoeuvring the Ford Escort out of the parking space and turning it around within the width of the drive required a degree of skill and a considerable amount of patience.

So Jill Sheridan had visited Downdale a few hours before Orchard had committed suicide? Landon shook his head. As if the beleaguered Deputy Director General of the SIS wasn't already in enough trouble. Until very recently Jill had been in the fast lane and destined to become the first woman to head the SIS. That had been apparent to her peer group from the day she had been appointed to run the Mid-East Department, five months before her thirty-sixth birthday. She was attractive, highly intelligent, had friends in high places and was an icon and role model for every ambitious woman in the SIS.

One of her powerful and intimate friends was Robin Urquhart, the senior of four deputy under secretaries at the Foreign and Commonwealth Office. He was the man who had promoted her meteoric rise to Deputy DG; ironically he was also the man who was indirectly responsible for derailing her career. Believing Ms Sheridan to be as in love with him as he was with her, Urquhart had decided to divorce his wife, Rosalind, something most people thought he should have done years ago. In keeping with her vindictive nature, Rosalind had gone public and launched a hate campaign against Jill Sheridan in the tabloid press. The fact that Rosalind had been paralysed from the waist down in a hunting accident had won her the sympathy vote initially. Unfortunately for Jill Sheridan the damage had already been done by the time the press discovered the truth about Rosalind. Although Jill had survived the fallout, it was common knowledge that she would go no further.

Now there were grounds for thinking Ms Eleanor Gadsby represented an even greater threat. Senior management might consider he was overreacting but Landon reckoned they should be apprised of the situation a.s.a.p. Trouble was, all incoming calls to Vauxhall Cross over an unguarded link were routinely monitored by friends and potential foes alike and his mobile didn't have a secure speech facility. However, he knew some-body who did have access to a scrambler. Keeping his eyes on the road, he tapped out the private number of the Ashtons' residence in Bosham and asked Harriet if she would relay a message to her husband on the other means.

Until 31 December 1996 Ashton had been a fourth-floor man with an office that afforded an unrivalled view of the rail tracks between Vauxhall and Waterloo. Never in his wildest dreams had he imagined that one day he would be given a department of his own and end up on the top floor with the other assistant directors. Neither had Rowan Garfield, Roger Benton, Winston Reid and Roy Kelso, who were respectively in charge of the European, Pacific Basin and the Rest of the World and Mid-East departments and the Admin Wing. They were not alone; there was a fairly large body of opinion in Whitehall, particularly within the Foreign and Commonwealth Office, that regarded Ashton as a loose cannon.

Ashton reckoned he had three people to thank for his unexpected promotion – Rowan Garfield, Victor Hazelwood, the Director General, and Jill Sheridan in that order. Following the collapse of the Soviet Union, the Warsaw Pact Countries had ceased to be a separate entity and they had been merged with the European Department. The Treasury had also insisted the number of desk officers should be reduced. As a result Garfield had ended up running the largest department in the SIS with a much-diminished establishment. His bailiwick extended from Vladivostock in the east to Lisbon in the west; from Vadsø in the far north of Norway to Reggio in the toe of Italy. It was an impossibly large land mass for one assistant director to oversee and Garfield had said so time and time again until the Treasury had given way.

It had been Victor Hazelwood, Ashton's guide and mentor from the day he had joined the SIS, who had hived off the whole of what had once been the Soviet Union from the European Department and had fought tooth and nail to give the new organisation to his protégé.

Finally, Ashton had to thank Jill Sheridan for the way she had justified the proposed establishment by anticipating every possible objection the Treasury might raise. To give even more weight to the proposed East European Department she had included the Balkan hotspots of Serbia, Bosnia, Hertzegovina and Kosovo. To round things off, the Assistant Director of the new department would be responsible for the SIS element in MO(SP). Since this stood for Military Operations (Special Projects) Ashton could only assume the Foreign and Commonwealth Office had no idea what the abbreviation meant, otherwise this cell within the Ministry of Defence would have been wrested from him.

Ashton was reading the latest intelligence update on the political situation in Bosnia Hertzegovina when the telephone rang. Recognising the distinctive treble, he reached beyond the unguarded British Telecom extension and lifted the transceiver from the Mozart. Harriet was the last person he expected to hear on the secure link.

'What's happened?' he asked. 'Don't tell me that wretched oil-fired boiler is acting up again?' The ancient Wallflame 90 had been the only drawback to the house in Bosham Harriet had found.

'Relax, it's working perfectly since the central heating man looked at it.' Harriet paused to tell Edward not to poke his baby sister Carolyn in the stomach with his finger, then said, 'Better have your scratch pad handy. I've just had a long phone call from Will Landon.'

'Sounds ominous.'   .

'It is. Mary's sister claims that Bill Orchard was murdered by The Firm. Ms Eleanor Gadsby also claims that Jill Sheridan was the last person outside the family to see Bill before his death. Seems she called at the house the night Bill decided to end it all.'

'Jill never mentioned that she had been down to Wrotham. Isn't she the sly one?'

'I thought you would be surprised.'

'I don't suppose Will told you when I might expect to see him?'

'That's where you're wrong,' Harriet said. 'Provided the rush hour isn't too horrendous Will reckons to be with you by six or thereabouts.'

The phone picked up a faint wailing noise and Harriet told him she would have to go before Edward did something awful to Carolyn. Ashton replaced the transceiver, than rang Brian Thomas, Head of the Security Vetting and Technical Services Division to warn the ex-detective chief superintendent that he was on his way down to the third floor to see him.

Thomas had joined the SIS as a Grade III intelligence officer on his retirement from the Met. In those days he had been one of a team of three officers who had conducted the in-depth subject interview, the final crucial stage of the positive vetting procedure. His laid-back approach enabled him to strike an immediate rapport with the people he was interviewing to such an extent that they felt a need to disclose some adverse character trait that raised doubts concerning their suitability for positive vetting clearance. In that respect he was like a priest in a confessional. But it wasn't only his skill as an interrogator that made him such a valuable intelligence officer. A significant number of the police officers who'd served under Brian Thomas in the Met were now themselves chief superintendents and above, and they were prepared to do him the odd favour now and again.

'So what brings you here, Peter?' Thomas enquired when Ashton tapped on the open door to his office.

'Bill Orchard. I want to have a look at his security file.'

'Fine. Have you got an access slip signed by the Director or Roy Kelso?'

'No.'

'Well, I'm sorry but I can't let you have it.'

'Oh, come on, Brian, the guy's dead.'

'Doesn't make any difference. And you should know the rules, you were in charge of this division not so very long ago.'

'OK. The fact is certain allegations were made at the funeral by a member of the family,' Ashton said carefully. 'I want to have a quick look at the file to see if we have anything on this relative.'

'What about the family history I prepared for Will Landon?'

'It's not detailed enough.'

Thomas sighed. 'I could get shot for this,' he said, then went over to the combination safe and returned with Orchard's security file. 'You mind reading it in my presence, Peter?'

'Not a bit.'

Ashton went through the file, reading every subject interview, starting with the initial clearance by PV. He paid special attention to the supplementary interview that occurred when Orchard informed the SIS that he was getting married. Mary Orchard, he learned, had a brother but no sister called Eleanor Gadsby.

Chapter 2

Victor Hazelwood assured his wife that he hadn't forgotten they were having people to dinner and promised he wouldn't stay late at the office, then put the phone down. He wasn't sure who derived the most pleasure from the knighthood, which had appeared in the New Year Honours List – Alice, his wife, or his personal assistant, Mrs Dilys Crowther. The day after the list had been published it had given Alice enormous pleasure to place an order with their local printer for five hundred invitation cards that began with the regal phrase 'Sir Victor and Lady Hazelwood'. As for Mrs Crowther, she never missed an opportunity to refer to him as Sir Victor when conveying some imagined desire of his to one of the lesser mortals of the administrative staff. Assistant directors and below who wished to see the DG had always had to go through Mrs Crowther. However, the recent installation of a new office intercom that did not make her voice sound tinny meant that instead of ringing Hazelwood's extension, she was able to announce the name of his visitor like some major domo.

Now a faint click told him Dilys was about to use the wretched instrument for the umpteenth time that day.

'Mr Ashton's here to see you, Sir Victor,' Dilys Crowther informed him.

'So send the man in,' Hazelwood said, and simultaneously reached for yet another Burma cheroot in the ornately carved cigar box on his desk.

Hazelwood was conscious that to a certain extent he

wouldn't be where he was today had it not been for Ashton. In the intelligence world there were those who liked to sit back and analyse events as they occurred with a view to anticipating what might follow. Hazelwood, on the other hand, had earned himself the reputation of being a thruster, a man who made things happen by taking the fight to the potential enemy. Ashton had been the cutting edge of his policy and no matter how you looked at it, he hadn't always done right by the younger man.

He had failed to support Ashton over TRIPWIRE, the Soviet plan to lay a nuclear minefield with Atomic Demolition Munitions as the Red Army withdrew from East Germany. Almost single-handed Ashton had forced Colonel General Lobanov, Commander of 6 Guards Tank Army to remove the ADMs that had already been planted. Ashton should have been lionised; instead he had been put out to grass in the Admin Wing because the then Director General had believed that he had got too friendly with Lieutenant-Colonel Alexi Leven, the GRU officer in charge of the Arms Control Unit at Potsdam, and had been contaminated in the process. Hazelwood knew he should have defended Ashton but he had just taken over the Eastern Bloc following the sudden death of his predecessor and he had felt too insecure to take on the DG.

But that hadn't been an isolated instance. Only a few months ago he had bowed to political pressure and hadn't lifted a finger to safeguard Ashton's anonymity after he had been subpoenaed to give evidence at a coroner's inquest into the death of Kevin Hayes of the Provisional IRA. The Ashtons, of course, had been given new identities. Unfortunately their cover had lasted a bare seven weeks, thanks to an IRA sympathiser in the Civil Service. It could only have happened to Ashton.

'You're not about to upset the apple cart, are you?' Hazelwood asked, giving voice to his thoughts as Ashton entered the office.

'I could be,' Ashton said and proceeded to tell him about the strange encounter Will Landon had had at Bill Orchard's funeral.

Hazelwood listened to what Ashton had to say and didn't like what he heard. Orchard had had a sister-in-law they knew nothing about? Why had Bill Orchard omitted to include Eleanor Gadsby in the names of next of kin he'd submitted before his wife-to-be was cleared by the Security Vetting and Technical Services Division? And what was Jill Sheridan doing at their house near Wrotham the night Bill Orchard had evidently decided to commit suicide?

'Where's Landon?' he asked, interrupting Ashton.

'Will's on the way back from Wrotham. He should be here shortly. I assume you'll want to see him?'

Hazelwood shook his head. 'Not immediately. In any case, Landon is on your team now so you should have first crack at him. Find out what he made of Eleanor Gadsby. Did he, for instance, think she wasn't quite the ticket?'

If the woman was mentally unbalanced her allegations could be safely ignored, though Hazelwood doubted if they would be that lucky. There would have to be an internal investigation and just who should head it was something of a problem. Ordinarily the job would go to the Deputy DG but Jill Sheridan was implicated. Kelso would only succeed in putting everyone's back up; Winston Reid, latterly of the Foreign and Commonwealth Office, hadn't been with the SIS long enough; and there was no telling where any investigation led by either Rowan Garfield or Roger Benton might wander. As a former detective chief superintendent, Brian Thomas would seem an ideal choice but he lacked the necessary seniority should MI5 become involved. That left Ashton.

'You'll have to do it, Peter.'

'Do what?'

'Head the investigation. I want chapter and verse on this sister-in-law who never was.'

'The lady would appear to know Jill,' Ashton said pointedly.

Hazelwood could well understand why the younger man would prefer to give Jill a wide berth. Eight years ago they had been lovers with a joint mortgage on a flat in Victoria Road, Surbiton. They had even set a date for the wedding, then a posting to Bahrain, which would really put Jill in the fast lane, had come up, and she had suddenly realised that she wasn't yet ready to rein in on such a promising career.

'You don't have to worry about Jill,' Hazelwood told him. 'I'll speak to her when she returns from Florida on Tuesday.'

'Thanks, Victor.'

'Landon is a newcomer to the Russian Desk and won't be missed. Get him to do the spadework.'

'I was planning to.'

'I'm glad to hear it.' Hazelwood lit the cheroot he'd been holding all this time between the index and second finger of his left hand, and savoured the aroma. 'I want blanket security on this investigation,' he continued. 'For the time being the need to know is restricted to you, me and Landon.'

'I'd like to include Brian Thomas.'

'Why?'

'We might want to run Eleanor Gadsby through the normal vetting process to see if she has ever come to the notice of MI5. We'd also learn whether or not the National Identification Bureau has anything on her.'

'You can't do that until you have ascertained the date and place of her birth. Talk to me again when you have those details.'

'OK.' Ashton paused, then said, 'Are there any restrictions I should know about?'

Hazelwood could tell that Ashton was angry and didn't like being reined in but that was something he would have to get used to.

'Listen to me, Peter. You're no longer a foot soldier; the days when you were the cutting edge have gone for good. You have people like Will Landon to do that; your job is to point them in the direct direction. Do I make myself clear?'

'Absolutely.'

Hazelwood toyed with the idea of warning Ashton to watch his step, before deciding that would be the equivalent of teaching his grandmother to suck eggs. Ashton was no fool. He knew there were any number of people in Whitehall who were just waiting for him to put his foot in it.

A splitting headache and the sun playing on her face finally roused Jill Sheridan. Rolling over on to her right side she reluctantly opened both eyes and peered at the clock radio on the bedside table. Eleven thirty: surely it couldn't be that late? Still only half awake, Jill kicked the sheet off, crawled out of bed and staggered over to what she thought was the bathroom, only to find the door opened into a walk-in cupboard. Backing out she tried the next door and for a split second wondered who was the ravaged-looking woman she could see in the full-length mirror on the facing wall. What the hell had she done with her satin pyjamas, and whose trendy clothes were hanging up in the cupboard?

And why had she applied mauve-coloured chocolate lipstick to her nipples, a black leather collar two inches wide around her neck and similar bands attached to the wrists and ankles? In God's name, who had done this to her? Jill felt the bile rise in her throat and just made it to the toilet before she threw up. As if in a trance, she flushed the lavatory, and rinsed out her mouth with a glass of water, then on legs that threatened to buckle under her, Jill returned to the other room and sat down on the double bed.

She examined the cuffs on her wrists and discovered that one had a hook, the other an eyelet. The same applied to the black leather bands around the ankles. Nobody had to tell Jill what they were for; sick with apprehension, she still managed to undo the straps even though her hands wouldn't stop shaking. The collar round her throat had been fastened behind the neck but although the buckle was easy to reach, it was shielded by some kind of metal attachment. The collar was, however, fairly loose and slipping her fingers inside the leather band, Jill moved the buckle round to the front. A hand-held mirror on what passed for a dressing table showed that the metal attachments consisted of two metal tags with eyelets, which had been stitched to the collar either side of the buckle and then fastened together with a tiny padlock.

How to pick a lock using a hairgrip, nail scissors or a pair of tweezers was one of the tricks Jill had been taught when she had attended the SIS induction course at Amberley Lodge. Hairgrips were out of fashion these days but there was a nail file among the contents of her handbag, which had been tipped out on the dressing table. Suddenly her heart started to palpitate and she found it difficult to breathe. Knowing this was the classic symptom of a panic attack was no help because whoever had brought her to this hotel had obviously been through her handbag. Her purse hadn't been taken but the two hundred and sixty-eight dollars it had contained plus forty-five pounds in sterling had gone. So too had all the American Express traveller's cheques and the United Airlines plane ticket. The thief had tossed her passport on to the floor and had shown similar contempt for the Gold Mastercard issued by Lloyds Bank, possibly because it looked too English.

The traveller's cheques could be replaced within twenty-four hours and she could purchase a flight ticket to Heathrow with the credit card. But right now she was marooned stark naked in some sleazy hotel without so much as a nickel to her name.

'Calm down and stay cool. You've got a good brain so try using it to get out of this mess.' It was sound advice but not easy to put into practice when you couldn't even recall what you had been wearing last night. Jesus, this had to be the foul-up to end all foul-ups. With Victor Hazelwood's agreement she had taken three weeks off to sort herself out. Robin Urquhart had got his decree absolute and was pressing her to marry him but she had only just turned thirty-eight, and the idea of spending the rest of her life with a man eighteen years her senior was a daunting prospect. She had chosen to go to Florida because the average temperature was practically guaranteed to be in the high seventies and February was pure hell in England.

All senior intelligence officers were required to lodge their travel plans with the Admin Wing, and for the first six days Jill hadn't deviated from her itinerary. Departing Heathrow on Tuesday, 21 January she had flown to Tampa via Washington DC by United Airlines. On arrival at Tampa International Airport, she'd rented a Chevrolet Beretta from Hertz and had then spent two nights at the Wyndham Harbor Hotel before driving on down the Gulf Coast to Marco Island. On her third day at the Marriot Hotel she had made the acquaintance of Tom Kransky, a media consultant from Baltimore. For Jill the attraction had been immediate. Kransky was her age, a shade over six feet and handsome with it. He had an engaging personality and was the only man she had met who could best be described as charismatic. She had left for Miami on the Monday; twenty-four hours later Tom Kransky had checked into the same hotel. Thereafter her planned itinerary had gone by the board. Key West was out, Ford Lauderdale was in, and the Chevrolet Beretta had suddenly become surplus to requirement.

Jill racked her brains trying to recall what had happened after they had checked into The Breakers early yesterday evening. She remembered visiting some bar in North Palm Beach and subsequently they had driven up and down the coast road between Jupiter and Boca Raton, sampling the local colour, as Tom had put it, but mostly her mind remained an obstinate blank. Wherever it was she had spent the night no way did this place resemble the five-star hotel built by one of the railroad barons whose name was just one more thing she couldn't recall.

No money, no clothes, no telephone in the room: everything she needed was back at The Breakers and only Tom Kransky could help her. As far as she knew this was one of his free days but that could be wishful thinking on her part. Jill picked up her bits and pieces on the dressing table and put them back in the handbag, then went over to the walk-in cupboard. The clothes had to be the working outfits of some hooker. Abbreviated miniskirts in PVC and denim that barely covered the crotch, satin blouses in lurid colours, six-inch-high heels and patent-leather boots. The hooker who wore them was about her height and build, and took a shoe at least one size smaller. Jill went through the entire wardrobe until she found a mini that hadn't been cut to emphasise the buttocks. A pale-violet-coloured shirtwaister was the least trashy item of clothing in that line, and while it didn't match any of the other items she'd taken, the blue denim jacket was almost modest in comparison with the others on the rail.

Before dressing, Jill went into the bathroom to freshen up. She would have given anything to stand under the shower but the wherewithal was lacking. There was only a small face towel resembling Jacob's coat of many colours that had not been laundered recently and the tiny cake of soap had obviously been used by the previous occupant. The face flannel, however, just about passed inspection. After what amounted to no more than a lick and a promise, Jill dressed in record time, ran a comb through her hair and left the room to make her way down to the lobby three floors below.

The desk clerk was a swarthy unkempt-looking man in an off-white undershirt and a pair of dark brown slacks that could have done with a visit to the dry-cleaners. His eyes were fixed on the portable TV on the counter and he didn't answer Jill when she asked if she might use the telephone. The desk clerk believed in treating everybody alike; he didn't take any notice of the hooker and her client either when they came in off the street and made straight for the elevator.

'I'm going to use the phone,' Jill snapped. 'I assume that's OK with you?'

'Cost you a dollar,' the man said, still totally engrossed in some long-running soap that had been dubbed in Spanish.

'I don't have any money,' Jill told him.

'Go out and earn some, you got the butt for it.'

Jill wasn't aware that anybody was standing close behind her until a man sniggered and began fondling her buttocks. At the height of Rosalind Urquhart's vilification when she was being hounded by the press, Jill had worked off her anger and humiliation in the gym, honing her skills at martial arts, which had lain dormant since the induction course. As the groper raised the miniskirt with one hand while unzipping his pants with the other, all her suppressed rage came bubbling to the surface. Pivoting on the balls of her bare feet, Jill swung round in an anticlockwise direction, left arm extended and rigid as a steel bar. The blow caught the groper high up on the left side of his head and sent him cannoning into the one armchair in the lobby. Arms flailing in an attempt to stay on his feet, his back hit the wall with a resounding thud as he went down. The people who had trained her all those years ago had included an element of kickboxing. Turning sideways on to her would-be rapist, she pumped out her right leg, driving the foot into his face with enough venomous force to break his nose and jaw. At Vauxhall Cross, Jill enjoyed a reputation for being ruthless: this was the physical side of it which nobody, not even Ashton, had been aware of.

The Cuban rapidly lost interest in the soap opera on the TV and stood up, one hand stealing under the counter.

'Don't even think about it,' Jill told him ominously.

'I do nothing,' the man said, and showed her both hands as proof of his good intentions.

'Step away from the counter.'

'What you want?'

'Just do it.'

'I am, I am,' the Cuban assured her.

Jill walked round the counter, opened the nearest drawer underneath and took out an old Smith & Wesson .38 she assumed the clerk had been groping for.

'Please, I give you no trouble.'

'Too right. Now get me The Breakers at Palm Beach.'

'Whaaat?'

'It's a hotel.'

'I not know the number.'

'Then look it up in the phone book.'

Another hooker, coming in off the street with a John in tow, immediately turned tail and left, unnerved by the revolver Jill was holding and at the sight of a man slumped against the wall bleeding profusely from the nose and mouth.

Anxious to please, the Cuban desk clerk rang The Breakers for Jill and handed her the phone when the switchboard operator at the hotel came on the line. There was no answer from Room 678 but the concierge was able to tell her that Mr Kransky could be reached on his mobile number 9361440275.

The swift response Jill got when she rang the mobile number suggested to her that Tom Kransky was not doing business with a client.

'I need your help,' she told him. 'I don't know what happened to me last night but I'm stranded. I've no money and no clothes, please come and get me.'

'Where are you?'

Jill cupped a hand over the mouthpiece while she asked the desk clerk the same question, then said, 'Apparently I'm at the Regal Hotel, Sixth and Atlantic Avenue, Highland Beach.'

'Apparently? Boy, you must have tied one on last night.'

'Can we talk about that later?'

'Sure we can. Expect me in forty minutes from now.'

Jill put the phone down. The adrenalin had ceased to flow and she suddenly felt spent.

Before it had been converted into an office for the head of the newly created East European Department, the room had been occupied by the code breakers. Situated on the west side of the building, the top-floor office afforded Ashton a glimpse of the river and an even better view of the rail tracks, this time between Vauxhall and Queenstown Road, Battersea. This evening, however, he had great difficulty in seeing the lights on Nine Elms Lane, which were a lot closer. The occasional flurries earlier in the day had been superseded by a moderately heavy snowfall, which made for hazardous driving conditions, particularly down in Kent. Ashton was therefore a little surprised when Landon walked into his office a mere ten minutes later than he had estimated.

'There was an accident on the A20 just beyond Swanley,' Landon said, as if an explanation was called for. 'Traffic was reduced to one lane on the dual carriageway.'

'That's OK, Will. I used the extra time to look up Mary Orchard's side of the family and we don't have any record of an older sister called Eleanor. There's a brother, Lawrence Gadsby, aged fifty-eight, whose last known address was in Church Stretton, but that was donkey's years ago.' Ashton paused, then said, 'Did you happen to meet him at the funeral?'

'No. Apart from conveying the usual condolences to Mary Orchard, I only talked to Eleanor Gadsby. I didn't see any man sitting next to Mary in the church or supporting her at the graveside. Truth is, I kept a low profile, which is what you wanted me to do.'

Ashton nodded. Victor Hazelwood had told him to detail

a middle-ranking intelligence officer to accompany Roy Kelso when he visited Mary Orchard on 22 January to explain her pension rights as a widow. Knowing how the Admin King could offend people, Victor had wanted someone there who could intervene should Mary become overwrought. Ashton had chosen Will Landon because he had only recently joined the department from the South American Desk and could be spared. Having made the acquaintance of Mary Orchard he had subsequently been the right man to represent The Firm at the funeral.

'So what do you know about Eleanor Gadsby, Will?' he asked.

'Very little, I'm afraid. She told me she was older than Mary but not by how much. At a guess I wouldn't have thought there was more than a couple of years between them. I know I didn't like her. She also struck me as being a very dangerous woman who is out to make trouble for us.'

'Which is why I want you to find out all you can about her.'

Ashton ripped the top sheet of paper from his scratch pad and gave it to Landon. 'Mary's date and place of birth, also her brother's. Put it through the shredder as soon as you've memorised the details.'

'Right.'

'Nobody, but nobody, is to know about this enquiry until I say so. No file is to be opened, nothing is to be recorded in writing. You report only to me. Got it?'

'You're the boss,' Landon told him cheerfully.

'Damn right I am,' Ashton said.

Tom Kransky was as good as his word and arrived at the Regal Hotel in exactly forty minutes from the time Jill had spoken to him. He had collected her suitcase from their room at The Breakers and no quick-change artist could have switched clothes faster than she did. Returning to the lobby from the hooker's room on the third floor, Jill released the cylinder from the frame of the Smith & Wesson, ejected six rounds and handed the empty revolver to the Cuban desk clerk.

'Give the man a dollar, Tom,' she said.

'What for?' Kransky asked.

'The phone call I made to you.'

The Cuban waved his hands in protest. 'No please, lady, is no charge. You not report unpleasantness to the police. Yes?'

There was nothing to show there had been any unpleasantness; the groper had crawled away somewhere while she had been upstairs changing.

'Let's get out of here, Tom,' Jill said.

'Yeah, the atmosphere is more than a little polluted.'

Kransky prised the suitcase from her grasp and, carrying it out to his Corvette, put it in the trunk. Then he opened the nearside door for her before walking round the car to get in behind the wheel.

'What's the matter?' Jill asked after he had been silent for a good five minutes. 'Cat got your tongue?'

'I'm waiting for an explanation.'

'What!'

'I'd like to know why you dumped me last night.'

'I think you had better tell me what happened.'

'You mean you don't remember?'

'Would I be asking if I did?' Jill said angrily.

'Yeah. I'm sorry, forget I said that.'

'So what happened?'

'We drove south to Boca Raton, took in a couple of bars, then headed back to Delray Beach where we stopped off at a place called Michael's.' Kransky paused as if uncertain how to continue, then said, 'That's where things started to go wrong. We'd had a couple of drinks before reaching Michael's; you were on Bloody Marys, I was sticking to plain tomato juice. We'd been there about twenty minutes when you had to use the facilities . . .'

'The what?'

'The powder room – a public lavatory for women.'

'Oh.'

'You were gone a long time.'

Tom had become concerned that something had happened to her and had been about to send in a rescue party when she had reappeared arm in arm with a blonde in her mid-to-late twenties.

'You told me her name was Sara and that we were going to make up a foursome with her husband, Dan, who was holding a booth for us.'

Michael's was one of those so-called sophisticated bars where the lights were dimmed in the belief this helped to create an air of intimacy. A dance floor with scarcely enough room for half a dozen couples and a three-piece combo did the rest.

'You got kind of friendly with husband, Dan,' Kransky said, choosing his words with care.

'How friendly?'

'There's no easy way to tell you this, Jill, but when you were on the dance floor together it looked like he was trying to hump you and you were enjoying it.'

'How did his wife take it?' she asked in a husky voice.

'Sara didn't seem to mind; she told me they had an open marriage.'

'Was I really that drunk?'

'I'd say you'd had more than enough to drink by then.'

Jill began to wish she hadn't probed quite so deeply because what Tom Kransky was telling her was getting worse by the minute. The way he told it, he had kept on at her to leave but she wouldn't have it. There had been no unpleasant scene in Michael's; that had happened outside in the parking lot when she had announced she was going home with Sara and Dan, and he could go fuck himself.

'That's when I took the hint and returned to The Breakers without you.'

'I don't remember any of this. I wake up naked in a strange hotel room, my money has been stolen and all my clothes have gone. I must have been drugged.'

'Maybe later, but not when you left me.'

'This swinging couple, what do we know about them?'

'I can't answer for you, but very little as far as I'm concerned. Dan told me he's an attorney and Sara is supposed to own several boutiques in Miami. They looked very presentable, otherwise I would never have left you in their company.'

Something wasn't right. She was getting a series of fleeting images, like photoflashes popping in front of her eyes. The girl she was seeing in her mind's eye was a blonde all right, but she was a lot older than Kransky had led her to believe and Michael's was not how he had described the bar either.

Chapter 3

Landon kept one eye on the clock behind reception, the other on the entrance to Vauxhall Cross. There was less than ten minutes to morning prayers, the daily briefing chaired by the DG and attended by the Deputy DG and heads of departments. Ashton normally arrived a good half-hour before the eight thirty deadline but this morning it was beginning to look as if his fast train to Waterloo was running late. Landon watched the minute hand move forward another notch and was resigned to catching him after the conference when he entered the lobby.

'If you are waiting for me,' Ashton told him, 'you've got less than nine minutes.'

'I think I'd better catch you after morning prayers.'

'Then you're in for a long wait.' Ashton continued walking towards the lifts and pressed the nearest call button. 'We're getting less money for the financial year 'ninety-seven-'ninety-eight than we asked for. Every assistant director will be fighting his own corner to make sure his department gets off lightly. Rowan Garfield is going to fight me tooth and nail because my little organisation was part of his empire when the estimates were submitted back in October.'

A bell pinged behind them, signalling the arrival of an empty car.

'Does this have anything to do with our conversation last night?' Ashton enquired as they stepped into the lift with half a dozen linguists from the fifth floor.

'Everything,' Landon said quietly.

'I thought it might.' Nothing further was said until they alighted at the top floor and were walking along the corridor towards the conference room.

'So what is it you want from me, Will?'

'Money,' Landon said bluntly. 'Without it we will get nowhere. Unless I can give the exact date and place of birth of Eleanor Gadsby the staff of the Office of Population Censuses and Surveys at St Catherine's House will be unable to produce a birth certificate for her, at least not at the drop of a hat. If I push them to do a trawl, their head man will want to know why—'

'And you know an easier way of doing it,' Ashton said, cutting him short.

'I think so.'

'Well, don't keep me in suspense, Will.'

'We go for a credit rating using a third party to obtain it.'

'Is this a theoretical solution or do you have some practical experience?'

'Between leaving Nottingham University and attending the SIS induction course at Amberley Lodge I worked for a finance company.'

'How much do you want?'

One of the things Landon liked about Ashton was his decisiveness. He also let you get on with the job, unlike his previous boss, Roger Benton, who was forever breathing down his neck.

'A hundred and fifty should do it, Peter.'

'You can go up to three hundred. If that's not enough, come and see me again.' Ashton opened the door to his office, shucked off the topcoat he was wearing and hung it up on an old-fashioned hat stand. 'Three minutes to go,' he said, glancing at his wristwatch. 'Is there anything else we need to discuss?'

'Not that I can think of.'

'Well, I'll tell you one thing, Will. Right now I wish I was in your shoes.'

'Why's that?'

'Because this is Roy Kelso's big day and he is going to make the most of it,' Ashton said, and disappeared into the conference room.

When Landon had worked for the Unicorn Trust Group a sizeable percentage of the working population did not have a bank account or a credit card. People in that socioeconomic group who wished to buy some major household item or a car were able to do so by entering into a hire purchase agreement with a finance company such as the Unicorn Trust Group. Before selling the item, the retailer checked the credit worthiness of the purchaser against the list of known bad debtors in the area. Among the questions on the hire purchase application form was one requesting details of any other agreements entered into. Any such previous agreement was, of course, a valuable means of assessing the financial prudence of the applicant. This was, however, no deterrent to a lot of people, who made livings by obtaining goods under false pretences.

Technically the item remained the property of the finance company until the final instalment had been paid. The finance company therefore had a special interest in tracing people who, for one reason or another, defaulted on their repayments. In Landon's day with the company, Unicorn Trust had used Fasttrack Associates, a debt-collecting agency, to deal with the problem.

Fasttrack Associates was still operating from the same address in Acton, a fact Landon had verified from the phone book. Before leaving Vauxhall Cross he'd also rung the firm on his own mobile and made an appointment to see a Mr Harry

Bennet, one of Fasttrack's foremost risk assessors, as the office manager had quaintly put it.

Landon judged Bennet to be roughly his own age. It was difficult to say immediately how tall the man was because he only half rose from his chair to greet Landon. He had a somewhat limp handshake, a plump round face, plump fingers, plump waistline and thighs to match. To Landon, he looked like a man who enjoyed his food and wasn't too fussed about his physique.

'So what made you come to us?' Bennet said after waving Landon to an upright chair. 'That's an obligatory question I'm obliged to ask.' A rather oily smile appeared on his mouth. 'Management is keen to know whether their new advertising campaign is attracting new clients.'

'Steve Allen, a friend of mine, recommended your firm. He used to work for the Unicorn Trust Group.'

Bennet half turned to the right in his swivel chair, gazed at the VDU on his desk and moved the mouse around to select a file. 'Thought so,' he murmured presently. 'It's more than four years since we had any dealings with Unicorn. Are they still in business?'

'I wouldn't know,' Landon said calmly. 'Steve left them in 'ninety-two and went to work for William Hill the bookmakers.'

Like all good fabrications, the story contained more than a grain of truth. A Steve Allen had worked for Unicorn Trust when Landon had been there, and he was still in touch with a fellow student at Nottingham University who had abandoned the law after two years to become an on-course bookie.

'That's enough market research for one day, Mr Landon.' Another oily smile made a brief appearance. 'Now what can we do for you?'

'Well, first of all I have to be satisfied that whatever I tell you will go no further than this room. Nothing on file, no recorded conversations and nothing in writing. Do you think you can live with that or should I go some place else?'

'Am I allowed to make notes? Purely for my own use, you understand?'

'I've no objections provided the notes don't make sense to a third party.'

'You can bank on it, Mr Landon.'

'All right. I was named as the sole executor in the last will and testament of the late Mr William Gadsby. This didn't come as a total surprise to me because despite the age difference of thirty years between us, we were good friends. I'm a keen angler, so was Bill. That's how we met.'

Sticking to the legend he had prepared to conceal the true identity of the deceased, Landon told him that apart from a few minor bequests, the estate was to go to his wife, Mary.

'It was all pretty straightforward and probate was about to be granted when a Ms Eleanor Gadsby intervened. I knew Bill had had a brother out in New Zealand who was killed in a plane crash when his Cessna had ploughed into a mountain in adverse weather conditions. But never once had he or Mary spoken of a younger sister. Anyway, the fact is Bill owned a thriving antiques business in Sevenoaks before he died. Now this woman comes along and claims she was a silent partner and has a half-share in the business.'

'Can she prove it?' Bennet asked.

'At the moment it looks as if Eleanor Gadsby will get what she wants without contesting the will in court. She must have been badgering her sister-in-law because Mary has apparently agreed the woman should have half the residual value of the business after it has been wound up.'

'Somehow I get the impression this settlement doesn't meet with your approval, Mr Landon?'

'You're right, it doesn't. Mary has no idea what she's doing half the time. She had a stroke eighteen months ago which affected her brain. She's not a complete vegetable, just a little childlike and naïve.'

'What does the family solicitor have to say about it?'

'Well, now we're getting into hot water,' Landon told him. 'I don't trust the man. I think he is in league with this Eleanor Gadsby and is planning to defraud the widow. Of course I can't prove it yet awhile, and I would be sued for libel if this ever got back to either of them.'

'Don't worry, I understand the need for discretion. However, at the moment you haven't indicated what you want from us.'

'That's easy. I want to know where and when Eleanor Gadsby was born. I particularly want to know if Gadsby was her birth name of if she acquired it by deed poll sometime during the last four years. I can deal with the family solicitor and Eleanor Gadsby if it turns out she's an impostor.'

'Do you have a home address for her?' Bennet asked.

Landon shook his head. 'All I can tell you is that she is part-owner of Gadstar Promotions in Bruton Place off Berkeley Square.

'It's not much to go on,' Bennet said, frowning.

'Are you saying you can't deliver?'

'No, it'll just take a little longer, that's all.'

'What are we talking about?'

Bennet thought it could take him up to six working days to obtain the information Landon wanted. Fasttrack Associates charged seventy-five a day plus expenses for his services and he would need Landon's home address and office number. It was also customary to pay for the first three days in advance. Landon gave him a cheque for £225 drawn on his own current account with Lloyds Bank in Gloucester Road and printed his home address and mobile phone number on the back. When the cheque was presented, it would leave him with under sixty in his account. He hoped Ashton had held his own in the battle of the budget cuts.

The view from his office window of Big Ben and the Houses of Parliament a mile downriver was wasted on Hugo Calthorpe. Dr Johnson might have observed, 'When a man is tired of London, he is tired of life; for there is in London all that life can afford' but Calthorpe had always hated the place, as did his wife. With the exception of eighteen months on the Soviet Armed Forces Desk as a Grade III intelligence officer back in 1971, Calthorpe had spent his entire service abroad. He had done two stints with the British Embassy in Washington and had had a lively time in Rome with the anarchist Brigate Rosse, who specialised in kidnapping and murdering members of the judiciary. He had also spent six years in Moscow as Head of Station.

On Calthorpe's return to London after his extended tour in Moscow, Sir Stuart Dunglass, then Director General, had made it known that he intended to employ him as the chief instructor at the Training School before making him Deputy DG to Victor Hazelwood when the latter eventually moved into the Director's chair. To avoid this fate, Calthorpe had immediately applied for an appointment in Asia on the grounds that he had never served east of Suez. Dunglass had been sympathetic but Calthorpe had been assigned to Delhi only because the resident physician to the British High Commission had insisted the Head of Station should be sent home on medical grounds. Now the wheel had turned full circle and he had been recalled to London to head up the Asian Department following the death of Bill Orchard.

Calthorpe had feared this might happen when he'd learned that Bill Orchard had committed suicide, but as the days passed with no word from London he had begun to hope that Hazelwood had found somebody younger to fill the post. No such luck. London had caught up with him last Friday with orders to complete the handover to his deputy by Monday, 3 February and catch the British Airways First Class Sleeper service departing at 01.10 hours the following morning. The Calthorpes had been allocated one of the flats retained by the Foreign and Commonwealth Office in Dolphin Square, and Victor Hazelwood seemed to think he had been extraordinarily generous in allowing Calthorpe three days to settle in. Officially he wasn't supposed to assume the appointment until Monday, the tenth, but what Hazelwood gave with one hand he took away with the other, and Calthorpe had been asked to show his face at morning prayers today.

He had not found himself among strangers. Benton he'd met during his first stint in Washington when the Head of the Pacific Basin and the Rest of the World Department had then been in charge of the China Desk and was a frequent visitor to Langley, liaising with his opposite number in the CIA. Ashton wasn't a stranger either. Calthorpe had met him when he was Head of Station, Moscow and the younger man had been sidelined into the Security Vetting and Technical Services Division. Ashton and an electronics wizard called Hicks, who managed to get up everybody's nose, had visited the British Embassy on the Maurice Thorez Embankment to carry out the annual security check.

That had been more years ago than Calthorpe cared to think about. Not that he had worn all that badly, he thought, and instinctively patted his stomach. Five feet eight and still tipping the scales between 141 and 145 pounds, which wasn't bad for a fifty-one-year-old.

A faint tapping noise didn't register with Calthorpe, lost in thought as he was. Then Ashton asked if he could spare a few minutes and he flinched as if someone had struck him.

'I'm sorry,' Ashton said, 'I didn't mean to startle you.'

'That's all right. What can I do for you, Peter?'

Try as he might, Calthorpe couldn't get used to the idea that Ashton was now an assistant director in charge of a department. He had little difficulty seeing him as a case officer out on the streets running his agents, or going it alone, which was much more likely. But desk-bound and exercising the grey matter? He didn't believe Ashton would stay the course.

'Tell me about Bill Orchard.'

'Tell you what?' Calthorpe asked, genuinely puzzled.

'Bill killed himself four days after returning from Sri Lanka, Pakistan and India in that order. You must have been one of the last people to see him alive, Hugo—'

'And you would like to know if I had found his behaviour somewhat withdrawn?' Calthorpe said, cutting in.

'Yes. Did you?'

'We dined with the Hazelwoods last night. We were asked to arrive fifteen minutes earlier than the other guests so that Victor and I could have "a little chat", as he put it.'

'About Bill Orchard?' Ashton said.

'Yes, and before you start asking the inevitable questions, what I said to Victor was strictly in confidence.'

'Did Victor mention Bill's mysterious sister-in-law, by any chance? The one we'd never heard of until she turned up for the funeral?'

Calthorpe hesitated, uncertain just how much Ashton knew and how much he was entitled to know.

'The lady reckons Bill didn't commit suicide. Right? Apparently we did away with him.' It was almost as if Ashton could read the doubts in his mind and was doing all he could to assuage them. 'Did Bill give you the impression he was heading for a nervous breakdown?' Ashton asked.

It was exactly the same question Victor had asked in the privacy of his study, the only room in the house where Alice Hazelwood permitted smoking.

'I'll give you the same answer as I gave Victor,' Calthorpe

said quietly. 'I'm not a clinical psychiatrist and I didn't know him well enough to give an opinion. The people to ask are surely his colleagues here at Vauxhall Cross.'

'We regarded him as a pretty laid-back character. Nothing seemed to bother him.' Ashton smiled. 'Except when his Audi was stolen. That made him angry. Flying was his pet hate, especially long haul. Made him a bit introspective afterwards.'

'So I noticed.'

'He was out of sorts when he flew in from Islamabad?'

'Bill was very quiet for the best part of the following day. On a number of occasions he didn't hear what I said to him. Turned out he was simply exhausted. Evidently Bill had eaten something which had violently disagreed with him and he hadn't had a wink of sleep when he boarded the flight to Delhi. He was much better the next day, though he still looked very pale. I thought Bill might have picked up some bug but he didn't have a temperature. I couldn't believe it when I heard he had committed suicide; I never saw a man looking so happy to be going home as he did when he left during the early hours of Friday morning. Obviously you didn't notice any change in him.'

'I didn't see Bill after he returned from India. None of us did.'

'What about morning prayers on the Monday?'

'Bill wasn't there,' Ashton told him. 'His wife phoned in to say he was sick.'

'That's funny, I wonder why Victor never mentioned it.'

'Possibly because he didn't want to influence your impression of Bill.'

'What of the inquest?'

'No real problem there,' Ashton said. 'Mrs Orchard stuck to the script we had prepared for her.'

Virtually overnight Orchard had become a diplomat. Like all SIS officers his name appeared in the Foreign and

Commonwealth Office Blue List, a security measure intended to make it difficult for hostile intelligence services to identify individual SIS personnel serving in embassies. One of the four deputy undersecretaries at the Foreign Office had told the coroner that Orchard had been sent to Sri Lanka, Pakistan and India to brief consular officers on the measures being taken to prevent illegal immigrants entering the UK from the sub-continent. He further stated Orchard had been regarded as a well-adjusted officer by his superiors and had been popular with his peers. The deceased would also have been aware from his last annual assessment that he could look forward to a bright future in the Diplomatic Service, which meant he most certainly had not reached his ceiling.

'Mrs Orchard didn't upset the apple cart,' Ashton continued. 'She went along with the party line that her late husband had been a Foreign Office official but she did say that in recent weeks he had been under a lot of strain. They had no financial problems and she would have known if he had been having an affair. She could only think it was pressure of work which had unhinged him.'

'That's a bit rich.'

'We thought so too.'

'What did Bill have to say in his tour report?'

'There was no tour report,' Ashton said, and edged towards the door. 'He was taken ill and didn't come to the office on the Monday. Remember?'

'But surely he would have made some notes?'

'You would have thought so but we can't find any.'

The reference library was on the second floor of Vauxhall Cross. The available floor space amounted to just under two thousand square feet, which had been subdivided to provide a small reading room some fifteen feet by twenty-eight. The remaining 1,540 square feet contained 5,000 titles arranged on shelves to a height of twelve feet. The heavier volumes, which included the current editions of Jane's *Fighting Ships, All the World's Aircraft, Infantry Weapons, Armour and Artillery, Military Communications,* and *Railways of the World* were to be found on the lower shelves. The topmost shelves represented the last resting place for typescript translations of Soviet technical and scientific papers dating back to 1950, which the chief librarian was reluctant to dispose of in case somebody asked for them one day.

The library also ran an up-to-date copy of every BT phone book, which *in toto* listed every subscriber in the UK other than those individuals who chose to be ex-directory. The phone books were displayed in numerical order: the man Landon was looking for lived in Church Stretton in Shropshire, an area covered by book number 613.

Every member of the Gadsby family had been looked at by the Security Service before Orchard's wedding on 9 April 1966. Anything could have happened to Lawrence Gadsby in the intervening thirty-one years. He could have died, moved house, gone to live abroad, or could simply be ex-directory, in which case enquiries would refuse to give Landon the number. If that should be the case, somebody with a lot more clout than he had would have to persuade the Driver and Vehicle Licensing Agency, Swansea to do a trawl of their records. Draw another blank there and he would have to go to St Catherine's House to see if they could produce a death certificate for Lawrence Gadsby.

The odds against tracing the widow's brother with the phone book were astronomical. But some people don't move house for years on end. The entry on page 17 of the phone book was proof of that contention. It read: 'Gadsby L.P., Faraday Road, Church Stretton'.

Landon made a note of the number and returned the directory to the shelf. At that moment he had little use for the information but it would be a different story when he knew a good deal more about Eleanor Gadsby.

At any other time Jill Sheridan would have regarded Palm Beach and The Breakers as the nearest thing to paradise on earth but her attitude was coloured by what had happened to her in the last twenty-four hours. To wake up in a crummy hotel bedroom with no idea how you came to be there, only to discover you were wearing various items associated with bondage was enough to make anybody sick. And having to put up with Tom Kransky's sanctimonious disapproval on top of all that was the last bloody straw. The way he told it, she had embarrassed him with her lewd behaviour; that was why he'd left her in the parking lot. And who had taken her to Michael's in the first place? A twosome had become a foursome. Tom, Sara and Dan: one of them had spiked her Bloody Mary with Rohypriol, the soluble substance known as the date rape drug; with perhaps a touch of LSD. It had to be Tom Kransky; the whole sorry business had started when she'd met Sara in the powder room. For her to subsequently reappear arm in arm with the blonde woman was something she would never have done had she been in possession of her faculties.

Right now Kransky was on his way to Orlando, allegedly to see the Features Editor of the *Sentinel* to drum up a few column inches of free publicity for a client. He had broken the news to her last night and had invited her to come along for the ride if she had nothing better to do. It had been a meaningless invitation because he knew she had arranged for American Express to deliver the replacement traveller's cheques to the hotel in the morning. In any event, home was the only place Jill wanted to go and soon – before some bloodsucker started to demand money with menaces.

It angered Jill that she daren't go to the police. Nobody had attempted to blackmail her yet but she had been drugged, abducted and held against her will. Technically she had been kidnapped, which meant the local FBI office in Miami would be involved in an investigation. She had survived every malicious thing Rosalind Urquhart had done to destroy her reputation and was still the Deputy Director General of the Secret Intelligence Service. That she would never become Head of the SIS was the collective wisdom around Whitehall, but times change and who could possibly say if current attitudes would prevail in five or ten years' time? But once the FBI became involved the investigation wouldn't be confined to the local office. Sooner or later her name would get back to Washington where she would be identified at the Deputy DG of the SIS. That really would spell the end of all her ambitions, no matter how liberal society might become in the next millennium.

It was, Jill decided, time to cut and run. After taking delivery of the traveller's cheques from American Express, she settled the hotel bill and booked herself on to British Airways Flight BA252 departing Miami at 17.55 hours, using her Mastercard in both cases. Then she rented a car from Hertz.

Chapter 4

Morning prayers started at eight thirty but this timing wasn't set in stone and occasionally there were exceptions. That Thursday morning happened to be one such exception. The meeting had been put back by two hours because the leader of Her Majesty's Loyal Opposition wished to meet the Directors General of the SIS and MI5, and since, according to the opinion polls, the leader of the opposition was almost certainly going to be the next Prime Minister when the Government called a general election in three months' time, the daily routine went by the board. In the event, a ten thirty start proved unduly optimistic and the meeting didn't get underway until eleven fifteen.

Rowan Garfield led off, because he happened to be the longest serving assistant director next to Roy Kelso, whose great day with the budget had come and gone almost a week ago, which meant he had nothing further to offer. Neither had Rowan, but he still managed to take an inordinate amount of time saying so. Benton's input for the Pacific Basin and the Rest of the World was simply a rehash of the latest intelligence summary, which his department circulated twice a month.

Although familiar with the digest that he'd read yesterday, Ashton made a few personal notes on his scratch pad. At the top of a blank sheet of A4 he wrote '16 February', a reminder that in three days' time Harriet would be celebrating her thirty-third birthday, if celebrating was the appropriate word. Underneath he added, 'Get birthday card today', followed by a series of question marks, which indicated he didn't know what to buy her. After some thought he wrote 'Perfume? Make-up? Lingerie?'. And then in desperation he printed in block capitals – 'TRY HARRODS. SEE IF THEY HAVE ANY BRIGHT IDEAS.'

'Peter.'

Ashton looked up.

'What have you got for us?' Hazelwood asked.

'Not a lot. Kosovo is going to be the next flash point in the Balkans but that's hardly news—'

'You're right, it isn't,' Jill said, interrupting him. 'Rowan's been telling us that for ages.'

'What's new is that the Kosovo Liberation Army is beginning to look less of a ragtag and bobtail outfit. There isn't the mix of small arms within a unit we used to see. The KLA is now uniformly equipped with Kalashnikov AK-47s.'

'Who is supplying them, Peter?'

'We think the Albanians.'

'You think,' Jill said disparagingly.

Same old Jill, Ashton thought wryly. She had returned from Florida earlier than expected and had looked on edge on her first day back in the office, but now she was on song again, oozing confidence and scoring points whenever an opportunity presented itself.

'How about your department, Hugo? Have we found Bill Orchard's tour notes yet?'

Calthorpe shook his head. 'Personally I don't believe Bill put pen to paper. What I have done is signal Heads of Stations Colombo and Islamabad requesting they submit detailed reports of his visit – whom he saw, where he went, what was discussed. I'm hoping to hear from them by the end of the week.'

'Which is tomorrow.'

'Yes indeed.'

Hazelwood looked round the table. 'Any other points?' he asked. 'None?'

He pushed his chair back and stood up. 'A word with you, Peter, in my office now.'

Hazelwood sounded for all the world like a headmaster about to deal with a troublesome sixth former in his study. But it wasn't like that at all. Hazelwood just wanted him to know that he had spoken to Jill about her flying visit to Wrotham some eight hours before Bill Orchard had committed suicide.

'Mary Orchard phoned Jill at six to say that Bill wanted to see her urgently before she left for Florida. When Jill arrived at Downdale she was informed by Mary Orchard that Bill was behaving very irrationally and no longer wanted to see her. She apologised profusely and said that if Bill had only known Jill's mobile number she could have saved her an unnecessary journey. There was a woman with Mary Orchard whom she introduced simply as Eleanor. She offered no explanation for her presence in the house and she certainly didn't tell Jill that they were related.'

'So Jill merely turned round and drove straight back to London?'

'No, she insisted on seeing Bill.' Hazelwood helped himself to a Burma cheroot from the cigar box and lit it. 'First of the day,' he said with evident relish.

'So what did Jill make of him?' Ashton asked impatiently.

'She thought he was running a temperature and advised Mary to call their doctor and get him to examine Bill. However, as Jill was leaving Eleanor told her she thought Bill had been drinking heavily all day.'

'Was there any evidence that he had?'

'According to Jill he was rambling a lot but she couldn't smell alcohol on his breath.' Hazelwood pursed his lips. 'About Eleanor: have we heard anything from the Fasttrack agency yet?'

'No.'

'I think we should dispense with their services. We don't want to court any bad publicity.'

'Landon has been very discreet,' Ashton told him.

'I'll be sixty in June, Peter. Part of the reason for my knighthood is the fact that I will then have reached retirement age. I'd like to stay on even if they only extend me twelve months at a time.' Hazelwood cleared his throat. 'The thing is, we'll have a new Prime Minister before then and he is determined his administration is going to be squeaky clean. That includes the Civil Service et cetera, et cetera.'

'OK, Victor. I don't want to see you go either.'

'What does that mean?'

'It means I will tell Landon to terminate the contract with Fasttrack.'

It was, however, too late for remedial action. When Ashton returned to his office he found a note from Will Landon informing him that Bennet had been in touch and he'd gone to Acton.

Landon could see why the office manager at Fasttrack Associates had described Harry Bennet as one of their foremost risk assessors. The first thing Bennet did was to present him with his report, a detailed itemised list of expenses and an invoice for a further £375 in settlement of their account, all neatly put together in a plastic folder with the firm's logo on the front cover. The report itself was a model of brevity and took under four minutes to read and digest.

Eleanor Gadsby had been born Eleanor May Westwood on 16 June 1948 at Chipping Norton, Oxfordshire, the illegitimate daughter of Virginia Westwood and an unnamed airman in the United States Air Force. Virginia Westwood had died four years later after contracting meningitis and Eleanor had been taken in by Dr Barnardo's. The Gadsbys had adopted her in 1955 when she was aged seven.

'What about the maternal grandparents?' Landon asked. 'Didn't they have any say in the matter?'

'I wouldn't know,' Bennet told him. 'That wasn't in my brief.'

'Right. Do you mind if I ask you a question?'

'Depends what it is,' Bennet said with an oily smile.

'How did you obtain this information?'

'A sister doesn't suddenly appear out of the blue, Mr Landon. If the widow you are representing had never mentioned Eleanor before she started to contest the will, common sense told me there must have been a schism of some kind in the family. I figured she might have been an adopted daughter, so I tried the various agencies and finally got round to Barnardo's.'

'What did you tell them?'

'The same story as you gave me.'

'I see.' Landon weighed the file in his hand. 'And this is the only copy?'

'Yes. I destroyed my notes. There's nothing on file.'

Landon didn't know whether to believe him or not but if he pressed the oily Bennet any further it would only excite his obvious suspicion. Better to settle for the fact that he had obtained the information Ashton had wanted. Tomorrow, with his agreement, he would drive up to Church Stretton in Shropshire and make the acquaintance of Lawrence Gadsby . . .

'Will you take a credit card?' Landon asked, conscious of the sixty-odd pounds remaining in his current account.

'We love plastic,' Bennet told him.

The client was an inch or so under six feet and was physically in good shape for a man who had to be in his mid-to-late forties.

He had a broad face that tapered to a strong jaw, and a mouth that always seemed to be hovering on a smile. He had brown eyes set wide apart and short, reddish brown hair parted on the left side. Most women would probably find him attractive but the more discerning might suspect the auburn tint had come out of a bottle.

Tom Kransky knew him as Eric Christensen, a third-generation American whose great-grandfather had left Denmark with his young bride in March 1872 to seek his fortune in America. Other than having a fat billfold there was little else Kransky knew about him. Christensen was either an attorney or a private investigator acting on behalf of one party in a particularly messy divorce. He had wanted the wife presented in the worst possible light in order to reduce the amount of alimony a bleeding heart judge might award. That made him ruthless as well as unscrupulous, and in case he was being set up, Kransky had taken care to implicate Christensen in what they had done to their victim.

At three minutes to eight that evening, Kransky drove into the parking lot fronting the shopping centre on the outskirts of Ellicott City southwest of Baltimore. Alighting from the Chevrolet Corvette, he locked the car and walked into the local branch of K Mart. He picked up a basket from the stack inside the entrance, went on down the aisle between the fresh fruit and vegetables, then turned right at the bottom and headed for the liquor section at the other end of the supermarket. Christensen was already there waiting for him, apparently torn with indecision between a bottle of Jack Daniel's, Southern Comfort, and a Kentucky bourbon. Kransky lifted a six-pack of Budweiser from the shelf and dropped it into the plastic basket, then checked to make sure nobody was watching before he approached the client.

'I prefer Irish myself – Bushmills,' he muttered.

'It's a matter of taste,' Christensen told him in an equally low voice.

'So where's your car parked?' Kransky asked, catching a nod from Christensen that told him nobody was close enough to hear them.

'Fifth row back, far right as you face the lot, sixth vehicle in.'

'OK. Go through the checkout, I'll join you in five.'

Kransky moved past him, turned right before reaching the nearest checkout and began to snake up and down the aisles as if trying to find his way out of a maze. When he encountered her, Sara was wheeling a shopping basket up the aisle separating cans of pet food, biscuits and Kat Lit from washing-up liquids, rolls of multipurpose clingfilm, kitchen foil and freezer bags. Unlike his covert meeting with the client, Kransky acted as though they were old friends when he greeted her. In the course of their brief conversation, he slipped Sara the keys to the Corvette and told her where to find the car.

'You got a key to the studios?' he asked.

'In my purse,' she told him.

'Good. You'd better get moving then.'

'Yes, sir,' Sara said, and threw up a mock salute.

'Wear something modest,' he'd told her. 'Dress like a housewife for once.'

But Sara's idea of what that entailed differed from his. The sweater she had on was too tight, the jacket was too short, reaching only to her hips. The stretch pants drew attention to her ass and the pelvic motion did the rest as she sashayed up the aisle in four-inch heels to join the shortest line at the checkout.

Kransky walked on in the opposite direction, then doubled back up the adjoining aisle, to join the cash-only checkout. Leaving the supermarket, he picked out the car in the fifth row to the far right and made his way towards it. Christensen was one very cautious man. The first time they had met, he had been driving a Dodge Intrepid; on Monday when he'd delivered the second instalment it had been a Ford Probe; tonight he favoured a Chrysler Neon. All of them had been rented but obviously not from the same agency. Kransky opened the nearside door, dumped the paper bag containing the six-pack on the back seat, then got in beside Christensen.

'You bring the money?' he asked.

'You got the pics?' Christensen countered.

'They're on the way to the studio now.'

'Then I guess we're in business.'

'Not so fast. I want to see the colour of your money first.'

'What, here and now, in the parking lot?'

'No, some place quiet where we won't be disturbed.'

'And I bet you know just the spot.'

'I surely do. Head into Ellicott City and follow State 144 out of there.'

'That's fine by me, Mr Kransky.'

Christensen switched on the ignition, cranked the engine into life, then released the handbrake and shifted into drive. As he moved out of the parking lot, the driver behind him flashed his lights.

'What the hell's eating him?' Kransky said irritably.

'Nothing. My friend is just letting me know he's there covering my back.'

'He's your bodyguard; is that what you're telling me?'

'I'm carrying seventy-five grand and you're taking me some place nice and quiet to inspect it. You think I'm going to leave anything to chance?'

'Jesus, man, I'm in the same position as you and I haven't found it necessary to—'

'You're not in the same position,' Christensen told him curtly. 'I have something you want and it's right here in the trunk. You have something I want and I have no idea where your goddamned studio is.'

Fuck you, Kransky thought, but lacked the nerve to voice the sentiment aloud. To the adjectives of ruthless and unscrupulous he now added chilly. Retreating into his shell, Kransky confined himself to directing Christensen to Patapsco Valley State Park. 'Anywhere around here will do,' he said tersely.

Christensen turned off the track and, avoiding the few remaining patches of snow, made for a fold in the ground that would partially conceal the car, then killed the lights and switched off.

Kransky looked into the rear-view mirror but could see no sign of the vehicle that was allegedly following them, and wondered if the bodyguard actually existed. The treatment he received after they alighted from the car and moved round to the back fuelled the suspicion. Before he knew what was happening, Christensen had him spread against the trunk, arms braced, legs wide apart, body at an inclined angle. He had been frisked before by the police when a student at NYU, and Christensen was equally professional. No part of his body was left untouched, his chest, stomach, the flanks from armpit to hip, the outside of the legs to the ankles, then up the inside in case he had taped a flat-bladed knife to one of his thighs. Just as the cop had done all those years ago, the bastard suddenly crushed his testicles, which made Kransky buckle at the knees.

'Consider that a warning, Tom.'

Kransky didn't need a warning; he had no intention of tangling with a man like Christensen. Still feeling groggy, he straightened up and stepped back a pace. The pain in his groin eased rapidly when Christensen opened the trunk and revealed a suitcase of money.

'It's all there, Tom. Seventy-five thousand in hundreds, fifties and twenties, non-sequential dollar bills.'

In all there were seventy-five packets of varying thickness depending on the denominations of the dollar bills. Choosing a third of the total at random, Kransky riffed each packet in turn to see if any of them contained blank sheets of paper cut to size.

'Satisfied?' Christensen asked contemptuously.

'Yeah.'

'Then let's go to the movies.'

The studio was located in the run-down section of Baltimore across the Patapsco River from Fort McHenry. The two-storey building that housed Kransky Productions on the top floor had once been the head office and accounts department of a depository before the giant warehouse behind it had been reduced to a fire-blackened shell almost thirty years ago. On Kransky's instructions Christensen parked in front of the entrance to the studio next to the Chevrolet Corvette. The first floor had been converted into a garage for commercial vehicles, but this had gradually fallen into disuse and the individual bays had been bricked in to prevent the place becoming a garbage dump.

'The Corvette is mine,' Kransky told him unnecessarily, 'the other car belongs to Sara, and Dan, her partner.'

'No lights are showing upstairs,' Christensen observed.

'That's because the windows have been painted over in black. Good for the lighting. Discourages the Peeping Toms as well.'

Kransky got out of the car, waited for Christensen to collect the suitcase of money from the trunk, then led him up the external fire escape and entered the building. The available floor space had been partitioned to provide three stage sets and a projection room. There was, however, no wide screen or tip-up seats, merely a 27-inch TV, a VCR and four canvas-bottomed chairs.

'This is Sara and Dan,' Kransky said, introducing them.

'I don't need to know their names,' Christensen told him brusquely. 'This isn't a social occasion. Just switch off the lights and let's see how good a cameraman you are.'

'You won't be disappointed.'

The lights dimmed and gradually went out on the 27-inch screen '*It Happened One Night*' appeared in Gothic script.

'Great title, great movie,' Kransky opined. 'Claudette Colbert and Clark Gable.'

'Starring Sara Gay and Dan Swordsman.'

'Those are their professional names, Mr Christensen. Dan gives a whole new meaning to swordsman.'

The names of the stars dissolved and the words 'Introducing Jill Sheridan' suddenly appeared in blood-red letters filling the whole screen.

'Watch this for a great entrance.'

'Shut up,' Christensen told him angrily. 'Let the goddamned movie do the talking.'

The woman made her appearance in high-heeled sandals, hands shackled behind her back, a large brown paper bag over her head. Then Sara removed the bag to reveal Jill Sheridan full frontal. Her eyes were on the blank side but they were no more lifeless than some of the Hollywood starlets Christensen had seen. Most people watching the movie would think she was drunk; only a few would realise she was stoned out of her mind. Girl on girl, three in a bed, every position, every perversion known to man.

'Have you made copies for a British VCR?' Christensen asked.

Kransky nodded. 'Five, like you asked for.'

'And pics?'

'Thirty-six exposures, a complete roll of one two seven.

Kransky thought the sound effects were truly brilliant. You'd have to have been there to know that all the moans and heavy breathing were faked by Sara.

'How long does this movie last?' Christensen asked.
'The full one hundred and eighty minutes.'
'Then run it fast forward until I tell you to stop.'

His name was Samir Abbas. He was a highly qualified geologist and had worked for the state-owned oil company before leaving Iraq. In America he had had a succession of low-paid jobs, which was the lot of an illegal immigrant with no social security number and no hope of getting a work permit. Currently he was employed as a forecourt attendant at a filling station outside Tuxedo. In another fortnight or so, he would have to move on to a different job or risk detection and arrest prior to deportation. What he needed was some high-flier in the law, banking, business or in Congress who was desperate to find a live-in domestic and was prepared to turn a blind eye to his lack of a long-stay visa. Chef, chauffeur, gardener, general handyman – he was qualified to undertake any of these.

Tonight he was shadowing Christensen in a five-year-old Volkswagen Polo that had been fitted with a tracking device that picked up the signals emitting from the miniature transmitter on the underside of the American's Chrysler. The transmitter had an operating range of one mile, and the signal was displayed as a moving dot on the 4-inch screen fitted next to the instrument panel. He had followed Christensen out of the parking lot and had flashed his lights to let him know he was there when the American had stopped, waiting for a break in the traffic before turning right on to State 144. Thereafter he had dropped back and had tracked the Chrysler Neon from a distance slightly in excess of half a mile.

The only worrying moment had occurred when Christensen had turned off the highway on to a track leading to the Patapsco Valley State Park. The dot had suddenly stopped moving and Abbas had been slow to react. At a rough guess he thought the separation distance between the two vehicles had narrowed to something like five hundred yards by the time he'd switched off the lights, and there was a chance Kransky might have spotted the beams in the door mirror on his side. More bad luck had followed when he had pulled over on to the grass and headed away from the track before his eyes had become accustomed to the dark. The nearside front wheel had dropped into a shallow ditch that had been partially hidden by a patch of snow that had survived the thaw that had come with the warmer weather and rain three days ago.

Abbas had sat there, eyes fixed on the TV screen. Four minutes had passed, then five, six, seven, and he'd begun to wonder if Christensen was in trouble. The dot was stationary but that didn't prove anything. Kransky had guided him to this place and maybe he had arranged for his friends to be waiting for them. Men had been known to kill for less than $75,000.

After what had seemed an eternity, the dot had started moving again, this time heading in his direction. A minute later the Chrysler had swept past him to make a right on State 144. Somehow Abbas had managed to extricate the Volkswagen from the ditch at the third attempt but he'd lost an awful lot of ground. The blank screen had told him that Christensen had to be at least a mile ahead. He'd floored the accelerator and driven like a maniac to catch up, and had only succeeded in doing so by backing a hunch. He had turned right on to State 166 and had just gone past Cantonsville Community College on Rolling Road when the blip had made a welcome reappearance on the screen. Thereafter he had closed to within a hundred yards of Christensen as they headed into Baltimore. Nevertheless, the last few miles hadn't been exactly trouble-free. When it became evident that Christensen was heading towards the run-down section of Baltimore across the river from Fort McHenry, Abbas had been forced to drop back. In doing so, he'd lost the Chrysler again.

Abbas had quartered the area, trying to pick up a signal from the transmitter. It had taken him the best part of twenty nerve-racking minutes to get the blip back on screen and run the Chrysler to ground. It was parked in front of a two-storey building with the faded legend 'Brogan's Depository' painted on the wall midway between the two floors. With a sigh of relief he cut the ignition and reached under his seat for the semi-automatic. The pistol was a 7.65mm Type 64 manufactured by the People's Republic of China. Incorporating a silencer, it was the only handgun in the world produced solely as an assassination weapon.

Like all pornographic material *It Happened One Night* was repetitive and ultimately boring. Christensen had zipped through the video, making frequent use of the fast forward button to move on to the next sexually explicit act, which had reduced the viewing time to under twenty minutes. But that hadn't been the end of it; the porno movie producer and director had made five copies from the master tape and Christensen had wanted to make sure Kransky wasn't about to palm him off with five blank cassettes. Kransky hadn't minded but the actor had had plenty to say about it in a snide manner that grated on Christensen. He was the sort of clown who didn't know when to stop, especially when every quip at Christensen's expense provoked a cackle of laughter from Sara.

'Satisfied now?' he asked belligerently as Christensen rewound the fifth and last copy.

'I think so.' Christensen reached into his jacket pocket, took out a split ring with two keys attached and tossed it to Kransky. 'Both will open the suitcase,' he said. 'The seventy-five grand is yours to split three ways as you see fit.'

'Seventy-five!' Dan echoed. 'That's all there is? You're not going to let him get away with this, are you, Tom? Jesus, man, we kidnapped the fucking woman and raped her. We could spend the rest of our lives in jail if ever she identifies us.'

'This is the third payment,' Christensen informed him calmly, 'and nobody is shaking me down for another dime.'

'The third!' Dan screeched in disbelief.

'I put down twenty-five thousand to cover preproduction expenses, then I handed over another twenty-five allegedly to grease a few palms.'

'Is he lying or what, Tom? I mean, how deep are your pockets?'

'I took the most risks,' Kransky said, jabbing a finger at the actor. 'I was with Sheridan night and day for the best part of a week. If there is a face she is going to remember it's mine. I also collected her from the Regal Hotel, Highland Beach after the show was over and stayed with her the following night. I had to find out what, if anything, she remembered.'

'Give yourself a Medal of Honour, Tom.'

'Are all your brains in your prick?' Kransky demanded savagely. 'Don't you understand, if the police get to me, they would start looking at Kransky Productions, then sooner or later they would get around to you two.'

Christensen put the porn material into two large Jiffy bags and left them to it. He let himself out of the building and ran down the external staircase, relieved to find that Abbas was where he was supposed to be, parked next to his Chrysler. Opening the nearside door, he tossed the Jiffy bags on to the back seat.

'They're upstairs, all three of them,' he said. 'First room on your left.'

Abbas got out of the Volkswagen. 'Are you going to wait for me?' he asked.

'No, I've got a house call to make.'

Abbas jacked a 7.65 round into the breach of the Type 64 pistol and pushed the selector bar to the right for semi-automatic. The silencer was only a hundred per cent effective when the bullet was fired in a locked breech, which meant the empty case had to be ejected manually. This was a time-consuming process, and when faced with three targets, the delay could prove fatal.

As Christensen started the Chrysler Neon, Abbas climbed the staircase, the sound of his footsteps on the metal treads deadened by the two-litre engine. He moved into the building and opened the first door on the left where he could hear raised voices. All three, the two men and the woman, stopped talking simultaneously and stared at him wide-eyed.

'Are you Kransky?' he asked the nearest man.

Kransky nodded. 'You want the money?' he said. 'It's yours. OK?'

'It was mine anyway,' Abbas told him, and shot the movie producer in the chest.

The other man threw up both hands to cover his eyes as if he didn't want to see death coming. Abbas squeezed the trigger a second time, the bullet drilling through the right palm before hitting the man between the eyes and blowing his skull apart like an overripe watermelon. The woman screamed just the once, then turned about and started to run from him but there was no way out and he shot her high up in the back. A methodical killer who didn't believe in leaving anything to chance. Abbas shot the woman again, this time in the head and then did the same to Kransky. There was no need for him to dispatch the actor.

There were packets of dollar bills scattered all over the floor. Completely unruffled, he picked up the wads, repacked them into the suitcase and left the office with the money, switching off the lights as he went. The whole business had taken him less than four minutes to accomplish.

Chapter 5

It would be the third time Christensen had been to Kransky's apartment on Federal Hill. Approaching Belmont House from William Street, he turned into Warren Avenue, and then, some forty yards beyond the intersection, signalled a left. The basement garage at Belmont House was secured by a steel shutter, which was controlled by a photoelectric cell, programmed to recognise a coded signal that was supposedly unique to the apartment house. Each resident was therefore issued with a battery-powered activator that automatically emitted a signal when aimed at the photoelectric cell mounted outside the garage. An allegedly secure system was made vulnerable by the very fact that residents were given a spare in case they temporarily mislaid their activator. Such was the nature of his job that Christensen had no difficulty in obtaining one for his own use.

Christensen stopped the car just short of the garage, aimed the activator at the photoelectric cell and set the machinery in motion. The steel shutter was still moving upward when he shifted into drive, went down the ramp and entered the garage to park the Chrysler in the space allocated to Kransky. As soon as he had reversed into the vacant slot, Christensen switched off the ignition and reached under the seat for the .38 Police Positive and hip holster he'd secreted there. Alighting from the Chrysler, he buckled the belt round his waist and tucked the revolver into the holster, then moved round to the back and opened the trunk. From the spare wheel housing where the basic tool kit was stored he recovered a small executive-style briefcase containing a battery-powered drill and a sealed packet of rubber gloves.

He walked over to the elevator at the bottom end of the garage and pressed the call button. By a stroke of good fortune the car was already at the basement level. Although Kransky's apartment was on the fifth floor, Christensen got out at the third in case the doorman in the lobby looked up from his desk and noticed the car was on the move. Christensen met nobody on the internal fire escape, nor did he encounter any residents as he made his way along the corridor to Apartment 56.

He had in his possession a bunch of skeleton keys that were guaranteed to open any lock. All the same, he put the power drill down and pressed the door bell just in case some girl or boyfriend was in the apartment waiting for Kransky to come home. Presently a tinny voice asked who was calling.

'Police,' Christensen told her, and held up his badge in front of the spyhole.

'What do you want?'

'Are you Mrs Kransky, mam?' he asked in a cool professional voice.

'You could say that.'

'Then please open the door. I'm afraid my partner, Officer Diane Olberg, and I have some very bad news for you.'

It was a calculated risk; if the woman asked to see Diane Olberg in the spyhole, he was done for. On balance, however, he thought it was more likely she would accept his story if she believed he had a woman officer in tow. A faint rattle as the security chain was removed told Christensen he had got it right. He waited until the bolts top and bottom had been withdrawn and the handle itself was rotating, then picked up the briefcase and put his shoulder to the door to send the woman staggering back into the hall. Arms flailing like windmills in a vain attempt to retain her balance, she sat down hard on her rump and toppled over backwards, her head striking the floor with a muffled hump. Christensen left the briefcase on the hall table and pulled the .38 from the hip holster.

There was a momentary stunned silence before the woman let rip with a string of four-letter words. The tirade died instantly when she raised her head off the floor and found herself looking into the barrel of a snub-nose revolver.

'Who are you?' she asked in a shaky voice.

'I've already told you, I'm a police officer,' Christensen said, and flashed the badge at her again. 'Now get up, keep your mouth shut and take me through the apartment.'

He stepped back a couple of paces to give her space and position himself out of harm's way in case she took it into her head to kick him in the ankles. But in the event all she wanted was to please him. Her first name, she told him, was Paula and she was the third Mrs Kransky.

'And the last,' he suggested mockingly, and wondered where she had been on the other two occasions he'd been to the apartment.

'I hope so,' Paula told him with unconscious irony.

The apartment had two large bedrooms, one with a bathroom en suite as well as a Jacuzzi, a kitchen out of *Good Housekeeping*, with a serving hatch to the dining area off the large sitting room, and a den, which Paula told him was Kransky's domain. Christensen had come to Belmont House because he suspected the porno movie director and producer had made an extra copy of *It Happened One Night* for his own use. A hundred and twenty-five thousand dollars wasn't enough for him; double or treble that amount and Kransky was the sort of man who would still be looking to make a little extra on the side.

'What exactly are you looking for?' Paula asked.

'Your husband and I are in business. He has something that belongs to me, photographs and the like. Where's the safe?'

'In the master bedroom behind the picture.'

The picture was a copy of *American Gothic* by Grant Wood, the diameter of the safe behind it didn't look big enough to take a video cassette. Nevertheless Christensen decided he would drill it open to make sure.

'I don't know the combination,' Paula said nervously. 'Tom refused to tell me.'

'No problem, I'll wait for him to come home.'

'Oh.'

Christensen had never heard so much apprehension and resignation expressed in a single word. 'You don't mind, do you?' he asked, smiling.

'No, no, of course I don't.'

Her rapid breathing and strained voice told him otherwise. Paula Kransky was undoubtedly scared of him but not to the extent that she was paralysed with fear. As they moved from room to room he'd noticed that she had tried to get ahead of him with the intention of slamming the communicating door in his face and locking it. He had returned the Police Positive to the hip holster and done everything he could to put Paula Kransky at her ease, but she had seen through him and knew he wasn't just a neighbourhood cop on the take.

'Tell you what,' Christensen said, 'why don't we have a drink and try to relax?'

'Sounds good to me.'

She tried to put space between them again as they left the bedroom, crossed the hall and entered the sitting room. Paula was even more obvious when she pointed to a well-stocked bar abutting the dining area and invited Christensen to help himself and fix her a Gimlet while he was at it. As Paula made for the sofa, he knew that the moment he passed her on the way to the bar, she would double back to the hall and lock him in. Timing it to perfection, Christensen sent her flying with a violent shove between the shoulders so that in colliding with one of the arms, she ended up face down in the upholstered seat of the sofa. Before Paula had time to recover, he grabbed one of the scatter cushions, held it against her head and put two .38 rounds into her skull. The cushion smouldered around the bullet holes and particles of the stuffing were expelled into the air. Her body jerked twice and was then still.

Although the scatter cushion had served to deaden the sound of each discharge, it was not a perfèct silencer. He went out into the hall and listened intently to see if there was any reaction from the apartments on either side. The possibility that one of the neighbours had heard the disturbance and was even now making a 911 call excited him more than any woman ever could.

Christensen picked up the plastic case containing the power drill from the hall table and walked it through to the bedroom. The rubber gloves made his hands sweat, wrinkling the fingers like dried prunes, but that was a small price to pay to protect his identity. He started on the wall safe and drilled through the combination lock, eventually forcing it open. It was apparent that the cash inside represented the greater part of the first two instalments Kransky had received from him. He stuffed the packets of dollar bills into a pillowcase taken from the linen cupboard, then went through the rest of the apartment, upending every item of furniture to dump the contents on the floor. He found two additional copies of *It Happened One Night* in the den which came as no surprise to him. What he did find surprising was the fact that Kransky had made no attempt to hide them away.

At 1.06 a.m. some sixty-eight minutes after murdering Paula Kransky in cold blood, Christensen left the apartment, rode the elevator down to the basement garage and drove back to Washington without incident. When he arrived at his house in

Alexandria he went down into the cellar and burned the rubber gloves and forty-one thousand dollars in the furnace.

The distance from London to Church Stretton was 169 miles, according to Landon's calculations. Whether the route he had chosen was the most direct was another matter. Leaving the flat in Gloucester Road he'd headed out of London on the M40, bypassed Oxford and picked up the A44 trunk road, which skirted Evesham and Worcester to link up with the A49 south of Leominster. Thereafter Landon hadn't needed to consult the directions he'd taped to the instrument panel. He had hoped to average fifty miles in the hour but roadworks and heavy rain had put paid to that ambition and the journey had taken him three and three-quarter hours. Had the ten-year-old Aston Martin he was busily restoring been fit for the road, he could probably have clipped a good twenty minutes off the time, even allowing for weather conditions. But the V8 Vantage model was still in bits and pieces in a lock-up garage near his flat, and making deep inroads in his bank account.

Once in Church Stretton Landon found his way to Faraday Road in no time at all, thanks to the explicit directions he'd received from Lawrence Gadsby. He had telephoned Gadsby yesterday afternoon to explain why he wanted to see him, which had not been the easiest thing to do without courting a serious breach of security. 'Give him the facts,' Ashton had advised. 'Tell Gadsby what his adopted sister has alleged but make out Bill was a senior official in the Management and Personnel Office.'

The Management and Personnel Office was responsible for the organisation of the Civil Service, recruitment into it, personnel management, and the staffing of senior appointments. As such, MPO, as it was commonly referred to in Whitehall, came under the supervision of the Prime Minister. Somewhat to his surprise Gadsby had accepted Landon's story without comment and he had made an appointment to see him at eleven o'clock, which should have given Landon an opportunity to look round the town before going to his house in Faraday Road. In the event he only just made it on time.

Gadsby was a large, florid-looking man in his late fifties. Had he attended the funeral, Landon would certainly have recalled his face. By profession he was a chartered accountant with offices in both Shrewsbury and Church Stretton. It was evident from the size of his house, never mind the cook/housekeeper, daily cleaning woman and full-time gardener, that the head of Gadsby and Company enjoyed a sizeable income. Golf was the one great passion of his life and, as he told Landon, thanks to his efficient junior partners he was out on the links more often than he was in the office. He had the trophies to prove it on display in walnut cabinets either side of the fireplace in the drawing room. Gadsby was still discoursing on his favourite subject when the cook/housekeeper appeared with a pot of coffee and a plate of shortbread biscuits.

'Care for anything stronger to go with the coffee and biscuits?' Gadsby asked.

Landon shook his head, 'It's a little too early in the day for me,' he said.

'Quite right.' Gadsby leaned forward in his armchair and helped himself to a shortbread. 'Next to whisky, this is the best thing to come out of Scotland,' he said.

'About your adopted sister—' Landon began hesitantly.

'Eleanor is an evil, poisonous bitch, always has been, even as a child. Can't think what our parents saw in her. They were Quakers, you know; perhaps that's why they adopted her. The Christian thing to do.' Gadsby snorted. 'I can tell you, Mary and I were pretty unhappy about it. She took great pleasure in bullying Mary. One time Eleanor picked up her favourite doll and deliberately smashed it to pieces, then told our parents that Mary had accidentally dropped it and was blaming her because she knew they would be angry. And the incredible thing was they actually believed her and poor Mary was sent to bed early without any supper. She was seven when that happened and Eleanor was going on eleven. Of course, there were many, many other incidents in later life.'

'Such as, for instance?' Landon asked, probing gently.

'Well, there was the St Valentine's Day card she sent me after I'd been married five years. The message, in Dymo tape, which she'd put inside the card, read, "Do you miss those long and deeply satisfying nights we spent together? I do." It upset Audrey, my wife, no end.'

Gadsby waved a hand towards a gallery of photographs in silver frames, which were displayed on every available surface in the sitting room. The subject was the same in every one – a woman, at various stages in her life: the young bride on the arm of Gadsby, as a mother with a new-born baby and in the autumn years of their marriage.

'Eleanor wrote a so-called letter of sympathy when our daughter and only child was knocked down and killed on her way home from school by a reckless driver. Said all the right things, only to twist the knife in the last sentence. Eleanor claimed she wasn't surprised to hear Julie had been fatally injured in a traffic accident because from what she had heard, our daughter walked around in a dream half the time. Somehow she made it sound as if the accident had been Julie's fault.'

After that disgraceful episode Gadsby had had nothing further to do with his adopted sister. Any letters from her had not been answered and he'd made a point of putting the phone down when he heard her voice on the line. He had thought of changing his phone number and going ex-directory but in the end had rejected the idea.

'It would have meant informing God knows how many relatives, friends, acquaintances and clients, and Audrey said why should we be put to all that trouble? And of course she was right.' Gadsby helped himself to another cup of coffee. 'Did you go to the funeral?' he asked, abruptly changing the subject.

'Yes I did,' Landon said.

'Out of respect for a former colleague, I suppose.'

Gadsby's conversation was about as erratic as a grasshopper. It was virtually impossible to anticipate what he would say next.

'I rang Mary as soon as I saw the notice of Bill's death in the *Daily Telegraph*,' he went on. 'Couldn't believe it when she told me Eleanor had been staying with her when Bill killed himself. Didn't make sense. I mean, it isn't as if she hadn't been left on her own before when Bill was away on his travels.'

What had puzzled Gadsby more than anything else was the fact that Mary had taken up with Eleanor again. If anybody had suffered at her hands it had been Mary. Her adopted sister had missed no opportunity to humiliate her.

'Eleanor told her she had only to snap her fingers and Bill Orchard would jump into bed with her, then set out to prove it.'

'And did she?'

'Well, Mary was certainly convinced Bill had been unfaithful but I'm not so sure. Truth is, in my opinion, Bill didn't have the requisite hormones to be a womaniser and I know damned well Mary would have left him if there had been the slightest evidence that he had committed adultery.'

Gadsby paused as if to gather his thoughts, then invited Landon to help himself to another biscuit before doing the same.

'Naturally, Mary wanted to have nothing more to do with her adopted sister. Of course, that was donkey's years ago,' he continued in his inimitable fashion. 'Let's see now, they had been married four years when the shenanigans were supposed to have taken place so it must have been 1970. I attended their silver wedding in 1991.'

'And Eleanor wasn't invited?' Landon said tentatively.

Gadsby looked at him and shook his head as if amazed that he could have asked such a stupid question. 'Absolutely not. That's why I was completely dumbfounded when Mary told me she had been staying with her. Made me wonder just who was unbalanced.'

'Are you saying Eleanor Gadsby is irrational?'

'I'm surprised you should ask.'

Landon could think of at least two people in Vauxhall Cross who would be pleased to hear Gadsby say that. The last thing Ashton had said to him yesterday evening concerning his flying visit to Church Stretton was in effect to watch his step. It had been so unlike Ashton that at first he'd assumed Peter was simply passing on the message he'd received from the Director General. Then, thinking about it later at home, Landon wondered if he had witnessed the emergence of the new Ashton, a more cautious version of the old. Maybe that was what happened to you when you joined the top table?

'The jury at the inquest didn't believe Bill had been murdered, did they, Mr Landon?'

'No, they were satisfied he had committed suicide.'

'Well. There you are then.' Gadsby paused to brush a crumb from the corner of his mouth. 'Of course, it wouldn't be the first time a coroner's jury brought in a wrong verdict. Now, I wouldn't mind betting Eleanor could find somebody to do away with Bill if she was so inclined.'

'You are joking, aren't you?'

Gadsby didn't answer his question. Instead he told Landon that Eleanor's PR firm, Gadstar Promotions, had some pretty odd clients in the Middle East, North and South Africa. He had gleaned this information from his sister Mary during the course of a long telephone conversation in which he had remonstrated with her for taking up with Eleanor again. Stung by the inference she was being silly, Mary had reeled off a list of Gadstar clients, presumably to impress him.

'If that had been Mary's intention, it misfired. I hadn't heard of any of the firms, though a couple of names did sound vaguely familiar. Reminded me of those two armament kings you read about from time to time.'

'Ahmed Shirawai and Abdel Mohammed Zubair?' Landon suggested.

'Could be, could be.'

Gadsby glanced at his wristwatch, mumbled something about time running on and a lunch date and immediately brightened up when Landon took the hint and said he must be going.

They said their goodbyes on the doorstep, Landon thanking him for being so helpful even though he had his doubts. It seemed to him that Eleanor wasn't the only dysfunctional member of the family, that when a push came to shove, Gadsby could be pretty vindictive. Driving southeast to London he decided the best thing he could do was check with MI5 to see what the Security Service knew about Gadstar Promotions and their clients.

At a quarter to eight that morning Samir Abbas made two phone calls on his mobile. The first was to the Caltex filling station outside Tuxedo to inform his employer that he was feeling pretty sick and wouldn't be coming to work. The other call was to a Lebanese businessman whose journeys to and from London qualified him as a frequent flier with American, United and British Airways. To Abbas he was simply known as Emile.

The Lebanese was light-skinned and matched the classic medium-height, medium-build description witnesses to an incident invariably give the police. In Emile's case, women, generally being more observant than men, would probably have added that he was good-looking, was possibly a bit of a lady's man, had an infectious smile and was obviously in his early thirties. He had in fact turned forty, travelled for the most part on an American passport and was used as a courier by Samir Abbas.

From the public low-cost housing development on New York Avenue, Abbas made his way by Metrobus to Union Station. The morning rush hour on Metrorail started at five thirty and ended four hours later. During this peak period there was a train every five minutes. Abbas took one of the down escalators to the free area below ground, walked through the uncluttered mezzanines and purchased a fare card from one of the vending machines, then went on down to the platform. The time was eight minutes past eight and all being well, he knew Emile was about to board a Blue Line train at L'Enfant Plaza metro station.

The peak period was already beginning to wind down and there was no need for anyone to stand. Boarding the fourth car of six, Abbas found a seat midway between the doors and sat down nursing a thin black zip folder, fifteen inches long by nine and a half deep, on his lap. The folder contained two video cassettes in Jiffy bags, both of which were addressed by Ms J. Sheridan, 47 Bisham Gardens, Highgate, London NW3 IJJ. Familiar with the line, he didn't need to look at the route map or pay much attention to the station announcements on the public address system in the railcar. Judiciary Square came and went, then Gallery Square; at Metro Center he got off the train and walked through the mezzanine towards the Blue Line platforms. Emile was waiting for him near the escalator for the disabled. They greeted each other like old acquaintances who were mutually delighted and surprised to encounter one another on the metro. Clutching the slim, black folder in his right hand, Abbas spread his arms as if to embrace Emile: the transfer of the zip folder was done so deftly that only somebody loitering within a few feet of them could possibly have noticed that the Lebanese was now holding it in his left hand.

'Are you all set?' Abbas enquired.

Emile nodded. 'I'm flying to New York this afternoon, then catching British Airways flight BA174 out of JFK at 20.00 hours, arriving Heathrow at 08.55 hours tomorrow.'

'Good, very good.'

Abbas turned away and walked towards the nearest up escalator to emerge on 13th and G Streets, content in the knowledge that, unless something went badly wrong, Jill Sheridan, the Deputy DG of the British Secret Intelligence Service, would receive a very nasty surprise bright and early on the Monday morning.

Chapter 6

If there was one month in the year Ashton really hated it was February. The end of the winter was still a long way off and all you had to look forward to was twenty-eight days of unremitting greyness. Provided you could get away, February was a good month for escaping to warmer climes. But it seemed a change of climate didn't suit everybody; Jill Sheridan had returned from Florida a week ago looking absolutely fragile and this morning she had phoned in sick. Jill had taken her time about doing so, leaving it until 8.40 a.m. ten minutes after morning prayers should have started.

For some inexplicable reason, a meeting that started late invariably lasted almost twice as long. This morning's had been no exception. When he returned to his office Ashton found a note from Will Landon on his desk asking if he would let him know when he was free. Lifting the receiver on the internal phone, he tapped out the number of Landon's extension, and told him to come on up.

Ashton already had a fair idea of the subject they were about to discuss because Landon had called him late on Friday afternoon on his way back from Church Stretton. However, mindful that their conversation was taking place over an unguarded link, Landon had made it clear there were certain matters that would have to wait until they were face to face. Can it wait that long? Ashton had enquired, and had been informed there was no immediate hurry. The fact that Landon appeared so quickly after Ashton had spoken to him suggested a sense of urgency had developed between five o'clock on Friday evening and ten minutes after ten on Monday morning.

'Take a seat, Will, and tell me all about it,' Ashton said, and waved him to a chair.

'Well, as I told you on Friday, Gadsby was very frank but I've done a lot of thinking since then, and it seems to me vindictive would be a more accurate description.'

'And you're wondering just how much of what he told you can be taken literally?' Ashton suggested.

'Yes. To put it bluntly, if most of what he said was true, then Eleanor Gadsby was born evil.'

The thing that really puzzled Landon was why the parents had always taken Eleanor's part against their own natural children. They had been Quakers and therefore predisposed to see the best in people, but they would have had to have been wilfully blind to ignore Eleanor's basic nastiness. And for Mary Orchard to take up with Eleanor again after all she had allegedly done to her beggared belief. There was therefore a case for disregarding everything Gadsby had said.

'Eleanor is an attractive woman,' Landon continued. 'It occurred to me that Lawrence might have it in for his adopted sister because he had tried it on with her when he reached puberty and had been slapped down for his pains.'

'In other words, Gadsby made Eleanor out to be a lot worse than she really is?'

'Yes. But that doesn't mean the lady isn't pretty weird anyway. Look what she said to me about 'The Firm' doing away with Bill Orchard. That's hardly rational.'

'So what do you want to do, Will?'

'I'd like to run Gadstar Promotions and Eleanor Gadsby past MI5 to see if she or her public relations firm has come to their notice.'

'As long as it's unofficial,' Ashton said quietly.

'Yeah, well, there's the problem. I've never had much to do

with the Security Service and don't know who to approach.'

Ashton reached for a memo slip, wrote down a name and number and passed it across the desk to Landon. 'You should know this lady,' he said.

'Francesca York?' Landon looked up. 'The name sounds vaguely familiar.'

'She was a member of the Combined Anti-Terrorist Organisation, as were you, Will, at one time.'

'I don't recall meeting her.'

'Then you certainly haven't met her,' Ashton said drily. 'Fran is not the sort of young woman you forget in a hurry.'

A former lieutenant in the army's Special Counter-Intelligence Team, commonly known as SCIT, Francesca York had been taken on by MI5 at the end of her five-year short-service commission. When Ashton had first met her she had been inclined to see herself as God's own gift to the Security Service. But that had been almost eighteen months ago and her ego had taken a bit of a battering since then. The old innate air of superiority had disappeared and she was a much nicer person for it.

'She's like that, is she?' Landon said.

'Like what?'

'A prickly lady.'

'Don't be put off by her voice on the phone. It can be a bit precise, as if somebody decided Fran should have elocution lessons when she was very young.'

'Sounds grim.'

'Not at all. Francesca is blonde, twenty-seven and quite good-looking. Anyway, if Gadstar and/or Eleanor Gadsby are known to MI5 Francesca will have all the information at her fingertips.' Ashton pointed to the memo slip Landon was holding. 'That's her direct line you've got there, five-nine-four-seven.

'Right.'

'Let me know if you encounter any difficulties,' Ashton said, and immediately regretted it. Even a probationer just out of the Training School would automatically do that and Will had practically run the South American Desk single-handed. 'Forget I said that,' he added.

'I already have,' Landon said, and grinned.

Not so very long ago Hazelwood had told Ashton that he would never amount to more than a Grade I intelligence officer because he lacked the necessary ruthlessness to sack a subordinate for an error of judgement. Well, maybe Victor was right but for all the wrong reasons. He wasn't cut out to be in charge of a department, he was a foot soldier at heart and always would be.

Ashton reached for the millboard in the pending tray and looked at the notes he had made during morning prayers when Hugo Calthorpe was paraphrasing the reports he'd received from Heads of Stations Islamabad and Colombo. The minutes of the meeting were actually recorded by Hazelwood's PA, Mrs Dilys Crowther, and all the Heads of Departments would receive a fair copy of the proceedings by four o'clock that afternoon. The minutes, however, would not encompass the notes he had made. In block capitals he had printed 'ISLAMABAD' and 'DELHI'. Under each heading Ashton had then drawn a face, one smiling, the other downcast. The picture represented Orchard on leaving Pakistan and his subsequent arrival in India. Head of Station, Islamabad had said that when Orchard had left him to go on through the departure lounge, he had been smiling. But when Hugo Calthorpe had met him off the plane at Delhi, Bill had looked pale and withdrawn. He'd also been very quiet for most of the following day. Orchard had claimed he hadn't had a wink of sleep the night before leaving Islamabad because he'd eaten something that had disagreed with him, a condition Head of Station, with whom Bill had been staying, had apparently failed to notice.

As Ashton saw it, Bill's condition had to be the result of something that had happened to him while he'd been waiting in the departure lounge. To ascertain what that might have been would be a monumental task, and right now Ashton couldn't think of a way to go about it, at least not while the present restrictions were in force. He toyed with the idea of asking Hazelwood if the scope of the inquiry couldn't be enlarged but was interrupted by the Mozart secure speech facility before he came to a decision.

When Ashton lifted the receiver, a familiar voice warned him to be careful how he answered, then asked if he was alone.

'Like a hermit, Jill,' he told her.

'I want your help, Peter.'

'To do what?'

'Your advice then. I'm in trouble.'

'Well, I knew this couldn't be a social call.'

'I can do without the snide remarks,' Jill said tersely. 'I want to see you, Peter, right now at my place.'

'Let's get this straight, you expect me to drop everything and nip across town to Highgate?'

'I suppose that is what it amounts to. I don't really know how to beg, Peter, but please, please don't turn your back on me.'

Jill was right, she didn't know how to beg but he didn't want her to because it would demean them both. A long time ago, when they had been an item, Ashton would have gone to the moon and back for Jill but now he could think of a dozen good reasons why he shouldn't lift a finger to help her, but he knew he wasn't hard enough to walk away from her. He told himself it would do no harm to hear what Jill had to say and then take it from there.

'I'll be with you in an hour,' Ashton told her quietly.

'Thank you, thank you,' she said breathlessly.

'You don't have to thank me. I haven't done anything yet.'

'Are you coming by Tube?'

'I don't have much option, I left my car at Havant.'

'OK, I'll pick you up from Archway station.'

'Good.'

'And, Peter – please don't tell Victor where you are going.'

'I wasn't planning to,' Ashton said, and hung up.

Jill shopped at Jaeger, Liberty, Burberry, Austin Reed and Aquascutum, neatly covering Regent Street from one end to the other. Her taste and dress sense were impeccable and she always looked as if she had just stepped out of the pages of *Vogue*. This morning, however, Ashton thought she was less than glamorous. Her tan-coloured slacks were well and truly out of fashion while the grey woollen turtleneck sweater had obviously stretched in the wash and was decidedly loose around the collar. The three-quarter-length coat had been to the dry-cleaners once too often and comfortable-looking was the best that could be said for a pair of scuffed moccasins. Her auburn-tinted hair was concealed by a pull-on hat, and had she not been wearing a pair of sunglasses on what was a bitterly cold day, nobody would have spared her a second glance.

'I take it you're in disguise,' Ashton said.

'I can do without the jokes, even the funny ones, which yours never are.'

Brittle, nerves on edge, worse than she had been on her first day back in the office after returning from Florida. She had left the Porsche 911 in Macdonald Road on a double yellow line right by a fire hydrant and the sight of a parking ticket taped to the windscreen triggered an hysterical outburst. Jill tore the offending Cellophane-wrapped package from the windscreen and would have ripped the ticket to shreds if Ashton hadn't taken it from her.

'Calm down,' he told her. 'Throwing a tantrum won't solve anything.'

'It might just make me feel better.'

'Give me the keys.'

'What?'

'I'm going to drive, you're in too much of a temper.'

'Like hell you will. Get in the car.'

'The keys,' Ashton repeated, and held out his hand. 'Or I leave you here and now.'

'Well, if you feel like that . . .' Jill said, and slapped them into his palm. Ashton walked round the Porsche, got in behind the wheel and started the engine, then shifted into gear, checked the wing mirror to make sure the road behind was clear and pulled away from the kerb. With Jill directing him he turned left at the road junction, went up Highgate Hill into the High Street, and turned left into Bisham Gardens at the top of Waterlow Park. Like the Porsche, the four-bedroom house called Freemantle had belonged to her former husband, Henry Clayburn. She had kept both in lieu of maintenance.

From the integral garage, Jill led through the utility room and kitchen, across the hall and into the large sitting room. Opening the tantalus on top of the drinks cabinet, she removed a cut-glass decanter of whisky and poured two generous measures into Waterford tumblers.

'Ginger ale, soda water or Highland Spring?' Jill asked, her back still towards him.

'I think you'd better drown it in soda water.'

'Literally?'

'Literally, right to the brim.'

Jill filled the tumbler from a bottle of Schweppes, then turned round and handed the glass to Ashton. 'Sit down and make yourself comfortable.'

'I will, but what's this all about?'

'That package arrived this morning,' Jill said, and gestured at the Jiffy bag on the low coffee table in front of the settee. 'Have a look at the contents.'

Ashton picked up the bag and extracted a video cassette

entitled *It Happened One Night*. Half a dozen photographs also spilled out of the bag.

'Don't be shy,' Jill told him, 'take a good look at them.'

Ashton gathered the photographs together. The one on top told him why Jill had been so guarded on the Mozart secure speech facility. All she was wearing in the photograph was a collar, and cuffs on both wrists. A naked man whose face had been deliberately obscured was standing behind Jill cupping a breast in each hand while a girl with dark hair knelt in front of her.

'The next one's better still.'

'I've seen enough,' Ashton told her.

'No, no, you haven't. I want you to look at the next one, taking particular note of my expression and tell me what you make of it.'

The naked man was out of the picture except for his hands, which were on Jill's hips apparently supporting her as she leaned back. The photographer had obviously been standing behind the kneeling woman to catch Jill full frontal.

'Go on, tell me how I look,' Jill demanded angrily. 'Ecstatic? Enraptured? In seventh heaven?'

'None of them is appropriate.'

'Don't go all gallant on me, Peter.'

'I'm not.'

'Let me make it easier for you. Suppose you were a stranger and saw those photographs, wouldn't you think I was participating on my own free will?'

'I would have said you were high on something.'

'Thanks.'

Ashton watched Jill open her handbag, take out a packet of Silk Cut and light one. In all the time he had known her, he had never seen Jill with a cigarette in her mouth before.

'It's a habit I acquired in Florida,' she said as if reading his thoughts.

'Because of this?' Ashton said, pointing to the photographs on the coffee table.

'Yes. I thought it might be a little too obvious if I took to the bottle.'

Jill gazed at the cigarette as if seeing it for the first time. 'I was drug raped,' she said in a dull voice. 'Can you believe it? I wake up in this crummy room in the Regal Hotel, Highland Beach to find all my clothes, US dollars, sterling and traveller's cheques had been stolen. They had also been through my purse but hadn't bothered to steal my credit card, which was a good thing because otherwise I don't know how I would have managed.'

'Maybe you'd better start at the beginning and tell me how you met the naked man and the kneeling woman?'

'Their names are Dan Swordsman and Sara Gay, or at least they are according to the credits on the video. I knew them only as Dan and Sara until the post arrived this morning. I was with a man called Tom Kransky when I met them.'

Ashton waited for her to continue but she had dried up, apparently too embarrassed or ashamed of her part in the affair to go on.

'It began with Kransky, didn't it?' Ashton said bluntly.

'Yes.' Jill leaned forward and stubbed out her cigarette, crushing it to pieces in the heavy glass ashtray on the coffee table. 'We were staying at the same hotel on Marco Island.'

From a smile and a cheerful good morning their relationship had progressed to drinks at the bar and dinner for two. When Kransky had arrived at the hotel where she was staying in Miami they had rapidly become an item. Kransky was about her age, was good-looking, attentive, had a great sense of humour and was definitely charismatic.

'He opened my eyes to what life with Robin Urquhart would be like in the years to come and I knew then that if I did marry Robin it would be an even bigger disaster than my marriage to

Henry. I had taken three weeks' leave of absence to get away from Robin and buy some time to sort myself out. So maybe I was vulnerable to somebody like Tom Kransky.'

After checking into The Breakers, Tom Kransky had suggested they take in some of the night spots. They had started in Boca Raton, then headed back to Delray Beach and a place called Michael's, where, according to Kransky, things had started to go wrong. She had arrived feeling pleasantly mellow on two Bloody Marys, only to wake up in a seedy hotel bedroom with no idea how she came to be there. It had, however, been very evident to her that she had been an involuntary participant in a sexual orgy.

'You know the best part,' Jill continued angrily. 'Kransky accused me of dumping him and had the gall to suggest my behaviour had embarrassed him. Anyway, he took off without saying goodbye to me.' A lopsided smile briefly appeared. 'Still, I can't complain when I intended to do the same to him. I was frightened, Peter, really frightened. I assumed Dan and Sara had taken a number of compromising photographs and my one idea was to return home before they had a chance to blackmail me. I thought I had got away with it until the postman arrived this morning.'

'What time was this?'

'Nine, nine fifteen.'

'Lucky you were in,' Ashton said.

'Luck didn't enter into it. A man phoned on Sunday evening and left a message on the answer machine. He said he was ringing on behalf of the concierge at the Regal Hotel who wanted me to know that some personal items I'd left behind were in the mail and should arrive sometime on Monday.' Jill lit another cigarette, drew the smoke down on to her lungs and slowly exhaled. 'Fortunately, Robin wasn't here.'

Urquhart, Ashton learned, had spent the weekend at his sister's house in Edinburgh and had returned to London on the night sleeper. Robin had phoned her from the FCO as soon as he discovered she had phoned in sick.

'I told him there was nothing to worry about; it was just one of those womanly things and I would be back to normal tomorrow.'

'He knows nothing of this?' Ashton said, pointing to the Jiffy bag again.

'Are you mad? I've told no one but you. Why would I seek your advice if I'd already put my hand up?'

'The bag was posted in London.'

'I had noticed,' Jill said acidly.

'So did the man who left the message on your answer machine have an American accent?'

'Not that I could tell, and before you ask to hear the message, I wiped the tape after I had listened to it.'

'That's a pity. Did he say what he wanted for the master video and all the other copies they have made?'

'Nothing was said about payment and no threats were made.'

'The blackmailer has phoned you again, hasn't he?'

'Yes, this morning. That's why I phoned you.' Jill vented her anger on the cigarette, stubbing it out with vicious jabs. 'He asked for the number of my mobile and wanted to know what was the best time of day to get in touch with me. What should I do, Peter?'

'You already know the answer to that,' Ashton told her. 'You must submit a Change of Circumstance report.'

It would hardly be a new experience for Jill. She had already submitted five such reports, three of which had been inconsequential. The initial one had been submitted when she had become engaged to Ashton, the second after she had broken it off and the third when she had announced her intention of marrying Henry Clayburn. The fourth had been written when she had decided to divorce the despicable Henry after being married to him for a mere eighteen months. The fifth had been triggered by Rosalind Urquhart, who had cited Jill as the co-respondent in an action to divorce her husband on the grounds of his adultery.

'I might just as well submit my resignation,' Jill said after a long silence.

'That's up to you.'

Jill had retained her security clearances on the previous five occasions but she would not be so lucky this time. Her positive vetting status would be withdrawn, as would every other clearance, which meant she would become unemployable.

'I was set up, damn it. Whatever happened in that hotel room was not of my volition. I wasn't drunk, I hadn't been sniffing coke, I was drugged and then raped.'

'Some people would say you merely looked spaced out.'

'And what do you say?'

'Well, I know you better than most. You're not a nun, Jill, nor are you a sex-crazy nymphomaniac.'

'Thanks for damning me with faint praise.'

'On the other hand,' Ashton continued bluntly, 'there's such a thing as guilt by association.'

'Who are you talking about?'

'Your ex and a letter a British contract officer in the Bahrain Police Force wrote to the ambassador concerning the business activities of Henry Clayburn.'

The relevant folio, together with the accompanying photograph, had been removed from Jill's file by Roy Kelso and subsequently destroyed by Stuart Dunglass, the previous Director General of the SIS. But not all had been lost because Victor Hazelwood had lodged a reconstructed version in his Demi-Official file.

Henry Clayburn had made his fortune on the back of the oil revenues enjoyed by the Gulf sheikdoms. He had started at the age of twenty-six in Abu Dhabi when the money was beginning to flow into the country from the oil strike on Dás Island.

Suddenly the nomadic way of life in the sheikdom changed: goats, dates and camels lost much of their attraction; Chevrolets, Ford Mustangs, Lincoln Continentals, fridge-freezers, TVs, Rolex watches and music centres were in – durable commodities that Clayburn had been happy to supply. After establishing other emporia in the neighbouring Emirates, he had moved to Bahrain, where he had been faced with much stiffer competition.

He had overcome this problem by making himself useful to some of the well-connected young blades about town. In practical terms this had meant pandering to their not-so-little fantasies concerning European women. Clayburn had, in short, become a procurer. One member of his stable was said to have been the wife of an insurance undermanager at the British Bank of the Middle East; another had been an air hostess with Lufthansa.

But it was the colour snapshot the British contract officer had sent to the ambassador that could really damage Jill, even though it no longer existed. The subject was a young woman who had discarded all her clothing except for a pair of high-heeled shoes, black stockings and a suspender belt. She had been wearing a yashmak so that all that could be seen of her features were her blue eyes. For added eroticism, Clayburn had been photographed standing behind the woman, cupping her breasts in the palms of his hands.

The woman had been identified as Clayburn's first wife, Helen, whom he had divorced on the grounds of her adultery with Inspector Leslie North, the contract police officer. All this had happened eight years before Jill had even met Henry Clayburn. There was, however, every reason to suppose she had known all about his nefarious activities when she had married him because North, believing Clayburn had been instrumental in getting him sacked, had fired off his infamous letter to the British Ambassador.

'I don't suppose it will count for anything that I divorced Henry when I realised what sort of man I had married?'

'I think it's fair to say you've had too many near misses,' Ashton told her.

Jill lit a third cigarette, her hands shaking. 'Will you do me a favour?' she asked, still in a nervous voice.

'Depends what it is.'

'Can you prepare the ground for me with Victor?'

'Are you out of your mind?'

'Hear me out, Peter. At least you can do that. It's always been Victor's hallmark that he makes things happen instead of reacting to events. Right?'

'Yes.'

OK, if I put my hand up I'm out on my ear and everybody says that's one security risk the less. But if I'm allowed to stay on and the "hostiles" believe I'm in their pocket, we could achieve much, much more. I think Victor might go for that solution.'

In spite of everything, Ashton found himself hanging on to her every word.

Chapter 7

The one question he should have asked Jill only occurred to Ashton on the way back to Vauxhall Cross. It was so obvious and so pertinent that he couldn't think why it hadn't been on the tip of his tongue. If she had been set up and Kransky had been actively involved, as Jill now believed, how would he have known her itinerary? Since joining SIS Ashton had left the country only on official business with the exception of a weekend in Paris a long, long time ago. Just who had to be informed and whose approval was required when planning a vacation abroad was now something of a closed book to him. If there was one man in the organisation who would know the procedure backwards it was Roy Kelso, the Assistant Director in charge of the Admin Wing.

Roy Kelso had held the appointment of Assistant Director, Administration for as long as most people could remember. His empire comprised the Financial Branch, the Motor Transport and General Stores Section plus the Security Vetting and Technical Services Division. He was responsible for claims and expenses, control of expenditure, internal audits, Boards of Inquiry, clerical support, travel arrangements, and legal representation when required. He was not the most popular senior officer in the SIS. Promoted to Assistant Director a week after his thirty-ninth birthday, Kelso had convinced himself that he was destined to go right to the top. Ten years later it had become evident even to him that he had been passed over and would go no further. In a fit of pique he had applied for early retirement, only to have second thoughts. Consequently he had been obliged to write what had amounted to a begging letter requesting permission to withdraw the application, which had made him even more embittered.

Kelso could not forget that Hazelwood had been a Grade I intelligence officer when he had joined the top table. Worse still, Kelso had attained his present rank only a few months after Jill Sheridan had completed her induction course at the Training School. If there was one person he couldn't stand above all others it was Jill Sheridan, of whom he was a little afraid. It was no secret that it would give him enormous satisfaction if he could somehow pull the rug from under her feet. Aware of his ambition, Ashton knew he would need to be very careful how he obtained the information he wanted from the Admin King.

Kelso's office was a tiny cubbyhole but it was on the top floor, which was very much a status symbol for some people. He had fought very hard to join the eyrie and had justified the move on the curious grounds that since the Financial Branch, Motor Transport and General Stores Section, and the Security Vetting and Technical Services Division were all on different floors of the building, he would be divorced from them wherever his office was located. In theory Kelso was more accessible to the other heads of departments; in practice he was frequently out of the office visiting the various branches of his empire, as Ashton had already discovered, having visited his lair twice before. On this occasion, however, it was a case of third time lucky.

'Are you busy, Roy?' Ashton enquired.

'One doesn't have to look for work in this job,' Kelso told him pompously. 'There's always something which needs to be done.'

'In that case I'll come back later.'

'Don't go. There's nothing so urgent that I can't spare you a few minutes, Peter.'

There was a certain oiliness about Roy Kelso, especially when he wanted to project himself as Mr Nice Guy. If he was dropping everything to make time for Ashton, the nearly empty state of his in- and pending trays suggested he was doing so more out of curiosity than a genuine desire to be helpful.

'Harriet and I are thinking of adding a few extra days to the Easter break so I've been looking at standing orders regarding travel abroad.'

'I only wish the other assistant directors would follow your example.'

Weasel words and creepy with it; somehow Ashton managed to hide his contempt.

'I was looking at the list of high-risk countries and wondered if mine was up to date. It shows the whole of the former Eastern Bloc. No account has been taken of the reunification of East and West Germany, nor the break-up of Czechoslovakia.'

'You're right, your copy is out of date,' Kelso told him. 'Where are you and Harriet thinking of going?'

'We fancy Egypt. All being well, Harriet's sister-in-law will look after the children.'

'I would avoid Egypt if I were you. Gamaat al-Islamiyah terrorists massacred seventeen Greek tourists outside a hotel in Cairo near the pyramids in April last year. There's every likelihood Gamaat al-Islamiyah will continue with their policy of targeting Europeans. They're out to destroy the tourist trade and thereby bring down the Government.'

'I guess that rules out the Valley of the Kings for the next few years. Is it true to say China, Cuba, Burma, Vietnam, Cambodia, Laos, the Lebanon and Iran are all off limits to people like me?'

'You've left out Iraq,' Kelso said gleefully. 'We wouldn't be too happy about you going to the Baltic States or Russia either.'

'Neither would I,' Ashton said drily. 'Nobody's got anything against the States, have they? I wouldn't mind doing a fly-drive from New Orleans going up the Mississippi to Natchez and Vicksburg, see some of the antebellum homes and take in the Civil War battlefields.'

'How many days will you be tagging on to Easter?'

'Seven' – ten if Victor is willing.'

'I don't see how he could object; after all, he allowed Jill Sheridan to get away for three weeks and she is Deputy DG.'

'Good point. I might just remind Victor if he raises any objection.'

'With your record I would have thought they were more likely to be raised by the State Department.'

Lake Arrowhead, St Louis, Nine Mile Drive outside Richmond, St Clare's Hospital in New York, Denver and more recently, Chesapeake Bay: Ashton had to admit trouble seemed to follow him around. But what the State Department thought of him was immaterial in this instance; his whole line of enquiry was bogus and was intended for another purpose.

'If you do decide to take a holiday in America, I shall need three copies of your detailed itinerary – dates, places to be visited, hotels et cetera.'

'Three copies?'

'Yes, one for the file, one for Head of Station, Washington, and one to the CIA.'

'That's news to me. When was this procedure introduced?'

'In 1995 by the previous DG, Sir Stuart Dunglass, and you won't have heard of it before now because it only applies to senior officers.'

The procedure had come into being because Dunglass had decided it was only common courtesy to let the CIA know when a senior officer of the SIS was visiting the United States for personal reasons. The detailed itinerary was intended to allay any suspicion that the individual concerned was operating illegally inside the US of A. It so happened Jill Sheridan had been the first person to be affected by this new standing order.

'Two questions,' Ashton said. 'What do the CIA do with their copy when Continental America is off limits to any operations they might want to conduct?'

'That's entirely up to them.'

'And Head of Station?'

'Delacombe is responsible for ensuring the FBI is aware of the impending visit, in case the CIA omit to pass on the information.'

'Thank you, Roy, you've been most helpful.'

'One small point,' Kelso said, arresting him as he was about to leave, 'I must have your detailed itinerary a minimum of three weeks before your departure date.'

'Good Friday is March the twenty-eighth, which gives me a little over five weeks.'

'Then you'd better get a move on.'

Three weeks' notice, three copies, and Jill's itinerary known to the CIA, the FBI, Head of Station, Washington and God knows how many clerks. If one had a mind to believe Jill's story, it was possible to see how Kransky might have known about her movements at least a fortnight in advance. Just who had passed him the information was, however, another matter altogether, one that Ashton had no desire to resolve.

There was a note from Landon waiting for Ashton when he returned to his office. In effect it said that Francesca York had told Will that the person he ought to see was Colin Wales, the Head of K2 Section, which monitored the activities of suspected subversives. Unfortunately Wales was out of the office and was unlikely to be available until five o'clock. As Ms York had kindly offered to introduce him to Wales, he had arranged to meet her at MI5's Gower Street address at four thirty.

Louella Kay Lincoln was the great-granddaughter four times removed of a slave owned by General John Bell Hood,

Confederate States Army. Louella was fifty-three and although only five feet six she weighed over 180 pounds. She had never had much luck with the men in her life. The hot-shot quarter back who'd been her boyfriend in High School had walked away from Louella after making her pregnant at the age of fifteen. At nineteen she had married an insurance salesman ten years older than herself who had been regarded as a good catch by her parents. However, the so-called good catch was by nature a violent man who liked nothing better than to knock his wife about when he'd had a few beers. Five years on and three children later he had walked out of the house one summer's morn and never returned, which Louella had regarded as a blessed relief.

Life in general had not been exactly kind to Louella Lincoln either. She had come through all her normal childhood illnesses but had then caught diphtheria and nearly died. In the winter of '81 she had slipped on an icy patch on the sidewalk and, falling over backwards, had fractured her skull. Louella Kay had spent the next eight days on a life-support machine and the doctors and nurses at the John Hopkins had feared she would not regain consciousness. She did not, however, make a complete recovery. There had been collateral brain damage to the extent that her attention span became progressively limited and she found it difficult to concentrate on the minutiae of her job.

When still a young woman she had put herself through night school and had qualified as a legal executive. No longer able to cope with the work, she had left the law practice of her own accord to seek less demanding work. She had, in short, become a domestic, and was currently employed by Mr and Mrs Thomas Kransky, Apartment 56, Belmont House, Warren Avenue on Federal Hill.

Following a bad attack of angina, Louella Kay had not been into work since last Wednesday. She had, of course, telephoned her employers on the Thursday morning to explain the situation and Mrs Kransky had been very understanding. Paula Kransky had told her there was nothing so urgent it couldn't wait a day or two and she was to stay at home until she was feeling much better. Louella Kay had rung the apartment again yesterday morning and, getting no answer, had left a message on the answer phone to the effect that the rest had done her the world of good and she would be coming in on the Monday at the usual time.

A foul smell was the first thing to strike Louella as she let herself into the Kranskys' apartment. Because no one answered when she called out, Louella immediately assumed her employers had gone away on an extended weekend and that the fridge-freezer had blown a fuse and defrosted in their absence. Acting on that assumption she walked down the hall, opened the last door on her left and looked inside the kitchen. There was nothing wrong, the fridge-freezer was quietly humming away and the only smell was coming from the rose-scented air freshener.

The living room told a different story. Paula Kransky was lying face down across one arm of the sofa, her toes barely touching the carpet. A cushion had been placed over her head and it was all too obvious that she had been shot twice at point-blank range. A great deal of blood and grey matter, which had seeped through the cushion before the onset of rigor mortis, had now dried out, forming an obscene crust around the skull like a halo. At the moment of death Paula Kransky had fouled her pantihose.

Although there was a telephone in the sitting room Louella Lincoln could not bring herself to use it. She retreated into the kitchen where there was a second phone and collapsed into a wooden upright chair, her hands shaking, the taste of bile in her mouth. It was a good ten minutes before she felt able to lift the receiver off the hook and make a 911 call. The response was virtually immediate. Two officers arrived at the apartment in half the time it had taken Louella to phone the police. They had a whole raft of questions for her. How long had she been working for Mrs Kransky? When did she last see her? How well did she know Mr Kransky? How often had Louella seen them together? Did the Kranskys appear to get on well? Who else had a key to the apartment?

Two detectives from Homicide put in an appearance while Louella was still being interrogated by the responding officers. Naturally they took her over the same ground again before pitching a whole lot more questions, many of which she couldn't answer. How could she tell them what the Kranskys kept in the wall safe in the master bedroom when she didn't know there was one concealed behind the picture? No, she couldn't say what had been stolen. Goddamnit, the sight of Mrs Kransky bent over the sofa and the awful smell had completely unnerved her. The fact that the apartment had been ransacked had scarcely registered with her. Mr Kransky was a movie producer with an office somewhere in town. He was frequently away for days at a time – probably in Hollywood. Sometimes Mrs Kransky accompanied him.

Louella wanted the detectives to know Mr Kransky was a kind man, he'd run her home a couple of times when she'd had an attack of angina. Lots of employers had fired her when they had learned of her condition but not Paula and Tom. What sort of car did he drive? A dark blue Chevvy Corvette – had a broad stripe from the hood, across the roof and trunk to below the plate. No, she couldn't remember the licence plate – couldn't they find that out for themselves?

The medical examiner came and went, Paula was carried out of the apartment in a body bag and the police photographer shot a load of film. Two men from Forensic were busy taking the sofa apart looking for a bullet that had apparently exited through the forehead. All this Louella witnessed, a familiar pain making itself felt in her chest and getting worse by the minute because she had forgotten to transfer the pills for her angina when she had changed handbags that morning.

In Ashton's experience the end of the day was not a good time to catch Hazelwood since he was never in a hurry to go home. Rumour had it that his reluctance to leave the office was entirely due to his wife, Alice, and her penchant for entertaining all and sundry. It wasn't true: Alice gave only one dinner party a week and Victor didn't stay late on those occasions. He had once told Ashton that he did some of his best work after everybody else had gone home. What he really liked to do was bounce his ideas off a captive audience and if you went to see him shortly before five thirty, chances were you would become the captive sounding board of the day. Ashton hadn't minded staying late when he had been living in Ravenscourt Park but since setting up house in Bosham, down on the coast, he had avoided seeing Victor after 4 p.m. whenever possible. This afternoon, however, was one of those occasions when Ashton didn't have any choice.

Although he wasn't going to plead her case, Jill Sheridan was in deep trouble and Victor was entitled to know the facts before the whole thing blew up in his face. A faint hope that Dilys Crowther would tell him the DG was too busy was dashed when he walked into her office and saw the green light above the communicating door was on. Had the red light been showing he could have put off briefing Victor until tomorrow.

'Please go straight in, Mr Ashton,' Dilys told him with a saccharine smile.

There was no easy way of breaking the news to Victor that his deputy had had a starring role in a porno movie. In a neutral voice Ashton related everything that had happened to Jill from the moment she had met Tom Kransky to the anonymous phone call she had received early that morning. Hazelwood didn't interrupt him once. His only reaction was to help himself to a Burma cheroot from the ornate cigar box on his desk.

'Why did Jill tell you?' Hazelwood asked when he had finished.

'Because she wanted me to prepare the ground.'

'Prepare the ground? If there's one person who should know the drill backwards it's Jill Sheridan. God knows, she has submitted enough Change of Circumstance reports. The only difference this time is that her resignation should accompany the report.'

'Jill maintains she was set up,' Ashton said tentatively.

'That's as good an excuse as any.'

'There could be something to her claim.'

'You're going soft in the head,' Hazelwood told him bluntly.

'Why? Because I could be persuaded that what happened to Jill could be a variation of the honey trap the KGB used back in the good old bad days? The people who set Jill up haven't demanded money, they're out to recruit her.'

'That's her story. The only evidence you've seen are the photographs and a video cassette which you haven't viewed. Jill is a quick-witted, resourceful woman whose footwork can't be faulted. She is quite capable of fabricating a convincing explanation for what happened after meeting Kransky. And her suggestion that she should be used as bait to entrap some unknown hostile intelligence service is a stroke of genius.'

'What if her story is true?'

Hazelwood gazed at him in disbelief, his right hand outstretched towards the cut-down brass shellcase, which served as an ashtray. 'Have you taken leave of your senses?' he asked rhetorically, then tapped the ash from the cheroot, neatly missing the target to deposit it on the desk. 'If we did act on Jill's suggestion we'd have to forego a Change of Circumstance report. We couldn't risk placing one on her security file, and where would that leave us if word of Jill's antics in Florida did get out and made the front page of the tabloids? We wouldn't have a leg to stand on.'

'Jill, you and I are not going to leak anything,' Ashton told him. 'Neither are the blackmailers.'

'You're gifted with second sight, are you?'

'They knew who they were targeting—'

'You're right,' Hazelwood said, interrupting him. 'They know how ambitious Jill is and just how far she is prepared to go in order to slide into my chair when I retire.'

'I think you've just accepted the case Jill made for herself. The only thing is, whoever set Jill up clearly misjudged her. They were banking on her remaining silent but she didn't.' Ashton paused, then said, 'I wouldn't like you to get the wrong idea, I'm merely acting as devil's advocate.'

'I don't care for your acting.' Hazelwood crushed what was left of the Burma cheroot in the ashtray. 'Get back to Jill and tell her to submit a Change of Circumstance report.'

'Right.'

'And this conversation never took place. Understand?'

'Perfectly.'

Ashton was about to open the communicating door when Hazelwood asked him what, if anything, Landon had discovered about Eleanor Gadsby. The short answer was very little other than the fact that the lady was a spiteful piece of work. Will might return from Gower Street having learned something about her and/or Gadstar Promotions from MI5 but Ashton was inclined to doubt it. Francesca York hadn't been able to give Landon an answer off the cuff when he had phoned her shortly after morning prayers.

'York is in the Irish Section, isn't she?' Hazelwood asked.

'Yes. She also happens to be a member of the Combined Anti-Terrorist Organisation. That's why I thought she might have the information at her fingertips if Eleanor Gadsby or Gadstar Promotions were known to Five.'

'Let's not jump to conclusions before we hear from Landon.'

'I'd like to get shot of this inquiry no matter what Landon brings back from Gower Street.'

The whole business had started because Eleanor Gadsby had alleged the SIS had murdered her brother-in-law. Since Hugo Calthorpe was now in charge of the Asian Department and was already investigating Orchard's demeanour on leaving Islamabad, Ashton thought it would make sense if Calthorpe took over the inquiry. Unfortunately, Hazelwood didn't agree with him and said so vehemently.

Will Landon had to admit Francesca York's voice on the telephone had sounded exactly as Ashton had described it. Her diction was clear, measured and careful; like Ashton, he believed an ambitious mother had arranged for her to have elocution lessons when she was very young. Down the years she had also cultivated a pseudo-upper class accent with a gentle 'orf' instead of 'off'. On meeting her, however, Landon felt Ashton hadn't done Francesca justice. According to him, she wore her blonde hair long to soften her hard features. Maybe her face had filled out a little since Ashton had seen her last because personally Landon found her quite appealing. He also thought if he had met the former Intelligence Corps officer when they had both been members of the Combined Anti-Terrorist Organisation he would certainly have remembered her.

Landon had expected to be introduced to Colin Wales but it seemed the head of K2 had been called to yet another meeting and Francesca York was deputising for him. It was an arrangement that met with his approval and he happily followed Francesca up to her small office on the second floor.

'Tea or coffee?' she asked. 'I hasten to add both are better than the tea and coffee dispensed by your vending machines.'

The clerks had been plying him with cups of coffee at regular intervals throughout the day until it was practically running out of his ears. The last thing he needed was another cup but it would be churlish to refuse.

'I'm going to have one,' Francesca said as if to encourage him.

'OK. Black then, please, no sugar.'

She buzzed the clerks, asked if she could please have two cups of coffee, one white with, one black without, then made small talk while they waited. Learning that he lived off Gloucester Road, Francesca told him they were practically neighbours because she had a flat in Derry Street just off Kensington High Street. In the next couple of minutes she also discovered he had a pilot's licence, was busy rebuilding a ten-year-old Aston Martin V8 model and held a black belt in judo. But for the arrival of the coffee Landon reckoned there would have been few areas of his life that she hadn't uncovered.

'I'm afraid I've drawn a blank with Gadstar Promotions,' Francesca said as soon as the clerk left the office. 'The company hasn't come to our notice. Do you know who or what they promote?'

'I was hoping you were going to tell me.'

'When did you say Eleanor Gadsby was born?'

'The sixteenth of June nineteen forty-eight at Chipping Norton. She's the illegitimate daughter of Virginia Westwood.'

'An Eleanor May Westwood was convicted of assaulting a police officer in nineteen seventy during the Grosvenor Square riot and was sentenced to one month's imprisonment. It has to be the same woman.'

Apart from being violently opposed to the Vietnam War, Eleanor Gadsby had also been active in the Campaign for Nuclear Disarmament and had often been observed outside South Africa House demonstrating against apartheid. She had not, however, committed any further offences that would have warranted her arrest after Grosvenor Square and by

1976 she had disappeared from the protest scene altogether.

'What has that lady done to excite your interest?' Francesca asked.

Landon hesitated. When Hazelwood had appointed Ashton to investigate Orchard's suicide he had been the only person Peter had been allowed to brief but that restriction had already been breached to some extent. You couldn't go to Five and ask them what they had on Eleanor Gadsby and Gadstar Promotions without the Security Service expecting a trade-off.

'The lady accuses us of murdering her brother-in-law, Bill Orchard,' Landon told her bluntly.

'And did you?' Francesca asked with a mischievous grin.

'But of course. We broke into the Orchards' house in the dead of night, dragged Bill out of bed without waking Mary Orchard and put him to sleep in his garage with carbon monoxide fumes from the car.'

'So what is Eleanor really like?'

'According to her adoptive brother she is a thoroughly nasty piece of work. Evil is the word he actually used. Personally, I think the whole family is dysfunctional.'

'Is that the official line, Will?'

The sudden use of his first name almost threw him. 'It will be if I have anything to do with it,' he said.

'Well, like you, we are no longer interested in Eleanor Gadsby.'

Landon recognised the declaration for what it was – an example of the official denial so popular with politicians and civil servants. Intended to allay suspicion, it invariably had the opposite effect.

Chapter 8

Officer Jamieson made a right on O'Donnell Street and headed for the waterfront and the run-down area of Baltimore across the Patapsco River from Fort McHenry. Beside him his partner, Frank Zigmund, rocked backwards and forwards, his head lolling, his mouth open. It was twenty after five in the morning, this was their first graveyard shift and they had been on duty for three hours twenty. If Frank Zigmund was going to do this to him every night, Jamieson could see he was going to have a fun time over the next month.

He didn't greatly care for his partner; Zigmund was a lazy cop who did the minimum to get by. He was unfit, at least twenty pounds overweight, smoked like a chimney and had a bad attitude towards women. Other than being police officers they had nothing in common. More than once Jamieson had considered asking to be rerostered with another officer or transferred to a different precinct but each time he'd had second thoughts. Fact was, someone had to put up with Zigmund.

'Hey, Frank, wake up,' he said, and gave Zigmund a none-too-gentle punch on the arm. 'Look alive and throw some light on the neighbourhood.'

'What the hell's got into you, punching me like that? You've bruised my fucking arm.'

'Put the spot on and stop bellyaching.'

On the edge of Dundalk, Hawks Point had once been a thriving mercantile centre. Its now derelict buildings were not, however, the happy hunting ground of the criminal fraternity. The drug pushers, hookers and muggers did their business in central downtown Baltimore where the pickings were richer. What you got in Hawks Point were the winos, the homeless and the occasional crazy. In Jamieson's book that didn't mean you closed your eyes to what was going on.

'I need to take a leak,' Zigmund suddenly announced. 'Right now before I pee in my pants.'

Jamieson sighed. That was another reason why he didn't like Zigmund: the guy had a weak bladder. 'Don't take all night about it,' he said, and stopped the car opposite the two-storey building fronting the burned-out warehouse.

Muttering under his breath, Zigmund got out and slammed the door behind him, then walked away from the shaft of light cast by the spot. It was then that Jamieson thought he could see something just outside the beam. Switching off the engine, he grabbed a flashlight and got out. He walked towards the two-storey building that had once been the head office of a depository company and found his eyes hadn't deceived him. As he stood there mentally congratulating himself, Zigmund called out, asking what he was doing.

'Come and see for yourself,' Jamieson told him.

There were two cars parked outside the low building, a red Ford Taurus LX and a Chevrolet Corvette. Both vehicles were up on blocks, their wheels removed.

'So what's the big deal?' Zigmund demanded. 'What you've got here is a couple of wrecks. You see 'em all the time in this neck of the woods.'

'I think the Corvette belongs to Tom Kransky, the movie producer who killed his wife over in Federal Hill.'

'How do you know? The plate's missing.'

'The vehicle matches the description Homicide were given.'

'You wish,' Zigmund said contemptuously.

Jamieson ignored him and climbed the external fire escape.

He tried the door facing him at the top of the metal staircase and found it wasn't locked. A foul, sickly sweet odour hit him as soon as he stepped inside the narrow passageway. Tracing the source to the first room on the left, he held a handkerchief over his nose and mouth, then opened the door and walked into a slaughterhouse.

Jill Sheridan was the last person Ashton had expected to see at morning prayers on Wednesday. He had phoned Jill on Monday evening from his home to inform her that Hazelwood wanted a Change of Circumstance report and her letter of resignation in the post the following morning. Her absence on Tuesday suggested she had complied with Victor's instructions and would never set foot inside Vauxhall Cross again. Yet, barely thirty-six hours after he'd given her the news, there she was sitting in her rightful place at the conference table, apparently without a care in the world. Even more surprising was the fact that Hazelwood seemed to be completely at ease with the situation.

Cool to the point of iciness, that was Jill Sheridan. There were no telltale signs to indicate she hadn't been sleeping too well, nor did she look pale, tense or nervous. The smile that Jill gave him when she became aware that Ashton was staring at her was more serene than wry.

'What have you got for us this morning, Peter?'

'Me?' Ashton said, caught off guard.

'As far as I know there is only one Peter here,' Hazelwood said pithily.

Ashton glanced at the notes Chris Neighbour, the senior collator on the Russian Desk, had prepared for him.

'The CIA can't agree the figures the Russians have released concerning their stocks of chemical weapons.'

'How big is the discrepancy?'

'Minister of Defence, Marshal Konstantin Nikolayevich

Talanov claims their war reserve has never mounted to more than forty thousand tons—'

'How much?' Benton asked, interrupting him, his voice practically an octave higher than normal.

'More than enough to kill every man, woman and child on this planet twice over,' Hazelwood told him, then turned to Ashton again. 'You were saying?'

'The Agency calculates the Ivans had approximately three hundred thousand tons, meaning just over a quarter of a million is unaccounted for.'

'What's the strength of their allegation?'

'It's not without substance,' Ashton told him. 'The figure is based on satellite photographs of chemical plants and obvious supply depots. With this data they were able to calculate the production and storage capacity of each installation.'

'Have you consulted Defence Intelligence and sought their opinion?' Hazelwood asked.

'We're in the process of doing so. Chris Neighbour is over at the Ministry of Defence now.'

Ashton didn't offer any comment. Victor knew as well as he did that Chris Neighbour was unlikely to return from the MoD with a conflicting opinion. Every week the USAF delivered a planeload of satellite photographs to Brize Norton, which were then dispatched to RAF Brampton where they were studied at the Joint Air Reconnaissance Interpretation Centre. The Photo Interpreters and analysts, Special Intelligence who examined this material had nothing to compare it against. Such discrepancies they did find were likely to be of a minor nature and would have been routinely addressed by the appropriate US intelligence agency. Nobody at Brampton was going to find an error in the region of a quarter of a million tons.

'Any other titbits?' Hazelwood asked.

'Yes.' Ashton checked his notes again. 'We have confirmation from a reliable source that Vladimir Aleksandrovich

Labur, Director of Chemical Defence Research, resigned on December thirty-first nineteen ninety-six on the grounds of ill health. He is said to have an inoperable cancer.'

'Good Lord, I thought he was dead,' Calthorpe said. 'Labur was involved in a traffic accident and was in a coma for eleven weeks before they switched off the life-support machine. At least that was the story going the rounds when I was serving in Moscow.'

'When was this, Hugo?'

'Early February 'ninety-one.'

It was the time when Ashton had been put out to grass with the Security Vetting and Technical Services Division where he had been denied access to sensitive information coming out of the former Soviet Union. But it transpired Hazelwood had no recollection of the incident either and he had been the Assistant Director of the Eastern Bloc in those days.

'Any other points? No?' Hazelwood eased his chair away from the table and stood up. 'Same time tomorrow, gentlemen,' he added, and swept out of the conference room.

Ashton followed suit and caught up with Hazelwood in the corridor before he entered the PA's office.

'I hope you can spare me a few minutes, Director?' he said with barely suppressed anger.

'I've always got time for you, Peter. You know that.'

Ashton could think of a number of instances when this hadn't been the case but as always he let it pass. Harriet had never understood their relationship and couldn't fathom why Victor had commanded his loyalty for so long. In her opinion loyalty extended in both directions, down as well as up. The funny thing was that whenever Ashton was inclined to agree with Harriet, Victor always did something that restored his faith in him.

'You want to know what Jill's doing here,' he said after closing the communicating door on Dilys Crowther.

'Yes I do. Everything seemed to be cut and dried on Monday. On your instruction I told Jill to submit her resignation with a Change of Circumstance report.'

'The situation has changed since then. We're letting things run their course.'

'In other words, you've changed your mind and have decided to use Jill in the role of double agent.'

'Let's say I was persuaded to do so.'

The noticeable lack of enthusiasm in Hazelwood's voice said all. One of Jill's friends in high places must have brought pressure to bear, and for some reason he had folded.

'Who talked you into it?' Ashton asked. 'Robin Urquhart?'

'He was the spokesman. There were other, more powerful figures behind him.'

'And they were obviously in a hurry. On Monday afternoon Jill gets her marching orders, by Wednesday morning they have been rescinded.' Ashton shook his head, perplexed. 'Or did it happen even quicker?'

'I spent most of yesterday sorting the mess out with the Foreign and Commonwealth Office. When Robin Urquhart went home to Bisham Gardens last night he was able to tell Jill she would be retained for the foreseeable future as a controlled agent in place.'

An agent in place, especially one as senior as Jill Sheridan, was the biggest asset any intelligence service could hope to acquire. To use that agent in place against the people who had recruited him or her was a high-risk operation that could prove extremely costly should it go badly wrong. To play the double-cross game successfully the agent in place had to disclose certain items of highly classified information to the case officer in order to maintain credibility. As always the difficulty lay in deciding what price you were prepared to pay in terms of damage and, in an extreme case, how many lives you were willing to sacrifice simply to stay in the game. With Jill as a player, a committee would have to agree what information she could be allowed to pass on. Hazelwood would obviously be a member but aside from Robin Urquhart, Ashton couldn't think who else would be co-opted.

'Why don't you share them with me?' Hazelwood suddenly asked.

'What?'

'Your thoughts.'

'Actually I was wondering who else will be vetting the information you give Jill.'

'Robin Urquhart and two Privy Councillors whose names I'm not going to disclose.'

'Can I be frank?'

'You've never asked for my permission before,' Hazelwood told him.

'Is this another of those conversations that never took place?'

'If the whole business ends in tears, Peter, feigning ignorance will be your best defence.'

'Is that what you're telling me to do?'

'In a word – yes.'

'Are you covered?'

'That's my problem.' Hazelwood reached for the Burma cheroot, then quickly withdrew his hand from the box as if he had been stung by a wasp. 'I'm trying to cut down, perhaps give them up altogether,' he said by way of explanation.

'You could have picked a better time,' Ashton observed.

'Maybe. What did Landon get from Five on Monday?'

'Very little. According to Francesca York, Gadstar Promotions hasn't come to their notice. However, K2, the section responsible for monitoring subversives, admits to being aware of Eleanor Gadsby's existence. Apparently she was sentenced to one month's imprisonment for assaulting a police officer during the Grosvenor Square riot. By nineteen seventy-six she had dropped out of the protest scene and hasn't been in trouble since then. York maintains Five has lost interest in the lady; Will thought she was fibbing. He could be right. The way I see it, Five had to tell us about Eleanor Gadsby's conviction because they knew we could get that information for ourselves from the National Identification Bureau.'

'So what do you propose we do?'

They had enough evidence already to show that Eleanor Gadsby nursed a lasting hatred for her adoptive siblings and was out to make trouble for them in any way she could. In Hazelwood's shoes Ashton knew he would forget the damned woman for the time being and concentrate all their resources on discovering what it was that had driven Bill Orchard to commit suicide. And that was unquestionably a job for Hugo Calthorpe. But before committing himself to any course of action Ashton would want to satisfy himself that Francesca York was not trying to pull a fast one.

'I recommend you have a word with K and ask him point blank as one Director General to another whether or not MI5 is keeping an eye on Gadstar Promotions.'

'And then?'

'And then you have to decide whether or not to investigate Orchard's financial position during the last six months of his life.'

Amongst other things it would mean obtaining a sight of his bank accounts, current and deposit, if the latter was applicable. Given the whole-hearted co-operation of the solicitor handling the probate, they would have a detailed picture of Bill's assets. Of course, no judge would give them the necessary court order but there were other ways of acquiring the information. The expression on Hazelwood's face when Ashton began to explain just how this could be done killed that line of enquiry stone dead.

'You'd better rein Landon in,' Hazelwood told him.

'And Gadstar Promotions?'

'I'll talk to MI5. Meantime you need only concern yourself with matters affecting the Russian Desk.'

It was what Ashton wanted to hear, what he had been angling for all along.

Defence Intelligence was located in what used to be the Air Ministry but was known as the Main Building. The organisation was split into departments numbered consecutively from DI1 to DI24 with the odd gap here and there caused by branches that were now defunct. DI7, which was staffed by RAF personnel, dealt with photo reconnaissance and satellite intelligence. One of the first things Chris Neighbour had been issued with after being expelled from Russia was a plastic entry card that enabled the holder to gain admittance to every government office in Whitehall. Predominantly white in colour, the central motif was a broad, green directional arrow directly above which the registration number of the card had been embossed. The system did away with the visitor's pass; all Neighbour had to do was insert the card in the slot, tap out the entry code he had committed to memory and the turnstile gate was released. It was, however, essential to leave by the same gateway otherwise the computer controlling that access would have him logged as still inside the building. Consequently his card would not be actioned the next time he went there.

Although not a frequent visitor to DI7 Neighbour had got to know Group Captain Keith Amesbury-Cotton RAF pretty well and would be sorry to see him go when he was replaced in April. Amesbury-Cotton was an easy man to like; he was unfailingly cheerful, had a keen sense of humour, and had a knack of putting everybody at their ease. He was forty-three years old, married to a former nursing sister and had three children, two girls aged fifteen and twelve and a boy of nine. A fighter pilot, he had flown a Harrier jump jet off HMS *Hermes* during the Falklands campaign, shooting down two Mirage III planes in one action and winning a Distinguished Flying Cross in the process. In '91 he had taken part in Desert Storm, leading Tornado fighter bombers in night raids directed against airfields, radar installations and surface-to-air missile batteries defending Baghdad. Amesbury-Cotton had never spoken of this, nor had he mentioned the Air Force Cross he had been awarded when seconded as a test pilot to British Aerospace for three years, or the OBE that had appeared in the New Year Honours List in 1988. Neighbour only knew about the honours and awards because the Ministry of Defence had sent Amesbury-Cotton's CV to the SIS when he had been appointed head of DI7.

'Good to see you again, Chris,' he said, waving Neighbour to a chair. 'I gather this is another episode in the great missing gas conspiracy.'

'I fear so. The CIA reckons the Russians have over two hundred and fifty thousand tons of nerve gas they haven't declared in accordance with the Memorandum of Understanding with the United States which they signed in September 'eighty-nine.'

From his time in Moscow Neighbour was aware that, on coming to power, Gorbachev had declared that henceforth the Soviet Union would cease developing chemical warfare agents. However, despite this assurance, compelling evidence had subsequently emerged to show Moscow had continued to develop third-generation nerve agents into the early nineties.

'What do you want, Chris, the ten-minute burst or the hour-long presentation?' Amesbury-Cotton asked with a grin.

'Something in between,' Neighbour told him.

'Well, the short answer is the CIA could be right about the tonnage but not the type of agent. The Russians were producing chemical warfare agents before, during, and after World War Two.'

The Soviet chemical warfare arsenal comprised mustard gas and lewisite blister agents, the more lethal choking chemicals like phosgene, chlorine, hydrogen cyanide and their various derivatives where the lethal effects were felt, at one end of the scale up to twenty-four hours after inhalation to, at the other extreme, within fifteen seconds. Most deadly of all, however, were the nerve agents, tabun, sarin, soman and VX. One tiny drop the size of a pinhead on the exposed skin and death would follow in one minute unless the casualty was equipped with an auto-injector of atropine.

'At the height of the Cold War the Soviets had the biggest stockpile of chemical weapons in the world.' Amesbury-Cotton left his desk, went over to the combination safe and returned with an A4 box of aerial photographs. 'The munitions were dispersed, tucked away in forest hides to avoid detection and minimise the effects of enemy air action,' he continued, and placed a selection of photographs in front of Neighbour.

The photographs were annotated to show where and when they had been taken, which Neighbour thought just as well because without the legend he couldn't have told one from another. Each one showed a forest clearing with the ground cover uprooted and the earth scarred. Examining them more closely he noticed that in two of the photographs the soil appeared to be contaminated.

'A hell of a lot of their bombs, shells and surface-to-surface missiles have been stockpiled for close on fifty years, exposed to the elements. As a result the casings have become corroded and the chemical filling unstable and dangerous to handle. The Soviet method of dealing with the hazard was to move the material to another site and bury it. The paperwork wasn't always up to scratch and the whereabouts of many of the sites established in the nineteen sixties is now unknown. I doubt if even the current Defence Minister could tell you just how many tons of chemical agents were stockpiled by the Soviet armed forces at the height of the Cold War.'

However, under the terms of the 1993 Chemical Weapons Convention the Russians had formally declared they held forty thousand tons of chemical weapons of which eighty per cent were nerve agents. Moscow had also signed up to destroy their entire stockpile of chemical weapons in stages. The first four hundred tons were to be destroyed by 2000; two years later they were required to have disposed of a further six thousand tons. In papers that Neighbour had seen at the British Embassy in Moscow, the cost of the operation had been estimated at 5.7 billion US dollars, a sum way beyond the means of the Russian economy.

'CWPFs are another source of mistrust,' Amesbury-Cotton said.

'What are they when they're at home?' Neighbour asked.

'Sorry, I mean chemical weapon production facilities. American CWPFs are all single-purpose military facilities that have lain dormant for years, whereas the Russian equivalents are buried within massive civilian chemical industrial complexes like Volgograd. With some justification Moscow claims that to raze the Volgograd type of CWPF would be uneconomical, irrational and ruinous financially. The Russians would like to convert such chemical weapon production facilities to normal civilian use. The fear is they could reconvert them for military usage in the event of mobilisation.'

Amesbury-Cotton also thought it conceivable that senior military officers would wish to retain some CWPFs illegally to meet such an eventuality.

'The fact is we're not sure they have disclosed the locations of all their production facilities.'

'That is good news,' Neighbour said drily.

'Well, here's another item to cheer you up. The raw materials for making sarin are reasonably easy to get hold of and a second-year chemistry student wouldn't find it difficult to mix you a cocktail. Dispersing the agent is, however, another matter.'

Jill Sheridan left the office at ten after six and walked to Vauxhall station. Usually she drove into work and parked the Porsche 911 in the space reserved for the Deputy DG in the basement garage at Vauxhall Cross. Her routine had been altered as a result of a phone call she had received yesterday from the man who had called her twice before. He had told her to leave the car at home and use the Underground. He had also demanded that she finish work for the day at five o'clock sharp. Instinct had told Jill she was being tested and it wouldn't sit right if she complied with all his instructions without a word of protest.

'What are you trying to do?' she'd asked him in a shrill voice. 'Get me noticed? I've never left the office before six. Most nights it's more like seven o'clock.'

Ten minutes past six had been the resultant compromise.

Hazelwood had assured her the home team would stay out of it and leave the field clear to the visitors, whoever they were. Special Branch might have elevated surveillance to an art form but it was impossible to guarantee there was no chance of the opposition spotting one of their officers. If that should happen, the man who had contacted her would assume she had told the Director General of the SIS everything, and walk away. She would then be of no further use to either the Secret Intelligence Service or the Foreign and Commonwealth Office. Robin Urquhart had obtained a stay of execution by arguing that Kransky and his associates had deliberately targeted her knowing she was Deputy DG. He had persuaded the Chairman of the Joint Intelligence Committee and a reluctant Victor Hazelwood that they should endeavour to discover who had gone to so much trouble to make her open to blackmail and why. Once that argument ceased to be valid the Change of Circumstance report would be acted on and her career abruptly ended.

Although the evening rush hour was just beginning to tail off it was still standing room only when Jill boarded a northbound Victoria Line train. The only instructions she had received from the man was to travel on the Underground and leave the office at ten past six. But if she had acquired a shadow since leaving Vauxhall Cross she hadn't spotted him or her. Not that she had tried to; convinced this was a trial run she wanted to appear compliant.

Jill alighted at Euston and followed the directional signs for the Northern Line, which, as she had had reconfirmed to her that morning, provided the worst service of the whole Underground network. Even now, in what was a peak period, trains were running at five-minute intervals. Furthermore the information screen showed the one due in three minutes was going to Edgware, which was no good to her. When the High Barnet train finally arrived the commuters were lined up three deep along the entire platform.

Jill stood all the way from Euston to Mornington Crescent and on through Camden Town, and Kentish Town. A seat did become available at Tufnell Park but this was one stop from her destination and she couldn't be bothered to sit down.

From Archway station to the house in Bisham Gardens was just under three-quarters of a mile. It was going to seem a lot further on this blustery night with a gusting wind threatening to turn her umbrella inside out. Head down and leaning into the wind Jill trudged up Highgate Hill towards the High Street. She had just passed the junction with Dartmouth Park Hill and was abreast of Waterlow Park when she was attacked. They came up behind her, two men moving swiftly and silently in trainers. Umbrella clutched in her left hand, the right keeping a tight grip on the leather straps of the Vuiton handbag carried over the shoulder, Jill was powerless to defend herself. Knocked off balance by a violent shove in the back, she stumbled forward, then someone hacked the legs from under her and she went down flat. Instinctively Jill let go of the umbrella and put out a hand to cushion the fall. Even so, blood flowed from the nose a split second after her face struck the pavement. The second man started kicking her in the left rib cage while his friend ripped the handbag from her grasp. That such a thing could happen to her on a busy main road was beyond belief.

Everything the Training School had taught her about self-defence on the induction course all those years ago was useless when the odds were two to one against and you were already half unconscious. Jill opened her mouth and screamed, a high-pitch, blood-curdling shriek. From somewhere she found the wind to do it again.

The world started rotating and she felt herself being drawn into the vortex. Her screams found an echo across the street as some driver heading in the opposite direction slammed on the brakes and skidded to a halt. Then suddenly the men stopped kicking her and she heard them running away. Moment later the whirlpool sucked her down.

Chapter 9

The voices were unintelligible and sounded a long way off until her ears seemed to pop and she heard a man with a deep voice pleading with her not to move because an ambulance was already on the way and would arrive any second. For a few brief moments Jill wondered what she was doing there flat on her stomach, apparently fascinated by a grass-filled crack in one of the paving slabs. Total recall came when, ignoring the man's advice, she tried to get up and a knife went into her left side. Two men had been kicking her as she lay helpless on the ground, and the pain just now had been sharp enough to suggest the man on her left had fractured one or more of her ribs.

Blood was still oozing from her nose and she could only breathe through the mouth. Jill touched her nostrils gingerly, trying to gauge the damage for herself. The nose didn't feel broken but it was certainly swollen. Continuing with her own medical examination, she plucked up courage and took a deep breath, then started coughing and almost choked when she tried to stifle the paroxysm.

The ambulance arrived when the attack was just beginning to subside. With Whittington Hospital little more than a mile away, Jill was seen by a junior houseman barely three minutes later. There was a well-organised, long-established routine for dealing with casualties brought into A and E. Following a brief physical examination she received first-aid treatment for the injuries to her nose and face. While this was being done, her name, address, and details of the next of kin were recorded, together with a contact number. She was then wheeled into the X-ray department where various photographs subsequently confirmed the houseman's initial examination that, although there was extensive bruising to the left side of the body, no ribs had been fractured. Despite the fact there was nothing to suggest Jill was suffering from concussion, it was decided to detain her in hospital overnight under observation.

There was a bed available and Jill had needed very little persuading. She had been given a mild sedative and was in that euphoric state engendered by a feeling of being cosseted by the nursing staff. Before falling asleep she recalled being interviewed by a woman police officer who had hoped to obtain a description of the two men who had attacked her. But she had gone away disappointed because Jill hadn't seen their faces. The next time Jill opened her eyes Robin Urquhart was occupying the chair at her bedside.

'How long have you been sitting there?' Jill asked in a thick voice that sounded quite unlike her own.

'About an hour. How are you feeling now?'

'Fragile, but I'll live. What time is it, Robin?'

'Five to ten.'

Five minutes to ten? Surely that was wrong? It meant nearly four hours had passed since she had left the office. Her mind jumped, focused on another subject. It wasn't just her purse, pocket diary, powder compact, lipstick, tissues, Chanel No.5, eyeliner, house keys, nail scissors and credit cards she had lost when the muggers had stolen her handbag. They had also taken her mobile. Her pulse racing, Jill looked about her. She wasn't in a private room but the curtains around the bed had been drawn, affording some privacy from the other patients in the ward. Reaching out, she seized Robin by the wrist and drew him closer.

'Has he phoned the house this evening?' she whispered.

'There were no messages on the answer phone,' Urquhart told her quietly.

'My mobile was in the handbag.'

'We can buy another, darling.'

Robin enjoyed a reputation for being exceptionally cool when under pressure and this, Jill supposed, was another example of his sang-froid. In this instance, however, it owed everything to stupidity. His patronising tone also angered her because if there was one thing guaranteed to make her hackles rise it was being talked down to as if she were some empty-headed bimbo.

'Of course I can buy another,' Jill said through gritted teeth, 'but how will the man know the phone number?'

'We'll wait for him to contact you the way he did the first time.'

It was, Jill realised, the only thing she could do, and Robin was right to presume he would get in touch with her. After all, she was a prize catch and they had gone to a lot of trouble to snare her. What had happened to her on Highgate Hill had been an unrelated incident, and she wasn't going to attach any significance to it. But she knew someone who would.

'Has Victor been told?' she asked.

'Yes, I rang him before I came here.'

'Damn.'

'He had to know sometime, Jill.'

'Why? I'll be at my desk as usual tomorrow morning.'

'You obviously haven't looked at yourself in the mirror. Believe me, your appearance would only set tongues wagging at Vauxhall Cross. Besides, even walking about the house will cause you considerable discomfort for the next few days.'

'And in the meantime Victor will do his best to get rid of me. He's less than enthusiastic about this operation.'

'You needn't worry about Victor. He will be sixty in June, the retirement age for officers of his seniority.'

'Four months from now,' Jill mused. 'What makes you think I will last that long?'

'Well, Victor is hoping to be extended in post a year at a time and he has to have our approval.' Urquhart smiled and looked incredibly pleased with himself. 'Need I say more?'

'No.'

'Good. I'll be here bright and early in the morning with a change of clothes.'

'You think of everything,' she murmured, suddenly drowsy.

'I try to.' Urquhart leaned over the bed and kissed her lightly on the cheek. 'Sleep tight.'

The exhortation was unnecessary; her eyes were already closed and she was breathing deeply before he finished opening the curtains enclosing the bed.

Until a few months ago Jill Sheridan was rarely absent from morning prayers. From the time she had been promoted to head the Mid-East Department Jill had never taken her annual entitlement of leave in full or phoned in sick. If in the last five years a league table had been kept showing who had attended the most sessions, Jill would have been far ahead of everybody else, including the Director General. That record had been slipping ever since Rosalind Urquhart had cross-petitioned her husband for divorce on the grounds of his adultery with Jill.

There had been the enforced absence from Vauxhall Cross while Rosalind commanded the sympathy vote in the tabloids. But even after the press had seen through Rosalind and revised their opinions, there had still been the odd day here and there when Jill had felt unable to face her colleagues. That aberration had been followed by the three-week vacation in Florida, which had taken everybody aback. Since returning from America she had already phoned in sick once; the fact that she hadn't appeared for morning prayers for the second time in three days surprised few people round the table, most of whom thought she had looked peaky when they saw her yesterday. What did surprise everybody, including Ashton, was Hazelwood's announcement that she had been mugged on her way home. Colleagues like Roger Benton and Rowan Garfield, who'd never had much time for Jill Sheridan, were the ones who had fired the most questions at Victor. Was Jill going to be all right? How serious were her injuries? Had she been detained in hospital? Where and when had she been attacked? Garfield wanted to know why she had used public transport to and from the office and he had still looked perplexed when curtly informed the Porsche was being serviced. He had, however, known better than to pursue the subject after Victor had called the meeting to order.

Unlike the Head of the European Department, Ashton had no desire to pursue the subject but he wasn't given any choice. At ten fifteen, an hour and a quarter after morning prayers had ended, Dilys Crowther rang to say Sir Victor Hazelwood would like to see him. 'It's to do with the memo you sent him on nerve agents,' she added helpfully.

Ashton thanked her, then cleared his desk locking the in-, out- and pending trays with their contents in the safe before leaving the office. Victor was one of those people who never put off until tomorrow anything that could be done today. Had he really wanted to discuss the information Chris Neighbour had obtained from DI7 Ashton knew the DG would have grabbed him before he went home. Consequently he wasn't surprised when Hazelwood reverted to the subject of Jill Sheridan and told him in greater detail what had happened to her and why she had left the car in the garage yesterday.

'We believe the assault had nothing to do with the people who are running her,' Hazelwood said in conclusion, and waited expectantly.

Yesterday Victor had told him feigning ignorance would be his best defence should things go badly wrong. Today he seemed to be imparting a different message.

'Why are you telling me all this?' Ashton asked.

'Because I value your opinion.'

'Well, OK. I'm sure you're right on both counts. Yesterday the opposition was testing Jill to see how malleable she was. The mugging was unscripted and must have taken them by surprise too. All the same they may see the assault as an unexpected bonus.'

'In what respect?'

'The fact that nobody came rushing to Jill's defence might convince them we weren't keeping a watchful eye on her.'

'I don't think I'd mention that possibility to Ms Sheridan. After the beating those two muggers gave her I doubt she would like to be told it was all to the good.' Hazelwood eyed the cigar box with longing and almost yielded to temptation. 'Who are you thinking of sending to the CIA-sponsored symposium on International Terrorism?' he asked, changing the subject with a breathtaking suddenness that left Ashton floundering.

The symposium was to be held at Langley from Tuesday, 4 March to Thursday, 6th. It had been discussed back in January at the very first session of morning prayers that Ashton had attended following his promotion to Assistant Director. In addition to the SIS, invitations had also been sent to the intelligence services of Australia, Canada and New Zealand. All were member countries of Echelon, the exclusive intelligence-sharing organisation, which had come into being in 1948 and was still extant. Because no other country from the European Union has been invited, it had been decided on the grounds of political expediency that the SIS should be represented by Rowan Garfield and two of his Grade I intelligence officers.

'I didn't think my department was involved,' Ashton said.

'It is now. One of Rowan's team has been stood down to make room for your man.'

'I don't have a Grade I intelligence officer on my establishment, and I doubt if Langley would welcome my presence.'

In August of last year Ashton had been seconded to the CIA interrogation team who were debriefing a top-ranking defector. From day one he had been at loggerheads with the team leader. Worse still, the defector had ended up on a slab and the CIA had lost their prize acquisition before they had learned anything of significance.

'I had in mind one of your Grade II officers,' Hazelwood told him.

'What qualities are you looking for?'

'A man with an enquiring mind, a cool head, and who can lie with conviction, should this be necessary. I want to know if the name of Tom Kransky means anything to the intelligence community or the FBI.'

'You want Will Landon. He's the man for the job.'

'Fine. Now go away and prepare a cover story with him.'

'I should point out that Landon doesn't know a thing about Jill's involvement with Kransky.'

'Good, make sure you keep it that way,' Hazelwood said, and reached for a Burma cheroot, finally yielding to temptation.

Landon's telephone was never so busy that no sooner had he answered one incoming call and put the receiver down than it started ringing again. But it did that morning. At a quarter to eleven Francesca had phoned to inform him that, contrary to what she had told him on Monday, Gadstar Promotions had now come to their notice. Apparently they represented TTF, which stood for Tiny Tots Fashions. Why the rag trade should have excited MI5 had become evident when Francesca had invited Landon to guess the name of the principal shareholder and had then told him it was Ahmed Shirawai, the arms dealer, before he had a chance to answer her question. The information had carried a price tag and he had found himself agreeing to a dinner date for Friday.

The second caller had been Mary Orchard, the very last person he had expected to hear from. She had been upset, so much so that at times her speech had been incoherent. Her distress had everything to do with her late husband and she had to talk to Landon about it because he was the only person she trusted. The conversation was largely one-sided and lasted over ten minutes, Landon making notes on his scratch pad as she rambled on. As soon as Mary Orchard put the phone down, Landon walked the problem upstairs to Ashton.

'I was about to send for you,' Ashton told him, 'but what I have to say will keep. What's on the scratch pad you're holding?'

'I've just had a phone call from Mary Orchard, going on about her husband's suicide. Claims she knows what made him take his own life.'

'What sort of state was Mary in?'

'Definitely overwrought but I didn't get the impression she was fantasising. I don't know what she proposes to tell us but my gut tells me it will be worth listening to.'

'All right, I'll pass your message on to Hugo Calthorpe.'

'Mary won't speak to him, she made that very clear. The same goes for Roy Kelso.'

'So who is she willing to confide in?'

'Me,' Landon told him. 'Apparently I'm the only one she trusts.'

'Lucky you.'

'So do I go and see her?'

Ashton mulled the question over. 'We don't have the manpower to do the work of other departments as well as our own.'

'Do I take that as a no?'

'It's just an observation. Have you got anything else for me?'

Landon gave him an edited version of the conversation he'd had with Francesca York, and the reason why Five had suddenly begun to take an interest in Eleanor Gadsby's company.

'Ahmed Shirawai was one of the two names I ran past her stepbrother, Lawrence Gadsby. Maybe there's a lot more to that family than we thought.'

'Where's your car?' Ashton asked.

'At home.'

'OK. Ring the MT section and order one. If the transport supervisor proves difficult refer him to me.' Ashton reached for the phone. 'Meantime, I'll have a word with Hugo Calthorpe and tell him what's happening before he hears it from some-body else.'

'You want me to report to him on my return?' Landon asked as he edged towards the door.

'No. You brief me first, then you see Hugo.'

There was more to come. Ashton caught him again before he disappeared into the corridor. On no account was he to mention Eleanor Gadsby's Gadstar Promotions or her brother. His task was simply to listen to what Mary Orchard had to say and soak up the information like a sponge.

As Landon rapidly discovered it was amazing how quickly difficulties were resolved when Ashton was mentioned. The transport supervisor had been adamant that every vehicle was already tasked and there was no way he could provide a car for him. However, the moment Landon asked if he could use his phone to inform Ashton, the transport supervisor suddenly remembered that he had a Ford Granada that had been taken off the roster for a valeting job on the interior. He also found a driver for the car, a former sergeant in the Royal Military Police named Eric Daniels, who had joined the SIS in 1979 after completing twelve years' service in the army.

The Royal Corps of Transport had taught Daniels the skills of defensive driving and he was one of the very few people who'd had occasion to put theory into practice. The former SIS Head of Station, Athens was alive today and living in retirement at Salcombe thanks to Daniels. In 1985, while he had been serving with the British Embassy as specialist driver-cum-bodyguard, an active service unit of the Provisional IRA had tried to ambush the SIS man on the way to the International Airport. The terrorists had opened fire much too soon and Daniels had been able to execute a 180 degree turn at speed. He had then run down and killed the gunman whom the IRA had put out as a backstop.

Landon had no need of his skills as a defensive driver; Daniels earned the respect of the younger man with his encyclopaedic knowledge of London. When it came to finding his way around the capital south of the river few cab drivers could rival him. Between Vauxhall Cross and the M20 beyond Swanley he knew every quick cut and how to avoid roadworks that were likely to delay them. The only thing Landon had to tell him was the way to Downdale after they had reached the outskirts of Wrotham.

The last time Landon had been to the house half a dozen cars parked at irregular intervals in the drive had taken up most of the available space. Today they were spoiled for choice. And this time round Mary Orchard was waiting to greet him at the top of the Portland stone flight of steps leading to the front door.

'So good of you to come, Mr Landon,' she murmured, and led him through the hall to the drawing room. 'None of my late husband's colleagues in the Asian Department would have responded so quickly to a cry for help.'

Landon made no comment; even a self-deprecating smile could be taken the wrong way. Instead, he moved to the French windows and stood there gazing out at the ornamental pond.

'What do you keep?' he asked. 'Comet? Golden orfe?'

'Those and shubunkin and some fantail. The pond was Bill's domain, mine was the garden. We had a gardener come in three days a week to mow the lawn and do all the hard work. Shan't be able to afford him now. Not that it matters; the bank owns sixty per cent of the house and I don't have the wherewithal to redeem the mortgage.'

There was no reason for Landon to ask Mary Orchard why she had wanted to see him urgently. It rapidly became evident that she required no prompting from him to unburden herself.

The deeds of the house were in their joint names and she had no recollection of signing a document in October '95, which in effect remortgaged Downdale for the sum of three hundred and fifty thousand. The money so raised had not gone into their joint current account.

'I only learned of the loan from my solicitor the day before yesterday. In fact, he was equally mystified and was hoping I could throw some light on the subject.'

Further enquiries had revealed that the money had been lodged in a deposit account for two months. The three hundred and fifty thousand pounds plus the accrued interest net of tax had then been paid to Charles Yarpole Associates on 18 December.

'Who are Charles Yarpole Associates?' Landon asked.

'Brokers. Apparently my husband was a name at Lloyd's, which was another thing he neglected to tell me.'

Bill had become a name on 2 January when Lloyd's was already in turmoil. If that wasn't bad enough, he had also joined a syndicate that faced being hammered. Charles Yarpole Associates had cornered a large share of the Fire Insurance market. Sight unseen, they had insured property in the Bronx, which no American company would touch, for a lot more than the tenements were worth. Unscrupulous landlords, and there were any number of them, had torched their derelict buildings and taken the syndicate to the cleaners. But it had been the policies Charles Yarpole Associates had sold to the oil, gas and pharmaceutical companies that had really been their undoing. American courts might award punitive damages for polluting the atmosphere but it was like water off a duck's back to the offending corporations.

'It's the British middle class who pick up the bill, people like my late husband.'

And now Mary Orchard was about to discover what unlimited liability really meant. Lloyd's could take her house and everything in it, her savings and every penny she might earn, less the amount deemed necessary for her subsistence. There was no escaping the burden; even if she gave notice today of her intention to leave the syndicate, they would still have their claws into her for the next five years. It was, Landon thought, a lousy deal.

'The three hundred and fifty thousand was not a final payment,' she continued. 'There was another demand waiting for Bill when he returned from India. I didn't open the envelope in his absence. I wish I had now because then I would have known what was troubling Bill over that last weekend. Then maybe things would . . .'

Her voice broke and the tears began to well in her eyes. Bill Orchard had deceived his wife and unbeknown to his colleagues was faced with financial ruin. The demand for even more money that had been waiting for him when he returned home must have been the final straw.

'Of course I blame Jill Sheridan.'

'What?'

'Bill always said she had a good financial head on her shoulders and respected the advice she gave him from time to time. I'm sure it was Jill who persuaded him to become a name at Lloyd's.'

No sooner had one can of worms been disposed of than you were presented with another. This, however, was one can Landon didn't intend to open.

Although his given name was William, he had called himself Wes from an early age because it sounded menacing and gave him greater street cred than if he had been known as Willie Sharples. Between the ages of twelve and sixteen he had totted up forty-one convictions, mostly for taking and driving away a motor vehicle without the owner's consent, an offence euphemistically referred to as joyriding. The rest of his crime sheet as a juvenile comprised five convictions for housebreaking, eight for thieving and two for common assault. On leaving school shortly before his sixteenth birthday, Sharples had found employment at a car wash in Stoke Newington. Other jobs had followed at irregular intervals over the next seven years, ranging from stacking shelves at the local branch of Tesco to labouring on building sites. During that time he had actually gone straight for sixteen months, which had got the police off his back.

Currently Sharples was the part-owner of a mini cab firm, which was a good front for his more lucrative work. He was, loosely speaking, in the second-hand car market. If some dishonest garage proprietor wanted a '97 Mercedes Benz S Class at a reasonable price for a valued client, then Sharples went out and stole it to order. Although housebreaking was now a thing of the past, no lockup within a ten-mile radius of Stoke Newington was safe from him. That evening he had visited a lockup in Harrow with a Transit van driven by his partner, Carl Ivers. They'd had no specific information to go on but, in keeping with their usual practice, they had visited Harrow at the beginning of February and cruised around the town looking for a target that might be worth hitting on spec.

The target they had chosen was on a side road beyond the old Territorial Army centre on Ferndale. There were six lockups in all and it had taken them less than four minutes to open up the lot. Two were full of materials that had been salvaged or stolen from various building sites, another contained a load of domestic electrical appliances, some of which were being reconditioned, while the fourth was a veritable treasure-trove, stacked with cases of imported beer, wine and Scotch whisky. They hadn't bothered to check out the last two lockups; instead they had taken all eighteen cases of whisky and driven off in ten minutes flat.

Their storeroom was a cellar that had been dug underneath the kitchen in the ground-floor flat that the two men shared. The cellar had been constructed long before Sharples had moved into the place and the fact that the landlord hadn't mentioned it when Sharples had signed the lease suggested he hadn't known of its existence. Sharples had only discovered it by accident when he'd tried to unblock the U-bend under the sink and had made a hash of it, creating a miniature flood. However, instead of lying there, the water had rapidly drained away. He thought the cellar had been constructed as an air-raid shelter by the family that had then occupied the whole house, and had later become a hiding place for a deserter. Either way, Sharples couldn't have asked for a better storeroom.

In celebration of what had been a good night, Sharples opened one of the cases and removed a bottle of Scotch. Returning to the kitchen he found a couple of mugs and poured a large tot for Carl Ivers and one for himself. The whisky looked the right colour but it was tasteless. Sharples raised the mug to his nose and sniffed it; then suddenly his vision became blurred and mucus began to stream from both nostrils and the mouth. A steel band rapidly tightened around his chest, making it very difficult for him to breathe, then his eyes felt as if they were burning in their sockets. He supposed the same thing was happening to Carl Ivers but the thought brought him little comfort. His legs gave way under him and he collapsed on to the floor, every limb, every muscle twitching violently. Thirty seconds later he was as dead as Ivers.

Chapter 10

Military Operations (Special Projects) was staffed by the army and the SIS. The army element comprised a lieutenant-colonel drawn from one of the combat arms, and two majors, one of whom had to be an officer in the Royal Signals. Clerical support was provided by a staff sergeant chief clerk and two Ministry of Defence civil servants, one a clerical officer, the other a clerical assistant. Currently, the SIS personnel were led by a retired commander RN whose name was Max Brabazon.

Ashton had served briefly in MO(SP) when he was being rehabilitated after being put out to grass in the Security Vetting and Technical Services Division, which in those days had been located at Benbow House in Southwark. He sometimes wondered if this was the reason why Jill Sheridan had included the SIS element of the organisation when justifying the establishment of a separate East European Department under an assistant director. On the diagram of the family tree that accompanied the proposal, MO(SP) had been linked to Russia, Serbia, Bosnia Hertzegovina and Kosovo by a dotted line, which indicated a tenuous connection. Tenuous or not, it had got past the Treasury, and Ashton had visited MO(SP) to show his face to the staff the day after he had been promoted to assistant director.

During his courtesy visit he had taken Max Brabazon aside and had assured the retired naval commander there would be no change to the current working practices. Ashton had also said there was no need for Max to consult him on routine day-to-day matters. In the seven intervening weeks since then Brabazon had been as silent as a Trappist monk.

Ashton had Will Landon in his office working on the cover story he would need when attending the CIA symposium on International Terrorism when the Mozart secure speech facility was activated. Lifting the receiver, Ashton found he had Max Brabazon on the line.

'I think you may want to get involved in this, Peter,' he said crisply. 'There's been a rather disturbing incident in Stoke Newington which indicates a probable terrorist involvement.'

Ashton told him to hang on for a second, then hooked the receiver into the amplifier and set the tape running before inviting him to continue.

'Two men were found dead in the ground-floor flat at forty-four Kimberley Road. They were discovered by a member of the public who is now in hospital under intensive care. He was having convulsions, which suggests he had been exposed to some chemical agent. Anyway, the police aren't taking any chances, they've evacuated everybody living in Kimberley Road and the adjoining streets. Scientists from the Chemical Warfare Research Establishment at Porton Down have also been called in. I'm afraid that's all I have at the present moment.'

'Does Five know all about this?' Ashton asked.

'Yes. As a matter of fact Richard Neagle from the Anti-Terrorist branch is on his way there as we speak.'

'Thank you, Max. I'll make sure he won't be lonely.' Ashton broke the connection and turned to Landon. 'Did you get the address, Will?' he asked.

Landon nodded. 'I presume I'm the one who's going to keep Neagle company?' he said.

'You are. I want a complete rundown on the two dead men. If they were gassed, try to find out how the agent was administered. In that connection, you'd better visit the General Stores Section and sign out an NBC suit.'

The nuclear, biological and chemical warfare suit was charcoal-lined and was designed to protect the wearer from low-level radiation and contamination from liquid nerve agents. The suit also came with atropine, pralidoxime and chloride auto-injection kits.

'If the supervisor denies all knowledge of the kit tell him to open one of the RSG pallets.'

'What the hell is that?' Landon asked.

'It's short for Regional Seat of Government. There were twelve of them at the height of the Cold War. They were composed of personnel drawn from the police, armed forces, the medical profession, local government, British Telecom and engineers from the sanitary department. They were the people who were charged with restoring some kind of order in their region after a nuclear attack. To help them to survive the strike, deep shelters were constructed and there were NBC suits in store for the chosen, something which ninety-nine per cent of the population didn't have. Naturally it would have been bad for morale if the population at large knew of this so the existence of these pallets was classified Secret. It probably still is; that's why the supervisor may pretend there is no such item in his store.'

'You're having me on.'

'You want to bet?' Ashton enquired.

'No, thanks. I'd lose.'

'Check to make sure your respirator is a perfect fit, Will. Some of the vapour may still be hanging about inside the house. Also, make sure you are issued with rubber gloves and cotton liners.'

'Anything else?'

'Yes. Call Francesca York and ask her to let Neagle know you're on the way.' Ashton smiled. 'It might just persuade him you have some right to be there.'

★

Jill sat at the dressing table gazing at the face in the mirror. The
nose was not nearly so swollen as it had been and the congealed
blood had been removed from both nostrils. But her ribs on the
left side still hurt like hell. Turning sideways on to the mirror,
she raised the roll-neck sweater above her bra. The bruises were
out now, purple in the centre, fading to the colour of an overripe banana on the periphery. The consultant who'd looked at
her before she was discharged from hospital had said it was
fortunate she had reacted instinctively and had protected the
rib cage with her left arm, otherwise the injuries would have
been much more serious, possibly life-threatening. The
wonder was that the left arm hadn't been broken in two places.
Even so, it was pure agony to raise it above shoulder level.
Robin had been right: just walking around the house was
painful enough. At her present rate of recovery she would be
lucky if she was fit enough to go into work on Monday. She
was bored out of her skull with nothing to do and all day to do
it in. She was also very worried because the only phone calls
she had received yesterday had been from well-wishers at
Vauxhall Cross. No word from Ashton, of course, despite their
once close relationship. Dammit, Ashton should have called to
find out how she was. He owed her, for Christ's sake. He would
still be a Grade I intelligence officer if it hadn't been for the way
she had written up the establishment proposal. The phone
interrupted her silent monologue of self-pity and she left the
dressing table to pick up the extension on the bedside table. A
man with a harsh voice wished her good morning then
observed that she was staying at home for the second day
running.

'You noticed,' Jill said in mock amazement.

'We saw what happened. How soon will you recover?'

Jill didn't recognise the voice and was sure he was not the
man who had told her to travel into work on the Underground.
'Who are you?' she demanded.

'I am the one who posted the video to you. *It Happened One Night*. Remember?'

'Do you have a name?'

'Yes, but it is not for you to know.'

'That's too bad,' Jill said, and hung up.

'We saw what happened'; the import of what the man said a few moments ago sank in and made her incredibly angry. They had been on the scene when she had been attacked and they hadn't lifted a finger to help her.

Five minutes passed, then ten, and still the phone remained silent. Jill wondered if she had tried him too far and immediately told herself she was being stupid. The man would phone again because he needed her. Didn't he? She went downstairs and had just reached the hall when the slimline started trilling like a myna bird.

A confident belief that she had been proved right was shattered when she answered the phone in the large sitting room and Eileen Garfield asked how she was feeling. Nothing could have been more hypocritical than Eileen pretending to be worried about her. They had met only half a dozen times at the most but on each occasion Eileen Garfield had deliberately set out to make Jill feel small. Try as she might to end their conversation there was no stopping Rowan's wife. Eileen simply went on and on for a good ten minutes until she finally said, 'Good heavens, is that the time?' and put the phone down.

It rang again a few minutes later. 'My name is Emile,' said the man with the harsh voice. 'Who have you been talking to?'

'The wife of a colleague.'

'And what is his name?'

Jill hesitated. The identity of an SIS officer was sacrosanct. On the other hand her first priority was to win the trust of Emile and whoever else was involved. There was no time to consult Victor Hazelwood or the Privy Counsellors who had been appointed to vet the classified material she would be allowed to pass on. She alone had to make the decision.

'His name is Rowan Garfield.'

'Rowan Garfield. Why did you hesitate to disclose his name, Miss Sheridan?'

'I thought you were going to ask me his wife's given name and it had slipped my memory temporarily. It's Eileen, of course.'

'Why have you switched your mobile off?'

'I haven't. It was in my handbag and was stolen along with my other possessions. Naturally I have acquired a replacement.'

Jill was about to give Emile her new number when the receiver started purring and she realised he had hung up. There were two possibilities, either Emile was paying her back for what she had done to him some twenty-odd minutes ago or else he had been using a pay phone on both occasions and was making sure he didn't stay in one place long enough for British Telecom to get a fix on him. The only thing was, she couldn't recall hearing the coins go down in the meter when she picked up the phone and gave her number.

It soon became evident that Emile was in no hurry to resume their conversation. To kill time Jill went into the kitchen and made herself a cup of coffee from a jar of instant, then sat down at the breakfast bar to linger over a cigarette. Even though she had been expecting it, the sudden jangle from the telephone made her flinch. The voice on the other end of the line identified himself as Emile but he definitely wasn't the same man Jill had spoken to earlier. He was, however, fully conversant with everything that had gone before.

'What is your new mobile number?' he asked without any kind of preamble.

She told him it slowly and distinctly.

'Who purchased this phone for you? Was it Mr Urquhart?'

'Yes, as a matter of fact he did.'

If Emile Mark II had intended to provoke an attack of the jitters by springing Robin's name on her he had failed lamentably. In considering the feasibility of mounting a double-cross operation Victor Hazelwood had insisted they assess how much of her private life was in the public domain. Emile and his friends could have got their information about her relationship with Robin from the tabloids, thanks to Rosalind.

'Is he a colleague, this Mr Robin Urquhart?'

'No, he's Foreign and Commonwealth.'

'And you are lovers?'

'We used to be.'

'You lie, he lives with you.'

'Not any more.'

'Liar, liar.'

It had been recognised that her affair with Robin Urquhart was going to be tricky. Merely to assert that he was completely in the dark wouldn't be enough. She had to convince the Emiles of this world that Urquhart had been history long before they had appeared on the scene.

'Listen to me,' Jill snapped. 'Yes, he does still have a key to my house because he refuses to return it. The man simply won't believe we are finished. That's why I'm having all the locks changed.'

'When?'

'The locksmith said he would come tomorrow.'

Big mistake! She hadn't been in touch with a locksmith, didn't even know the name of one, and the Yellow Pages was in the drawer of the hall table. If Emile pursued that line she was going to be in serious trouble. Anxiety was replaced by relief when he reverted to the subject of Robin Urquhart and demanded to know why they had split up.

'Let's say he was too old for me.' Jill stubbed out the cigarette in the saucer. 'His age never bothered me while he was still married to Rosalind and we were casual lovers. I saw him in a different light after he started divorce proceedings so that he would be free to marry me. I couldn't face the idea of spending the rest of my life with a man whose virility was already diminishing.'

'Tell me something, Miss Sheridan, why do people refer to you as "the Ice Maiden"?'

Jill froze. Although nobody had ever said it to her face, she was aware of the nickname. But who the hell had told Emile?

'You should have a word with Tom Kransky,' she told him in a brittle voice. 'He certainly had no complaints about my performance in bed.'

'I'm not interested in your sex life and I don't believe you would end your affair with Mr Urquhart because of his inadequacies.'

'You're right, sex was not the main reason. I finished with him because there was nothing more he could do for my career. His influence was on the wane and thanks to his wife and her thirst for vengeance, my name has become mud in Whitehall. Consequently any hope of being the first woman to become Director General of the SIS is finished.'

It was the plain, unadulterated truth and the injustice of it all in her eyes touched a raw nerve. Jill didn't have to act the part; her anger and bitterness were genuine. Loud in the condemnation of those colleagues whom she thought had been quick to distance themselves when the tabloids were dishing out the dirt, it was some moments before she realised Emile had severed the connection.

Stoke Newington was not a part of London that Eric Daniels could claim to know like the back of his hand. In fact he could not recall an occasion when he'd had cause to visit the area. However, having looked up the address in the *London A–Z Street Atlas* before leaving Vauxhall Cross, he had found his way to Kimberley Road without having to stop and ask for directions.

The exclusion zone was centred on Kimberley Road and included the parallel streets east and west of the affected area. The barrier at the south end of Kimberley Road was the usual thin strip of blue and white plastic tape, one end tied to a lamppost, the other to the front gate of the first terraced house on the left. A police constable was stationed in front of the tape but there were no onlookers and no sign of the media.

'Nothing like a whiff of poison gas to disperse a crowd,' Daniels observed cheerfully.

The police officer waved an arm, inviting them to move on. When they failed to do so he repeated the hand signal with a good deal of vigour and, still getting no reaction, walked purposefully towards the Ford Granada. Landon got out of the car and went forward to meet him.

Landon was wearing a first generation chemical weapons protection suit over his street clothes and was already feeling uncomfortably warm. The material was a kind of sackcloth coated with wax and lined with charcoal on the inside. Self-adhesive tapes sealed the blouse type jacket at the waist, throat and around the wrists. The bottom half of the protective suit went over a pair of calf-length jump boots and the trouser-legs were fastened tight around the ankles by the ubiquitous adhesive tapes. Instead of a steel helmet Landon wore a charcoal impregnated baseball cap and carried a respirator in his left hand and a pair of rubber gloves in the other. Attached to a canvas belt around his waist was an auto-injector containing atropine. The police officer wanted to know if he could help him, which was another way of asking why the hell he had ignored his signal to move away from the prohibited area.

'I'm here to see Mr Neagle,' Landon told him, then added, 'from the Ministry of Defence.'

'And your name, sir?'

'Landon. I'm also with the MoD.'

'Do you have an identity card, Mr Landon?'

The ID card was in the breast pocket of the civilian jacket, which meant he had to put the rubber gloves and respirator down, then remove the auto-injector and unfasten the adhesive tapes before he could raise the blouse with one hand while groping for the plastic ID card with the other. The cotton gloves Landon was wearing deadened his sense of touch and much to the amusement of the police officer, he found it difficult to extract the card.

'Satisfied?' Landon demanded, and thrust the card at him.

'I'm only doing my job, Mr Landon.'

'Sure you are. Now let me do mine.'

Landon returned the ID card to the breast pocket, buckled the auto-injector around his waist and put the rubber gloves on over the cotton ones, then picked up the respirator and ducked under the plastic tape.

Number forty-four Kimberley Road lay beyond a tight bend and couldn't be seen from the southern end of the street. When the terraced house came into view it was evident that the incident was a long way from being under control. Four body bags were being loaded into military ambulances by medics wearing respirators and protective clothing, as was everybody else in the vicinity. Taking his cue from them, Landon donned his respirator, then checked to make sure it was airtight by cupping a palm over the intake filter while attempting to inhale. By cutting off the supply of oxygen he could tell the gas mask fitted the contours of his features like a second skin.

Although Neagle had been warned to expect him, Landon had never met the Head of the Irish Section and the description he had been given wasn't much help when it was impossible to see anyone's face. As he approached the group standing outside the house, a burly figure left the others and came forward to meet him.

'Mr Landon?' he enquired.

'Yes, and you are Richard Neagle?'

'What?'

The respirator distorted Landon's voice and he repeated the question slowly, pausing briefly after each word.

'No, I'm Colin Wales. Richard's over at Hackney General waiting to interview the man who raised the alarm, should he recover.'

'It's touch and go, is it?'

'I'm afraid so,' Wales said.

'How many people were living in number forty-four?'

'We've brought out six bodies, four men, two women. I don't think there can be any more. It's only a two-up, two-down terrace house.'

One male Caucasian victim thought to be in his late teens or early twenties had been found lying down in the hall, his feet within touching distance of the front door. Wales thought he had been on the point of leaving for work when he had been overcome and had turned back for some unaccountable reason after opening the front door.

'I'm only guessing but it would explain why there are no signs of a forcible entry.'

Two other male victims, one of whom was of Caribbean origin, had been found in the kitchen-cum-living room on the ground floor at the back. Two young females and a male of approximately the same age had died in the room upstairs.

'The team from Porton Down found an opened bottle of Scotch whisky on the kitchen table.'

'The chemical agent was in liquid form?'

'It would appear so,' Wales said. 'Two large tots had been poured from the bottle of The Famous Grouse into mugs, which the two men dropped on to the floor when they each went into cardiac arrest. The liquid vaporised and gradually spread through the house, killing the other occupants. Traces of the nerve agent were still present when the team arrived. It was odourless, colourless and invisible to the naked eye.'

'So how did they know it was present?'

'Fortunately they were equipped with an American M8.'

'I presume that's some kind of gas detector?'

Wales nodded. 'It's the only instrument capable of detecting the downwind hazard from a nerve agent following the detonation of the munition.'

'What have we got here?' Landon asked. 'A terrorist incident?'

'Not in the conventional sense. There is reason to believe the bottle of whisky was purchased off the shelf at a well-known supermarket.'

'Which one? Sainsbury's? Tesco? Somerfield? Safeway?'

'I'm not saying.'

Wales seemed to be implying that some ruthless criminal was trying to extort money from one of the supermarket chains. It wouldn't be the first time that had happened but usually the blackmailer added powdered glass to a packet of sugar or doctored face cream with an irritant. From what he'd read in the newspapers Landon understood that as yet no would-be extortionist had resorted to life-threatening tactics. Of course there was always a first time for everything but a nerve agent was a sure-fire killer. At least an innocent victim would stand a chance with phosgene, which gave off a smell like new-mown hay.

'There was just one bottle of whisky?' Landon asked.

'Yes, isn't that enough?'

'I'm going to take a look inside.'

'But they're about to decontaminate the building,' Wales objected.

Landon ignored him, brushed aside an officious police inspector who tried to bar his way and walked into the terraced house. Two soldiers in protective clothing were swabbing out the kitchen-cum-living room, hosing the floor, walls, furniture with a stirrup pump. The team from Porton Down had identified the agent, pinpointed the source and ascertained the boundaries of the contaminated area. Five and possibly Special Branch as well had given them to understand the incident had been perpetrated by an extortionist who was prepared to kill innocent people to make a supermarket chain pay him a fortune. In view of this assessment they were not looking for a cache of chemical weapons. But Landon was.

He walked round the room tapping the walls to see if any part sounded hollow, then went to work on the floor, ending up on hands and knees under the sink. The hollow sound produced by a clenched hand was like music to his ears, and he lifted the square of linoleum that covered the trapdoor. The shaft underneath was brick-lined, wide enough for a man of Landon's build and approximately six feet deep as far as he could tell. Turning round, he backed under the sink, then lay flat on his stomach and slowly lowered himself into the shaft.

The brick wall facing him was in fact a door that opened into a pitch-dark chamber. Groping around, Landon found there was a flashlight hanging from a hook on the back of the door. The first thing he saw in the beam of light was eighteen cases of Scotch whisky. There were other attractive items – music centres, VCRs, radios, televisions – but none as significant as the eighteen cases of The Famous Grouse.

Landon climbed out of the hole and left the house to inform Colin Wales they were faced with a wholly different ball game.

The lights were on in Bisham Gardens but not in Jill Sheridan's house. She sat there in the darkness of the large sitting room nursing a stiff whisky and soda, waiting for the telephone to ring. It had been silent ever since Emile had cut her off in mid-sentence that morning. She would not hear from him again or the other man who called himself Emile because they didn't trust her. That was the plain inescapable truth. She hadn't eaten anything all day but she had smoked like a chimney and had put away far too many whiskies for her own good. Jill was in fact slightly drunk, and in her befuddled state was unable to differentiate between the ringing tone of the fixed link and the mobile. When finally she did answer on the right one, Emile Mark III, a man she had never spoken to before, told her to wake her ideas up.

'I'm sorry,' Jill said contritely, 'I was catnapping and—'

'We're not interested in your excuses,' Emile Mark III told her. 'All we want from you is some answers.'

'To what? I've observed every instruction I've been given.'

'Before Mr Urquhart there was another lover.'

'I was married briefly to Henry Clayburn—'

'I'm referring to Peter Ashton. You were engaged to him, were you not?'

'Yes.'

'Where is he living now?'

'Bosham, he lives in Bosham on the coast near Chichester.'

'And the address?'

This was worse, far worse than what she had told them about Rowan Garfield. At least she hadn't been asked for his address. But she was being tested and it was essential to win their trust, or so she persuaded herself yet again.

'Roseland Cottage, Church Lane.'

'There now, that wasn't difficult, was it?' Emile said, and hung up.

Chapter 11

For Ashton the incident in Kimberley Road had ensured he would be in the limelight when everybody assembled for morning prayers after the weekend. He had faced a barrage of questions but there was little he could tell them that wasn't already public knowledge. The names of the victims had been released by the police after the next of kin had been informed and had appeared in all the Sunday newspapers. Porton Down was still examining the eighteen cases of whisky and had let it be known they didn't intend to submit an interim report. Mr Erwin Zeigler, a dispatcher at the mini cab firm partly owned by Sharples, and the man who had raised the alarm, had died at four o'clock that morning, bringing the total death toll to seven. But this had been reported on every newscast broadcast by local and national radio stations, and everybody present had caught at least one of the bulletins.

In briefing the press the police spokesman had attributed the fatalities to highly toxic chemical waste, the exact composition of which was still under investigation. Although extortion hadn't been mentioned by the spokesman, several reporters had gone away with the impression that what had happened in Kimberley Road had been the aftermath of a criminal conspiracy that had gone wildly wrong. Garfield wondered how long that would hold up and had then asked Ashton if Five suspected an IRA involvement. Before Ashton could tell him the Security Service had no evidence to suggest this might be the case, Garfield had had another thought. Had Head of

Station, Moscow, heard anything more about Vladimir Aleksandrovich Labur, Director of Chemical Defence Research, who had retired on 31 December 1996, supposedly on the grounds of ill health? And what about General Stanislav V. Petrov, Chief of Chemical and Biological Defence Troops? Had anybody thought to seek his advice?

Those two questions rankled with Ashton a good hour after Hazelwood had terminated the daily briefing. Garfield's whole purpose had been to score a few points off the new boy at the top table and make himself look good in the eyes of the DG. Ashton had hoped his old guide and mentor would have seen through the gambit but, as if to give him an opportunity to address both questions, Victor had waited expectantly for some moments before allowing Roy Kelso to have his say.

Labur and Petrov, partners in the business of chemical warfare. Ashton knew there was no point in firing off another signal to Head of Station, Moscow, politely telling him to get his finger out and do something about the dearth of up-to-date information on the two Russians. Head of Station was doing his best but it wasn't easy to suborn someone close to a man like Labur, who'd retired and moved out of Moscow to God knows where. And such information as they did have on General Petrov was mostly low-grade stuff from an unproven source. The Chief of Chemical and Biological Defence Troops kept a low profile, as did his principal officers, which meant Head of Station, Moscow, had precious little chance of cultivating a primary source.

The way forward was to enlist the help of Government Communications Headquarters, Cheltenham. The eavesdroppers had the ability to monitor every known means of communication from radio transmissions to fax and e-mail. Ashton wasn't looking for the high-level, high-grade intercepts the Director General of GCHQ would impart at the weekly meeting of the Joint Intelligence Committee. He wanted whatever snippets they had on Labur since the date of his alleged retirement, which might prompt the SIS to start looking in another direction. From the wall safe Ashton took out the combined Top Secret staff list and telephone directory of GCHQ. Early on in his career he had been seconded to Cheltenham for three years and he wanted to see if any of the people he'd known then were still around. He had just reached V in the alphabetical list when Dilys Crowther rang to say Sir Victor wanted to see him. The presence of Ms Sheridan, she added gratuitously, had also been requested.

The extractor fan in Hazelwood's office was proving inadequate now that Jill Sheridan had taken to smoking cigarettes and Victor had reverted to his old habit. The greyish haze in the room matched the sky outside.

'Sit yourself down, Peter,' Hazelwood said. 'I want you to hear everything Jill has just told me.'

The alarm bells started ringing in Ashton's head the moment Jill told him the name of her case officer. Five days ago Hazelwood had advised him that feigning ignorance of the double-cross operation would be his best defence if the whole business ended in tears.

'I don't think I should be listening to this,' Ashton said.

'Well, I do,' Hazelwood snapped, 'and I am aware of the advice I gave you last Wednesday.' He nodded to Jill, inviting her to continue.

'I had four telephone calls on Friday,' she said. 'Two were from the same man who had a harsh voice and called himself Emile.'

'And the other two?' Ashton asked in spite of his reservations.

'They were from different men, both of whom wished to be known as Emile. At least one of the three Emiles had been following me when I was mugged on Wednesday night.'

The disconcerting thing was that none of the Emiles had sounded like the man who had left a message on her answer phone that Sunday evening eight days ago warning Jill that some personal items she had left at the Regal Hotel would arrive the next morning in the post. She was also sure Emile Mark One was not the joker who had told her to travel into work on the Underground.

'Between them they knew an awful lot about my personal life.'

'Like what, for instance?' asked Ashton.

'They were aware of my relationship with Robin Urquhart. Emile Mark One wanted to know if he was a colleague. I had to tell him Robin was Foreign and Commonwealth.'

'What else did you tell him?'

'Eileen Garfield was on the phone when Emile Mark One was trying to ring back. He wanted to know who I had been talking to and I told him it had been the wife of a colleague.'

'Let me guess,' Ashton said derisively, 'you had no choice but to give him Rowan Garfield.'

'Just his name, nothing else.' Jill turned away from him to look at Hazelwood as if pleading for his understanding. 'I had to make him believe they had succeeded in manipulating me. There was no time to consult anyone.'

'So what did those Emiles actually know before you so obligingly answered their questions?' Ashton demanded.

'They knew you and I were once engaged, Peter.'

'And Henry Clayburn?'

'Him too. Look, maybe Emile Mark One was using something which distorted his voice but the more I think about it, the more I'm sure he's from the Mid-East.'

Jill went on to say the Emiles now had her new mobile phone number and why she believed they were planning to use the Porsche as a mobile drop, but Ashton wasn't really listening to her. How he was known to the men who called themselves Emile wasn't such a big mystery. The source was certainly Henry Clayburn, whom Jill had met when she was running the intelligence setup in the United Arab Emirates from Bahrain. Clayburn, being the sort of man he was, would have asked Jill about the previous men in her life when he was wooing her. Hell, the bloody man had been present when Jill had telephoned from Bahrain demanding that he drop the asking price for the flat in Surbiton they had been buying on a joint mortgage. The story of their rows would have gone the rounds and been picked up by a hostile intelligence service. The identification of an agent often started with a piece of tittle-tattle like that. But how they had got on to Urquhart was a different matter.

Ashton pointed an accusing finger at Jill. 'You told Kransky about Robin, didn't you? Don't bother to deny it. You took three weeks' leave of absence, something you've never done before, because now that Robin was free you couldn't face the thought of spending the rest of your life with him. You needed time and space to work things out. A few days into your vacation you meet Kransky and suddenly your itinerary goes haywire. Who else but Robin would you have talked about the first time you went to bed with Kransky?'

'Have you quite finished?' Jill said furiously.

'Yes he has.' Hazelwood stubbed out the Burma cheroot in the cut-down shell case that served as an ashtray. 'You and I will talk later, Jill.'

'Whatever pleases you, Victor,' she said, and stalked out of the room.

'Well, what do you make of Jill?' Hazelwood asked when they were alone. 'Can we believe what she is telling us?'

'Why ask me?'

'Because you should know Jill better than anyone. After all, there was a time when you two were lovers and were about to marry.'

Ashton could now understand why Victor had gone back on his word not to involve him in the double-cross operation. It did not, however, make him any the happier.

'She dumped me when the fast-track posting to Bahrain was offered to her. Remember?' Ashton smiled. 'I might be considered prejudiced.'

Hazelwood got up from the desk, walked over to the window and stood there, hands in pockets, gazing at the Houses of Parliament across the river.

'I was never in favour of this operation,' he said. 'Jill waited until Monday before reporting she was open to blackmail. Then instead of submitting a Change of Circumstance report she persuades Robin Urquhart and other influential friends to leave her in place and wait developments. As a result of these delays there was no time to implement any electronic surveillance measures.'

'What exactly are you implying, Victor?'

'How do we know a hostile intelligence service is hellbent on manipulating her? Dammit, we've only Jill's word for it. There is no audio record of her conversation with various Emiles. On her own admission, she wiped the first message she received from the opposition.' Hazelwood shook his head. 'For all we know this man Kransky may make a decent living from blackmailing women like Jill. And let's face it, she is clever enough to invent the Emiles, knowing the longer she keeps up the pretence, the more hush money we will have to fork out to keep her mouth shut.'

'No, you're wrong. Jill is intelligent enough to know she would be rumbled sooner rather than later and for what it's worth I believe her story.'

'Thank you, Peter.'

'You're welcome.' Ashton stood up and moved towards the communicating door, then suddenly turned about. 'All the same, in your place I would be inclined to put the foot soldiers on to her.'

*

Landon stacked the in-, pending and out-trays on top of one another, and placed them in the bricked-in safe, then closed the locking bars and spun the combination dial. Leaving the fourth-floor office, which he had inherited from Ashton, he walked down the corridor to the bank of lifts and pressed the nearest call button. He couldn't think why Eric Daniels should want to have a word with him in private but apparently it had something to do with the conversation they'd had last Friday on the way back from Stoke Newington. Whatever it was, Daniels had been reluctant to show his face on the fourth floor and Landon had agreed to meet him in the basement garage. Alighting from the lift, Landon spotted the one-time military policemen working on the Ford Granada at the far end of the garage near the entrance to the badminton court. As he walked towards the car, Daniels stopped tinkering with the engine and closed the bonnet, then turned to face him.

'Morning, Mr Landon,' he said quietly. 'There's a friend of mine I'd like you to meet.'

'A friend?'

'Yeah, a detective sergeant in Special Branch.' Daniels opened the nearside front door and ushered him into the Granada, then walked round the front of the car and got in beside the wheel. 'I think you should hear what O'Meara has to say,' he added, and cranked the engine into life.

Landon assumed they were going to meet O'Meara at Scotland Yard and was mildly surprised when they turned right outside Vauxhall Cross and were obviously staying south of the river.

'So where are we going, Eric?' he asked.

'So far as the transport supervisor is concerned we're off to Gower Street. In practice we're dropping by my place in Worcester Park.'

'Will Detective Sergeant O'Meara be there?'

'Yeah, it's her rest day.'

There was a longish pause while Daniels mentally wrestled with some personal matter. Finally he told Landon there were a couple of things he should know about O'Meara. Ashton had once asked her what the initials G. D. stood for and she had told him she had been christened Geraldine Dawn, two names she had disliked from childhood. In fact, on joining the Met she had informed all and sundry that she would answer only to O'Meara. The preamble led to the disclosure that O'Meara was black and had two children, a nineteen-year-old son called Wesley, who was reading computer sciences at Portsmouth University, and a pain-in-the-arse daughter, Lisette, who couldn't wait for her sixteenth birthday when she would be free to leave school.

'O'Meara has had it pretty tough,' Daniels continued. 'Her husband walked out on the family eight years ago, which is when Lisette started being difficult. Wesley isn't so bad these days but if there were two things those kids had in common it was a strong aversion to all white people and a deep hatred of the police. They had undoubtedly made an exception in her case before I came on the scene but two years on they're still unwilling to accept me.'

'I can see a situation like that would be very stressful,' Landon said, trying not to sound pompous.

'It didn't help when O'Meara was badly wounded in a terrorist incident a year ago.'

Landon snapped his fingers. 'I remember now – the Warlock Estate in North Harringay. The Provisional IRA had booby-trapped a lock-up garage they were using as an arms cache. Am I right in thinking a detective constable was killed?'

'Yeah. His name was Kenny Browne. O'Meara was lucky: he was blown to pieces; she just had both legs mangled. Of course, her face looked as if it had been run over by a dumper truck and she had flash burns from the neck to the buttocks.

By the time O'Meara was discharged from hospital she had one leg shorter than the other and will never be fully mobile again.'

'I don't know what to say,' Landon told him. 'Rotten luck is so bloody inadequate.'

'What other way is there to describe it? Fact is, O'Meara returned to duty a month ago and was put to work in the office, running what Special Branch calls the Case Index. The thing is, she believes they will never use her in the field again, which means her career is blighted.'

'You don't think she is being unduly pessimistic?'

'Could be. The point is, she blames Francesca York for what happened to her.'

Although O'Meara was the vastly more experienced, York had been in charge of the surveillance team simply because when it came to anti-terrorist operations, MI5 was calling the tune. The trouble was the two women disliked each other. Whenever O'Meara ventured an opinion, York had taken it the wrong way and had been convinced the Special Branch officer was finding fault with her judgement.

'The arms cache was supposed to be in lockup number six,' Daniels continued, 'but nobody had come near it in the four or five days they'd had the place under observation. On the final day of their watch a dark blue van drove slowly past their observation post and backed up to number seven in such a way that O'Meara couldn't see what they were up to inside the lockup. A nagging suspicion that the driver and his mate were Provisional IRA became a stone-cold certainty within a matter of a few hours. But York wasn't having it, not even when they learned the van was displaying false number plates.'

It was nightfall when York finally agreed they should have a look inside lockup number seven. Detective Constable Kenny Browne had picked the lock on the up-and-over door and, once they saw a number of breeze blocks had been loosened, it was painfully obvious what had happened. Supposition became an established fact after Browne had opened up the hole in the dividing wall.

O'Meara's hand-held radio was being screened by the building and since York couldn't hear her she went outside to transmit. It was then that Kenny Browne went through the hole in the dividing wall and blundered into a tripwire. This detonated the booby trap the IRA had armed after they had emptied the arms cache.

'End of story, except that much later O'Meara learned that York had tried to put the blame for the fiasco on her – said she had been headstrong and impatient.'

'Did Miss York actually do that?'

'O'Meara had it on good authority,' Daniels said.

Landon shook his head. What Daniels had just said made him see Francesca in a different light. She had made quite an impression on him when they had dined at Mario's in South Kensington on Saturday and he had planned to see more of her. Now he wasn't so sure.

'I've only told you all this,' Daniels said, 'because I think you should know that O'Meara has really got it in for MI5. Truth is, she can't say anything bad enough about the Security Service.'

'Thanks for warning me.'

Daniels nodded sagely and didn't say another word until he stopped outside 26 Victoria Gardens and announced they had arrived. The house was semidetached, post World War One and part of the ribbon development stretching out from London in the era of building homes in a land fit for heroes. There were two narrow flowerbeds either side of the tiled path leading to the front door and a semicircular one fronting the bow windows. In the centre of a lawn not much bigger than a double blanket there was a rose bed of sorts. O'Meara opened the door to them before Daniels had the key out of his pocket.

O'Meara was wearing a beige-coloured roll-neck lambswool

sweater, loose-fitting black trousers and low-heeled shoes. Landon estimated she was about five feet nine inches tall and noted that her figure was as slim as any weight-conscious teenager's. There were a few streaks of grey in the sleek black hair but he was inclined to think this was down to the IRA bomb rather than the normal ageing process. Because O'Meara had a nineteen-year-old son, he assumed she was nudging the big four 0. She had a nice smile and it wasn't difficult to see why Daniels was smitten with her.

'This is Mr Landon, love,' Daniels said, introducing him on the doorstep.

'It's a pleasure to meet you,' O'Meara said, and shook his hand. 'I've heard a lot about you.'

'It's Will,' Landon told her, 'and the pleasure is mutual.'

Daniels suggested O'Meara should take him into the drawing room and he would make the coffee. He sounded like a fussy old maid which, even though Landon hardly knew him he was aware was completely out of character.

A three-piece suite, which included a sofa large enough to seat four people in comfort, made the drawing room seem a mite crowded, never mind the nest of tables and an overly large television. French windows opened on to a long rectangular garden, which didn't look as if it had received much attention before the onset of winter.

'What did Eric tell you about me?' O'Meara asked him quietly.

'Only that you had been blown up and seriously injured when a colleague set off an IRA booby trap. He also said you had only returned to duty a month ago and Special Branch had given you a desk job, which didn't thrill you.'

O'Meara smiled. 'Don't tell me he forgot to mention I'm not exactly a fan of MI5?'

'I believe he did say something to that effect,' Landon told her in an equally droll voice.

'I understand you attended the incident at forty-four Kimberley Road on Friday.'

'Yes I did.'

'What do you know about Wes Sharples and Carl Ivers?'

'Who are they, the two victims found in the kitchen?'

'Yes. Sharples had a string of convictions as long as your arm when he was under the age of sixteen, but nothing since then. Doesn't mean he was a reformed character, just that he was a hell of a lot smarter.'

Landon wasn't surprised; he'd already figured the two men were thieves. You didn't hide away eighteen cases of whisky for personal consumption.

'The official story is that the bottle of contaminated Scotch was purchased at a supermarket, the local branch of Tesco to be precise.'

'Why Tesco?'

'Because they are under attack by an extortionist. By the way, that's not public knowledge.'

'The official story makes sense to me,' Landon said. 'I mean, the last thing you want is widespread panic while you're looking for the perpetrators.'

'If that's what you're intent on doing,' O'Meara said coolly.

'What are you saying?'

'Was there only the one contaminated bottle of whisky or were there more?'

'We're still waiting to hear from Porton Down.'

'So are we, Will, but the Security Service is still prepared for every eventuality. If some journalist discovers the local police regard Sharples and Ivers as two out-and-out villains, the press will be informed that they had stolen the whisky from Tesco. The newspapers will then be persuaded not to publish the story until the extortionist is caught.'

'Suppose this mythical reporter learns there were eighteen

cases of Scotch and more than one bottle contained nerve gas? What then?'

'MI5 will simply modify the story. Instead of taking it off the shelf, Sharples and Ivers broke into a Tesco warehouse. If this does go public it will be enough to make the extortionist crap in his pants. Suddenly he is down for seven murders. Ten to one he will break cover and try to sell his side of the story to the press.'

What the extortionist might or might not do didn't interest Landon. He wanted to know if O'Meara had any evidence to support the allegations she had made about MI5. Tact and diplomacy were called for if he was to make that point to O'Meara without offending her. It was like tiptoeing through an uncharted minefield and the end result was equally disastrous.

'Are you doubting my word, man?' O'Meara demanded, putting on a West Indian accent.

'Certainly not.'

'Sounded like it to me,' she said, her eyes still glinting.

'Look, if we are to nip the idea in the bud, I have to have names.'

'OK, you tell me first how you propose to demolish their fairy tale?'

Landon said demolishing the fairy tale was not on the agenda. As soon as Porton Down submitted their findings his superiors would contact MI5 and Special Branch. Specifically they would seek assurances that steps had been taken to discover where the eighteen cases of Scotch had been stored before they were stolen. There would be the unspoken assumption that the Security Service agreed the nerve agent had been stockpiled by some unidentified terrorist organisation for future use. The matter would also be raised at the weekly meeting of the Joint Intelligence Committee.

'Matter of fact, I can practically guarantee members of the JIC will be called to an emergency meeting. That should bring MI5 into line,' Landon said in conclusion.

O'Meara gave it some thought, then nodded in agreement. 'I saw an internal memo addressed to the Deputy Assistant Commissioner, Special Branch,' she said quietly. 'It was from the Commander, Operations, and referred to a conversation he'd had with a Mr Colin Wales.'

Ashton was thinking of leaving early for once. He had tickets for the Festival Theatre in Chichester, had arranged for a baby-sitter, and booked a table for an early dinner at the Millsteam in Bosham. He had just cleared his desk and locked the combination safe when the Mozart phone rang. Some people could ignore the strident summons of a telephone; Ashton was one of those who couldn't and as a result the dinner reservation and everything else went down the pan. The caller was Max Brabazon, the SIS representative at Military Operations (Special Projects), who wanted him to know that Porton Down had completed their investigation. The eighteen cases of Scotch contained a combined total of 216 one-litre bottles, every one of which was contaminated with VX, the persistent nerve agent. Given the right weather conditions and an appropriate means of delivery, there was enough VX to wipe out four million people, or half the population of London.

Chapter 12

At 21.00 hours the temperature in Washington DC was down to 37F and would fall to below 30 before dawn, when a further light snowfall was anticipated. This was the third winter Samir Abbas had spent in and around the nation's capital and he was no more acclimatised to the cold now than when he had first arrived in the country. In the last fortnight he had given up his job at the Caltex filling station outside Tuxedo and had found work as a cleaner at McDonald's in Hyattsville. He had also turned in the five-year-old Volkswagen Polo for a six-year-old Ford Probe, which was one of the reasons why he was feeling cold. Either the mileage on the clock had been turned back by the used car dealer or he'd fouled up the electrics when he had transferred the tracking device. Whatever the cause, the heater was malfunctioning.

Abbas drove south on Connecticut Avenue, branched off on to 24th Street and went on past the Sheraton Park Hotel. He crossed Calvert Street and entered Woodley Road, which led to Rock Creek Park. Descending into the valley bottom, Abbas pulled off the road and drove into the treeline approximately fifty yards from the bridge over the creek. He switched off the ignition and doused the main beams, then sat there in the darkness until his eyes had adjusted to the preventing light. Sprawled behind him on the back seat was a cross-bred bull terrier. Alighting from the Ford Probe Abbas pushed his seat forward so that the dog could jump out before he collected the pooper-scooper from the trunk. Then he crunched across a thin carpet of snow, making his way to the litter bin that served as the cardinal reference point, the small terrier walking obediently to heel. Abbas positioned himself facing north, his back to the litter bin, then walked thirty-five paces due west to the hollowed-out trunk of an oak tree, which was one of three drops in and around Washington he'd given to Christensen. He bent down, reached inside the cavity and pulled out a black bin bag. He knew what was in it without looking; just over an hour ago Christensen had phoned to inform him the order book had been mailed to the Woodley Road address.

Abbas returned to the car, the bull terrier stopping every now and again to cock his leg and urinate against a tree, staining the snow around the trunk a sickly shade of lemon. The bull terrier belonged to Abbas and in this instance was a useful accessory. There was, after all, nothing suspicious about a man out walking his dog late at night, especially when a pooper-scooper and black plastic bag indicated he was a very responsible owner.

The dog back on board, Abbas drove out of the wood, rejoined the road and continued heading in a southerly direction. Woodley Road merged into Waterside Drive; at the junction with P Street he made a left, went round Dupont Circle and filtered into Massachusetts Avenue. Scott Circle, the underpass beneath Thomas Circle, Mount Vernon Square: the familiar landmarks came and went.

Home for Abbas was a grim-looking low-cost housing complex on New York Avenue within a stone's throw of the railroad tracks. Once inside the three-room flat, he sat down at the kitchen table to examine the document Christensen had left for him in the black plastic bag. The document was a photocopy of Cyclops, which he thought was a singularly inappropriate codename for the CIA-sponsored conference on International Terrorism. Classified Secret, it contained the detailed programme and the names of delegates expected to attend. Among the list of the SIS representatives the name of the Deputy Director General was conspicuous by its absence.

Abbas switched on his mobile and tapped out the number of the Lebanese businessman resident in Washington. When Emile answered, he told him he had been looking at the latest consignment note from London.

'I see the figurine of the ballerina we purchased has not been dispatched. I think we should get on to the firm and find out what's happening.'

'Leave it to me,' Emile said.

'The sooner the better,' Abbas said meaningfully, and switched off his mobile.

As was usually the case these days Jill Sheridan was already awake when the alarm went at six fifteen. Rolling over on to her right side, she reached out and shut it off, then groped for the mobile, which she had left next to the extension on the bedside table. She closed her fingers round the battery-powered phone and used the other hand to erect the aerial and depress the power button.

Jill got out of bed, stripped off her satin pyjamas and, after slipping into a towelling robe, picked up the mobile and went into the en suite bathroom. She opened the glass door of the shower cabinet and ran the water from outside the cubicle, adjusting the temperature to her satisfaction. Wearing a plastic shower cap she then stood under the rose and soaped herself all over. That done, Jill turned the mixer to cold and gave a muffled scream as the jet of icy water cascaded over her shoulders and took her breath away. She held out for almost ten minutes before she gave in and turned off the shower. It was a masochistic performance but Jill was convinced it toned up her body and she was all the better for it.

The mobile came to life while she was still towelling herself dry. For some moments she stared at it on the laundry basket, sick with apprehension, because only one of the Emiles would phone her at this ungodly hour. Reluctantly she picked up the mobile and managed a breathless hello.

'Why you not go to Cyclops?' Emile Mark I demanded in his unmistakable hoarse voice and unique brand of English when excited.

'Because I have to answer for the Director General in his absence,' Jill told him.

'Liar, liar, liar,' Emile screamed. 'You are under suspicion, that's why they not send you to CIA conference.'

This situation had been anticipated by the gang of four who decided just what information she could disclose to the opposition. They had prepared a plausible legend to hoodwink the Emiles and were confident it would hold up under interrogation. The problem for Jill, however, lay in persuading Emile Mark I to shut up and listen to her.

'You don't understand—'

'I understand everything,' Emile snapped.

'I'm not putting up with this,' Jill told him. 'Phone me again when you've calmed down.'

The gang of four had also decided controlled aggression was the best way to deal with Emile Mark I when he was in one of his hectoring moods. For all his intimidating personality they believed he was just a messenger like the other two Emiles, only more excitable. With careful handling he might commit some breach of security that would reveal the organisation he was working for. At least that was the theory.

Jill finished towelling herself dry, dressed for the office and went downstairs to breakfast off fresh orange juice, a cup of black coffee and a thin slice of wholemeal toast. The mobile rang again as she was loading the crockery into the dishwasher.

'Why are you not going to America?' Emile demanded as soon as she answered his call.

'I'm not going because my Director has not taken a holiday in two and a half years. Furthermore, his wife has not been feeling at all well lately and the doctors have advised a complete change of scenery.'

'This is a joke. Yes?'

'No, they leave for Arosa tomorrow, the first of March and return the following Saturday. The holiday was arranged long before the CIA decided to hold a seminar on International Terrorism.'

'The hotel where he's staying?'

'He isn't. My Director has borrowed a chalet from a very old friend in the banking world. Admittedly it's not far from the Wald Hotel in Arosa.'

'Do you take me for a fool?'

'I don't take you for anything,' Jill said tersely. 'Some things you have to take on trust but if you doubt me, go to Heathrow tomorrow, the VIP lounge in Terminal 2. He's on Swissair Flight SR803 departing 09.50 for Zurich.'

Jill waited for Emile to come back at her and even said hello a couple of times but again there was no reaction and she assumed he'd switched off his mobile. It was coming up to 7 a.m. and although Victor always left the house on the dot of seven, Jill thought she might catch him. She went into the drawing room and used the Mozart secure speech facility to call him at home. He sounded just a touch irritated when he picked up the phone and was in no way mollified by her half-hearted apology.

'Whatever it is, can't it wait?' Hazelwood demanded.

'We can leave it until after morning prayers.'

'Good.'

'But I think Alice would appreciate a little forewarning.'

'Don't tell me, we're going on holiday.'

'I'm afraid so.'

'You did the right thing in phoning me,' Hazelwood told her after a brief pause.

'Thanks, Victor.'

There were aspects of her conversation with Emile which Jill thought Victor should know before they met in the office, but then the mobile started trilling and she had to go. The caller was Emile Mark III, the one man of the trio who didn't have a guttural voice. He also happened to have a far better command of English than the other two and was particularly adept at catching her offguard.

'What name is he travelling under?' Emile asked.

'Who are we talking about?'

'Your Director General, Sir Victor Hazelwood and his wife, Alice. I assume she will be accompanying him?'

Jill caught her breath as though suddenly winded. How the hell did they know Victor was the DG? She could not recall his name appearing in print linked to the SIS. And what about Alice?

'Well?' Emile said belligerently, making it apparent he believed she was trying to stall him.

'They are travelling as Mr and Mrs Vernon Hunter.'

'Thank you, Miss Sheridan,' Emile said, and cut her off.

Ever since Porton Down had discovered that all 216 bottles of whisky had been contaminated with VX, Ashton had found himself wearing two hats. He supposed that having once been the Grade I Intelligence Officer in charge of the Combined Anti-Terrorist Organisation, he was the obvious choice to run the show when the moribund cell was given a new lease of life following the incident in Stoke Newington. The job wasn't demanding: at present more information flowed into the SIS from other agencies than out of it. The reason was simple enough: MI5 was the home team and was responsible for co-ordinating anti-terrorist measures within the UK.

The decision to treat the incident in Kimberley Road as a terrorist outrage had been taken by the Joint Intelligence Committee. That the nerve agent had been released accidentally had been irrelevant in their eyes, the deciding factor had been the nature and quantity of the chemical agent. Thereafter the next step was to discover where the whisky had been stored before it was stolen by Sharples and Ivers. This was never going to be an easy task for the police; the official press release had merely added to their difficulties. Newspaper editors had been given all the facts on the understanding that nothing would be published until the threat had been resolved. In the meantime they had agreed to run the story Colin Wales had proposed to the Commander, Operations, Special Branch. Consequently the search for the original hiding place had to be conducted discreetly.

Every day before morning prayers Ashton rang Colin Wales at MI5 to see what progress had been made. The answer on Tuesday, Wednesday and Thursday had been zero; today, however, had been different and he actually had something tangible to say at morning prayers when Hazelwood turned to him.

'Six lockups in Harrow were broken into during the night, twentieth, twenty-first of February—'

'But that's a week ago,' Garfield said, interrupting him in a voice that rose a full octave in disbelief. 'Are you telling us the police have only just learned about it?'

'Yes I am and there's reason for the time lag. Nothing had been taken from five of the lockups; the sixth appeared to be full of wine, cans of lager, cigarettes and cigars. The police secured the place and then looked for the tenant.'

'And I suppose he had vanished without trace?'

'I'll tell you one thing, Rowan,' Ashton said, his eyes narrowing, 'We'll get through this a lot quicker if you don't keep interrupting.'

Garfield opened his mouth to protest, then caught a warning glance from Hazelwood and closed it again. 'Sorry,' he mumbled.

'That's OK, Rowan. As a matter of fact none of the other tenants could recall ever meeting him.'

The garages had once belonged to the old Territorial Army drill hall and had been sold off when the reserve army units had been amalgamated and the centre closed. The property developer who'd bought the TA drill hall had then discovered there was a preservation order on the building and had promptly put it on the market. Thereafter the property had regularly changed hands until finally it had become a leisure centre.

The garages had also changed hands many times, principally because would-be entrepreneurs couldn't get planning permission to build a housing estate so close to what had been a refuse tip until it was closed by the urban district council in 1988. In the end the premises had gone for a song and the new owners had rented the garages out to various retailers in and around Harrow.

'The lockup the police are interested in is rented by a Mr Allum of Woodcock Lane, Kenton. On the sixth of September last year, Mr Allum signed an agreement leasing the property for three years and paid six months' rent in advance. The next payment was due in five days' time. However, the agent acting for the owners received a banker's draft on the tenth of January. There is no Woodcock Lane in Kenton, there is no Mr Allum on the electoral roll, there is no business registered in his name.'

'Who pays the community charge on the business?' Hazelwood asked.

'The agent. It's included in the rent.'

'So what line are the Met pursuing now, Peter?'

'They are interviewing the agent, hoping to jog his memory and the Central Cheque Squad of C1 is endeavouring to trace the banker's draft. Forensic is examining every bottle; they don't really expect to find any latent prints but there's always a faint chance somebody might have got careless. The distillers are adamant that the whisky bottles found at forty-four Kimberley Road differ in a few, very minor aspects from the type they use. Same applies to the labels, which gives Forensic a couple of additional avenues to explore.'

'Anything else?'

'No, that's it from Five. I do have a possible fix on Vladimir Aleksandrovich Labur, former Director of Chemical Defence Research. On Monday the sixth of January this year he called his wife in Odintsovo and told her he would be home in a day or two.'

'Where is Odintsovo?' Jill asked.

'It's approximately sixty miles south of Moscow.'

'He called his wife,' Hazelwood repeated slowly, 'meaning Labur phoned her. From where?'

'Baghdad.'

'I don't remember hearing that at the last meeting of the Joint Intelligence Committee.'

'Well, you wouldn't – it was low-grade stuff.' Ashton cleared his throat. 'A friend at GCHQ did me a favour. Purely on a hunch I asked him if Labur had received any communications from the Middle East shortly before or immediately after his retirement. He rang me when I got into the office this morning to say 9 Signal Regiment in Cyprus had picked up part of a conversation over an unguarded radio telephone link. GCHQ had Labur's voice on record and this man sounded like him. Against that, he called the woman Yevdokia, whereas we've always understood Raya was the first name of Labur's wife. Yevdokia also had a lewd nickname for the man in Baghdad – called him her big shag-happy bear, which is certainly at odds with his physical appearance.'

'I think it's out of character too,' Calthorpe observed quietly. 'Labur is a bit of an old maid, no sense of humour at all and very strait-laced.'

'Well, I did point out it was low-grade stuff, Hugo.'

There was a feeling round the table that a man of Labur's seniority and experience wouldn't be so foolish as to use an unguarded link. Ashton was about to point out that nobody was infallible and mistakes were made when Hazelwood beat him to it. He noticed Jill was looking disconcerted, just as she had when he had talked about Labur and the phone call from Baghdad. He had acted on a hunch but it had been inspired by Jill's suggestion that Emile Mark I had hailed from the Middle East. He had come close to saying as much and she had sensed it.

'What is your friend in GCHQ doing about this low-grade intercept, Peter?'

'Communications and Security up in Leicestershire has got a detachment monitoring the radio relay towers feeding Odintsovo. The whole of the Middle East is, of course, the responsibility of 9 Signal Regiment. I don't believe there is anything more we can do at present.'

Hazelwood agreed and turned his attention on Rowan Garfield. But the European Department had nothing exciting for him and he moved on to Winston Reid, the former Foreign and Commonwealth diplomat who had brought to the SIS an encyclopaedic knowledge of the Middle East. Hazelwood continued on round the table, reluctantly allowed Roy Kelso to have his say regarding the allocation of funds for the financial year 1997/1998 and then ended morning prayers with a bombshell.

'I shall be away all next week,' Hazelwood announced calmly. 'Alice has not been feeling well of late and the doctors tell me she needs a complete rest and change of scenery. So we're off to Arosa in the morning. Naturally, Jill will be in the driving seat during my absence, and you, Rowan,' he added smiling, 'will head the SIS delegation at the CIA symposium on International Terrorism.'

Ashton tried to catch Victor's eye but his old guide and

mentor had suddenly developed a bad case of myopia. Had anybody deliberately set out to create a recipe for disaster, no one could have made a better job of it than Hazelwood. In his absence Jill was answerable to a couple of unknown Privy Counsellors and Robin Urquhart, a weak man whom she could twist round her little finger without even trying.

The FBI had more than a passing interest in the symposium on International Terrorism sponsored by the CIA. Counter-intelligence, especially within the United States, was very much their baby. The Bureau was therefore responsible for assessing what sort of threat delegates from Australia, New Zealand, Canada and Great Britain might be under while they were in Washington. So far as Director Louis Freeh was concerned the people most at risk were definitely the representatives of MI5 and the SIS, even though his Deputy Head of Counter-Intelligence didn't appear to think so. Despite the truce there were plenty of Irish Americans who would be prepared to do the leg work for a hit team from the Irish National Liberation Army or some other extremist group outside the control of the Provisional IRA.

'Not too many Brits are attending this symposium,' Freeh observed without looking up from the list of delegates he was studying. 'No Deputy Director General either from the Secret Intelligence Service or MI5. You're the Deputy Head of Counter-Intelligence, Eric – do they know something we don't?'

'I don't believe so, sir. Furthermore, I don't see the Provisionals shooting or bombing a British intelligence officer over here. It would make our Government pretty mad and we would be told to bear down on Noraid. Besides, it wouldn't be in the Provisionals' interest to resume hostilities while they're still talking to the British Government and getting somewhere.'

'People don't always do what is in their best interest,' Freeh said.

'Yes, sir.'

'I see you've persuaded the CIA to put all the Brits in the Loews L'Enfant Plaza Hotel?'

'They've also been allocated rooms on the fourth floor, and they will travel on the same bus to and from Langley. Makes it a lot easier to protect them.'

'Just be sure you do protect them, Eric.'

Freeh looked up. The Deputy Head of Counter-Intelligence was just a shade too cocksure of himself for his liking. Women were said to find Eric attractive and he was certainly a great socialiser. Freeh had seen him at a number of parties on the cocktail circuit and always with a different lady on his arm. But none of them seemed to want a permanent relationship with him. Maybe they too thought Christensen was as phoney as his auburn-tinted hair.

'Just be sure you do,' Freeh repeated.

The evening rush hour had started to wind down by the time Ashton finally left Vauxhall Cross to begin the long journey home. Suburban services into London had reverted to the off-peak schedule and he had to wait a good fifteen minutes for a train to Waterloo and therefore missed the fast service to Portsmouth Harbour. Rather than wait more than an hour for the next one, he caught a semi-fast, which meant the train stopped at every station from Woking onwards. If that wasn't enough there was a shortage of rolling stock and what should have been an eight-car unit was down to four, so that by the time he boarded the train it was standing room only. It was, Ashton supposed, a fitting end to what had been a bloody awful day.

Hazelwood had fought a delaying action all day long with considerable skill. In Dilys Crowther, Victor had an invaluable ally who'd never failed to provide a reason why the DG was far too busy at the moment to see Ashton. The impasse had finally been resolved when Hazelwood had summoned him on the squawk box after Dilys Crowther, Heads of Departments and Jill Sheridan had gone home. It had come as no surprise when Hazelwood had told him the real reason why he was taking a week off. Ashton had assumed Jill Sheridan was the root cause and had surmised she'd heard from one of the Emiles again. That they had known she wasn't attending the CIA symposium could only mean somebody in London or Washington was keeping them up to speed. However, provided Jill's account of her two conversations with the Emiles could be relied upon, it was evident they had simply wanted to satisfy themselves that she wasn't under a cloud. The trouble was, the SIS still had no independent means of assessing what had passed between Jill and the people who were controlling her. An ideal opportunity to wire the house in Bisham Gardens for sound had been lost when all the locks had been changed to support her story that she and Robin Urquhart had split up. The old need-to-know rule had been applied so rigorously that they had been afraid to involve the Positive Vetting and Technical Services Division, which had left Jill to find a locksmith in Yellow Pages.

That hadn't been the only nasty surprise. In his absence, Hazelwood expected Ashton to keep an eye on Jill and report any misgivings he might have to Robin Urquhart and the two Privy Counsellors. Ashton reached inside the breast pocket of his jacket to make sure he still had the slip of paper torn from a scratch pad on which Hazelwood had written the names and phone numbers of the Privy Counsellors. That slip of paper could prove invaluable if things went from bad to worse.

And things were doing just that. On Hazelwood's instruction he had briefed Will Landon to find out whether the name of Tom Kransky rang any bells with the FBI. Now, this evening, Victor wanted him to call on Miles Delacombe first to see if Head of Station, Washington, knew anything about the man. Landon was suspicious enough already. As a newcomer to the

Russia Desk he had gone through the card index but hadn't been able to find Tom Kransky among the list of hostile intelligence agents. The same applied to the Ukraine, Belorussia, Kazakhstan and Georgia and all the other former Soviet Republics, which had greatly puzzled him. He had asked Ashton several times how it was Kransky had come to notice when the man hadn't been carded, and had looked far from convinced by the explanation he had received. Landon was going to look a damned sight more sceptical when he called him into the office on Saturday for a further last-minute briefing.

Ashton finally got a seat at Hazelmere and dozed off moments after the train had pulled out of the station. The next thing he knew he was waking up with a start as the semi-fast train rattled over the points outside Havant and drew into the platform. Alighting from the train, he passed through the booking hall and out into the station yard where he had parked his six-year-old Ford Escort XR3. He was on the last leg of the journey now, just seven and a half miles left via the back streets of Havant and the A259 trunk road through Hermitage and Nutbourne to Walton.

The encounter with the Range Rover occurred a mile beyond Nutbourne. It had started raining shortly before Ashton had joined the A259 but visibility was good, the road was dead straight and there was no oncoming traffic. The vehicle came up behind Ashton, headlights on full beam. Although the rear-view mirror was on anti-dazzle the glare lit up the interior of the car and Ashton could see his head, shoulders and features clearly reflected in the windscreen. He thought the Range Rover driver was going to tailgate the Escort but then the man dropped back and started flashing his headlights as if to indicate there was something wrong with his vehicle. Ashton touched the brakes, slowing down to under forty as did the other man. Then suddenly the Range Rover driver pulled out and accelerated. As he came abreast of Ashton, he deliberately sideswiped the Ford Escort off the road.

The car mounted the grass verge and almost flipped over when Ashton pulled the steering wheel over to the right in a desperate attempt to avoid ramming a telephone pole head on. He didn't quite make it and the nearside front wing clipped the pole. The impact shattered the headlight assembly, put a deep V-shaped dent in the fender and drove the bodywork into the tyre, bursting it like a toy balloon. By the time Ashton managed to release the seat belt and get at the mobile in his raincoat pocket, the Range Rover was no longer in sight.

Chapter 13

The autoflash on the camera dazzled Ashton and led to the immediate loss of night vision. It flashed again but this time he was ready for it and he saw the Range Rover as clearly as one could expect to in the last light of the day. Dark blue or was it black? And the registration number? P38, something D – or was it E? – then L. Anything with DL in it was an Isle of Wight index. He knew that because he had taken Harriet and the children over to Freshwater for a long weekend back in late September while the SIS were still pondering what to do with him. The camera blinked again and this time Ashton saw a man running through the car park as he left the station yard in the Ford Escort.

Suddenly he was wide awake, conscious of the wind driving the rain against the bedroom window and the distant, almost inaudible noise of the sea breaking on the shore. Last night hadn't been the first time the driver of the Range Rover had played tag with him on the A259. He had been there sitting on his tail on Tuesday or was it Wednesday evening. Ashton whistled softly. What had happened had nothing to do with road rage; the truth was somebody had been stalking him.

'What are you doing awake at this unearthly hour?' Harriet complained sleepily.

'Just thinking,' he said. 'Go on back to sleep.'

'Fat chance.'

'You don't know until you've tried.'

'I'll make a deal with you,' Harriet told him. 'Tell me

what's on your mind first, then I'll shut up and close my eyes.'

'Do you remember seeing a black or dark blue Range Rover in Church Lane any time in the last few days?'

'No.'

'Or in the village?'

'Range Rovers are not exactly unknown in Bosham. They're so commonplace I don't take any notice of them.'

'OK, let's forget Range Rovers. Have any salesmen been knocking on the door, people claiming to be double glazing reps?'

'I think you had better give me the whole story,' Harriet said quietly.

Ashton hesitated. There had been a time when Harriet had been cleared for constant access to Top Secret Codeword material and just about every other security caveat under the sun. The moment she'd resigned from MI5 every clearance had been withdrawn and these days she wasn't even permitted to see a document classified Restricted, which was the kind of nothing grading you stuck on a pamphlet dealing with the training of guard dogs in twenty easy lessons. But what the hell? Harriet never needed a slip of paper to prove she could be trusted.

He told her about the fling Jill Sheridan had had with Tom Kransky while she was in Florida, how she had ended up the star attraction in a porno movie and what happened thereafter. He left nothing out, from Hazelwood's volte-face concerning the action to be taken against his Deputy DG, to the need-to-know restrictions that had left Ashton slightly vulnerable.

'You know what I find really alarming? The fact that Victor didn't turn a hair when Jill admitted disclosing Garfield's name and appointment to one of the Emiles.'

'And after last night you are wondering if Jill had told them even more about you?' Harriet suggested.

'What happened wasn't your normal spur-of-the-moment road rage. There was no face-to-face confrontation. I was deliberately sideswiped off the road; it would have happened on Tuesday or Wednesday evening if there had been less traffic on the road. If I'm right, it means Jill must have given them our home address.'

'Do you think the driver intended to kill you?'

Ashton grimaced, wryly amused by the directness of her question. You could, he thought, always rely on Harriet to get right down to the nitty-gritty. The fact was he had been damned lucky on two counts. A foot or so to the left and the Escort could have hit the telegraph pole head on, driving the steering column like a lance into his chest. Furthermore, how the car hadn't flipped over and burst into flames was a mystery to him.

'I guess he meant to,' Ashton said presently.

'Why?'

Harriet could have added, 'You're not that important', which was exactly what he himself was thinking. Kransky hadn't set up Jill so that the Emiles of this world could take him out.

'Maybe to implicate Jill. Every time one of the Emiles has contacted her, he's used a mobile phone. They've undoubtedly got her voice on tape when she gave them this address. The gang of four who are running Jill believe she can reel these people in, but Urquhart, the two Privy Counsellors and Victor have got it wrong. I'll give you any odds you like, Jill did not consult them first before she blew the whistle on me. I'm also betting she still hasn't told them and never will if she can help it. That's why Jill is such a liability; once she learns what the Emiles now have on her, she won't just collaborate with them, she will become their damned ally.'

'What time is it, Peter?'

Ashton rolled over on to his right side and peered at the

luminous figures on the alarm clock. 'Ten past seven,' he told her. 'We've got at least another twenty minutes before Edward decides to join us.'

'That's what you think,' Harriet said, and kicked the bedclothes off. 'While I'm having a shower, you go downstairs and have breakfast.'

'What's all this in aid of?'

'Then I'll wake the children and get them dressed.'

'You haven't answered my question.'

'I'm going to drive you to the station in the Volvo. All being well, you should be in London shortly after nine o'clock.'

'And then what?'

'Why ask me when you know what needs to be done?'

'I'd like to be sure we're both thinking along the same line and are prepared to take the consequences.'

'OK, you are going to bug Jill's office and Hazelwood's too in case she decides to keep his chair warm while he's away in Switzerland. Get what you need from Terry Hicks; he'll do anything for you.'

Hicks was the electronic whiz-kid in charge of Technical Services. When the Cold War had been at its height, he had spent the first three months of the year giving the embassies behind the Iron Curtain a good spring-clean. In Moscow the KGB had tried their best to bug the secure area of the embassy but had never been able to neutralise the electronic defences Hicks had installed. Thwarted, the KGB had directed powerful sound detectors at the upper-floor windows of the embassy on Maurice Thorez Embankment from the Kremlin watchtowers north of the Moscow River. Technical Services had responded to this threat by building a soundproof igloo in the basement where it was impossible for the opposition to eavesdrop on a Top Secret briefing.

If Terry Hicks had a fault it was his uncanny knack of rubbing people up the wrong way. Roy Kelso referred to him as 'that bloody little insubordinate oik', but then Hicks didn't have much time for the Assistant Director in charge of the Admin Wing either.

'Of course, that's only part of the job,' Harriet continued. 'For a hundred per cent coverage every room in Jill's house should be bugged if possible.'

The task wasn't beyond Ashton technically, but Hicks would be in and out of the house in half the time it would take him. And Harriet was right: Hicks would go that extra yard and more for him. Best of all, he wouldn't ask why it was necessary to put the Deputy DG under electronic surveillance. The risks didn't bear thinking about.

Winter, summer, spring, autumn, weekdays and the Sabbath were all the same to Jill Sheridan. Not for her the long lie-in on her days off. Every morning she rose at six fifteen, took a hot shower followed by a cold one, then breakfasted off orange juice, black coffee and a thin slice of toast. Lately she had taken to smoking a cigarette after she had eaten; lately she had received the equivalent of a wake-up call on her mobile from one of the Emiles.

This morning, however, there had been no wake-up call at six forty-five, and thus far her mobile had remained silent. The phone that did come to life at eight forty-one was a BT Response 300 in the large sitting room.

'Thought I would give you a ring to let you know we're on our way,' Hazelwood said cheerfully.

'You're a little too early, aren't you, Vernon?' Jill said, using the alias he was travelling under. 'I understand your flight departs at nine fifty?'

'Well, that's Alice for you. She has a thing about making sure we have plenty of time in hand. It's a wonder she didn't insist on spending last night in a hotel near Heathrow.'

Jill gritted her teeth. She didn't know whether the opposition had the ability to eavesdrop on their conversation but if they could listen in, Victor was going to blow the whole double-cross operation. Maybe that was his intention? He had never been in favour of it, and had made it clear that easing her out of the SIS was, in his opinion, the best solution. No, she was allowing her imagination to run riot, that was the top and bottom of the matter. Victor hadn't deliberately sabotaged the operation, he had too much to lose. If he fouled things up there would be no extensions in post for him at yearly intervals and he would be under Alice's feet for the rest of his life, something he obviously dreaded. The trouble with Victor was his complete inability to make small talk, that was why he sounded so damned stilted. What she had to do was get him off the line a.s.a.p.

'Listen, Vernon,' Jill said forcefully, 'I have to go, there's somebody at the front door. Have a good time. Enjoy your stay at Arosa and forget about the office. I can handle things here.'

Jill put the phone down and went into the kitchen to make herself another cup of instant. She had just plugged the kettle in when the mobile demanded her immediate attention. Emile Mark III, the man with the best command of English, said good morning and then asked if G848 MAU meant anything to her.

'Golf eight four eight. Mike Alpha Uniform?' Jill repeated doubtfully.

'Yes.'

'No, I can't say it does.'

'You surprise me. It's the registration number of a Ford Escort belonging to Mr Peter Ashton.'

Jill waited for the inevitable bombshell, her stomach twisted in knots because she had an inkling of what was coming. Even so, to hear that Ashton had been a victim of road rage still gave her a nasty jolt.

'When did this happen?' she asked in a hollow voice.

'Last night on the A259 to Chichester between Nutbourne

and Walton. He was sideswiped off the road and ploughed into a telegraph pole.'

'Road rage!' Jill shouted. 'You must think I was born yesterday. You people did it in cold blood.'

'And you are partially responsible, Miss Sheridan. After all, it was you who gave us his name and address. The rest was easy.'

'You bastard.'

'Look on it as a timely warning,' Emile continued unperturbed. 'Something far worse could happen to you.'

'What am I supposed to have done?'

'Nothing as yet. Just keep it that way. Do you understand what I mean?'

'Yes.' Jill swallowed. 'How is Mr Ashton? Is he OK?'

'I wondered when you were going to ask after him. His car was badly damaged but he's all right,' Emile said, and switched off his mobile.

'Francesca York is blonde, twenty-seven and quite good-looking.' That had been Ashton's description of her and pretty inadequate it was too, in Landon's opinion. The former lieutenant in the army's Special Counter-Intelligence Team had a hell of a lot going for her. Maybe she wasn't a classical beauty like Harriet Ashton, the perfect symmetry of whose face claimed everyone's attention and remained firmly imprinted in their minds afterwards, but Francesca knew how to make a man feel special and she had certainly done that for him. He looked at her lying next to him in the double bed, knees drawn up to her stomach in the foetal position, blonde hair spread out on the pillow like a fan, the black and white check shirt he'd lent her unbuttoned from the neck to the thighs. The shirt was made to order by Charles Tyrwhitt of Jermyn Street but she fitted it far better than ever he could. Careful not to wake her, Landon slipped his right arm under her neck and moved closer to

Francesca. When her knees touched his stomach, she automatically straightened her legs and nestled against him, still
apparently asleep, though he wasn't inclined to bet on it. She
had rung him at the office late in the afternoon to suggest they
met for a drink. She had learned one or two things about
Eleanor Gadsby concerning her relationship with Bill Orchard.
Nothing secret, of course, but she thought he might be interested even if it was only gossip.

They had met in a wine bar off St James's Square and what
she had to tell him had taken no more than five minutes but it
had been interesting enough. It amounted to the fact that good
old Bill had been having a raging affair with his sister-in-law,
and it was Eleanor who had ruined him financially, not Ms
Sheridan as Mary Orchard had claimed. It only went to show
that no matter how well you might think you knew somebody,
there were dark corners in their life you never suspected.

They'd had a couple of glasses of Chardonnay and then
Francesca had persuaded him to accompany her to some
drinks party in the King's Road she'd been invited to. Looking
back now it was hard to say which of them had looked the most
out of place, Francesca in the little blackcocktail number she
had changed into at the office or him in his dark grey Italian-
style suit from Marks and Spencer. Compared to everybody
else, both men and women, in their turtle-neck sweaters,
moccasins, and tight fitting jeans, they had looked very over-
dressed.

They had stayed for half an hour. During that time one of
the party-goers had accidentally bumped into Francesca,
spilling a glass of wine over the front of her dress, while Landon
had been pinned in a corner by a woman with a metal stud in
her tongue who'd lectured him on the medicinal benefits of
cannabis.

They had gone back to his flat off Gloucester Road since
Francesca wasn't a bit domesticated and the only thing she had

in the cupboard was a half-empty packet of breakfast cereal. He'd served up bacon and eggs after Francesca had stripped off and taken a bath because, as she had pointed out, it was amazing how sopping wet a glass of wine could make you. After that, one thing had led to another and they had ended up in bed.

Francesca stirred against him and murmured contentedly. Her skin was smooth as silk to his touch and she excited him in a way that the barrister, his ex-fiancée, and her successors never had. When aroused she became uninhibited and it was questionable who was in control. He stroked her flank from knee to hip, then suddenly her open mouth was on his, their tongues entwining. She began to grind her teeth as she had done last night and a hand soft to the touch sought out his penis and fondled it gently.

'Oh, yes,' she breathed.

'And what does that mean?' he grunted.

'It means I am going to mount you like you've never been mounted before.'

Francesca pushed Landon over on to his back and straddled him. She hugged, kissed, cried out, moved up and down on him until no matter how hard he tried, he could no longer hold back. Landon suspected he had climaxed first but it could only have been by a split second. Totally spent, Francesca laid her head upon his chest and drifted off to sleep moments before he did. They had been dozing for roughly an hour when the telephone disturbed them.

The phone was on the bedside table within easy reach, but Landon turned the wrong way and drew a painful yelp from Francesca as his left knee sank into her abdomen. He rolled over to the other side and managed to catch her forehead a glancing blow with his elbow.

'Jesus, Landon,' she gasped, 'why don't you make a proper job of it and knock me unconscious while you're at it?'

He lifted the receiver and heard Ashton say there had been a last-minute change of plan. Convinced in his own mind he was no longer required to attend the symposium in Washington, he was taken aback when Ashton instructed him to see what Miles Delacombe knew about Kransky before he approached the Friends. Then before Landon had a chance to hint at the latest on Bill Orchard, Ashton was gone.

'Write him a letter,' Francesca said drowsily.

'That's funny.'

'No it isn't, it's perfectly sensible idea.'

'Ashton was using a mobile.'

'Bully for him.'

'I heard a train announcer in the background noise. I believe he's in London.'

'Oh, no, you're not thinking of going to Vauxhall Cross, are you? Write him a letter and deliver it tomorrow. Do that and I'll give you a juicy titbit.'

'What sort of titbit?' he asked.

'Gadstar Promotions does more than publicise their clients,' Francesca said. 'They are also into fund-raising. Right now they are raising money for Yassir Arafat and the PLO.'

Hicks checked the contents of the executive briefcase to make sure he had everything he needed, then left his semidetached on Sunleigh Road, Alperton, to make his way to Ravenscourt Park via Hanger Lane, Gunnersbury Avenue and Chiswick High Road. He could have got there on the Underground, changing from the Piccadilly Line to the District at Ealing Common, but it was a tedious journey and there was no telling where Ashton might send him. Even though the Ford Sierra belonged to Lorna, his wife, he took it in preference to his own Escort because the tank was three-parts full.

On a Saturday morning traffic into London wasn't a problem and he made good time. Parking near the District Line station was very much a hit-or-miss affair at weekends but luck favoured him today and he found a vacant slot just beyond the railway bridge opposite the entrance to the park.

It was a neighbourhood Hicks knew well from the time Kelso had purchased number 83 Rylett Close behind the Royal Masonic Hospital. The Edwardian semidetached had been converted into a safe house for a Russian family whose name he had long since forgotten. Later, it had been sold to the Ashtons when the Treasury had instructed the SIS and other government departments to reduce their housing stock as part of the so-called peace dividend. They had started stripping out most of the electronic defences he had installed only to put them back again when word got around that an IRA hit team was stalking Ashton.

Hicks glanced at the clock in the instrument panel and compared the time it was showing against his wristwatch. Five minutes to ten: Ashton would be arriving any moment now unless he had been hopelessly optimistic when he'd phoned him as his train approached Waterloo. Hicks grabbed the executive briefcase from the adjoining seat and got out, then locked the car and walked back to the station. As he entered the booking hall, a train drew into the island platform above; Ashton was one of the seven people who alighted.

'It's very good of you to give up your Saturday morning, Terry,' he said. 'I'm sure you must have better things to do.'

'Hey, there's no need to apologise; it's got me out of going to the supermarket with Lorna.'

'If you say so. Where did you leave your car?'

'It's up there a piece,' Hicks said, and pointed in the general direction of the Ford Sierra.

'Do you mind if I drive?'

'Be my guest.' Hicks aimed the remote control at the car and tripped the central locking, then handed the ignition key to Ashton. 'Just don't write it off,' he said, grinning.

'How did you know I'd been run off the road?'

'Christ, when did this happen?'

'Last night, on my way home. The guy who recovered the vehicle took one look at the Escort and told me it was a complete write-off.' Ashton opened the door on the driver's side, which happened to be next to the kerb, and got in. 'I had a quarrel with a telegraph pole and bent the chassis out of line,' he added.

'This was no accident?'

'It wasn't road rage either. I was stalked.'

The Escort was over six years old and had cost Ashton £2,750 on the road but he thought the insurance company was unlikely to give him more than the write-down value of the car, which was probably about £1,800.

Ashton started up, pulled away from the kerb and, further up the street, made a three-point turn. He drove back to Chiswick High Road, then headed on into London.

'Have you got all the equipment I requested?' he asked, glancing pointedly at the executive briefcase Hicks was nursing on his lap.

'I've got two transmitters half the size of your thumbnail. They are solar-powered, have a magnetic base, a maximum operating range of eight hundred metres and are voice activated. The tape recorder works on the same principle but it's somewhat larger.'

'How much larger?'

'The dimensions are six inches by four and a quarter.'

'Concealing it could be a problem' Ashton said thoughtfully.

'That depends how close you are to the targets.'

'I'll be within touching distance.'

'Within touching distance,' Hicks mused. 'Got your eye on someone down in Bosham? Maybe the burk who ran you off the road?'

'Could be.'

'Naw, I don't buy that. I think it's somebody in the workplace.'

Ashton didn't say anything, just sat there gazing ahead as if concentrating on the road. The rain which had petered out an hour ago, was now back again, driven before the prevailing wind. Still keeping his own counsel Ashton drove through Hammersmith and on into Kensington High Street.

'Am I allowed to know where we are going?' Hicks asked presently.

'You get the car back at Green Park.'

'Which is where you will catch a Victoria Line train to Vauxhall. Right?'

'Is there anything I should know about these transmitters?' Ashton said, ignoring the question. 'Does reception depend on line of sight, for instance?'

'Listen, you tell me where these bugs are to be installed and I'll do the job for you. So, OK, it's a totally illegal operation but it won't be the first one I've done for you. Remember Edwina's that ladies' hairdressing salon in Poplar High Street? I broke into that place without a warrant and exchanged one of the adaptors in the power point by the reception desk with an Ultimate Infinity Receiver.'

He reminded Ashton of that time in Hong Kong some years back when he had bugged two Rolls-Royce Corniches belonging to a Chinese businessman who fronted for the Black Dragon Triad and how, less than twelve hours later, he had broken into Chief Inspector Uttley's apartment on the eighth floor of Mirabar Court to wire the whole damned place for sound. Uttley had returned earlier than expected and if he hadn't nailed the Chief Inspector with a sucker punch as the bastard entered the room, he would have ended up doing time in Stanley Prison.

'You and I go back a long way,' Hicks said quietly, 'and I reckon we've done more bent operations than kosher ones on behalf of the country.'

'So?'

'So why are you suddenly looking out for me?'

'Because this one is different.'

'In what way?'

'Let me ask you a question. How many times have you walked into Vauxhall Cross on a Saturday morning?'

'There's always a first time for everything,' Hicks said lamely.

'Yeah, and tongues would start wagging, and pretty soon word would get back to Roy Kelso. The duty staff won't think twice about me.' Ashton paused, then said, 'Admit it, you know I'm right.'

'OK. Here's what you do. There's underfloor heating throughout the building; place the transmitters and tape recorders in the air vents at ground level.'

Hicks opened the briefcase and took out the electronic gadgetry Ashton needed, which included an earpiece to enable him to eavesdrop whenever he had an opportunity to do so. He also removed a plastic wallet containing a four-in-one screwdriver. Hicks then told him to start putting the gear away in his pockets when they were held at the next set of traffic lights.

'You may be an assistant director,' Hicks told him, 'but if you walk into Vauxhall Cross carrying a briefcase, the security guard will want to look inside it.'

Chapter 14

Ashton left the conference room and returned to his office. All through morning prayers, Jill Sheridan had studiously avoided his eyes, although on several occasions he had been conscious that she was watching him surreptitiously. There was not the slightest doubt in his mind that she knew he had been side-swiped off the road on Friday night. Terry Hicks was the only person he'd told and no way would the Electronics King have told her, or anyone else who worked at Vauxhall Cross for that matter. She had heard it from one of the Emiles; the lack of any kind of evidence to support his assumption didn't bother Ashton. In this instance the balance of probabilities was enough for him.

He opened the combination safe for the second time that morning, removed the filing trays and continued reading the latest intelligence summary from Head of Station, Moscow. He had hardly got to grips with the report when the chief clerk deposited a clutch of files in the appropriate tray, and informed him that the unopened brown envelope on top was from Mr Landon.

'He delivered it to the duty officer on Sunday morning.'

'Thank you.'

'I don't know whether the letter is classified or not because Mr Landon was adamant that the envelope should only be opened by you.'

'So I see.'

In capital letters Landon had printed: PERSONAL FOR AND TO BE OPENED ONLY BY MR P. ASHTON, ASSISTANT DIRECTOR EAST EUROPEAN AND BALKANS DEPARTMENT. He had also sealed the envelope with Scotch Tape in such a way that no filing clerk could inadvertently open it. Not content with that, Will Landon had affixed two red star labels across the flap and signed both, which had probably put a few noses out of joint in Central Registry.

Ashton picked up the paperknife on the desk, slit the envelope open and extracted two pages of A4 covered in Landon's familiar scrawl.

'As I thought, personal and demi-official,' Ashton said, looking up at the chief clerk. 'No need to book it in, it's unclassified.'

The information it contained, however, could prove embarrassing if seen by the wrong person. Ashton assumed Will had got the story from Francesca York, whom he was dating fairly frequently. It was apparent she hadn't disclosed her source or sources to him but in her shoes Ashton would have played it close to his chest too. He accepted her information because it supplied the missing piece of the jigsaw puzzle and explained Bill Orchard's up and down mood when he had visited Islamabad, Colombo and Delhi. Bill Orchard was the one person Ashton would never have suspected of cheating on his wife but then as the old saying went, 'still waters run deep'. Eleanor Gadsby had claimed that she had only to snap her fingers and Bill would jump into bed with her, and events had proved this had been no idle boast.

According to Francesca York, Bill's affair with his sister-in-law had started in April 1995, almost two years ago. No one at Vauxhall Cross had noticed any change in his behaviour; for as long as Rowan Garfield and the other senior heads of departments could remember, Bill had always been a clock-watcher and had habitually left the office on the dot of five o'clock. It had never entered anybody's head to question what time he arrived home. Wives never attended the office Christmas party and of the intelligence fraternity only Will Landon and Roy Kelso had ever met Mary Orchard. In the pursuit of his love life circumstances had certainly favoured Bill Orchard. Even so, he'd had to be damned careful not to arouse Mary's suspicion. No coming home in the middle of the night, nothing, in short, that would have led his wife to phone the duty officer at Vauxhall Cross to find out what had happened to him.

It would have been better for him and Mary herself if she had learned of his infidelity. Bill might still be alive today and maybe she would have been in time to prevent her husband remortgaging their house and losing all three hundred and fifty thousand on becoming a name at Lloyd's. Mary Orchard believed she had Jill Sheridan to thank for that and there was no prize for deducing who had planted the idea in her head.

Lawrence Gadsby had described his adopted sister as an evil, poisonous bitch, before proceeding to tell Will Landon what she had done to Mary. For reasons known only to her perverted mind, she had set out to destroy Bill Orchard as well as her younger sister and had succeeded brilliantly. Eleanor had enticed Bill into an adulterous relationship and within a few months had introduced him to Charles Yarpole Associates, the Lloyd's Syndicate that had swallowed up all his money.

Landon had returned from Wrotham believing quite rightly that the further demand for money that had awaited Orchard on his return from Delhi had pushed him over the edge. Hazelwood had been happy with that explanation; so too had Hugo Calthorpe. No security implications, just a sad tale of greed and lust. The news that Gadstar Promotions was in the fund-raising business on behalf of the Palestine Liberation

Organisation had put a different slant on things for Landon.

'You're wrong,' Ashton said aloud.

'Who is?' Jill asked from the doorway.

'Will Landon.' Ashton held out the latter to her. 'Read the last paragraph and you'll see what I mean.'

He didn't care if Jill read the whole damned letter and learned that Mary Orchard blamed her for their financial disaster.

'Why wasn't I informed of this earlier, Peter?'

'Because I've only just received the letter. OK?'

'There's no need to be aggressive, it was a perfectly reasonable question.'

Ashton gazed at Jill in wonder. Her gall never ceased to amaze him.

'Will is obviously hedging his bets,' she observed presently. 'He's saying that Eleanor told Orchard about the PLO business either to bring him to heel or else he had become too big a risk and he had to go.'

'It doesn't hold up, Jill. Whatever else she might be, Eleanor Gadsby is no fool. She wouldn't deliberately push Bill over the edge because there was a good chance he would leave a note behind explaining why he had decided to commit suicide. No, Bill discovered the PLO connection all by himself and that, coming on top of everything else, unhinged him.'

'Well, only time will tell who's right and who's wrong.' Jill returned the letter to Ashton and half turned away from him as if to leave when another thought occurred to her. 'What are we doing about Gadstar Promotions?' she asked.

'Nothing,' Ashton said tersely. 'They're being looked at by MI5.'

'I trust the Security Service will keep us informed?'

'I think you'll have no worries on that score. Will Landon has established a very close liaison with MI5.'

Jill Sheridan was almost in the corridor when he asked her if there was anything else she wanted to discuss with him.

Although there had been no hint of menace in his voice, she froze as if suddenly paralysed with fear. Moments later, when Jill turned about, she had regained her composure and there was a smile on her lips.

'Why yes, there is. What's this I hear about you having an accident on Friday night?'

'Who told you?'

'At least three people, that woman on the reception desk for one. I tell you it's all over the building by now.'

'Enid Sly,' he said.

'What?'

'The woman on the reception desk.'

A bossy and inquisitive person, Enid Sly had asked him why he'd arrived later than usual and he'd said Harriet had been obliged to drive him to the station because his car had been written off in a traffic accident.

'Whose fault was it?'

'I got shunted off the road. I was all right but the car is only good for scrap. Don't tell me you didn't know that?'

'Enid Sly didn't,' Jill countered, 'and she was my source.'

Game, set and match, Ashton thought wryly. Occasionally he was able to get the better of Jill but not in this instance when it really mattered.

Max Brabazon had become a member of the 'Rag' in St James's Square thirty-one years ago when a junior lieutenant RN. Ashton, on the other hand, had joined the Army and Navy Club on 1 January 1997, a little over eight weeks ago. For Ashton to invite him to lunch didn't seem right to Brabazon, who felt it should have been the other way round. The fact that Ashton had intimated his invitation hadn't been extended for social reasons had helped to salve Brabazon's conscience.

They had arranged to meet in the members' bar adjoining the entrance hall between twelve forty-five and one p.m.

Brabazon was on his second pink gin when Ashton arrived three minutes late for their appointment.

'I don't think I want a drink just now,' Ashton told him. 'Why don't you bring yours with you?'

'Not quite the done thing,' Brabazon muttered, then swallowed the rest of his gin and left the glass on the bar.

That a newcomer like Ashton could arrange at short notice to have a table in the window overlooking the square and enclosed garden was something of an eye-opener. So too was the way the head waiter danced attendance on them. They settled for the table d'hôte menu and decided on a carafe of claret, Ashton making small talk as he wrote out their order and signed it. He continued in the same vein until Brabazon began to think he must have got it wrong and this really was a social occasion. His original assumption was, however, confirmed once the head waiter had moved away from their table.

'Tell me something, Max,' Ashton said quietly, 'are you running a surveillance operation I don't know about?'

Brabazon gazed at him dumbfounded. 'I'm not with you, Peter.'

'Let me be more specific then. Are you using military personnel to mount a surveillance operation against a target I'm unaware of?'

'You're my boss, Peter. I'd never do anything behind your back.'

'Knowingly.'

'What?'

'You'd never knowingly do anything behind my back. But supposing you received your instructions direct from the DG, wouldn't you assume Victor Hazelwood had already briefed me?'

'I probably would but nothing of the kind has happened.'

'Well, the way things are you may have to set up such an operation in conjunction with your military colleagues. It will be a plainclothes job, round the clock, seven days a week, and the SAS are just the people to do it.'

Ashton was right about that. The Special Air Service was attuned to conducting clandestine operations and had had plenty of experience at it all over the world. They were the best in the business when it came to gathering intelligence.

'How much notice are we likely to get?' Brabazon asked cautiously.

'We'll need three teams of four. The first one will be at an hour's notice to move from noon tomorrow, all other things being equal.'

'What does that mean?'

'It's possible the operation is already underway but I'll know whether Special Branch is involved before you need to stand up the SAS.'

'We're talking about playing on the home turf?'

'Yes.'

Brabazon recalled the political furore when the SAS had shot down three IRA terrorists in Gibraltar whom they were shadowing. If a similar incident occurred within the UK the political fallout would be ten times worse.

'Have we cleared this with the Government?'

'You may rest assured the Cabinet Office has been briefed,' Ashton said coolly.

'So who are we putting under the microscope?'

'Jill Sheridan.'

'You're joking!'

Ashton shook his head. 'I've never been more serious in my life, Max,' he said.

The fasten seat belt signs were on and despite the pressurised cabin Landon felt his ears pop as the 777 began its descent into Dulles International airport. A few moments ago the airline attendant in business class had announced that British Airways

Flight BA217 was on time and would be landing at 16.30 hours local time. In London it was now 21.30 hours and ordinarily Landon would be cleaning himself up after tinkering with the Aston Martin.

He checked the customs declaration one more time, then turned his attention to the visa application, taking particular note of the answers he'd given to the questions on the reverse side of the green form. A cross in the box marked 'Yes' when he should have put it in the one headed 'No' would guarantee him a seat on the next flight to London.

The 777 touched down, shimmied just a fraction when full flap and the brakes were applied, then taxied sedately to the BA terminal building, a mere three minutes behind schedule by the time the plane reached the gate. Although Landon had never flown into Dulles International before, he knew the airport was a good half-hour drive from the centre of Washington, and was also aware that Miles Delacombe usually left the embassy at 6 p.m. Whether he would be able to catch the Head of Station before he went home depended on how swiftly the UK delegation was processed by Immigration.

Ashton had told him to see what Head of Station knew about Kransky before he approached the Friends. However, nothing had been said about calling on Delacombe the day he arrived in Washington. That had been his idea and the trouble was, Head of Station had had no forewarning of his intention. To use one of the on-board telephones to call embassy over what was an unguarded link would be a gross breach of security. Fort Meade, home of the National Security Agency, the American equivalent of Government Communication Headquarters, was no distance from Washington and any call he made was bound to be monitored.

Landon retrieved his carry-on bag from the overhead bin and followed the other business-class passengers out of the cabin. Francesca York had been sitting next to Colin Wales three rows in front of him and she was now even further ahead, striding out to keep up with her department head. In the departure lounge at Heathrow she had acted as if they were no more than casual acquaintances and he wondered if she was going off him or was worried her superiors might think she had become too friendly with an SIS officer and had been talking out of turn.

Much to Landon's relief there was no delay at Immigration. A gofer from the CIA was waiting for them in arrivals hall, holding up a sign that said 'UK Delegation'. They numbered ten in all: Rowan Garfield, Ralph Symes and himself representing the SIS; from MI5 there was Colin Wales, Francesca York and a man called Geraint whose surname Landon hadn't caught. Finally there were three senior officers from GCHQ whom he had nicknamed Tom, Dick and Harry, plus Group Captain Amesbury-Cotton RAF of DI7 representing the Defence Intelligence staff. Marshalled by the gofer they went through Immigration virtually on the nod. There was a brief hold-up while Tom, Dick and Harry, who were going to Fort Meade after the symposium, collected their suitcases from the baggage claim area but thereafter all Customs wanted from them were their declaration forms.

A Ford mini bus conveyed them into Washington, the gofer using the public address system to brief them about the programme for Cyclops, which he did step by step even though they had received a copy a week ago. Occasionally he would break off to point out some landmark as the driver made his way to L'Enfant Plaza via Falls Church, Arlington, the Theodore Roosevelt Bridge over the Potomac River, Constitution Avenue, and across the Mall on 7th Street. Landon's eyes were, for the most part, on his wristwatch, counting off the minutes and wondering if he would make it to the embassy in time.

Room numbers on the fourth floor of the L'Enfant Plaza

Hotel had already been allocated, which speeded things up. Nevertheless the hotel still needed to take an impression of his credit card to cover personal expenses like the minibar. Although this only took a minute it seemed more like five. Landon stopped by the bell captain's desk and asked if he would call a cab for him. After dumping his bag in the room, he had exactly nine minutes in hand and a rush hour to contend with. The driver told him he had no chance of reaching the British Embassy on Massachusetts Avenue North by six. He was right; they arrived at ten after, but luck was on Landon's side because Head of Station was working later than usual.

Miles Delacombe was a small man, no taller than five feet seven and definitely overweight for his height. He had a smooth round face, the makings of a double chin and a stomach that made him look four months pregnant. Delacombe had thin, sandy hair and affected a trim military-style moustache. He was fifty-one years old and a leading light of the Caledonian Society in Washington. He did not make Landon feel welcome. He was, Delacombe informed him, in a hurry because he was hosting a dinner party that evening for Rowan Garfield, Colin Wales and Keith Amesbury-Cotton amongst other guests.

'I'll be brief,' Landon told him. 'London wants to know—'

'You mean Ashton, don't you?' Delacombe said, interrupting him.

Landon knew there was little love lost between the two men. Office gossip had it that Delacombe regarded Ashton as a loose and dangerous cannon whom he never wanted to see on his patch again.

'Actually I mean the DG.'

'Oh!' Delacombe cleared his throat. 'Please continue.'

'Well, Sir Victor wants to know if you've come across a man called Tom Kransky?'

'In what connection?' Delacombe asked, his face darkening.

Landon hadn't the faintest idea because Ashton hadn't seen fit to tell him, but it was evident the name meant something to the Head of Station. There were moments when you needed to be inventive and this was one of them.

He recalled what Francesca York had told him about Gadstar Promotions and had a flash of inspiration.

'We've heard Kransky is fronting for the Palestine Liberation Organisation.'

'What's his nationality?'

'American, possibly of Polish or Russian extraction.'

'The only Kransky who has come to our notice is a pornographic film producer. He was murdered with two of his actors just over a fortnight ago. I doubt if Yassir Arafat would touch him with a bargepole . . . I didn't regard his murder as an intelligence matter. However, if you want to know more about the case you'd better see Dick Mycroft, the embassy Security Officer. Criminology is one of his hobbies. Now, if you will excuse me . . .'

'Where do I find Mycroft?'

'I've just buzzed my PA. She will escort you to his office on the ground floor.' Delacombe snapped his fingers and held out his left hand. 'Your visitor's pass,' he said. 'I need to sign you off.'

There was no please, much less a thank you when he handed the pass to Delacombe. Inwardly seething with anger, Landon thanked the Head of Station with icy politeness when he returned the visitor's pass with his signature and date/time group on it.

Delacombe's PA was a charming, smartly dressed, mature woman in her forties. In the course of their brief acquaintance, which ended at the door to Mycroft's office, Landon came to the conclusion that she must spend much of her time smoothing the feathers of those whom Head of Station had ruffled. He was equally certain Delacombe showed a different face to the Americans and senior diplomats.

Mycroft was MI5 had been posted to the embassy in May 1993 and next to Delacombe was the longest serving member of the staff.

'I hear you want to know what happened to Tom Kransky,' Mycroft said as they shook hands.

'Yes. Who told you?'

'God upstairs,' Mycroft told him, jerking a thumb at the ceiling. 'He rang me the moment you left his office. Did he tell you I was the greatest living expert on Kransky?'

'More or less,' Landon said.

'Well, I'd never heard of the man before he made the front page of the *Baltimore Sun*. The story began when Kransky's cleaning lady discovered the body of Paula Kransky a fortnight ago today. The apartment had been ransacked but the police could find no sign of a forcible entry. They concluded that either Paula Kransky had opened the door to the killer because she knew him or else he had a key to the apartment. Since the car belonging to Kransky wasn't in the parking lot and as the man himself was missing, he became a prime suspect.

'Paula was the third Mrs Kransky and divorcing the other two had cost him an arm and a leg. The theory was, Kransky had found a new love life but was determined he wasn't going to pay through the nose to be rid of Paula. So he faked a burglary that had gone badly wrong. Forty-eight hours later the bodies of Tom Kransky and two of his actors, a man and a woman known as Dan Swordsman and Sara Gay, had been found at his studio in Hawks Point.

'They had been dead for several days when their bodies were discovered,' Mycroft continued. 'Establishing Paula Kransky's time of death proved even more difficult because the central heating in the apartment was registering over eighty degrees Farenheit and the corpse was beginning to putrefy. The pathologists decided that Paula Kransky was murdered sometime during the night of Thursday the thirteenth and the early hours of Friday the fourteenth of February. Paula Kransky had been shot twice in the head with a .38. The others had been gunned down by a man armed with a semi-automatic 7.65mm pistol.

'The Baltimore Police Department concluded the murders were connected, mainly on the grounds that it would be too much of a coincidence if husband and wife were killed within a few hours of one another for wholly different reasons. The bullets removed from Tom Kransky and the two actors were sent to the FBI for analysis where the Forensic Department reported that the spiral grooves indicated that the murder weapon was a Type 64 pistol produced by the People's Republic of China.

'That's purely an assassination weapon,' Mycroft continued. 'From this, the Bureau concluded that they had been executed by a professional hit man.'

'Has any law enforcement agency come up with a motive for the killings?'

'There have been lots of theories but none has stood up under examination.' Mycroft regarded him thoughtfully. 'Anyway, why is the SIS interested in Kransky?'

'There have been rumours – political connections – that sort of thing.' Landon said, improvising.

'The man produced dirty movies.' Mycroft pursed his lips. 'Still, I suppose one of his actors could have been a diplomat, an MP, or even some junior minister. After all, from porno king to blackmailer is not such a gigantic stride.'

The possibility that it could just have easily have been a high-ranking member of the intelligence community suddenly occurred to Landon. Like who, he asked himself and immediately rejected the answer when Jill Sheridan came to mind. And yet . . . ? And yet it would explain why Ashton had been less than forthcoming about Kransky.

'You've gone all silent on me,' Mycroft observed.

'I was thinking about Kransky.'

'I'd be surprised if you weren't.'

Mycroft was reacting like the human equivalent of a sniffer dog, trained to detect the presence of Semtex or cocaine. Landon guessed his nose told him there was a bad smell about the Kransky business and, terrier-like, he wasn't about to let go. The way to deal with a sniffer dog was to throw the animal off the scent by confusing his sense of smell.

'What did the *Baltimore Sun* have to say concerning his other interests?'

'Not a thing.'

'Well, we know he is of Polish extraction and had travelled a bit in the Mid-East – Egypt, the Arab Emirates, the Gaza Strip. He was allegedly making a propaganda film for the Palestinians, vilifying Israel and by inference the United States.'

'I don't think we gave you that information.'

'No, you didn't. It came from a source in Cairo, who is pretty low-grade, according to Head of Station. Could be he embellished what few facts there were . . .'

'When was Kransky in the Middle East?'

'Just over eight months ago,' Landon said, lying effortlessly. 'Why do you ask?'

'Because I believe you should have a word with the FBI's Deputy Chief of Counter-Intelligence. He will know if Kransky was something more than a pornographer.'

Landon frowned, 'I've not had much to do with the FBI. In fact, I don't even know who is the Deputy Chief of Counter-Intelligence.'

'His name is Eric Christensen and he is attending the symposium. I can arrange for you to meet him if you like?'

Landon didn't like the idea one bit but Mycroft would know something was up if he tried to wriggle out of seeing the American.

'I'd certainly appreciate it if you could set up a meeting,' Landon said, and tried to sound as if he meant it.

Chapter 15

To watch Jill Sheridan conduct morning prayers as the acting Director General was an eerie experience, knowing what Ashton did about the lady. Even when Victor Hazelwood was present to monitor Jill's access to Top Secret Codeword material the risks they were taking with national security appalled him. With Victor away she had complete freedom of action and consequently the risks were, in his opinion, increased by a factor of ten. It was also a fact that since late on Monday afternoon Ashton had been the recipient of certain information that could possibly be of interest to the Emiles. As the junior Assistant Director he would be the last to be called, which would give him at least ten minutes' grace to decide just how much he was prepared to disclose. Ashton was still weighing the pros and cons when suddenly it was his turn to be the focus of attention.

'Vladimir Aleksandrovich Labur,' Jill said crisply. 'What's the latest on his present whereabouts, Peter?'

Labur, the former Director of Chemical Defence Research, had now acquired the codename of 'Feliks', and there were indications that Feliks could be travelling to Beirut in the not-too-distant future. It took Ashton no time at all to decide this was one piece of information he would keep to himself.

'Labur is still in Odintsovo,' he said blandly.

'Really?' Jill raised an eyebrow in apparent disbelief. 'Is that what your contact at GCHQ is telling you?'

'Yes. Do you have a source at Cheltenham who's given you a different story?'

'Of course I don't.' The tight smile that appeared on her lips was a portent of the anger that he knew was about to spill over. 'What other negative information has crossed your desk?' she asked venomously.

Ashton ignored the jibe and proceeded to outline the data he had received from the Metropolitan Police Forensic Laboratory and the Chemical Warfare Research Establishment at Porton Down. In the opinion of the Ministry of Defence organisation the liquid VX agent in the whisky bottles stolen by Sharples and Ivers had been produced at least six months ago, most probably within the UK. Scotland Yard's Forensic Lab had identified the factory in Lancashire that had manufactured the bottles and hadn't bothered to report the theft of 144 bottles from a consignment destined for Matthew Gloag and Son Ltd, Perth, Scotland in April 1996 because the management had decided the actual loss was insignificant. They had also been mindful of the fact that in the eighteen months prior to April 1996, vandals had broken into the factory yard on four occasions, stealing or destroying goods, the market value of which had been far greater than that of the latest incident. There was a momentary silence when Ashton finished, then Hugo Calthorpe piped up to ask if any of the previous break-ins had been reported to the police.

'Yes, all four,' Ashton told him. 'However, the culprits were never apprehended even though security was tightened after every incident.'

Burglar alarms linked to the nearest police station were installed, a night watchman was employed, guard dogs were brought in to patrol the perimeter fence. A private security company was hired to visit the premises at irregular intervals during the hours of darkness until the whole area was finally under surveillance by closed-circuit TV. The burglar alarm frequently malfunctioned, so much so that the police gave notice that they would no longer respond to the alarm and the link was disconnected. The night watchman was sacked because in the small hours of the morning he was asleep more often than not.

'The guard dogs were out of control and had to be destroyed after one of them savaged a factory worker as he was clocking on. The patrolmen from the security company got into the habit of visiting the factory at the same time very night and rapidly ceased to be a deterrent.' Ashton smiled wryly. 'As for the CCTV units, their locations were known and from the word go intruders who were caught on camera always had their features masked.'

'Seems to me the opposition knew a thing or two about security,' Calthorpe said, and provoked a ripple of laughter.

'You're absolutely right, Hugo,' Ashton said quietly. 'They had been watching the factory for months, sizing up its defence before they went in and stole the bottles they needed.'

'Is that the line the police are taking?' Jill asked.

'It's the line they are pursuing.' Ashton looked round the table. 'Incidentally, that information is strictly need to know and is not for dissemination outside this room,' he said, and turned back to Jill. 'Agreed?'

'Of course.' Jill gathered her papers together. 'Unless there are any other points this meeting is over.'

Nobody had any points he wished to raise. When Ashton reached his office the phone was already ringing. It came as no surprise to him to hear from Dilys Crowther that the acting Director General would like to see him when he had a moment to spare. What did take Ashton aback was the conciliatory tone of her message.

For Jill to be sitting at Victor's desk was disturbing and just a little sad. It was common knowledge that her one great burning ambition was to become the first woman to head the

SIS but that dream was never going to materialise now. However, for the next four days until Hazelwood returned she was the Director General, free to squirrel away information for future use without let or hindrance. The only people who controlled her were Robin Urquhart and two Privy Counsellors whom Ashton knew by name but couldn't put faces to. That was enough to worry anyone stiff.

'Not to my taste,' Jill said, dragging her eyes away from the painting of a battered-looking corvette on a storm-tossed Atlantic, to greet him with a winsome smile.

He thought she wouldn't approve of the other two paintings in Hazelwood's office, like the vic of three Wellington bombers on a moonlight night approaching a smudge of land on the horizon, which was entitled *Enemy Coast Ahead*. And the signed print of Terence Cuneo's *The Bridge at Arnhem* was unlikely to strike a responsive chord with her either.

'I wouldn't worry about it,' Ashton told her. 'You won't be here long enough for the paintings to get you down. In your shoes, I'd enjoy my own art gallery while I could.'

On her promotion to Deputy DG Jill had selected an early L. S. Lowry, a Jackson Pollock and an Andy Warhol from the catalogue produced by the Property Services Agency. A lot of people believed her choice was governed by the fact that all three paintings were originals and hugely expensive.

'You're indulging in wistful thinking,' Jill told him calmly. 'Nobody is going to ease me out of my job. I'm going to be around for a long, long time.'

'That rather depends on the Emiles, doesn't it?'

'I mean to reel them in, Peter.' Jill took a cigarette from the packet of Silk Cut on the desk and lit it. 'With your help, of course,' she added.

'In what respect?'

'Who told you about the bottle factory?'

'Richard Neagle at MI5. I reminded him I was a member of

the Combined Anti-Terrorist Organisation and was there anything I should know. He then told me how the investigation of the Kimberley Road incident was progressing.'

'You said the factory admitted to the loss of a hundred and forty-four bottles. Correct?'

Ashton nodded, then anticipated the point Jill was about to make. 'Whereas two hundred and sixteen were found at forty-four Kimberley Road.'

'Exactly. What does the factory management have to say about that?'

'Nothing. The police haven't asked them.'

'Why not?'

'Because they are looking at other bottle factories to see if part of their stock has gone missing in the last six months. MI5 and Special Branch think there might be other dumps of the VX agent spread around the country. I don't have to tell you what a panic it would cause if that got out.'

'I'm glad you credit me with some imagination,' Jill said tartly.

'Sometimes I think you've got too much.' Ashton moved towards the communicating door. 'Especially when it goes hand in hand with your instinct for survival,' he added, and walked out through the PA's office.

Daniels glanced at his wristwatch, then looked in the direction of the lift at the far end of the basement garage and wondered how much longer it would be before Ashton put in an appearance. His Ford Granada was scheduled for a routine monthly inspection and the transport supervisor had needed a lot of persuading before he'd agreed to postpone it until twelve noon. That deadline was now only half an hour away and it was pointless to ask for another delay because he wouldn't get it. The inspection followed by a road test took all of six hours and the transport supervisor was not a man who enjoyed working overtime.

Daniels saw the transport supervisor leave his office and, knowing he had some kind of urinary infection, guessed the man was making for the toilets. The opportunity to phone Ashton on the internal line was too good to be missed and he walked purposefully towards the transport office. He was almost halfway there when the lift arrived and the man himself stepped out of the car.

'Where to, boss?' Daniels asked.

'What's on your work ticket?'

'Local running.'

'Then let's head out to Wimbledon Common.'

'Whatever pleases you.'

Daniels opened the door for Ashton, then walked round the front of the Granada, got in behind the wheel and started up. He didn't say another word until they were approaching Putney Heath on West Hill and were about two miles from Wimbledon Common. Neither did Ashton.

'About the conversation we had yesterday morning,' Daniels said tentatively. 'O'Meara was on the night shift – ten till six . . .'

'That was convenient.'

'Yeah, well, not too many of her colleagues were around to catch her prying into stuff she should have left well alone.'

'I didn't want O'Meara to do anything which could land her in hot water. I had hoped I'd made that clear.' Although Ashton hadn't raised his voice there was a cutting edge to it.

'You did,' Daniels said, colouring, 'and I repeated every word you'd said to O'Meara. But . . .'

'But what, Eric?'

'I guess it has escaped your notice, Mr Ashton, but a lot of people are prepared to go that extra mile for you without being asked.'

'And O'Meara is one such person?' Ashton shook his head. 'But I hardly know her.'

'It doesn't matter. She thinks you got dumped on ten months ago by the people on the top table.'

'The DG was under a lot of pressure from the politicians, Eric. The Government was desperate to maintain the cease-fire and keep the peace talks going. The Provisional IRA had lost Kevin Hayes and wanted somebody's head on a platter. There was no way the Director General could have protected my anonymity at the coroner's inquest.'

Daniels glanced sideways at Ashton and saw a faint smile appear on his lips.

'Anyway, why should I complain? It got me where I am today.'

'O'Meara reckons you're about to be dumped on again.'

'What's this, womanly intuition?' The smile on Ashton's face became more positive.

'That, and the number of questions you asked—'

'Turn left at the junction,' Ashton said, interrupting him.

'OK.' Daniels tripped the indicator, turned into Wimbledon Park Side and went on down the hill towards the High Street. 'The answer is Special Branch doesn't have an SIS officer under surveillance, as far as she can tell.'

'And just how far is that?'

'You didn't give her much to work on, no name, no address. For what it's worth, O'Meara says that Special Branch has been given three main tasks. In order of priority these are to discover the location of the makeshift chemical plant where the nerve agent was produced and apprehend everybody involved in the manufacture and distribution of the gas. Secondly, to maintain the present level of surveillance on two suspected active service units of the Provisional IRA, one located in the Kilburn – Cricklewood – Maida Vale area of London, the other in Romford. Last but not least, Special Branch is running a covert operation aimed at penetrating the White Dragon Triad, which is at the heart of the biggest drugs empire in South London.'

Daniels took his right hand off the wheel, dipped into the top pocket of his jacket and produced a folded slip of paper, which he passed to Ashton.

'O'Meara asked me to give you this with her compliments.'

Ashton unfolded the slip of paper. Each major Special Branch operation had been allocated a codeword apparently taken from a list of Disney characters. Donald Duck referred to the ongoing investigation of the Kimberley Road incident, Mickey Mouse 1 and Mickey Mouse 2 had been allocated to the Provisional IRA active service units and Goofy covered operations against the White Dragon Triad. There was a fourth codeword, which was apparently going begging.

'What is Minerva, Eric?'

'O'Meara told me she was some sort of Roman goddess but that's the limit of her knowledge.'

'It doesn't appear to refer to any specific operation' Ashton observed. 'There's no indication of the manpower involved other than the name of the police officer in charge.'

'That puzzled O'Meara too. Minerva is the only unattached codeword in the case index. She included the codeword in case it meant anything to you.'

'I regret to say it doesn't.' Ashton folded the slip of paper in two. 'O'Meara took one hell of a risk on my behalf and I don't want to be the one who landed her in deep shit. I don't intend to disclose any of the information she has given me. But this slip of paper is dangerous and for your own peace of mind, I think you personally should destroy it.'

Daniels opened the ashtray in the console and pushed the cigarette lighter home before taking the slip of folded paper from Ashton.

'I wouldn't burn it in the ashtray if I were you,' Ashton told him. 'You've got a vehicle inspection this afternoon and you can't be sure what the transport supervisor will look at. If he should take a peep inside that tray he will know it's not full of cigarette ash. Best thing you can do is tear the note up and flush the pieces down the toilet.'

'Why all this nonsense about my peace of mind?' Daniels asked. 'Are you telling me I can't trust you to do the right thing?'

'I'm not saying that . . .'

'Well then, you deal with this,' Daniels said, and passed the note back to Ashton.

'All right, I'll put it through the shredder soon as I'm back in the office.'

'Is that where we're going now?'

'No, you're going to drop me near Wimbledon station before making your way back to Vauxhall Cross. Should anybody ask where you have been, tell them I went to see a former intelligence officer who's living in Richmond.'

'Do we have a pensioner living in Richmond?'

'I haven't the faintest idea,' Ashton admitted cheerfully. 'But trying to discover who he might be will keep some nosy parker busy for hours.'

Daniels turned left into Alexandra Road at the bottom of Wimbledon Hill and then pulled into the kerb twenty yards or so beyond the T-junction to let Ashton off. By the time a gap in the traffic enabled him to move off, Ashton was no longer in sight.

Ashton could not remember a time when he had been so torn with indecision and self-doubt. He had asked a lot of O'Meara and she had come through for him but the information she had obtained was confusing. The armed forces had a golden rule when allocating a codeword to an operation in that it should never reveal the objective of the mission. Maybe he was wrong but it seemed to him that Special Branch believed in doing exactly the opposite. Mickey Mouse was the soldiers' contemptuous nickname for an active service unit of the IRA operating abroad or in mainland Britain. The White Dragon Triad had cornered the market in drugs and Goofy was not an inappropriate description for a crack addict who was on another planet.

But it was the reference to Minerva whom the Romans identified with Athene, the Greek goddess embodying wisdom and power, that bothered him the most. With friends in high places Jill Sheridan could be said to have power, and while her wisdom was often sadly lacking, she was certainly a fighter, especially when it was a question of survival. Where the other three codewords were concerned, O'Meara had been able to name the Special Branch officer in charge of the operation and provide details of the manpower resources committed to the task. Minerva, on the other hand, was just a waif. That could mean one of two things: either the codeword covered an inquiry into the conduct of the named officer or else the operation was so sensitive that all other details had been excluded from the case index. And what could be more sensitive than the surveillance of the Deputy Director General SIS?'

Ashton walked through the concourse and, ignoring the District Line service, went down onto the main line platform to catch a stopping train to Vauxhall. Distancing himself from the other passengers, he took out his mobile and called Max Brabazon at Military Operations (Special Projects).

'It's me,' he told the retired naval commander, 'and I'm on an open line, so it has to be veiled speech and no first names. OK?'

'That strikes a familiar chord. What can I do for you?'

'This refers to the conversation we had over lunch yesterday concerning our friends in Herefordshire.'

He had told Brabazon the first SAS team of four was to be at an hour's notice to move from noon today when he had expected to be in a position to decide whether or not to proceed with the operation. It was now five minutes to one and he wanted the patrol leader to be in London by 6 p.m. if possible.

'I know it's short notice, Max; the good news is the operation will terminate this coming Saturday, if not sooner.'

'I see,' Brabazon said in a noncommittal voice.

'I'll need somewhere to brief the SIS team leader.'

'As it happens I'm throwing a drinks party for some of the neighbours at six thirty,' Brabazon told him. 'You're invited.'

Ashton thanked him and terminated the link. Before the stopping train to Vauxhall arrived, he made two other phone calls, one to Harriet to warn her he would be staying in town for the night, the other to a barrister with whom he had served in 23 Special Air Service Regiment, Territorial Army.

Landon had slept fitfully, his body clock completely at odds with Eastern Standard Time. Back home, Landon usually went to bed about half-past eleven and he had deliberately stayed up until, in Washington, it was close on midnight. In theory he should have fallen asleep the moment his head touched the pillow but in fact he had been overtired and had spent most of the night awake. He had finally drifted off shortly before dawn and had been sound asleep when the wake-up call roused him at a quarter to six. He had considered giving breakfast a miss to catch an extra half-hour in bed but had rejected the idea, knowing it would be fatal.

Even so, he had cut it fine. The symposium started at a quarter to eight and the UK delegation was scheduled to be collected from L'Enfant Plaza Hotel on the dot of seven. By the time Landon had shaved, taken a shower and dressed, breakfast was reduced to orange juice, a cup of coffee and a croissant. The last person to join the UK delegation in the lobby, he noticed that they had instinctively divided into two distinct groups, those who had dined with Delacombe last night and those who hadn't, like Symes from the West European Department, Geraint, the supercilious Grade II officer from

MI5, Francesca York and himself. He barely had time to say good morning to the social outcasts before a twelve-seater bus drew up outside the hotel. The last to board the vehicle, Landon found that Francesca had saved a seat for him at the back.

'How are you feeling?' she asked softly.

'Hung over. I couldn't get to sleep until the early hours.'

'That's my fault.' Francesca told him and pressed her leg against his as if to remind him of the intimate pleasures they'd shared.

They had dined together and afterwards she had invited him into her bedroom for a good night drink from the minibar. One thing had led to another and it hadn't been easy to resist Francesca's unspoken invitation to spend the rest of the night with her.

'Not entirely,' Landon said, and tried unsuccessfully to stifle a yawn.

Landon had always found it difficult to stay awake on a bus and long before they reached the George Washington Memorial Parkway his head was lolling until it came to rest on a soft shoulder. It was a very comfortable feeling; then a hand patted his right arm and he woke up with a start.

The man standing above him was an inch or so under six feet. He had a broad face that tapered to a strong jaw, and a mouth that seemed to be hovering on a smile. He had brown eyes set wide apart and short reddish hair parted on the left side.

'Hi,' he said, 'I'm Eric Christensen. You must be Will Landon.'

'Yes. How did you know?'

'You're the only guy who isn't wearing a name tag.' Christensen told him, the smile becoming wider. 'Dick Mycroft tells me you're interested in Tom Kransky?'

Landon nodded. 'We've heard he was making a propaganda film for the Palestinians.'

'Did you get that from Miles Delacombe?'

'No, it was reported by our Head of Station, Cairo. He didn't attach much credence to the story because the information came from a low-grade source who has a poor track record.'

'Yeah, well, it could be his track record is improving because we had pretty much the same information from a friendly source in the Jordanian Embassy. Seems to me the three of us should get round a table and compare notes.'

'It's a thought,' Landon said cautiously.

'We'll have to see what can be arranged.' Christensen patted him on the shoulder. 'I'll get back to you over lunch,' he said, and moved away.

Everything Landon had told the Embassy Security Officer had been a cock-and-bull story but now Christensen was saying it was the naked truth.

'What was that all about?' Francesca asked quietly.

'I wish I knew,' he told her.

Chapter 16

Eleven years ago there had been just four barristers who were junior to Keith, and Harcourt Stanley, QC had been Head of Chambers. Now his name no longer appeared in gilt letters outside number 1 Pump Court and Keith had become one of the more senior members of the chambers. Ashton had met him when they had been patrol commanders in the same squadron of 23 SAS before the Falklands War. He had been 'Grubber' Keith's best man at his wedding in 1986, a duty he had performed at short notice when the bridegroom's first choice had fallen by the wayside at the last minute.

'Grubber' was a nickname Keith had acquired at Haileybury when in the First XI. A middle-order batsman, he had been noted for the dogged defence of his wicket and the ability to snatch a quick single. Although Keith's average for the season never fell below 42.6, cricket enthusiasts who like to see a batsman open his shoulders when hitting the ball, referred to his technique disparagingly as grubbing for runs. From grubbing to 'Grubber' was a natural progression and the nickname had stuck.

Ashton walked into the terraced house that was number 1 Pump Court, presented himself to the managing clerk and was escorted to Keith's office on the second floor. They hadn't seen one another for six years and he was taken aback by Keith's appearance. He remembered 'Grubber' as a slim, tremendously fit, young-looking man but middle-age spread had now caught up with him and his blond hair had retreated from his forehead until it was little more than a monk's fringe around the crown.

'It's good to see you again, Grubber.'

'And you,' Keith said, and shook hands with him in a perfunctory manner, then waved him to a chair.

'How's Fiona?' Ashton enquired.

'I wouldn't know. We split up in 'ninety-three and she took herself off to South Africa with a wine merchant in tow. Damned woman was awarded custody of the children by a senile judge who refused to believe she had a vile temper, drank like a fish, had the morals of an alley cat and was totally unfit to be a parent.'

What Ashton was hearing was not the impression he'd formed of Fiona, but then the first time he had met her had been at the wedding rehearsal the day before the event. First impressions were never a reliable guide to a person's character; all the same, Fiona had seemed a particularly nice girl.

'Do you get to see your children?' Ashton asked.

'Oh yes. I have access, the whole of the eight-week summer holiday, which they spend here in England, plus another fortnight at Easter when I have to go out to South Africa.'

'That's tough.'

'One gets used to it. How about you, Peter? Still the confirmed bachelor?'

'No, I'm married.'

'Really? I don't remember being invited to the wedding.'

'It was a very quiet affair. We got married in a registry office and the best man was Harriet's brother, who happened to be on leave at the time.'

'Why all the secrecy, Peter?'

'Harriet was in the same line of business as me. One time in Berlin, her skull was fractured by a stone when she got caught up in a race riot involving Turkish guest workers. The incident destroyed much of her self-confidence and she couldn't face all the palaver of a big wedding.'

'But she's OK now?'

'Yeah, she's fine,' Ashton said.

'So you're the one who's in trouble?'

'I guess I am.'

'Quite like old times,' Keith observed sardonically.

Ashton knew what he meant. Six years ago he had flown into Moscow on what amounted to a rescue mission which had not been sanctioned by his superiors. The whole business had come unstuck when he had missed his connection to Heathrow at Helsinki. A Board of Inquiry had been convened and he had been required to account for his movements when he'd been out of the country. Grubber Keith had provided Ashton with an alibi, supporting his claim that, needing some time to himself, he had borrowed the lawyer's cottage near Meopham in Kent.

'Am I right?' Keith asked, bringing him back to earth with a bump.

'Yes. I could be in serious trouble.' Ashton reached inside his jacket, took out a plain white envelope measuring approximately 8½ inches by 4¼ and, leaning forward in his chair, placed it on the desk. 'I'd like you to keep this,' he said.

Keith picked up the envelope and weighed it in his hand. 'What am I holding, Peter – a letter bomb?'

'You could say that. In fact it's a statement concerning a high-risk counter-intelligence operation which stands a good chance of going horribly wrong.'

'And if it does, what do I do about this envelope?'

'Nothing. You open it only if I am arrested and charged with an offence under the Official Secrets Acts.'

'And then what do I do with your statement?'

'That's up to you but I'm hoping you're still a bit of a crusader, fond of championing the underdog.'

'I must be mad.' Still clutching the envelope, Keith went over to the bricked-in Chubb safe in the corner of his office, unlocked one of the metal drawers beneath the shelf and dropped the statement inside. 'Feel better now?' he asked.

'Thanks, Grubber.'

'Think nothing of it. But don't let six years go by before you look me up again.'

There was a wry smile on his face that made Ashton feel small.

Landon reached inside his jacket, found the fleshy part of the upper arm and pinched the skin viciously between index finger and thumb in a desperate attempt to stay awake. Jet lag had really got to him and the CIA's Director of Humint was no help in combating an overwhelming desire to close his eyes and go to sleep. The American spoke in a low monotone, never once modulating his voice, which was a positive inducement to throw in the towel. It was also a fact that Landon had heard it all before and had had some practical experience of Humint. So he stopped pinching himself and presently his eyes began to droop.

Satellite photographs, signals intercepts and the ability to read e-mails weren't much help when waging a war against terrorism. A terrorist cell rarely numbered more than four or five and they communicated mainly by word of mouth. Human intelligence was the only effective way of penetrating their security. The aim was to recruit a snitch and keep him happy with folding money, which would get fatter and fatter as he wormed his way into the organisation. You started with somebody on the periphery because it was only once in a blue moon that you managed to get your hooks into anybody close to the inner council. And that was when your problems began and you were faced with stark choices. If your snitch was to establish himself, you couldn't always act on his information.

Sometimes it was for his own protection, sometimes for his advancement and occasionally, very occasionally, some innocent party was killed as a result of your decision.

A sharp elbow in the ribs made Landon rear back in his chair. 'For God's sake,' Garfield hissed, 'you're snoring like a grampus.'

'Sorry.'

'Being sorry isn't good enough. Don't nod off again. You're letting the side down.'

Up on the rostrum the Director of Humint rested both arms on the lectern and leaned forward in a confidential manner to ask if there were any questions. There was a longish silence. Then, as if to atone for Landon's heavy breathing, Colin Wales raised his hand and was rewarded with a grateful smile. It wasn't so much a question as a congratulatory speech on behalf of the entire UK delegation whom Wales claimed had benefited from the lecturer's dissertation. Buried somewhere in the dross was a question and Director Humint was happy to give a ten-minute burst on what he thought Wales had asked. He waited expectantly for another question but this time nobody obliged him and the morning session was over.

Lunch was taken in the staff cafeteria. Landon chose a bowl of clam chowder and a slice of apple pie *à la mode*, then found himself a vacant table.

'Slimming, are we?' Francesca said, joining Landon.

'Not really, I'm just leaving room for another desert.'

'Greedy pig,' Francesca said, joshing him, then caught sight of Christensen moving purposefully towards their table. 'Don't look now,' she murmured, the smile fading from her mouth, 'but I think your American friend is about to join us.'

'Are you guys expecting anyone?' Christensen enquired, indicating the two vacant chairs. 'Because if you are I can catch you later.'

'No, we're on our own. Please sit down, we'll be glad of your company.'

'Well, that's real nice of you, Will, but this won't take more than a minute. Are you still interested in learning about Kransky?'

'Of course I am. Is there a problem?'

'Only a minor one. My Jordanian friend can't get away tonight so it'll have to be tomorrow evening. Is that OK with you?'

'Yes, absolutely. Where and when do we meet?'

'That's his choice and we have to go along with it.' Christensen pushed his chair back and stood up. 'I'll let you know soon as I hear from him.'

'I assume I'm also invited?' Francesca gave the American a warm smile. 'At least that was what you gave me to understand on the bus this morning when you suggested the three of us should get together round a table.'

'I was referring to my Jordanian source,' Christensen informed her.

'That's a pity.' Although the smile was still there it was beginning to look a little icy. 'Will and I belong to the same organisation.'

'Yeah?' Christensen looked from one to the other. 'I thought you were SIS, Will?'

'I am,' Landon told him. 'Fran is referring to CATO, the Combined Anti-Terrorist Organisation.'

'I guess that makes a difference. Naturally, I'll have to clear it with my source. You know how it is: a woman is a second-class citizen in the Muslim world.'

'Only in certain parts surely?'

'Maybe.'

'What's the name of this source of yours?'

'Aw now, Will, you know better than to ask me that,' Christensen said, and waved a hand as he walked away.

'He's being a little sensitive about his Jordanian friend, isn't he?' Francesca muttered.

'I think there is more to it than that,' Landon told her.

Max Brabazon rented an apartment in Dolphin Square, which was almost directly opposite Vauxhall Cross on the other side of the river. Leaving Pump Court, Ashton walked to the Underground station in Chancery Lane and caught a Central Line train to Oxford Circus where he switched to the Victoria Line. He then alighted at Pimlico and made his way to Dolphin Square.

A confirmed bachelor, Brabazon had been wedded to the Royal Navy ever since he had been a cadet at Dartmouth. The evidence was there for all to see in the photographs of the ships he had served on like HMS *Gloucester*, the Type 42 destroyer, the frigate HMS *Broadsword*, and his first command, the 'Ton' Class minehunter HMS *Maxim*. Pride of place, however, went to his last command, the modified Type 12 Rothsay Class frigate, HMS *Plymouth*. There was a profusion of more personal photographs displayed in silver frames in the sitting room. They were perched on top of the bookcase, the mantelpiece and nest of tables, these friends Brabazon had made from midshipman to commander, in and out of uniform. Nowhere was there a photograph of a woman.

'There are a lot more in my bedroom,' Brabazon said with an infectious smile. 'In fact, it's a bit like sleeping in the Imperial War Museum.'

'I'll take your word for it,' Ashton told him, then asked if the friend from Hereford had arrived yet.

'Yes. He's checked into the Winchester Hotel, Bayswater under the name of Messenger. He has all the necessary.'

Messenger was the standard cover name used by SIS personnel when it was essential to protect their real identity. In this instance 'the necessary' was a credit card that enabled the holder to settle all expenses at source. Everything the agent signed for was automatically debited to a secret bank account administered by Roy Kelso.

'I told Messenger to come back at seven fifteen because there are things you and I need to discuss before we brief him.'

'Damn right there are,' Ashton said.

'So what would you like to drink?' Brabazon asked, crouching in front of a mahogany cabinet. 'I can offer you brandy, gin, whisky, vodka.'

'Whisky, please, with a dash of soda.'

Brabazon poured a generous double of Chivas Regal into a cut-glass tumbler, added a splash of soda water from a siphon, then fixed himself a brandy ginger with a slice of lemon.

'Cheers,' Ashton said, and raised his glass. 'Here's mud in your eye. Let's hope it doesn't stick.'

'It will if we're not careful,' Brabazon said gloomily. 'I've already had the commanding officer at 22 SAS on to me wanting to know what Operation Merlin is about. I told him his name wasn't on the briefing list, which didn't go down at all well. Ten minutes later, the Brigadier commanding Special Forces was on the phone threatening to take the matter up with the Chief of Defence Staff unless I tell him what we're up to.'

'And what did you say to that?'

'I said you would visit his headquarters in the Duke of York barracks tomorrow morning and give him a full briefing.' Brabazon frowned. 'Incidentally why did you choose Merlin as the codeword for this operation?'

'Because I knew it hadn't been listed for future use.'

'That will only make the Brigadier, Special Forces, even more determined to discover what Merlin is.'

'That won't be a problem,' Ashton said calmly. 'I will simply tell him the truth.'

'Which is?'

'That we are putting Jill Sheridan, the Deputy DG, under

surveillance for her own protection and without her knowledge.'

The most believable lies always contained a substantial element of truth. In what had been a very messy divorce, Rosalind Urquhart had done her level best to crucify Jill. That Rosalind's tactics had ultimately rebounded on her was another strand of truth which Ashton could use to good effect. So too was the fact that a fortnight ago Jill had been mugged on her way home from work.

'I'll tell both Messenger and the Brigadier that we have reason to believe Ms Sheridan is being stalked. I propose to tell him we are not so sure now that it was a random case of mugging when she was attacked a fortnight ago. Special Branch had been told by one of their snitches that the two men who pounced on Jill Sheridan had been paid to work her over. Rosalind Urquhart might conceivably have hired them, which is the possibility the police are investigating, but we can't afford to take any chances, especially in view of the large quantity of nerve agent found at forty-four Kimberley Road. If we can believe a news agency report from Jordan, Saddam Hussein is planning a revenge attack on this country for helping to impose the no-fly zone in southern Iraq. Head of Station, Amman, thinks there could be something to it. We've no idea whether the attack will be a spectacular, such as the destruction of both Houses of Parliament, or something less ambitious like the assassination of a senior intelligence officer.'

'You mean Jill Sheridan,' Brabazon said.

'The Iraqis might regard her as a prime target; she is one of our foremost experts on the Middle East terrorist groups.'

'How much of this is true, Peter?'

'Between thirty and thirty-five per cent.'

Ashton thought he was probably being generous. There had been a news agency report that an Iraqi-backed terrorist group had entered the UK secretly but this had been regarded as just another rumour. Head of Station, Amman had lost count of the number of identical reports he and his predecessor had received since the Gulf War in 'ninety-one. They were invariably conveyed by Jordanian and Palestinian truck drivers, some of whom were employed by UNO to transport medical supplies and essential foodstuffs to Baghdad. The only good intelligence coming out of Iraq was attributable to the United Nations inspection teams investigating Saddam Hussein's capability to produce chemical and biological weapons. The rest was just bazaar and coffee-house gossip.

'What else do you propose telling Messenger?' Brabazon asked.

'Exactly what is required of his team.'

'That might be difficult.'

Brabazon was right in more ways than one. There was nothing wrong with the basic scenario, which Ashton was confident he could sell to Messenger, the commanding officer of 22 SAS and the Brigadier, Special Forces. The tricky part would come when Messenger learned he was required to forget everything he'd been taught about close protection.

The task of the SAS team was to ascertain whether anybody was shadowing Jill Sheridan on her way to and from the office. When following her they were to stay at least three cars in rear of her Porsche and on no account was she to become aware of their presence. If Ms Sheridan was being stalked they were not to intervene unless the situation became life-threatening. The requirement bore no relationship to the drills the SAS had perfected and Ashton was only too aware that if the briefing went badly Messenger would be on the phone to his commanding officer in no time.

A bell rang faintly. 'That will be him,' Brabazon said, and went out into the hall to answer the door.

The postcard was the only item in the letter box. Glancing over her shoulder as she closed the front door, Jill saw that the rest of the mail delivered to her house had been neatly placed on a silver salver on the hall table by her cleaner. There was a Lebanese stamp on the postcard but it hadn't been franked and the picture on the reverse side showed the bust of Karl Marx in Highgate cemetery. Although not addressed to her the message printed in capitals left Jill in no doubt for whom it was intended. It read: LAST RESTING PLACE OF WILLIAM MORRIS IS SARCOPHAGUS WITH STATUE OF MADONNA DIRECTLY OPPOSITE AND TWENTY PACES BEYOND FOOTPATH. PART OF STONE PLINTH AT LEFT REAR BROKEN OFF. STRONGLY ADVISE YOU SEE FOR YOURSELF. Even without the Lebanese stamp she would have known the postcard was from one of the Emiles and, if not actually written by him, it had certainly been drafted by the one with the best command of English. She didn't need to be told the plinth was a mail drop that she was required to empty a.s.a.p.

For over a week now Jill Sheridan had been aware that Hazelwood and possibly others believed the Emiles didn't exist and had been invented to back up her story. Now she had something tangible to show them and felt all the better for it. The only worrying thing was the realisation that whoever had delivered the postcard must have known what time her cleaner finished work for the day. She wondered if there were any corners of her life that were still private.

Jill walked through the house putting all the lights on, then went upstairs to look out the tracksuit and trainers she kept in the boxroom. First thing tomorrow she would take up jogging again.

It seemed to Ashton that Brabazon was taking a hell of a long time to say good night to the SAS officer. He could hear the mumble of their voices out in the hall but even though the door to the sitting room was ajar he had no idea what they were saying. He hoped the officer they knew only as Messenger was not having some last-minute reservations. He thought he'd handled the briefing pretty well and had answered all the questions Messenger had raised without hesitation. So why the debate on the doormat? Then Messenger suddenly called out, 'Good night, Mr Ashton,' and the front door closed behind him.

'So what was that all about?' Ashton asked when Brabazon returned.

'What do you mean?'

'Your long conversation with Messenger.'

'Oh! Well, he wanted to know what practical experience you'd had in the field. I think he had certain misgivings concerning the way you wanted him to operate. Anyway, I told him you had spent six months with the army's Special Patrol Unit in Belfast and had taken part in the SAS raid on Pebble Island when eleven Pucarà ground attack aircraft were destroyed during the Falklands War. He went away mightily impressed.'

'What about his reservations, Max?'

'He withdrew them.'

'On the strength of my army record?' Ashton snorted. 'I don't believe it.'

'Messenger had you down for a ditherer when you postponed the operation for twelve hours to give him more time.'

Ashton had hoped the first SAS team would be operational by 06.00 hours tomorrow but in delaying his decision to call them in they had not had time to look at Jill's house in Bisham Gardens in daylight. The postponement would also allow the team to familiarise themselves with the route she would take to and from Vauxhall Cross.

'You restored his confidence,' Brabazon continued. 'I can practically guarantee you won't have Messenger's officer on your back. I don't know about the Brigadier, Special Forces.'

'I can handle him,' Ashton said confidently.

'Good.' Brabazon looked at his empty glass. 'I could do with another drink,' he said. 'How about you?'

'Thanks, but I need to be moving on. I've got to find a hotel for the night.'

'Where have you left your bag?'

'I didn't pack one.'

'I have a spare room, you'd better stay with me.'

'It's very kind of you but—'

'No buts,' Brabazon told him firmly. 'Something tells me you were very reluctant to call on the SAS and there are matters we should discuss if we're not to end up with a lot of egg on our faces.'

The Blue Marlin was half a mile up the road from the Sunrise Hotel on State Highway 650. Located just inside the Capital Beltway, it was a popular bar and grill with truck drivers heading north and south, and drew some trade from travellers staying overnight at the motel. It was not, however, the favourite night spot for most people living in nearby Carole Highlands. With its big parking lot, isolated position and transient clientele, the Blue Marlin had almost everything Samir Abbas was looking for.

Trying to look as if he enjoyed it, Abbas swallowed the rest of his beer, then left the bar and went into the men's room. Four urinals, four cubicles, two wash basins, no windows, no back door: he would have to effect an entrance through the kitchen. He zipped up his pants, washed his hands and dried them with a paper towel. As he walked out of the Blue Marlin he noted there were eighteen booths with a seating capacity of seventy-two, twelve stools at the bar, two waitresses, two bartenders and maybe two short-order cooks in the kitchen. The time was ten after nine and the place was two-thirds full.

Abbas made his way round the low wooden building and was approaching the kitchen when one of the short-order cooks opened the back door and dumped a load of garbage in one of the trash cans outside. As soon as the man went back inside, Abbas moved forward to take a closer look at the door and almost punched the air when he saw it wasn't self-locking. It would be risky, but a quick in-and-out job was feasible. He would, of course, have to create a major diversion but that wouldn't be a problem.

Chapter 17

It was still dark when Jill Sheridan left the house. It was also spitting with rain. Turning right outside the front gate, she jogged uphill, passing a milk float on her way to the junction of Bisham Gardens with Highgate High Street where she turned right again. Thereafter it was all downhill and she lengthened her stride and ignored the occasional twinge of pain in the left rib cage, which was still showing signs of bruising. Gritting her teeth, Jill swept past the spot where she had been mugged exactly a fortnight ago without realising it until she veered into Dartmouth Park Hill and Whittington Hospital came into sight. Towards the bottom of the hill she turned right a third time and some two hundred yards further on entered Highgate cemetery.

The footpath Jill was following lay in the old part of the cemetery, which was now full and showing signs of neglect. Grass had rooted in the asphalt path, which was potholed, the trees needed lopping and the shrubs had been allowed to get out of hand with the result that some of them were laced with brambles. The verges hadn't received a final cut before the onset of winter and were disfigured with clumps of couch grass. Presently she came to a track running east to west and halted; glancing to her right, she saw a black marble plinth on which rested the head and shoulders of Karl Marx, cast in bronze. The memorial was two hundred yards south of Whittington Hospital and from where Jill was standing it was easy to pick out the last resting place of William Morris. The statue of the

Madonna on the sarcophagus towered above all the other gravestones in the immediate area.

Jill looked around her to make sure she was alone, then, heart in her mouth, she ran diagonally across the track to reach the stone coffin. William Morris, born in Walthamstow on 24 March 1834 had died on 3 October 1896: in the last hundred and one years lichen had gradually eaten into the stone and enveloped the coffin and plinth with a green fungus.

The directions Jill had been given enabled her to find the broken piece of the plinth without too much difficulty. It was right at the edge, shaped like a slice of cake and was roughly two inches thick. It lifted out cleanly to reveal a recess no fatter than a wallet, which had obviously been gouged out with a chisel. Great pains had been taken to dispose of the chippings and disguise the scratch marks on the stone. Inside the hollow, and neatly folded in two, was a small sheet of grey-coloured paper, which blended in with the background. After fishing it out, Jill replaced the slice, pushing it home so that to the casual eye the jagged cracks appeared no more than surface-deep.

She started running again, the slip of paper clenched tight in her left hand. Rejoining the original track, she headed north towards Waterlow Park, picked up Swain's Lane and stayed on it until the junction with Bisham Gardens. On the way up the hill to her house Jill encountered the postman going down the road. He was the only pedestrian she had seen that morning but a car did pass her on the way down the hill as she opened the front gate.

Jill had no idea how far she had covered but it couldn't have been more than two miles because she was back inside the house sixteen minutes after leaving it and that included the time spent at the sarcophagus. The run had proved one thing: she was not as fit as she had thought. In the remarkably short time since being seduced by British American Tobacco plc, smoking had taken its toll on her. Not so very long ago she had stayed late at the office twice a week to play badminton and had also regularly worked out in the basement gym at Vauxhall Cross. But all that fitness training had gone by the board when Rosalind Urquhart had launched her hate campaign and now she was paying for it. Out of breath and nursing a stitch in her side, Jill went into the kitchen and examined the scrap of grey paper she had been nursing in her clenched hand. The information the Emiles wanted from her offered no indication of their future intentions. However, after reading their questions a second time she couldn't see that the security of the UK would be prejudiced if she answered them. Fortunately, what she could or could not disclose was up to Robin Urquhart and the two Privy Counsellors.

For once Jill changed her daily routine and did everything in the reverse order, eating the usual light breakfast of orange juice, coffee and a thin slice of brown toast before taking a shower and dressing for the office. Dumping her soiled clothing into the linen basket, she left a note asking her daily woman to put her tracksuit and sweatshirt through the washing machine. Thereafter she adhered to her normal timetable and arrived at Vauxhall Cross with over half an hour to spare before morning prayers.

Although Max Brabazon had provided him with an old electric shaver that he no longer used, Ashton knew there was nothing to beat a wet shave for freshening you up first thing in the morning. Having to wear yesterday's clothes and endure the look of disapproval from the redoubtable Enid Sly when he walked into Vauxhall Cross made Ashton feel even more of a tramp. He wondered if he would get the same look from the Brigadier, Special Forces and didn't much care if he did. He went up to his office, called the MT Section on the internal phone and asked the transport supervisor to have a car on standby to take him to the Duke of York barracks from

09.00 hours. He was about to open the combination safe when Jill Sheridan walked into the room.

'You want to tell me what all this is about?' she demanded, and slapped a Top Secret intelligence report on his desk.

The signal had been received and decrypted by the communications branch during silent hours. The originator was Head of Station, Washington and the subject matter concerned Thomas Kransky. The cringing tone of the text told Ashton that Delacombe was aware the request for information had come directly from the DG.

'I think you should ask Victor when he returns,' Ashton said quietly.

'Oh, do you? In his signal Delacombe said it was Landon who asked the question and he's one of yours, isn't he?'

'Of course he is and—'

'What are you trying to do?' Jill said angrily, 'sabotage the whole damned operation before it gets off the ground?'

Ashton walked past her and closed the door. 'Try shouting a bit louder. Some people may not have heard you.'

'I'm surprised you haven't told the whole fucking building by now.'

'Listen to me,' Ashton said, and clapped a hand over her mouth. 'On Victor's instructions I told Will to find out what he could about Tom Kransky. Then after I had briefed him Victor had another thought and decided that before approaching the CIA or FBI he should see what Miles Delacombe could tell him about the man. OK?'

Jill nodded, waited for Ashton to remove his hand, then said, 'So Will knows I'm involved?'

'He knows nothing of the kind. Your name was never mentioned.'

'I'd like to believe it but the thing is, you're the one who told me to submit my resignation.'

'On Victor's instructions.'

'You would say that, Peter, especially when he's not here to deny it.'

'This is ridiculous. Read the signal again; if anybody has given you cause for alarm it's Delacombe. He's told the world and his wife that Kransky made porno movies. Around the time you returned from Florida a hired gun killed him, his two principal actors and Mrs Kransky. According to the Baltimore Police Department his safe had been cleared out and no trace of his film productions was found at the studio. Some people might conclude a business rival decided to move in on Kransky and take over his operation. If that view became widespread, it wouldn't do your story a lot of good.'

'Are you trying to threaten me?'

'Hell no, I'm trying to point out the danger Delacombe has put you in. Fortunately he doesn't appear to have briefed the ambassador, but that could change any time.'

Delacombe was particularly adept at covering his back and it would be out of character for him not to inform the ambassador. What action the ambassador then took was a matter of conjecture, but Ashton thought it likely he would at least write a demi-official letter to the Head of Diplomatic Service, if only to seek enlightenment. But an even bigger threat to Jill was the possibility that Delacombe's signal had been captured and decoded by the National Security Agency at Fort Meade. He was wondering if he should draw Jill's attention to this possibility when it suddenly became evident the same thought had occurred to her.

'The Americans could have intercepted the signal,' Jill said breathlessly, and on the edge of panic. 'What am I going to do, Peter?'

'You could anticipate the event and tell Robin, then persuade him not to cancel the operation. Or you could sit back and hope for the best. Just because Fort Meade is on the doorstep, it doesn't necessarily follow their Signals Intercept Service has been eavesdropping on the British Embassy.'

'You mean I could get lucky?'

Luck was such a random factor that nobody in their right mind would count on it. Looking back on his time with the army's Special Patrol Unit in Belfast, with D Squadron of 22 SAS in the Falklands and the fifteen years he had spent in the Secret Intelligence Service since those days, Ashton could recall a dozen occasions when luck, good or bad, had decided the issue.

'Yes, that's what I do mean,' he said presently. 'Essentially you are a lucky person. Somehow you always manage to land on both feet.'

'Really? Well, this is one time I'm not going to leave anything to chance. I think I'll take your advice and talk to Robin.' Jill glanced at her wristwatch. 'Almost time for morning prayers,' she murmured, and then left him without another word.

Only a few minutes ago, Jill had been thoroughly despondent, now she was back on an even keel and had even sounded confident. Ashton had always known she was resilient but this latest manifestation fairly took his breath away.

The bomb-making factory was the cellar of an isolated clap-board house, up a mile-long track off US Highway 29, that had been burned to the ground in 1988. The property, enclosed by a belt of trees, had been built on a two-acre plot by a none-too-successful writer who, in a drunken stupor, had kicked over a space heater and died in the resultant fire. The only living relative had been an elderly sister in California, who'd been killed in a traffic accident while the property was still on the market. Efforts to trace any other relatives had ended in failure and nobody had been interested in acquiring the land at a knock-down price, not even the literary agent who'd represented the erstwhile writer. Eventually the realtor stopped advertising the plot and everybody forgot about its existence, with the exception of two fringe members of the Palestine Liberation Front. They had seen its potential and surreptitiously had begun to take possession of the property in 1995.

Samir Abbas had been there twice but last night was the first time he had used the place for real. After reconnoitring the Blue Marlin, he had returned to the low-cost housing development on New York Avenue and collected a sleeping-bag before driving out to the bomb factory.

On arrival Abbas had parked his recently acquired Ford Probe in a clearing among the trees and walked across the yard to where the house had once stood. All that remained of it now were the foundations and a fire-blackened brick chimney. A metal staircase eaten up with rust led to a small cellar, which was open to the elements. The munitions and equipment Abbas needed were stored at the far end of the cellar in a cache excavated under the cement floor. The entrance was concealed under a pile of junk, which included an old freezer chest. Hidden inside the cache were twenty pounds of Semtex explosive, sixty-five feet of safety fuse, the same amount of instantaneous, a box of fulminate of mercury detonators, eight electric detonators, a carton of slow-burning fuse 'E' matches and various timers. The cache also contained sections of steel piping cut to various lengths and serrated to assist fragmentation, plus a large number of metal barbs with razor-sharp cutting edges made from scrap. Finally there was a handbook that explained how to make a super bomb in excess of a thousand pounds from garden fertilisers.

Abbas, however, had no need of a blockbuster. Instead he'd chosen a length of steel piping three inches in diameter and threaded at both ends. As though rolling pastry he had then flattened a lump of Semtex and embedded dozens of barbs before lining the pipe with the explosive. After one end had been sealed with a screw cap, Abbas had filled the casing with roughly four pounds of plastic explosive. When the time came to arm the bomb, he would insert a thirty-minute time-delay pencil into the Semtex, withdraw the split pin and squeeze the tube with sufficient force to break the glass phial of acid inside. Only when this had been done would he use the second screw cap to plug the other end. When released, the acid would take thirty minutes to burn through a thick cardboard plug and ignite the detonator.

Although Abbas had assembled the bomb sooner than anticipated, he nevertheless unfolded the sleeping-bag and spent the night in the cellar. It was one thing to drive up the track without lights, quite another to do the same thing when rejoining the highway in the pitch dark. A concrete floor did not make a comfortable bed and he slept fitfully, waking every hour or so with a nagging ache in whatever hip he'd been lying on. At first light he rolled up the sleeping-bag, carried it over to the Ford Probe and dumped the bundle in the trunk, then returned to collect the pipe bomb. That done, he got into the Ford Probe and drove off down the track.

Luck favoured him with a break in the traffic heading in both directions and he was able to rejoin US Highway 29 unseen. Abbas headed north as far as Scaggsville, where he made a right and then picked up Interstate 95 at the interchange two miles further on.

The time was ten after six. He had one hour fifty in hand in which to return to the apartment house on New York Avenue, hide the bomb, freshen himself up and report to the supervisor in charge of the morning shift at McDonald's in Hyattsville. Abbas had no problem with that.

Ashton had never met the Brigadier, Special Forces, before; after a grilling that had lasted all of two hours, he had no desire to meet him a second time. His confident statement to Max Brabazon that he could handle the man had come within a whisker of being a hollow boast. Brigadier, Special Forces, was a slim, wiry-looking officer with birdlike features, who crinkled his eyes a lot as if smiling whereas his mouth did no such thing. He'd listened to Ashton without once interrupting him during the briefing and had appeared to accept his reasons why the surveillance operation had had to be mounted with so little warning.

The Spanish Inquisition had started the moment Ashton had asked if he had any questions. It turned out he had a whole raft of them. He had wanted to know the precise nature of the threat to Jill Sheridan, the Deputy DG, why the SAS teams were to be unarmed, which terrorist organisation posed the threat and how reliable was the information Ashton had received. He also couldn't understand why Special Branch and MI5 weren't involved. Finally he had let it be known that, as a simple matter of courtesy, he thought Headquarters, Special Forces, should have been informed before Brabazon approached 22 SAS direct.

Where an apology was called for, Ashton had made one. He had told the Brigadier that the terrorists were of Mid-East origin and probably belonged to Hezbollah, although this was by no means certain. There had been a grain of truth in this assertion but none whatever in his claim that Special Branch had been ruled out because MI5 had stated they were already overcommitted. Since it had been obvious the Brigadier was unhappy about the constraints placed upon the SAS, Ashton had offered to give him an assurance in writing that he would accept full responsibility should anything happen to Jill. To be regarded as a wimp was the last thing Brigadier, Special Forces, wanted, and he had spurned the offer angrily. Although they may not have parted the best of friends. Ashton was pretty sure that at least for the next few days, the Brigadier wouldn't do anything that might rock the boat. It was, Ashton thought, all the time he needed.

Returning to his office, Ashton opened the combination safe, placed the in- out- and pending trays on his desk, and then took out the tape recorder. He switched it on, turned the volume down low and, holding the recorder to his ear like a telephone, listened to the calls Jill had made yesterday. The transmitters he had placed in both her office and Victor's were voice activated and consequently had picked up everything Jill had said to her PA. Conversations with department heads and clerical staff were of no interest to Ashton, and with a judicious use of the fast forward button he was able to monitor what had happened the previous day in a matter of minutes. Nothing unusual had happened on Monday and so far, yesterday looked like being a repeat performance. Then somebody tapped on the door and he hurriedly switched off the recorder and managed to shove it in the top drawer of the desk a split second before the chief clerk walked into his office with a clutch of files.

'Nothing too urgent,' he said, and placed them in the appropriate tray. 'But you'll want to see the signal from GCHQ.'

Ashton reached for the signal lying on top of the files, read it quickly, then glanced at the originator's date/time group.

'When did we receive this?' he asked.

'Communications finished decoding it at 08.11 hours this morning. I was hoping to catch you before morning prayers but you were conferring with the Deputy DG. Then after the conference you'd disappeared somewhere. I thought of sending it on to the Asian Department but the signal was prefixed personal for you. I hope I did the right thing?'

'You did,' Ashton told him. 'This is something Jill Sheridan ought to see first.'

Ashton ushered the chief clerk out of the room, locked the

door behind him and, pocketing the key, went into the PA's office. Dilys Crowther told him the Deputy DG had given instructions she wasn't to be disturbed. Jill Sheridan also tried to fend him off when he walked in unannounced, but Ashton wasn't having that.

'This takes precedence,' he said, and thrust the signal at her. 'Vladimir Aleksandrovich Labur arrived in Islamabad yesterday and called his wife, Yevdokia, in Odintsovo to let her know he had arrived safely and would be going on to Peshawar today.'

'I can read,' Jill said tartly.

He watched Jill write a brief note and initial the signal before transferring it to the out-tray. Even looking at her scrawl upside down, he could see the note was merely addressed to the Asian Department for information.

'Labur is the former Director of Chemical Defence Research,' Ashton reminded her.

'So?'

'Well, I would have thought we would like to find out who he is meeting in Peshawar.'

'Hugo Calthorpe will know what to do.'

'I'm not disputing that, but to get the information we want, Head of Station, Islamabad will have to throw money about like confetti. We're nearing the end of the financial year and Hugo won't have much of his budget left. He will need every penny of his contingency fund.'

'I'll look into it.'

For all her earlier acid comments it was evident Jill was distracted.

'Well, don't leave it too long. We need to be up and running before Labur and his friends disappear.'

'Who do you think you are talking to, Ashton?'

'A clever woman whose mind is elsewhere this morning.'

On his way through the PA's office he told Dilys Crowther

to inform Hugo Calthorpe and Roy Kelso that the acting DG wished to see them a.s.a.p. As he turned the corner at the end of the corridor he could hear one of the phones in the office ringing. The Mozart secure speech facility was still ringing when he unlocked the door and walked into the room. Answering the phone he heard Brabazon say, 'Is that you, Peter?'

'It is, what's up?'

'Messenger just called in to ask if it was the practice of our mutual friend to go jogging first thing in the morning. I said I didn't know but would find out.'

'You'd better give me the whole story, Max.'

'It doesn't amount to much. Messenger decided he'd better have a look at the neighbourhood before briefing his team. He was coming down Bisham Gardens in a rented car when he saw a woman jogging up the hill from the direction of Swain's Lane. He was almost abreast of her when she turned into the house called Freemantle.'

'Did Jill make eyeball contact with him?'

'He says not.'

Ashton didn't like the situation one bit. If he told Messenger not to worry about it the SAS man was bound to have misgivings and would waste no time in communicating them to his commanding officer. Ashton could almost feel the Brigadier, Special Forces breathing down his neck.

'Tell Messenger it's months since our mutual friend went jogging and even then it wasn't part of the daily routine.'

'I don't think that will satisfy Messenger.'

'Neither do I,' Ashton said. 'Tell him I want to hear how he plans to cope with the problem, then book a private room at' the Rag for three o'clock this afternoon so that he can tell me in person. OK?'

'Yes. Do you want me to be present?'

'It would be helpful if you were,' Ashton said, and put the

phone down. The files in the in-tray claimed his attention but he decided he should put the recorder back where it belonged first. He took it out of the drawer and checked to see what else was on the tape before rewinding it. To his surprise Ashton found himself listening to a conversation between Jill Sheridan and apparently Robin Urquhart that could only have occurred earlier that morning. By the time Jill finished he knew why she had gone jogging at the crack of dawn.

Landon moved dutifully towards the table Francesca had grabbed for them. There were two other chairs at the table but she had planted her shoulder bag on one of them to give the impression she was holding it for another friend. He would have preferred to lunch with the CIA people he had been conversing with during the coffee break but Landon couldn't pretend he hadn't noticed her frantic hand signals. He liked Francesca, in fact he liked her a lot, but they weren't an item yet and it riled him that Rowan Garfield should pretend otherwise to all and sundry. If Garfield said so much as 'Ah, here come the lovebirds' one more time, Landon was going to accidentally hack the legs from under him.

'For a moment I thought you were going to ignore me,' Francesca said jokingly as he joined her.

'I wouldn't do a thing like that.'

'You hadn't better,' she told him, still joking, then suddenly changed the subject. 'What did he have to say?'

'Who?'

'Christensen. I saw him tap you on the shoulder and he sure as hell wasn't whispering sweet nothings in your ear.'

'You're right, he wasn't. His Jordanian source has come good and is going to meet us tonight.'

'By us, I take it I'm included?'

'You certainly are. I think Christensen has got the hots for you.'

'Much good it will do him.'

'You'd better sit in the back then. He's picking us up from the L'Enfant Plaza Hotel at eight p.m.'

'And where are we going?'

'Carole Highlands or, to be more precise, the Blue Marlin.'

Chapter 18

Sometimes Urquhart had to remind himself that he was the senior of four deputy undersecretaries at the Foreign and Commonwealth Office and not some lovesick callow youth of fourteen who was just beginning to discover what sex was all about. But that was the sort of effect Jill Sheridan had on him. He could not bring himself to accept that Jill's oft-expressed love for him had waned and gradually died from the moment his decree nisi had become absolute and he was free to marry her. In the dark corner of his mind an insidious voice alleged that she had only ever allowed him into her bed because of what he could do to further her career.

The double first in modern languages and politics, philosophy and history he'd obtained at Cambridge in no way equipped him to deal with Jill Sheridan. She was his blind spot and he was completely infatuated with her. Since last November when Rosalind had launched her hate campaign, Urquhart could count the number of times he had seen Jill on the fingers of one hand. Jill had had no reason to take herself off to Florida for three weeks in late January; the hate campaign had rebounded on Rosalind by then and the popular press were no longer hounding Jill. Victor Hazelwood had gone so far as to suggest she had wanted to distance herself from him but he had refused to accept that. Nor would he believe that Jill had only turned to him again because she was in serious trouble.

He did not care that a hostile intelligence service had

motivated Jill to seek him out; it was enough to know that he would be seeing her again at four thirty.

It was, of course, ridiculous, and the nearer it got to half-past four, the less able he was to concentrate on the paper dealing with the policy changes the FCO could expect in the event the Labour Party won the next general election. Impatient for the time to pass, he left the desk and went over to the window. His office was in the southwest corner of the building at the junction of King Charles Street and Horse Guards Road. From a commanding position on the top floor he enjoyed a view of St James's Park, the Serpentine and Buckingham Palace. To call the room an office was definitely a misnomer considering it was furnished on the scale of a grand salon.

His PA in the outer office tapped on the communicating door and opened it to announce that Miss Sheridan had arrived. From its inception the room had conveyed the pomp and circumstance of a world power, and although this was now out of date, visitors were still impressed by the sheer grandeur of the place and some were even intimidated by its ambience. But not Jill Sheridan; she hadn't been overawed the first time she had called on him a year ago. Despite the pressure she was under, things were no different today.

'It's good to see you again, Jill,' Urquhart said, turning away from the window to greet her as she walked into the room.

'And you, Robin.'

She was wearing a dark green business suit cut on simple lines with kick pleats in the skirt. He thought Jill had never looked so desirable, and he kissed her fiercely, something he would never have done twelve months ago for fear his PA might walk in unannounced. After the messy divorce and the exposure they had received in the popular press such modesty was irrelevant.

'What brought that on?' she murmured.

'As if you didn't know,' Urquhart said, and ushered her to a

Regency chair lavishly covered in silk, then moved round the low rosewood coffee table, and sat down facing her. 'Now where is this drop you alluded to?' he asked.

'In Highgate cemetery, not far from the tomb of Karl Marx.'

'And how did you know where to find it?'

Jill opened her handbag, took out a postcard and handed it to Urquhart.

'I found this in my letter box yesterday evening. The directions are on the back..'

'The stamp hasn't been franked,' Urquhart said, and mentally cursed himself for making such a banal observation when it was patently obvious the postcard hadn't been handled by Royal Mail.

'It was delivered by hand after my daily woman had left the house,' Jill informed him crisply. 'And yes, that does mean they have been watching me closely and are familiar with the household routine.' She dipped into her handbag again and produced a slip of grey-coloured paper. 'This is what I collected from the drop this morning.'

Urquhart took the slip of paper from her and read it carefully. According to Jill only the man she had dubbed Emile Mark III had a fairly good command of English. The style in which both the postcard and the demand for information had been couched suggested that they had been written by him. Urquhart noted that Emile had not stated when he expected her to deliver the information, nor had he indicated whether or not she was to use the same drop. He had also failed to say how he expected Jill to contact him when she had the information.

'I presume Emile will telephone to give you the necessary instructions when he sees fit?'

'That was my assumption,' Jill said.

'Exactly what is Excelsior?' Urquhart asked, looking up from the slip of paper in his hand.

'I looked it up on our data base and learned that Excelsior was the codename for the SIS network in Tehran. The agents were all recruited locally. Of the four names Emile has listed, three were executed after the Shah fled the country. The fourth got out in time and went to America.'

'How would Emile know the codename?'

'I imagine the Iranians must have given it to him. Head of Station, Tehran used to exchange information with his opposite number in the CIA. Although the Americans were aware that the British network was called Excelsior, sources were not disclosed with the exception of those four individuals.'

Jill half smiled. 'Their names appeared on both our list and the CIA's because it was discovered they were working for both agencies and getting paid twice for the same information. Unfortunately the CIA failed to destroy all their files when the United States Embassy was stormed.'

'And Scorpion?'

'That goes back to the war between Iraq and Iran. It was an assessment of the internal security situation in Iraq. Specifically we wanted to ascertain whether the marsh people in the south and the Kurds in the north of the country would take advantage of the war to turn against Saddam Hussein while the army was heavily engaged fighting the Iranians. The answer was an emphatic no, the Republican Guard had the whole country in an iron grip.

'It was called Scorpion because there was a sting in the tail. To put it in a nutshell, this assessment was conditional on the Iraqis continuing to receive the latest weapons in quantity. Twenty years ago Saddam Hussein was one of the good guys so we were quite happy for the Sovs to provide him with an arsenal of tanks, self-propelled guns, armoured personnel carriers and surface-to-surface missiles.'

'What's your opinion, Jill? Will it hurt us to answer Emile's questions in full?'

'They already know the answers. This is just one more test they are putting me through.'

Jill was right, there was no doubt about that in his mind, but it would be necessary to consult the two Privy Counsellors first and he would like to get Hazelwood's endorsement before giving her a green light.

'Victor returns from Arosa on Saturday. Correct?'

'Yes.'

'Can you stall Emile should he contact you before Monday?'

'If I have to,' Jill said, and made no attempt to conceal her impatience.

'You could tell him that you have to pick the right moment to access the information without arousing suspicion.'

Jill said this was precisely what she had already planned to do. Then in the very next breath she told him about the signal Delacombe had sent querying why Landon was interested in Thomas Kransky. There was a chance Delacombe might convey his misgivings to the ambassador.

'I thought you should know the facts, Robin,' she said.

'I'm glad you told me. What I don't understand is why this intelligence officer . . .' Urquhart snapped his fingers, unable to recall the name.

'Will Landon,' Jill reminded him. 'He's over there attending the CIA's symposium on International Terrorism. Ashton briefed him to find out what the FBI had on Kransky. Then the day before he left, Victor had another thought and gave instructions he was to approach Head of Station, Washington first.' Jill crossed her legs and the kick pleats fell away to afford Urquhart a tantalising glimpse of her thigh. 'Mind you, all this is according to Ashton.'

'Do you believe him?' Urquhart asked in a strained voice.

'Well, Ashton doesn't like this setup and thinks I should resign, but he has been very open about it. Again, according to Ashton, Victor was adamant that I should go, but he's never said so to my face. And he does give the impression he's solidly behind the operation. All the same, I have this feeling that one of them is determined to sabotage it. And that would be a pity when we've just got the Emiles nibbling at the bait.' Jill shook her head. 'I shouldn't be talking this way about Victor,' she said in a subdued voice.

'No, you've done the right thing, and you're not to worry about Victor. I promise you he will not be a problem. Neither will Ashton.'

Ashton suspected he was going home to a testy wife, and since he was feeling more than a little scratchy himself, their combined attitude had all the makings of a combustible mixture. On his instructions the first SAS team was now to be operational with effect from 18.00 hours. In arranging a meeting for 15.00 hours at the Rag, he had allowed himself a minimum of two hours in which to rein Messenger in and convince him it was impossible to tag Jill should she go jogging tomorrow morning. For a while the latter task looked as if it was going to be relatively easy. Having reconnoitred the neighbourhood, Messenger realised there was no way men in tracksuits could blend into the background when Jill was the only person seen exercising that morning.

What he had proposed to do instead was to position his team in four cars so that no matter which way Jill set off from the house, one of them would spot her. Whoever saw Jill first would alert the others using a personal hand-held transceiver, which fitted neatly into the palm. Individual team members lying up in the side streets off Highgate Hill and Dartmouth Park would remain in position until redeployed by Messenger.

The problem Ashton had to face was how to knock the plan on the head without Messenger getting the impression he was being obstructive. He had solved it by asking the SAS captain if he had taken into account the difficulties likely to be caused by on-street parking? Few of the houses in the side streets Messenger had mentioned had a garage and they would be lucky to find a vacant slot before the residents went to work. Ashton had also wanted to know what he proposed to do should Jill decide to run through Waterlow Park? The ensuing discussion had lasted well beyond the minimum time Ashton had calculated he had in hand, but finally Messenger had had to accept his plan was too risky.

There were, however, other aspects of the operation that bothered the SAS officer and it had become patently obvious to Ashton that they couldn't be left to fester overnight. He had sent Messenger away after telling him to return as soon as Jill was safely inside her house. He had then phoned Harriet to let her know he was unlikely to arrive at Havant before eight thirty. It had been the first of several phone calls as he was obliged to revise his estimated time of arrival. Each conversation had got progressively more fraught, with Harriet finally telling him that he would be lucky to find he still had a wife whenever he did get home.

Alighting from the train at Havant, Ashton walked through the booking hall and looked for a taxi in the yard. A horn blared somewhere over to his right and turning in that direction, he saw Harriet behind the wheel of the Volvo. He told himself the fact that she had turned out to meet him at the station had to be a good sign. Then, instead of making a fuss of Harriet, he'd asked her what she had done with the children, which didn't go down very well.

'Give me credit for some intelligence,' she said waspishly. 'I left Edward in charge, what did you think I did?'

'I'm sorry, I'm not thinking straight. It's been a bad day.'

'Our next-door neighbour is babysitting for me.'

'That's nice,' he said vaguely.

'You'd better tell me about it.'

'What?'

'Your bad day.'

'I've put Jill under surveillance, something Victor should have done at least a week ago. The trouble is, I couldn't tell Messenger the real reason why his team was being tasked to watch her. I told him she was under threat and had to be protected, which was pretty dumb of me because the way I told him to play it ran counter to all the drills the SAS have perfected.' Ashton glanced at the dashboard. 'Ten thirty-seven,' he muttered and shook his head. 'I must have spent a good four hours with Messenger trying to get him on my side without giving too much away.'

'And did you succeed?' Harriet asked.

'If I have it's only because in the end I had to tell him a damned sight more than I'd wanted to.'

Messenger had been led to believe Jill Sheridan was a senior official in the Foreign and Commonwealth Office, which was how the tabloids had described her at the time of Urquhart's messy divorce. Ashton liked to think Messenger was still under that impression even though he'd had to tell the SAS officer that the SIS were running a double-cross operation.

'I just hope he keeps that to himself and doesn't pass it on to his commanding officer.'

'Did you make it clear what would happen to him if he did?'

'He was warned of the possible consequence.' Ashton smiled. 'In a subtle manner, of course,' he added.

'I bet he wishes he hadn't been so damned nosy.'

'Well, when it comes to keeping a secret there's nothing like making a man aware that he has learned more than is good for him.'

Ashton fell silent. He glanced at the speedometer and somehow resisted the temptation to look at it again. A long time ago he had once told Harriet she had a heavy foot and when satisfied no motorway police were in sight she had retaliated by flooring the accelerator until the needle was past the hundred mark. Fast driver she might be but as Ashton had rapidly discovered she was also a skilful one with good anticipation and quick reflexes. After that short demonstration he had always felt safe with her at the wheel. They passed through Hermitage and Nutbourne, and were approaching Walton when Harriet suddenly announced that the police had found the Range Rover that had sideswiped him off the road.

'The driver had hidden it in a derelict barn not far from Lewes. Both offside doors were dented and there was a fair amount of paint from your Ford Escort on them. The vehicle was purchased at a car auction six months ago; the name and address of the registered owner are false.'

There was another surprise waiting for him when Harriet turned into Church Lane. Parked down the side of Roselands Cottage was a Citroën ZX.

'I thought you said our next-door neighbour was babysitting for us?'

'The Citroën is mine,' Harriet told him. 'Or yours. We need two cars in this family.'

'Can we afford it?' he asked.

'Oh, yes, I sold some of the shares in British Telecom I inherited from my father. They peaked at an all-time high and it seemed a good time to make a minor killing. Besides, your insurance company was only prepared to give you two thousand for that old banger.'

He didn't want to ask Harriet when she had cashed in the BT shares because it was her money and it was none of his business what she did with it. But all the same, he was curious to know.

'Which one do you prefer?' Harriet asked. 'The Volvo or the Citroën?'

'No, you choose whichever one suits you best.'

'I'll keep the Citroën then.'

'Good.' Ashton got out of the Volvo and walked round to open the offside door and help her out of the car.

'I'm not an old lady yet,' she told him, smiling.

'I know that, I'm just trying to molest you.'

He folded his arms around Harriet and kissed her warmly. The tip of her tongue flicked across his lips and she thrust her pelvis forward, grinding it against him. They stood there outside the cottage locked in an embrace that became more and more heated. Presently Harriet placed a hand on his chest and pushed him gently away.

'I think we'd better finish this indoors,' she murmured in a voice that was almost lost in the back of her throat.

Samir Abbas left the housing development on New York Avenue, crossed the Baltimore and Ohio Railroad tracks and, joining US Highway 1, made for Interchange 27 on the Capital Beltway. The pipe bomb was in the trunk, tucked inside a plumber's toolkit half hidden under a pair of overalls. The timer, screwcap and a small pair of pliers were in the glove compartment.

Instead of the Type 64 pistol, he had opted for a 9mm Ruger P85 semi-automatic with a 15-shot box magazine. His choice had been a matter of expediency. He had put two rounds into Kransky with the Type 64 pistol, two more into Sara Gay and one in the actor who had called himself Dan Swordsman. It was only sensible to assume the Baltimore Police Department had recovered all five bullets, some of which were bound to have been in good enough condition for forensics to make something of them. He did not want the FBI to link the multiple slayings at Hawks Point with the incident at the Blue Marlin. The Ruger was fitted with a noise suppressor, which, although nowhere nearly as effective as the Chinese assassination weapon, was perfectly adequate for the task.

Joining the Capital Beltway, Abbas headed east towards Interchange 25. Christensen had arranged to collect the English troublemakers from their hotel at 8 p.m. and by now they ought to be on Rhode Island Avenue, but still well within the District of Columbia. No operation ran like clockwork and the Hawks Point slaying had been no exception in that he had nearly lost track of Christensen on the way to Kransky's studio. Tonight it could be the timer that caused a foul-up. These delay pencils were unpredictable because it was impossible to gauge accurately how long the acid would take to eat through the cardboard plug. The pipe bomb should detonate half an hour after crushing the phial of acid but it could blow five minutes either way. It would serve the American right if his precious timetable was thrown out of kilter. While he personally didn't feel threatened by the English troublemakers it seemed Christensen did, and after he'd expressed his fears orders had come from above that executive action was to be taken against them.

Abbas left the Capital Beltway and headed towards Carole Highlands on State Highway 650. Roughly a mile short of the Blue Marlin, he turned into Branch Park and switched off all the lights. Once his eyes had become accustomed to the dark, he began to close on the roadside bar and grill, inching his way through the trees at a snail's pace. Every now and then he stopped to check the odometer with the aid of a pocket-size torch. After covering seven-tenths of a mile Abbas judged he was close enough and began to manoeuvre the Ford Probe backwards and forwards to face State Highway 650. There was limited space and he had almost completed what amounted to a seven-point turn when he backed into a tree and broke the taillight assembly. Mouthing obscenities, Abbas got out of the car and went round the back to inspect the damage. Two small fragments of glass remained in the taillight assembly and as far as he could tell with the pocket torch the lightbulbs were intact.

Suddenly, almost before he knew it, time was running short. Opening the trunk Abbas took out the pipe bomb, armed it with a timer, then withdrew the split pin and broke the phial of acid with the pliers. Somehow he managed to put the end cap on cross-threaded and valuable minutes were lost sorting it out. He reached inside his pea jacket took out the Ruger semi-automatic pistol and chambered a 9mm round, then checked the noise suppressor to make sure it was fully locked in before moving off.

Silent as a big cat stalking its prey, Abbas padded through the wood clutching the pipe bomb in his left hand. He had calculated it would take him no more than eight minutes to cover the five hundred yards to the Blue Marlin. However, the timing he'd allowed for turned out to be optimistic and it took him close on fifteen minutes to reach the tree line opposite the parking lot. The number of vehicles he could see from his position suggested the bar and grill was more crowded than it had been last night. Moving to his right, Abbas worked his way round to the back of the Blue Marlin to the far parking lot. He checked out the line of vehicles nearest the bar and grill and placed the pipe bomb under a rig and trailer, the muffler of which was still warm to the touch. He then retraced his steps as far as the men's room at the rear of the building.

Chapter 19

Francesca decided she was going off Will Landon. He hadn't wanted her to be present when Christensen produced his Jordanian friend like a rabbit out of a conjurer's hat and had gone out of his way to discourage her. Some of the things he had said had been ludicrous, such as his allegation that Christensen had the hots for her. Will had come close to alleging the FBI agent wasn't entirely kosher. What bothered him was the fact Christensen had seemingly bought the cock-and-bull story he'd given him concerning the SIS interest in the late Tom Kransky. Will had been rocked back on his heels when the American had told him the agency had also heard the porno movie producer was making a propaganda film for the Palestine Liberation Organisation. He couldn't accept that in playing his story back at him, Christensen was letting him know he was sure the SIS interest in Kransky had nothing to do with Palestine.

Will was jealous of the American, that was the crux of the matter – and there was no getting away from it, Christensen certainly had charm. Had Landon been driving with the American sitting up front with him she would definitely have been left out in the cold. But Christensen had included her in their conversation, and from time to time he'd glanced over his shoulder and smiled at her.

They had passed through Carole Highlands and were on the State Highway 650 heading north. Christensen had told her to look out for a motel on her side of the road because the Blue

Marlin was only half a mile beyond it. She had expected to see a large billboard by the roadside advising anybody who was looking for somewhere to stay that the Sunrise Motel was the next turning on the right. Apparently the current owner preferred something more discreet and was content with a small sign some two feet high planted on the grass verge bordering the access road. The proprietor of the Blue Marlin suffered from no such inhibition. The roadside bar and grill was ablaze with neon lights, which included a likeness of the large salt-water game fish above the entrance. According to Christensen the spearlike upper jaw was out of proportion. He also thought the name wasn't appropriate, considering Chesapeake Bay was over thirty miles away.

The place was crowded and not at all to Francesca York's taste. Apart from two waitresses there were only three other women present and even though none of the men was misbehaving, she was glad she had decided to wear a pair of trousers instead of one of her usual tight-fitting skirts. Every stool at the bar was occupied and although there were vacant spaces in some of the booths, there was nowhere all three of them could sit together.

While Christensen was gazing blankly round the room, Landon noticed that a party of four was about to vacate a booth near the entrance. Tapping the American on the shoulder to attract his attention he and Francesca then moved swiftly to grab it before anybody could beat them to it. Some moments later Christensen joined them.

'Anything wrong with this booth?' Landon asked him.

'No, it's just fine. I was looking for my Jordanian friend, that's all.'

'Is he late?'

'Not by his standard.'

'I thought you said he was going to meet us at ten minutes past nine?'

'I said I would pick you two up from the hotel at eight p.m. I don't remember mentioning what time the source would arrive.'

There was friction in the air. Francesca couldn't understand why Landon disliked the American, nor why he was making so little effort to hide it. Half turning his back on him, Christensen signalled one of the waitresses to come over to the booth.

'What are you guys going to have?' he asked without turning round.

Abbas had abandoned his original position and moved back into the tree line, then circled the building until he was facing the entrance to the kitchen. Although there was no exit from the men's room there was an emergency one opposite the facilities and there was no telling which way a panic-stricken crowd of diners would run when they spilled out of the bar and grill. For some of the mob to blunder into him was the last thing he needed.

He believed Christensen had arrived. The American was, of course, driving a car he hadn't seen before but that was almost his trademark. If anything, the FBI agent had been nine minutes earlier than he had indicated, which would have worried Abbas if Christensen hadn't been accompanied by a man and woman whom he was convinced were English troublemakers.

Abbas checked his wristwatch for the umpteenth time. Eight forty-eight; eleven minutes to go. For the umpteenth time he asked himself what he would do if the timer failed and he was still no nearer the solution. The thunderclap took him by surprise and he stood there, seemingly unable to move. Then he saw the swirling column of black smoke rising above the roof and he ran towards the kitchen door.

The blast from the home-made bomb rocked the rig and the trailer. Such was the destructive force unleashed by four pounds of Semtex explosive that a twenty-foot section of the wooden outside wall was demolished and every window in the Blue Marlin shattered. The pipe itself fragmented into a mass of red-hot steel splinters to complement the metal barbs Abbas had implanted in the casing. The splinters shredded most of the tyres on the truck and ripped open the diesel fuel tank. Moments later the tank erupted, spewing globules of burning fuel over the building.

The waitress had just taken their order and was moving diagonally across the room towards the bar when the explosion occurred and swept her off her feet. Arms and legs flapping like a scarecrow in a strong wind, she crunched head first into the bar and then lay there motionless on the floor. Somebody or something punched Francesca York in the ribs on her left side and breathing suddenly became very painful. Dense black smoke invaded the room reducing visibility to the point where she couldn't see Landon, who had been sitting across the table from her. Then all the lights fused and people were shouting so loudly Francesca couldn't make herself heard when she begged somebody to please help her. It dawned on her the place was on fire and she had to get out before the smoke overcame her. That meant crawling on her stomach, because the cleanest air was a narrow band from the floor up to a height of a foot. But the first thing she had to do was squeeze past the table.

She squirmed sideways along the bench seat, each movement causing a stab of pain in her left side. She felt for and touched the end of the table, half rose from the bench seat and collapsed on to the floor. Instinctively Francesca wrapped her right arm around the waist as if holding herself together. The left side of her body felt wet and sticky to the touch and she prayed to God the injury wasn't life-threatening. Where the hell was Christensen? What had happened to Will Landon?

The questions multiplied in her mind. Please God, don't say they had got out and left her to die?

From where Abbas had been waiting in the tree line, the distance to the kitchen door was roughly thirty yards. It seemed twice that, as he jinked through the rows of parked vehicles. There was a sudden whoomf as he got within touching distance of the door and for a moment he thought a Calor Gas cooker in the kitchen had blown up, then he smelled diesel and knew different. A member of the kitchen staff yanked the door open even as he reached for the handle. The short-order cook was a tall, powerfully built black man who was not the least bit intimidated when Abbas pointed the Ruger semi-automatic at him. Cursed with more courage than sense, he tried to wrest the pistol from him and got shot in the groin for his trouble. As he staggered back, clutching his abdomen, Abbas shot him again in the chest and the throat. Whatever the limitation of the noise suppressor, the bedlam inside the Blue Marlin completely obliterated the sound of gunfire. There was, however, a witness in the person of the other short-order cook. Abbas saw the man was holding a meat cleaver and immediately raised his left arm to ward off the heavy chopping tool as the cook hurled it at him. At the same time he opened fire a split second before the meat cleaver struck his forearm and cracked it. Although it was the weighted edge rather than the cutting surface that caught him, it still inflicted a nasty gash.

Abbas ignored the pain and went into the kitchen. The smoke was not yet so dense he couldn't see where the serving hatch was, but then the lights fused and spotting the English troublemakers was never going to be easy. It was about to become impossible. For the hit to be successful two conditions had to be fulfilled. The pipe bomb was intended to make everyone sitting up at the bar stampede for the exit, which it had. Christensen had been told to ensure his party occupied one of the three booths in line with the serving hatch, which it appeared he had failed to do. One of the English troublemakers was a woman and suddenly there she was, wearing the sort of indecently short skirt that made Abbas despise and hate all Western women for the whores they undoubtedly were. He didn't know either of the English troublemakers by sight but there were two men with the woman and although the taller one had his back to him, he looked to be the same height and build as Christensen.

The smoke was becoming denser by the second and it was a question of now or never. Seventy per cent certain in his own mind that he had correctly identified the English trouble-makers, Abbas shot them down. Normally he used a double-handed grip on the semi-automatic but his left arm was too painful to raise, so he stood sideways on to the targets, right arm extended like a nineteenth-century duellist. The range was less than five yards and he couldn't miss.

The smoke began to choke him and he turned away from the serving hatch. Coughing and spluttering, Abbas staggered to the exit, remembered just in time to tuck the semi-automatic away in his pea jacket before leaving the kitchen. The parking lot seemed to be full of people running about like headless chickens. Truckers whose vehicles were close to the Blue Marlin were trying to manoeuvre their rigs clear of the building. Nobody paid any attention to Abbas as he made for the tree line.

Landon found himself lying on the floor, his head throbbing as if a gang of workmen were doing a demolition job on his skull, and unable to see very much out of his right eye. He recalled Christensen grabbing hold of an arm a split second after the explosion, then dragging him from the booth and on towards the bar. The American had tripped over something on the floor and had gone down, taking Landon with him. Christensen had then released his arm and crawled off in a totally different direction. As Landon now remembered it, the American had kicked him in the face as he crawled away. Had it been deliberate or had he simply panicked? And where the hell was Francesca?

Landon thought he knew where the exit was and started crawling leopard-style, alternating left leg drawn up, right arm extended then right leg drawn up, left arm extended. A voice in pain murmured, 'Help me, please help me.' Guided by the voice Landon tracked Francesca down and found her lying on her stomach, head turned over to the left, one arm under the body hugging her left side. He turned Francesca over on to her back and provoked a muted scream of agony. He lay down beside her briefly, took a deep breath of uncontaminated air and then raised himself up on to his knees. There was no easy way of doing what had to be done and closing his ears to her cries, he picked Francesca up, one arm under her legs, the other around her shoulders. One of the swing doors was on fire, the flames licking hungrily towards the other one. There was no room to work up a turn of speed but he covered the distance in four lengthy strides. Turning his back on the fire, he hit the swing door with his right shoulder. As he staggered out of the building, a tongue of flame seared his neck and set his hair on fire.

He ran clear of the building carrying Francesca in his arms, then laid her down gently. With his bare hands he reached behind his neck and smothered the frizzled patch of hair that was still smouldering. Wasting no further time on himself, Landon removed his jacket and stripped off his shirt. To make a dressing he folded the shirt into a pad and pressed it over the entry wound, then used his tie to hold it in place.

'I need a paramedic,' he shouted. 'Somebody get me a paramedic.'

He looked up to see Christensen walking slowly towards him. As the FBI agent drew nearer he noticed his left trouser leg below the knee seemed damp and a darker shade of grey than the rest of his suit. The American was also limping quite badly.

'Got me a hole in the calf,' Christensen told him.

'That's too bad. Have you called for assistance?'

'What?'

'The emergency services – fire, police, ambulance.'

'Yeah. Just about everybody here has made a 911.' Christensen looked down at Francesca. 'Is she hurt real bad?' he asked casually.

Landon ignored him. Francesca was still semiconscious and the last thing she needed to hear was the extent of her injuries.

'This shouldn't have happened,' Christensen said in a detached voice. 'Nothing but a goddamned fuck-up.'

'What the hell are you on about?'

'The Blue Marlin, no fire doors, too few exits.' Christensen cocked his head on one side. 'You hear those sirens? It won't be long now.'

'You want to make yourself useful,' Landon said belligerently, 'go grab a paramedic and bring him over here.'

Francesca groaned. Her breathing was shallow and there was a bloodstained froth on her lips. Landon clasped her hand and squeezed it gently. 'Stay with me,' he said, and repeated it over and over again.

Abbas reached the Ford Probe, opened the offside front door with his right hand and crawled inside. With his left arm broken, even closing the door with his good hand was a painful business but that was nothing compared to the agony of drawing the seat belt across his chest and locking it into the housing. The long-drawn-out aggressive bla-a-a-p of a fire engine and the oscillating warble from a fleet of ambulances and police cars drawing nearer and nearer churned his stomach. He turned the ignition on, cranked the engine and shifted into drive. Steering the car with one hand, he weaved through the trees, making for the state highway, every jolt, every bump sheer agony. He drove without lights all the way to the grass verge in the knowledge that rejoining the highway was going to be a risky business. Abbas stopped just short of the divided road and looked both ways. He was no more than four hundred yards from the Blue Marlin and the traffic was already backing up and double-banked. Before too long he wouldn't be able to get out. It was the spur Abbas needed; switching on the main beams and hazard warning lights, he floored the gas pedal, shot across the highway in front of an oncoming truck and drew an angry blast on the horn. The Ford Probe mounted the central reservation, suffering damage to the muffler on the high kerbstone, bounced across the grass dividing strip and hit the road the other side with enough force to break a shock absorber. Somehow, Abbas managed to control the car and headed north to Interchange 25 on the Capital Beltway.

He had a defective taillight assembly, the noise from the damaged muffler constituted a public nuisance, and the Ford Probe probably appeared lopsided – three good reasons for a police officer to pull him over. And what would he do if that should happen? Shoot the cop or attempt to talk his way out of trouble? If he did stop, his blood-soaked arm would be the first thing a cop would notice and that would be it. How many rounds of 9mm had he expended? Six? Seven? What did one round either way matter when the box magazine held fifteen? So shoot the cop. And if there was more than one patrolman in the blue-and-white? Best thing he could do was keep a low profile. Abbas eased his foot on the gas pedal long enough for the speed to fall back to a respectable fifty. The noise emitted by the muffler sounded a good deal less intimidating.

Abbas reached the interchange without further incident and

headed in a westerly direction, only too aware there was a long way to go yet before he could feel reasonably safe.

To Landon every minute seemed like ten as he kneeled beside Francesca, holding her hand. He felt helpless and angry: helpless because he lacked the skills of a paramedic to do anything more for Francesca; angry because wherever he looked there was an ambulance yet Christensen was taking for ever to find one. If the son of a bitch didn't return in the next two minutes he would have to leave her and go find a paramedic himself.

'Don't leave me, please don't leave me,' Francesca breathed, as if reading his thoughts.

'I'm here, I'll never leave you,' he said, and squeezed her hand.

'It hurts. Oh, Mummy, it hurts so much.' Her eyes focused on him. 'I'm dying,' she whispered.

'The hell you are. I won't let you.'

'Neither will we.'

Landon raised his head. Two paramedics, one stretcher: was there ever a better sight? One of the medics gave Francesca a shot of morphine and recorded the dosage on a wrist tag before they lifted her on to a stretcher and ran across the parking lot to a waiting ambulance. Landon sprinted after the paramedics and caught up with them just as they were loading the stretcher into the vehicle.

'Where are you taking her?' he asked.

'Howard University Hospital.'

'I'm coming with you.' Landon saw the paramedics exchange glances and sensed they were going to object. 'She's my girl,' he added.

With two other less serious casualties in the ambulance the paramedics were pushed for space but after a brief discussion he was told to ride in front with Buzz, a tall, thin man with prematurely greying hair. Howard University Hospital was a touch over eight miles, he informed Landon, and they would make it in six minutes, then set out to prove it. Lights flashing, siren warbling, they thundered down State Highway 650 and on into Capital Street. Landon sat next to Buzz in a state of suspended animation. It wasn't necessary to understand what the paramedic was telling Emergency and Reception over the radio, his terse voice confirmed what Landon already knew instinctively; Francesca was in a bad way and hanging on to life by a thread.

Landon wished to God he had been a lot firmer with Francesca and had told her point blank there was no way she was going to meet the Jordanian source. If he had done that she wouldn't now be lying seriously injured in an ambulance on the way to a hospital and God knows how many hours on the operating table. Only how could you persuade an intelligence officer like Francesca that Christensen wasn't to be trusted when you couldn't prove it? And where the hell was the FBI agent now?

'Where did Christensen get to?' he asked the paramedic.

'Who?'

'The guy who told you where to find us – around six feet, mid-to-late forties, broad face, brown eyes set wide apart, reddish brown hair.'

'Never set eyes on the feller,' Buzz told him. 'A cop told us where to find you; said your girl needed urgent hospitalisation.'

Interchange 24 was no good to Abbas because State Highway 193 would lead him back to Carole Highlands before he could head south, and that locale would be crawling with police. So he'd gone on to the next interchange, picked up Alaska Avenue and headed into Rock Creek Park where he had pulled off the road at the first picnic area he came to. He was bathed in perspiration after what had been a nightmarish drive from the Blue Marlin. No offside taillight, exhaust blowing, broken shock absorber; he had been driving one of the most conspicuous vehicles on the Capital Beltway but luckily he hadn't encountered a single police car.

After a series of bad breaks he had deserved some luck. From the moment the pipe bomb had exploded everything that could go wrong had gone wrong. Some of it had been his fault. He shouldn't have put the pipe bomb so close to the Blue Marlin without first making sure the structure appeared solid enough to withstand the blast. As for the rest, he couldn't have foreseen how the cooks would react or that the place would be so crowded Christensen would be unable to secure a booth in line with the serving hatch. There was, however, no point dwelling on what had gone wrong; that wouldn't get him out of the mess he was in.

Abbas opened the door and got out of the car. His mobile phone was in the left-hand pocket of his pea jacket and retrieving it was a painful business. He extended the aerial with his teeth, switched on the phone and tapped out the residential number of a friendly Iraqi doctor.

'You are needed, Jassim,' he told the doctor when he answered the phone. 'I have had an accident.'

'How bad?'

'A broken arm and a deep laceration. No hospital treatment.'

'I understand. Where are you?'

Abbas gave the doctor explicit instructions how to find him and the procedure he was to follow. He had no need to remind Jassim what would happen to members of his family in both Iraq and America should he think of betraying him.

He made one other phone call, this time to a man who had a car repair shop in the ghetto area of Washington's northeast section. He was the man who had supplied Abbas with a five-year-old Volkswagen and subsequently changed the vehicle for a Ford Probe. If anyone could make a car disappear without trace, he could. There was another reason why Abbas had implicit faith in the owner of the car repair shop. He was a member of Islamic Jihad.

Christensen had ended up at the Walter Reed Army Medical Center. The hole in his leg had been made by one of the barbs Abbas had implanted in the bomb and was nothing like as serious as he had implied to Landon. A male nurse had cleaned the wound up, dusted it with sulphanilamide as a safeguard against bacterial infection and had then made a neat job of stitching the lips together before applying a dressing.

After identifying himself as a senior FBI special agent, Christensen was allocated one of the consulting rooms so that he could make a verbal report of the incident to the Bureau in private. He had contacted his immediate superior, the Head of Counter-Intelligence, and proceeded to give his version of events. He had told him exactly what had happened and why he had gone to the Blue Marlin with Landon and Francesca York. He regretted to say she had been severely injured and had been taken to Howard University Hospital. And yes, it did look as if the incident had been an underworld killing gone wrong but he couldn't think which gang was behind it. Maybe they should wait to hear what the police department had found?

It was going on one thirty in the morning when he returned to his house in Alexandria. Unwinding in the den with a bourbon and branch water, Christensen thought it had been one of the most exciting and satisfying nights of his life.

Landon's injury looked worse than it was. Nevertheless the intern who had treated him had elected to keep Landon overnight in hospital under observation in case he had concussion. He had phoned Colin Wales at the L'Enfant Plaza to let him know what had happened and had promised to call again the moment Francesca was transferred from the operating theatre to the recovery room. Unable to sleep, he had persuaded the intern that they could just as easily keep him under observation if he curled up in a chair outside the ward sister's office. At one fifty, just as he was nodding off, the surgeon who had carried out the operation came to see him.

'I'm afraid we lost her,' he said quietly. 'She went into cardiac arrest on the operating table and there was nothing we could do to save her.'

It was the blackest moment of the night.

Chapter 20

As ever bad news travelled fast. Francesca York had been pronounced dead at 06.50 hours Greenwich Mean Time, news of the occurrence was conveyed to Vauxhall Cross in an Op Immediate classified signal date/time group 060727 Z March. It was the first of many from Head of Station, Washington. The embassy staff were also busy, so too was MI5, which had its own channel of communications. Everybody kept everybody else informed with the result that Jill Sheridan, as the acting Director General, was deluged with reports from the Foreign and Commonwealth Office and the Security Service. Points of detail in earlier communications were corrected in later signals and it wasn't until late afternoon that the full extent of Landon's involvement became clear, which was the reason why Jill Sheridan sent for Ashton.

'You'd better read this first,' she said, and gave him the latest update from Delacombe.

According to the Head of Station, Landon was not the flavour of the month with the Americans. He had gone to the Bureau and made a statement implicating Special Agent Eric Christensen, Deputy Head of the Counter-Intelligence Branch, in the bombing of the Blue Marlin. He had in fact gone so far as to suggest that he had been the intended victim of the bombing and possibly Francesca York.

'Is he a megalomaniac or what?' Jill demanded. 'Anyway, why would anybody want to kill Will Landon, for God's sake?'

'I don't know. Only he can tell us that. But for my money it starts with Kransky and the questions Will asked about him. It also has to do with you.'

'Me?' Jill's voice was a full octave higher than normal. 'Don't be ridiculous,' she snapped.

'I'm not. When you went to Florida you had to submit three copies of your detailed itinerary. One copy was retained by Roy Kelso, the second went to Head of Station, Washington, and the CIA had the third. It was Delacombe's job to keep the FBI fully informed, which he did by giving the Bureau a photocopy of your programme. That's the normal practice in accordance with our permanent standing orders. Of course I'm only guessing here, but within the Bureau I think your itinerary would fetch up with the Counter-Intelligence Branch.'

'And hence Christensen had every last detail of me on file?'

'Yes. He also appears to be the leading authority on the late Tom Kransky.'

'You're forgetting something,' Jill told him. 'Nowhere in the Florida itinerary did I disclose my home address in Highgate.'

'You didn't have to. The CIA and the Bureau will have a file on you an inch thick.'

The two agencies would have started to take an interest in Jill Sheridan when she was posted to Bahrain. The nature of her appointment in the Persian Gulf would have indicated she was in the fast lane and could be expected to progress up the ladder. They were therefore likely to encounter her again in an even more sensitive job and it was in their interest to assess what sort of person they might be dealing with in the future. They wouldn't have written her off when she had thrown in the towel and requested a posting back to London. They would have appreciated that in the Gulf a woman was definitely a second-class citizen, which had made her job virtually impossible. Besides, there was another reason why they wouldn't have lost interest in Jill. By then she had taken up with Henry Clayburn, whose entrepreneurial activities in the

United Arab Emirates and Kuwait were of particular interest to the CIA.

'When you returned to Century House, the CIA station chief here in London was told to keep an eye on you.'

'Pure conjecture.'

Ashton shook his head. 'No, it's the way the CIA operate. They would have had your address in Bisham Gardens the day Clayburn's solicitor exchanged contracts with the former owners of the house. We do the same as the CIA.'

'Do we?'

'You know we do. Remember the CIA's last chief of the London station?'

'Walter Maryck.' Jill smiled. 'There was a man to gladden the hearts of every tailor in Savile Row. With his well-cut suits in varying shades of grey, he could have passed for a senior officer in the Brigade of Guards. He also looked pretty good at a point-to-point in green wellingtons, corduroys, a Barbour jacket and a peaked cap.'

'The point is, Jill, he did two tours of duty in Vietnam with the Green Berets and was awarded the Distinguished Service Cross and Silver Star. Yet his enemies within the CIA frequently accused him of being too pro-British, which, as anyone in London could have told them, was plain ridiculous. But Victor made use of that information whenever he needed some favour which might run counter to American interests. In a subtle way he would remind Walter what his enemies back home might say behind his back if word got out, and maybe he should forget what he'd been asked to do. Walter Maryck was a proud man and he wasn't going to have those SOBs at Langley telling him what he could do or could not do. It worked because Victor only resorted to that ploy now and again.'

'Victor didn't use his knowledge of Maryck for personal gain whereas Christensen did.' Jill pursed her lips. 'Is that what you are implying, Peter?'

'Well, you told me the Emiles you've been talking to come from the Mid-East. And somehow I don't see the FBI collaborating with Hezbollah, Hamas or any other terrorist group to extract information from a British intelligence officer.'

'So he's doing it for the money?' Jill said.

'Or maybe it's for the excitement.'

'That's too esoteric for me.' Jill picked up the signal Ashton had left on her desk and transferred it to the out-tray. 'Landon and the others will be arriving at Heathrow tomorrow at 06.25. I'd like you to meet him off the plane and find out what the hell he has been up to. Neighbour can stand in for you at morning prayers. OK?'

'I've no problem with that,' Ashton told her.

The arrangement lasted all of twenty minutes. Then Jill called him again to say she had had another signal from Delacombe, this time to inform her the FBI had asked if Landon could remain behind when the rest of the British contingent departed.

'Apparently the Bureau is holding an internal inquiry and they would like to record his version of what happened at the Blue Marlin. They've promised to put Landon on a plane the following evening. That's really the early hours of Saturday morning our time.'

'I'll be there to meet him,' Ashton told her, then asked if she knew who was conducting the inquiry.

'Just a minute.' There was a faint rustling noise and he guessed Jill was sorting through the loose papers in her pending tray. 'Yes, it's Special Agent Leroy Manfred.'

'I know a Leroy Manfull. Are you sure that isn't an error?'

'It says Manfred here. He's in charge of the Harrisburg office.'

'Mine worked out at Little Rock,' Ashton said, and put the phone down.

*

Officer Tynan was driving south on US 29 through Rock Creek Park when he spotted a dark blue Ford Probe, which had apparently had been left unattended in a picnic area just off the highway. Last night, some five hundred yards above the Blue Marlin a similar vehicle had shot out of Branch Park in front of a truck and had then jumped the central reservation. Tynan backed up, turned off the highway and drove into the picnic area.

The Ford Probe had been parked on the hardstanding and jacked up, allowing the offside front wheel to be removed. A strip of cardboard had been propped against the rear window on the inside. On it was printed 'Spare tire no good. Gone to nearest garage to get flat repaired.' Tynan hunkered down, looked at the underside and saw the muffler had been ripped open and was hanging loose. So too was the shock absorber. Right make, right model, right colour; there was, however, no defective taillight assembly, which raised a doubt in his mind. He walked round to the driver's side, peered through the window, then carefully opened the door, using a handkerchief in lieu of a rubber glove. The carpet on the floor was damp and somebody had sponged down the upholstery but he or she hadn't made a good job of it and traces of blood remained.

He called in the licence number and was told to wait by the suspect car until agents from the FBI arrived. The registered owner was Rudolph Bauer, 2915 Nebraska Avenue, Rockville. Unfortunately, there was no such address in Rockville and hence no Mr Rudolph Bauer.

The symposium on International Terrorism had finished at 15.00, leaving the UK delegation just over three hours to return to Loews L'Enfant Plaza Hotel, pack their bags and get out to Dulles International. Landon had also returned to the hotel and packed but there had been no ride out to the airport for him. Instead he had been taken back to Langley and allocated a room normally assigned to one of the duty officers. After Landon had unpacked his clothes, a security guard escorted him to an office on the fourth floor.

The man who stood up and greeted Landon as he entered the room was a couple of inches short of six feet and clearly tipped the scales at well over two hundred pounds. While no authority on regional variations, Landon thought he detected a faint southern accent, which, taken together with the man's florid complexion and overhanging stomach, fitted most people's preconceived idea of a typical redneck.

'My name's Leroy Manfull,' he said, 'not Manfred like it said in the message your people received. That was a clerical error. Manfred is just an extra Christian name.' The American paused, then said, 'I don't want to sound trite but I was really sorry to hear what happened to your . . . to your . . .'

'Colleague,' Landon said, rescuing him as he floundered.

'Yeah.' Manfull cleared his throat. 'I assume you've been informed that I've been charged with conducting an internal investigation?'

'I was told it was an inquiry.'

'It amounts to the same thing.' Manfull inserted a cassette into the tape recorder. 'Do you mind if I record our conversation?' he asked.

'Not a bit.'

'OK. Now I know you've probably been over this ground before more than once already but I'd really appreciate it if you would give your version of events.'

'Beginning where?'

'From the moment you first met Christensen.'

'It really started with an American called Thomas Kransky who had become known to SIS. Nobody told me in what context but my boss instructed me to find out whether our Head of Station had heard of him—'

'Who's your boss?' Manfull asked, interrupting him.

'Peter Ashton.'

'Well, it's a small world. How's he doing these days?'

'He's doing fine, has two children and was promoted to assistant director in January of this year.'

'About time. I met him in St Louis almost three years ago. He was tracking a Hezbollah group which had blown up the English Bookshop, the SIS station in Berlin, and I was looking for a woman called Louise Kay, whom the CIA was shielding in the mistaken belief she was one of theirs.'

Manfull had asked him to give his version of events and he had barely started before the American was wandering off down memory lane. It was all very interesting to hear how the Hezbollah terrorists had acquired a 130mm nuclear shell from the Russian Mafiozniki, and about the unholy alliance they had formed with the Missouri Militiamen, a ragtag and bobtail army ready to defend America against FBI agents like Leroy Manfull. But unless there was some purpose to it, all the reminiscing was a waste of time, and the American didn't strike Landon as the sort of man who was prone to digress from the subject.

'You know what those red-blooded Americans were planning to do with their nuclear shell? They were going to place it next to the old Union Station, which is now the Hyatt Regency Hotel, St Louis. All the railroad tracks below the hotel have been converted into a shopping mall. On behalf of the Palestinians they were going to kill as many of their compatriots as they could.' Manfull snapped his fingers. 'Didn't you tell Christensen the SIS believed Kransky was working for the Palestinians?'

'Yes I did, but it was a lie. I had no idea why Kransky was of interest to us. The fact is, I had to come up with something when Christensen asked me how the porno movie producer had come to our notice.'

'And what was his reaction?'

'Christensen said he had heard the same thing from his source and that maybe we should compare notes.'

'He tells a different story.'

'You do surprise me,' Landon said drily.

'Christensen maintains you told him the SIS Head of Station in Cairo didn't attach much credence to the report. He then offered to set up a meeting with his source in the Jordanian Embassy who would certainly know if Kransky had visited the Gaza Strip, and you jumped at it.'

'Clever,' Landon muttered.

'What is?'

'The way Christensen has twisted our conversation. The fact is, the first part is true, the second isn't.'

Landon waited, expecting Manfull to fire more questions at him. When none came he recounted everything that had occurred the night before in chronological order starting with the moment Christensen had collected them from the L'Enfant Plaza Hotel. Although unable to give the exact time of the explosion, he recalled glancing at the clock above the service hatch, which was showing ten past nine, and thinking it was a few minutes slow. The explosion had occurred between five and ten minutes later. The interrogation was resumed after Landon told him how Christensen had dragged him towards the serving hatch.

'The room was full of smoke and dust. Right?'

'Yes.'

'But you don't accept that he could have been disorientated?'

'Damned right I don't. We were sitting in a booth near the entrance just four strides from the swing doors. I know because I counted them when I carried Francesca out of the bar and grill. Believe me, Christensen knew where he was going. And he wasn't in a panic when he did this.' Landon removed the dark glasses he was wearing and showed Manfull his right eye. 'The building was on fire and in a last-minute change of plan, he figured it would be neater all round if I was rendered unconscious. That way the police might conclude I'd been a victim of smoke inhalation when my charred remains were found. You find a corpse with a hole in the head and it's murder, not accidental death.'

'How come Christensen didn't mete out the same treatment to Miss York?'

'Probably because he knew she had been severely injured and couldn't move. When I came to she was pleading for somebody to please help her.'

'You say Christensen was dragging you towards the serving hatch?'

'Yes.'

'Why would he do that?'

'Jesus, I don't know,' Landon said, exasperated. 'Maybe he had a trigger man hiding in the kitchen who was supposed to take us out.'

'Maybe,' Manfull repeated with heavy emphasis. 'In other words it's just a hunch?'

'Yeah, if you want to call it that. I can tell you this: Christensen wasn't happy when Francesca and I grabbed a booth near the entrance. He wanted one of the booths facing the serving hatch.'

Manfull stopped the tape recorder. From his shirt pocket he produced a packet of gum, waved it vaguely at Landon, then unwrapped a stick of Wrigley Spearmint and popped it into his mouth. His jaw worked slowly like a cow chewing the cud. For some moments he gazed blankly into space, then switching the tape recorder on again, he began to rewind the cassette, stopping it frequently to play back snatches of the interrogation until he found the section he wanted. When he set it running, Landon heard himself say, '. . . he figured it would be neater all round if I was rendered unconscious. That way the police might conclude I'd been a victim of smoke inhalation when my charred remains were found.' At that point Manfull ran the tape fast forward until the gobbledegook finished and gave way to a faint hissing.

'OK, there was a last-minute change of plan. My question is, why didn't Christensen go for the smoke inhalation angle in the first place?'

'Because I don't think the trigger man had intended to set the Blue Marlin on fire. It was a cockup; instead of functioning like a stun grenade, the bomb was too powerful. Maybe he used too much explosive or else the casing was too thick and retained the explosive energy just that split second longer, enhancing its destructive power. He also positioned the bomb in the wrong place.' Landon pinched the corners of his eyes between finger and thumb in an effort to stay awake. He had hardly slept a wink last night for thinking about Francesca. 'These mistakes happen,' he said wearily.

Manfull switched off the tape recorder. 'OK, that's it,' he said.

'What happens now?'

'I'm going to take you out to dinner, then we'll call it a day. You obviously didn't sleep too well last night.'

Landon didn't bother to deny it. He had been haunted by the conviction that if he had really been firm with Francesca and had told her to stay out of it, she would still be alive.

'Any idea when I might be going home?' he asked.

'That rather depends on the Director,' Manfull told him. 'But my guess is it will be sometime tomorrow.'

Samir Abbas kicked the duvet off, crawled out of bed and went over to the window. Drawing the curtains back with his right hand, he gazed out at the quiet residential street in Falls Church. Jassim had done very well for himself and his family since coming to America. Big house on an acre plot in a highly desirable neighbourhood, a TV in practically every room, two cars in the garage, the children at a private school: the good doctor had a lot to lose, as Abbas had reminded him last night. No doubt Jassim had pointed this out to his wife whose immodest style of dress labelled her for the whore she was.

The children were another problem altogether. You couldn't enforce their silence with threats as you could their parents. Nor could they be trusted to keep a secret. Little tongues had a habit of wagging at just the wrong moment. So yesterday morning their father had told them Uncle Samir, whom they had never met, had arrived during the night from Canada and would be staying with them for a few days.

Exactly how many days depended on what the police had discovered at the Blue Marlin, how much they knew about him and whether anybody had seen Jassim enter the Community Medical Center in Sleepy Hollow in the hours of darkness in order to collect the various drugs, painkillers, antibiotics, surgical dressings and other stuff he had needed to patch him up. There was also the question of how long it would take him to recover from the treatment he had received. Jassim had had to set his arm without the benefit of X-rays and there was a chance it wouldn't mend properly.

Abbas switched on the TV, sat down on the bed and found CNN with the remote control. The number of bodies pulled out of the roadside bar and grill had risen to seven and the police had found a trail of blood leading to a clearing in Branch Park where broken glass from a taillight assembly had been found. There was no mention of the Ford Probe and he assumed the police hadn't found it yet. It wouldn't matter if they had and were playing it close to their chest. The man who had a car repair shop had guaranteed Abbas there was no way the police would link the vehicle to him.

Leroy Manfull was not an ambitious man. All he had ever aspired to was getting himself assigned to the FBI office in

Little Rock so that his wife, who came from Pine Bluffs, Arkansas, could be near her folks. He had attained that desire four years after marrying Sandra-Lee and would still have been working out of Little Rock if it hadn't been for a bunch of home-grown Hezbollah terrorists who had gotten their hands on a 130mm nuclear shell and were going to change the world.

The first time Manfull had met Director Freeh was in 1994 when he had been tasked to run down Louise Kay, the driving force behind the plan to nuke St Louis. He had seen the director on two occasions since then, the most recent being when he was appointed Bureau Chief of the FBI office in Harrisburg, Pennsylvania. The first time he'd met the Director, Manfull had felt uncomfortable in more ways than one. The single-breasted suit he had been wearing no longer fitted him; the jacket was tight across the shoulders and pulled under the arms. Also the zipper in his pants had refused to stay up and had kept inching down in what had been a losing battle of the bulge. This morning he was wearing a made-to-measure suit that was tailored to hide the spare tyre around his waist but he still felt uncomfortable in Freeh's presence.

'So what do you think of Landon's claim?' Freeh asked, waving him to a chair.

'Well, he hasn't deviated from his original statement and I'm inclined to think there might be something in it, Director. He believes the bombing was meant to give the trigger man in the kitchen a clear field of fire. Of course, it's pure conjecture but it carries a ring of truth.'

'And Kransky?'

'I believe Landon when he claims London didn't say why they wanted him to make enquiries about Kransky. What he learned from Mycroft, the MI5 man in the British Embassy, was a nasty surprise, and if he could have gotten out of it, he would have avoided Christensen like the plague, but our Deputy Head of Counter-Intelligence had other ideas.'

Manfull sucked in his stomach to minimise the telltale bulge around his waistline. 'It's only a hunch but I'd bet a month's salary Kransky had a lot of compromising material on some big-shot in London. It would explain why London kept Landon in the dark.'

'Has he been watching CNN?' Freeh asked out of the blue.

'I don't know what Landon did after we had dinner but he certainly didn't watch TV while he was in my company.'

'The incident happened after the last edition of the *Washington News* and the *Star* had gone to press on Wednesday. The *Post* carried the story yesterday and ran it again today in greater detail.'

Manfull wondered where Freeh was going. It sounded as though he was holding some kind of debate with himself.

'If Landon read today's *Washington Post,* he will know that four of the victims inside the Blue Marlin had been shot to death. They were the two short-order cooks and an unidentified man and woman near the bar and in line with the serving hatch.'

'Yes, sir,' Manfull said, feeling that some kind of response was called for.

'I'm not saying that Christensen is in some way connected to a hostile intelligence service but he needs looking at and that's your job. I want you to check out every leakage of classified information to a foreign power since 1991 when Christensen was appointed Deputy Head of the Counter-Intelligence Branch and ascertain how much of the material passed across his desk. I will obtain a list from the CIA of the intelligence acquisitions they copied to us which they believe were subsequently passed to unauthorised recipients.'

Christensen's superior would provide Manfull with details of the FBI's losses; all he had to do then was check the movements of the affected files, papers and communications recorded on the bin cards. The task was to be conducted with the utmost secrecy and Manfull was to report his findings in person to the Director.

'Soon as we can see a definite link between what Christensen has seen and what has been leaked we'll move against him,' Freeh said in conclusion, then asked if he had any questions.

'Only one,' Manfull said. 'What do you want me to do about Landon?'

'Have his statement typed up and get him to sign it, then he can leave this evening.'

Chapter 21

To arrive at Heathrow at 06.25 hours on an overcast, wet and windy Saturday morning was not the most uplifting experience in the world. Landon felt pretty much like the weather – sombre and unsettled. He had travelled light on the outward journey, packing what he needed for three days in a carry-on bag. The same bag was looking slightly fatter on the return leg because it contained the blood-stained suit he had been wearing the night the Blue Marlin was bombed. He passed through immigration, went down to the baggage claim area and, having nothing to declare, made straight for the green channel and emerged in the arrivals hall of Terminal 3.

Ashton was the last person he expected to see.

'You're not here to meet me, are you?' Landon said. 'Victor's due back today, you're waiting for him. Right?'

'If I am, I'm in the wrong terminal building,' Ashton smiled. 'My Volvo's across the road.'

'I can get a cab.'

'Sure you can but you're coming with me.'

Somewhat reluctantly Landon followed Ashton out of the terminal building, across the access roads and into the short-stay car park. The Volvo was as far from the lift as it was possible to be. Dumping his bag in the boot, he closed the lid and got in beside Ashton.

'Is this where the inquest begins?' he asked morosely as they drove out of the car park.

'You're feeling terrible because you think Francesca's death is down to you.' Ashton shook his head. 'Well, you aren't responsible for what happened to her.'

'I wish I could believe that.'

'Listen to me. Francesca was one of the most insecure people I've met. She was a borderline case when MI5 took her on after she left the army, and Richard Neagle wasn't the easiest task-master to cope with. It was touch and go whether she would survive her probationary two years with the Security Service. She was eager to please and was forever trying to notch up Brownie points. She still was by all accounts. Nobody could have stopped Francesca from going to the Blue Marlin that night unless they were prepared to knock her out.'

'That's quite a speech,' Landon said.

'So long as you remember it the next time you are feeling guilty about Francesca.'

Ashton picked up the M4 and headed into town, tyres swishing on the wet surface of the road, the wipers clearing the windscreen methodically.

'Who's conducting the FBI's internal inquiry?' Ashton asked presently.

'A guy called Leroy Manfull, who claims to know you. He said some clerk had scrambled his surname.'

'What did you tell him?'

'What could I tell Manfull? I'd no idea who Kransky was or why the SIS were interested. I should have backed off when Delacombe informed me Kransky was a porno movie producer who'd been murdered along with two of his principal actors. Instead I saw Mycroft, who thought he was being terribly helpful when he put me in touch with Christensen. I wasn't thinking straight.'

'What do you mean?'

'I was told to find out what the FBI had on Kransky, then you instructed me to check with Head of Station first. Soon as I learned how Kransky made a living, I should have walked away from the whole business. Hell, it was Mycroft who suggested that maybe one of the actors was possibly a diplomat and Kransky had turned his hand to blackmail. It even occurred to me the blackmail victim could be a high-ranking member of the intelligence community.'

It was only in the aftermath of the Blue Marlin bombing that the pieces of the jigsaw puzzle had started to come together. Kransky wasn't the blackmailer but he was the man who had provided the material and had been paid for it. He had been shot to death because he could identify the client.

'For the SIS to be interested the intended victim had to be a senior diplomat or one of us. Furthermore, the timing of Kransky's murder suggests the attempt to suborn—'

'Suborn?' Ashton said, interrupting him. 'A moment ago you were talking about blackmail.'

'I'm going with suborn. According to the *Concise Oxford Dictionary* the word means to induce by bribery et cetera, to commit perjury or any other unlawful act. I'd say passing classified information to an authorised person was a pretty unlawful act, wouldn't you?'

'Yes, especially if you've signed the Official Secrets Act.'

'You want me to continue?'

'I'm listening,' Ashton said.

'OK. Kransky is commissioned by Christensen to make a pornographic film involving the intended victim.'

'That's a pretty wild assertion, Will.'

'Maybe, but don't tell me Christensen, with all his years in the FBI, had never heard of Kransky. The man had his studio in Baltimore; that's forty miles maximum from Washington.'

Landon was equally sure Kransky had never met Christensen before he was hired and had had absolutely no idea the client was in the FBI. In all probability Kransky, his wife and the actors had been killed just in case the movie producer did find out who he had been working for. No doubt

Christensen also wanted to make sure no copies of the video had been retained for personal gain at a later date.

'I reckon they were killed the night Christensen took delivery of the videos,' Landon said. 'He passed them on to a third party, which was the limit of his participation. If it hasn't happened already, Jill Sheridan will be hearing from the third party any day now.'

Landon stole a glance at Ashton. There had been no sudden intake of breath, no tightening of his grip on the steering wheel until his knuckles turned white; in fact he couldn't have shown less reaction had he been in a coma. Irritated by Ashton's detached attitude Landon felt compelled to further justify his supposition.

'It has to be Jill,' he said. 'The film was made in America, probably some time in February and she was in Florida only a month ago. If it isn't her, why the interest in Kransky?'

'Did you tell Manfull this?'

'Of course I didn't. If I had, the Friends would be looking at us sideways again, like they did after Burgess, Maclean and Philby. I stuck to Christensen and why I was sure he had tried to kill us.'

'You're right, Jill has been targeted.'

The disclosure had the impact of an IRA blockbuster yet Ashton didn't elaborate, he merely left it hanging in the air as if what he'd just said was of no consequence. The M4 motorway merged with the old Great West Road. He was still silent when they reached the Hammersmith flyover.

'Jill has been targeted: is that all you are going to tell me?' Landon demanded angrily.

'You don't want to know the rest.'

'That's not good enough. There's a chance Francesca died because I was working in the dark.'

'You can forget that premise. I'm afraid Francesca was a

disaster waiting to happen. That may sound harsh and un-feeling to you but it's the truth.'

'You're still planning to keep me in the dark, aren't you?'

Ashton sighed. 'OK, Jill Sheridan informed us an attempt had been made to suborn her. The decision was taken at the highest level to use her as a double agent.'

'And it's happening now?'

'Yes, they've made contact with her.'

'Who do you mean by "they"?'

'Hamas, Hezbollah, Islamic Jihad; take your pick.' Ashton shrugged. 'Could be some terrorist faction we've never heard of.'

'So what happens now?'

'Nothing special. We do what we usually do and go about our normal business looking for some kind of pattern to emerge from the intelligence data we receive.'

Something big had to be in the offing. You didn't set out to ensnare the Deputy DG of the SIS unless you had something spectacular in mind that depended on good up-to-date intelligence. Ashton also thought they were in for a long wait.

It was exactly what Landon had been thinking. The nerve agent found in Stoke Newington had made people extra vigilant and, if past experience was anything to go by, the terrorists would hang back until that wore off as it inevitably would in time. There was nothing so boring as routine security procedures, and observance of them would become more and more cursory as the weeks passed without a terrorist incident.

The street names changed from Great West Road to Talgarth and then Cromwell Road. On a normal workday the traffic would have been crawling from one set of traffic lights to the next. But this was the early hours of Saturday morning and since there was nothing like the same density on the road they made good time.

'My place is the next one on the right,' Landon said as they went past the entrance to Gloucester Road station.

Ashton nodded, moved out towards the centre line, then tripped the indicators and turned into Stanhope Gardens. As vehicles belonging to the residents were parked nose to tail on both sides of the road, Ashton was forced to double bank outside number sixty-two, where Landon had a flat on the second floor.

'You did a very good job over there, Will,' Ashton told him.

'Thanks.'

'What are your plans for the weekend?'

'I'm going to spend a fun morning at the Launderette, then I'll take my suit to the dry-cleaners and see what they can do with it.'

'You're very welcome to spend the weekend with us in Bosham.'

'That's very kind of you but—'

'Think about it,' Ashton said, cutting him short. 'Give me a ring; you've got our number.'

Landon thanked him again, got out of the Volvo, and collected his bag from the boot, then waved Ashton goodbye as he drove off. He walked up the steps and let himself into number sixty-two. Although he had known Francesca for less than a month and could count the number of times he'd seen her on the fingers of one hand, the flat on the second floor had never seemed more empty.

Jill Sheridan was one of those people who rarely went to bed before midnight, never slept more than six hours at a stretch, and didn't need an alarm clock to wake herself up. One moment she could be fast asleep, the next wide awake. The Mozart secure speech facility on the bedside table had been silent all night, which meant there was no reason for her to go into the office. Although the Hazelwoods were returning from

Arosa today their Swissair flight from Zurich arrived at 13.00 hours and Victor would undoubtedly ring her from home. Nevertheless she was, as usual, wide awake at six, some fifteen minutes before the alarm normally went off.

At seven thirty, having lazed in the bath for a good three-quarters of an hour, she went downstairs to enjoy an equally leisurely breakfast in the kitchen. By the time she had read Saturday's edition of the *Daily Telegraph* it was gone ten. It was only then that Jill remembered that she hadn't switched on her battery-powered mobile, which was still in her bedroom next to the Mozart. Heart thumping, she ran upstairs to retrieve it, hoping against hope none of the Emiles had tried to contact her. It was not her lucky day. No sooner had she erected the aerial and switched the power on than the mobile started to ring. Emile Mark III was abusive and almost incoherent with rage when she answered.

'Where have you been, whore?' he snarled. 'Admiring your starring role in Mr Kransky's movie? Bitch. Bitch. Bitch, your phone has been dead for hours.'

'I forgot to switch it on.'

'Lying, no good whore, you are playing games with us.'

'I'm not doing anything of the kind,' Jill told him, conscious of the tremor in her voice. 'I have done everything you have asked me.'

'Then you have the answers we asked for?'

'My God, I only learned what you wanted on Wednesday.'

'You received a postcard on Tuesday—'

'In the evening when I returned home. You didn't seriously think I would go jogging at that time of night after what happened to me?'

'Have you got the information? Yes or no?'

'Not all of it—'

'Why not?' Emile said, interrupting her. 'Where is the difficulty? You are the Deputy Director General and you are in charge because your superior is away on holiday. You told me so yourself.'

'I still need to be very careful how and when I access the files.'

'I think you are under control; someone decides what you can disclose. Since you are a puppet you are of no use to us.'

Jill closed her eyes, listened to Emile threatening to distribute the video to a much wider audience, and cursed Robin Urquhart. It was his fault she was in this mess. The information the Emiles had demanded was out of date and hardly a threat to national security. But timid, gutless man that Robin Urquhart was, he had insisted on waiting until Victor returned before coming to a decision.

'Listen to me,' she said desperately, 'I can give you the whole of Excelsior and seventy-five per cent of Scorpion . . .'

'Why only three-quarters?'

'Because I was interrupted and had to log off, before I had finished. Now do you want seventy-five per cent or nothing?'

'You are in no position to dictate to us.'

'I'm sorry,' Jill said contritely.

'Highgate Public Library twelve o'clock midday, nonfiction department, the section devoted to photography. Are you writing this down?'

'Yes.' Jill grabbed a little memo pad by the Mozart and scribbled 'H.P.L'.

'Good. Leave the material in the book entitled *Landscapes in Black and White*. It hasn't been taken out for months,' Emile told her, and switched off.

It hasn't been taken out for months. The bald statement made her blood run cold.

Ashton turned into the Duke of York barracks on the King's Road, showed his ID card to the armed MoD police officer on the gate, and then parked outside the block occupied by the Brigadier commanding Special Forces and his staff. After dropping Landon off at his flat in Stanhope Gardens, he had driven to Vauxhall Cross, ostensibly to write a report on what he had learned from the debriefing. However, his real purpose had been far different: the PAs worked a five-day week and he had taken advantage of their absence to debug the offices of the DG and Deputy DG before Hazelwood returned.

As had been arranged, Messenger was waiting for him in the entrance. What hadn't been arranged was the presence of the Brigadier, Special Forces to whose office Ashton was escorted. He had met the Brigadier for the first time just three days ago and had been given a hard time by him. Commander, Special Forces had regarded Operation Merlin with the utmost suspicion and in a number of subtle ways had wondered if it had been officially sanctioned. There was, Ashton judged, every prospect of a repeat performance.

'I take it Merlin was successful, Mr Ashton?' he said truculently.

'It served its purpose.'

'Which was?'

'To ascertain to what extent the Deputy DG was at risk.'

'And you have been able to do this in what? Seventy-two hours?'

'Yes.'

'You amaze me, Mr Ashton.'

'You may not be aware of this, Brigadier, but just under three weeks ago Miss Sheridan was mugged on her way home by two young men. Now, although she wouldn't admit it to us, it was obvious she had been badly shaken by the incident. Miss Sheridan became increasingly worried about a report Head of Station, Amman, had submitted at the beginning of the year concerning an Iraqi hit team which had allegedly entered the UK—'

'You've already told me this—'

'The report was from a low-grade source, a Jordanian truck

driver who was employed by UNO to deliver medical supplies to Baghdad. I don't believe I mentioned that in my briefing.'

'You didn't but it doesn't alter the fact—'

'We heard –' Ashton said, cutting him short yet again '– we heard yesterday evening that he had been sacked for stealing medical supplies and selling them on the black market. This was back in December. The man wasn't within four hundred miles of Baghdad when he was supposed to have picked up information in some damned coffee house.'

'A cynic would conclude the timing of that discovery was remarkably convenient.' The Brigadier crinkled his eyes in his characteristic non-smiling way. 'I, of course, am not a cynic. All the same I'm puzzled to know why a lady concerned for her safety should go jogging on a dark winter's morning.'

'Sheer bravado, Brigadier,' Ashton said coolly. 'Miss Sheridan wanted to prove to herself she wasn't afraid. It's the only interpretation we can put on her behaviour, which ran counter to the briefing she had received from our Head of Security.'

Everything Ashton had told him was a lie; now he was about to compound it in writing. From the breast pocket of his jacket he produced four copies of a letter addressed to the Headquarters, Special Forces. Classified Secret, it was headed 'Operation Merlin' and dated 8 March 1997. Typed two-finger-style on Dilys Crowther's word processor, the letter praised the SAS for the way they had successfully conducted a difficult surveillance operation, the requirements of which had been completely at variance with their standing operational procedures. It also singled out the officer known as Messenger for special praise. As a final gesture Ashton signed all four copies above the signature block, two of which he handed to the Brigadier, Special Forces.

'One is for 22 SAS, the other two are for my records and the DG,' Ashton told him.

'How are we to enter this document in a secret register when it doesn't have a reference?'

Ashton produced his pen again and wrote 'DO 1' on all four copies.

'You have quite a sense of humour,' the Brigadier observed. 'In the army, DO means demi-official.'

'Doesn't make the document any less valid. In signing it, I've taken full responsibility for initiating Merlin and closing the operation down. I'd say you were covered, Brigadier.'

'I think we understand one another, Mr Ashton.' The eyes crinkled again but for the first time a faint smile touched the mouth at the corners. 'Let's go across to the mess and have a cup of coffee or something stronger. Merlin doesn't officially close down until 12.00 hours.'

Well, why not? Ashton thought. 'Thank you, I'd like that,' he said.

Before leaving the house, Jill checked the pockets of her leather bomber jacket to make sure she hadn't forgotten anything. Shopping list in the left pocket, the printouts taken from the files relating to operations Excelsior and Scorpion in the other. The latter had been edited to make it appear she had been disturbed by one of the Heads of Departments and had been unable to complete the task. Finally she unfastened her shoulder bag and looked inside to see if she had remembered to transfer her driving licence along with all the other items from the handbag she had been using yesterday. She didn't have a library card but the woman she had spoken to on the phone had assured her one could be issued on the spot provided she produced some means of identification. At eleven twenty-five she left the house, backed the Porsche out of the garage and drove round to the library.

Jill couldn't remember the last time she'd been inside a library, never mind the one in Highgate. It was a lot more crowded than she had anticipated and, with a queue of people at the desk waiting to return and take out books, it was some minutes before anyone could attend to her. There was a nerve-racking hiatus when the librarian asked for proof of her address. Just when it seemed she might have to go back to the house and collect a receipted bill, she discovered a postcard her parents had sent her when they were holidaying in Bermuda eighteen months ago.

From the desk Jill moved to the fiction department and began browsing the shelves. It wouldn't do to choose a book too quickly and then make straight for the section devoted to photography. At the same time she was loath to make the drop too soon. Emile had stipulated twelve o'clock midday; the trick was to leave it until the last few minutes. *Landscapes in Black and White* might not have been taken out for months but that didn't mean someone hadn't leafed through it to see if the book was worth perusing at leisure. Reaching the authors whose surnames began with a T, she took a book by Joanna Trollope from the shelf, then moved to the non-fiction department.

Nobody was interested in photography. Politics wasn't attracting any potential readers either. As casually as she knew how, Jill reached for *Landscapes in Black and White*, flipped the book open and, taking the printouts from the jacket pocket, slipped them between the pages. She then had *A Village Affair* date-stamped at the desk and left. By the time she drove into the car park for the local supermarket, the butterflies in her stomach had all but died.

Ashton had been ready to leave at eleven thirty. He had stayed on drinking coffee and making small talk with the Brigadier because Messenger had left the officers' mess anteroom to take a call on the mobile. Instinct told him the caller was a member of the surveillance detail; it was also unlikely that Messenger was being detained by mere social chitchat. At ten minutes past twelve the SAS officer returned to prove him right on both counts.

'There's been a development,' Messenger said, addressing a fixed point somewhere between Ashton and the Brigadier. 'Miss Sheridan left the house shortly after eleven twenty-five and drove to the public library in Highgate where she spent approximately half an hour. She then left carrying a book in one hand and drove to the supermarket.'

During the time they lived together in Surbiton, Ashton could not recall a single occasion when he had seen Jill with her nose in a book. On Wednesday morning she had gone jogging, later that afternoon she had phoned Robin Urquhart and arranged to see him at the FCO. This morning she had gone to the library to deliver the information the Emiles had asked for. There was not the slightest doubt of that in his mind.

'Well, Mr Ashton?'

'The lady has been known to read a book and she does need to eat, Brigadier.'

'But she stopped at a supermarket on her way home last night,' Messenger said.

'That doesn't surprise me,' Ashton told him coolly. 'I lived with Miss Sheridan for a year or so and I have to tell you she is a lousy housekeeper.'

Chapter 22

Will Landon had been more or less detailed to attend Bill Orchard's funeral on 6 February. No pressure had been exerted upon him to be present at Francesca's; he had gone of his own volition and it had been a journey of discovery that had depressed and saddened him. Francesca had led him to believe she had been born and bred in Scarborough, that her mother was a teacher while her father was a transport manager. In reality Francesca had grown up in Halifax, her mother was a school dinner lady, and her father was a bus driver. The only connection the family had with Scarborough was a fortnight every summer during the school holidays. The comprehensive Francesca had attended had become a minor public school for girls in her imagination.

Both parents had been proud of their daughter and had admired her determination to better herself. The widespread rumour that Francesca had had elocution lessons was proved correct, the assumption that an ambitious mother had arranged them had had no foundation. At age sixteen Francesca had found a teacher in Yellow Pages and had paid for the lessons with the money she had earned working Saturdays as a checkout girl at the local supermarket. After taking her A levels she had enlisted in the army and within six months had been selected for officer training. Listening to the parents, Landon got the impression she hadn't wanted them to attend her passing out parade but in the end they had and that day at

Sandhurst had been one of their happiest memories. That she rarely came home on leave they accepted as a fact of life. Francesca had her own life to lead but she had been a good daughter, never forgotten her mother's birthday and if they didn't see much of her she was always phoning to see how they were.

But the saddest part had been how few had attended her funeral service at the crematorium. Her former colleagues had sent a wreath through Interflora, as had Landon, but neither Colin Wales nor Richard Neagle had been present, and one of them at least should have attended incognito. He still felt badly about that, especially when he recalled how particularly grateful Francesca's parents had been that he had made the effort to be there. Landon knew he should put the whole business behind him and move on. Unfortunately that was easier said than done when you were meeting Wales and Neagle face to face every Tuesday morning. The unresolved incident in Kimberley Road in which seven people had succumbed to nerve agent had given the Combined Anti-Terrorist Organisation a new impetus. Whereas members had previously exchanged information on an as-and-when basis, they now met once a week under the chairmanship of Colin Wales. Today was the fifth such meeting Landon had attended since Ashton had made him the SIS representative. The other members of CATO were a detective chief superintendent from Special Branch, the second in command of 10 Intelligence and Security company, Northern Ireland.

10 Int. and Sy had little to add since the last meeting. The Garda were continuing to monitor the activities of various IRA splinter groups in hiding south of the border. And a fatal shooting outside Carrickmacross in County Monaghan was now thought to herald the start of another wave of internecine killings involving members of the Irish National Liberation Army. Landon didn't have much to say either. Vladimir

Aleksandrovich Labur, the former Director of Chemical Defence Research, had returned to Odintsovo a month ago and despite the expenditure of a small fortune, Head of Station, Islamabad still had no idea who Labur had met while he was in Peshawar.

Special Branch was in a quietly confident mood. Although they were no nearer in tracing the bogus Mr Allum who'd rented the lockups where the nerve agent had been found, their investigation into the business affairs of Gadstar Promotions ordered by MI5 was beginning to bear fruit.

'We've been to Companies House,' the Chief Superintendent informed them, 'and looked at their audited accounts, and in the last two years their turnover has quadrupled. Their list of clients isn't strong enough to result in such a rapid expanse. This leads us to believe they are in the money-laundering business for one of the drug barons in the Golden Triangle or one of the new boys on the block from Afghanistan.'

'Could they have acted for the nonexistent Mr Allum?' Landon asked. 'After all, they're already acting on behalf of Ahmed Shirawai and Abdel Mohammed Zubair, two of the biggest arms dealers in the Mid-East.'

'We may know the answer to that after we have impounded all of Gadstar's records.'

'And when do you see this happening?'

'We're going to make house calls at three o'clock tomorrow morning, Mr Landon.'

'Anything else?' Wales asked, addressing the question to the Detective Chief Superintendent from Special Branch.

'No, that's it for the time being.'

Wales nodded, looked down at the jottings on his millboard and was about to continue when one of the clerks tapped on the door and entered the conference room.

'I'm sorry to disturb you . . .' she began.

'I hope this is important, Alison,' Wales said irritably.

'We think it could be,' Alison said, and handed him a slip of paper.

Wales scanned the note, then stood there transfixed, seemingly unable to comprehend what he had just read. Recovering his wits, he told Alison she was quite right to interrupt the meeting, then turned to Landon.

'This should interest you, Will,' he said. 'CNN is covering a siege situation in Falls Church. The house the FBI and the SWAT team from Washington are watching belongs to a Dr Jassim. The gunman inside is said to be Samir Abbas, who is wanted in connection with the bombing of the Blue Marlin.'

Until nine months ago it had been true to say the admin staff at Vauxhall Cross had never seen a clerical officer quite like Nancy Wilkins. She had joined the SIS from a local radio station where, despite a first in media studies, she had been employed on the front desk answering the phone and making cups of tea for visiting dignitaries with no prospect of advancement. On her first day at Vauxhall Cross Nancy had appeared in trainers, jeans and a denim jacket over a dark blue cotton shirt. She had a taste for wearing some pretty outrageous outfit in leather, suede or PVC. Then suddenly the wet look, the skin-tight toreador pants and the microminis, which Jill Sheridan in a moment of crudity had once described as a pussy pelmet, were out. In were low-heeled shoes and smart business suits.

In assessing her when she was finishing probationary period as a clerical assistant Kelso had described Nancy Wilkins as bright, keen, conscientious and cheerful. For once Ashton had found himself in complete agreement with the Admin King. In the time he had known her she had gone from strength to strength and was, in his opinion, better than a lot of Grade III intelligence officers. Nancy could read a situation, anticipate events and was prepared to take whatever action was necessary in the absence of her superior officer. These days she normally answered to Will Landon. Since he was attending a meeting of the Combined Anti-Terrorist Organisation in Gower Street, she went straight to Ashton.

'I've just been watching the on-going CNN newscast on Sky,' Nancy said, coming straight to the point. 'I think you should pop down to the reference library and take a look.'

'OK, let's go.' Ashton collected the key to his office from the top shelf of the combination safe and followed Nancy out of the room, locking the door behind him. 'What am I going to see?' he asked as they made their way to the bank of lifts.

'A house in Falls Church where Samir Abbas, the man who allegedly bombed the Blue Marlin, has been hiding out for the past five weeks.'

'How did you learn this story was breaking?'

'On Will's instructions I watch CNN news every morning. He instituted the regime on his return from Washington. He was expecting something to happen and told me to look out for anything to do with the Blue Marlin.'

They reached the bank of lifts in time for Nancy to hold an empty car before it began to descend. Once inside the car she pressed the button for the second floor.

'The great thing about CNN, Mr Ashton, is the way they continually update any major story. This means I can register, file, and flag up the incoming mail knowing I won't miss anything of importance.'

The TV was in the small reading room, which formed part of the reference library. When they walked in, the cameras were focused on a large white house, the lawns front and back edged on three sides by trees and shrubs virtually isolating the property from the neighbouring houses. In Washington it was five thirty-two in the morning and first light was just beginning to show. The house, however, was illuminated by floodlights, which the SWAT team had set up. What was going on inside was impossible to see because all the curtains were drawn. As always when nothing was happening, the anchor man in the studio and the reporter on the ground were reduced to speculation. The main talking point was the length of time Samir Abbas had spent in the house. It was assumed that Dr Jassim had sheltered him under duress to begin with but during the five weeks Abbas had been in hiding it was felt the family must have had a number of opportunities to contact the police. That Jassim had done so in the end was beyond doubt; what puzzled newsmen was why he had waited so long. It was known Abbas had been injured in the bombing of the Blue Marlin and they assumed the good doctor must have obtained what he needed from his practice at the Community Health Centre in Sleepy Hollow.

'I think I've seen enough,' Ashton said. 'Could you continue to monitor the newscast until we hear from Head of Station, Washington?'

'I'd be happy to,' Nancy told him.

Ashton thanked her, left the library and returned to the top floor. What was happening in Falls Church could spell the end of the double-cross game before it was really up and running. He walked into the PA's office and tapped on the communicating door. Dilys Crowther didn't like anybody entering the inner sanctum unannounced but no red light was showing above the door and there wasn't much she could do about it.

'Do come in and make yourself comfortable,' Hazelwood said acerbically.

'I'm sorry but this is important.'

'It had better be.'

Ashton saw him reach under the desk and knew Hazelwood had pressed the red button. In a few brief words he told Victor what was going on at Falls Church and the probable relationship between Samir Abbas and Christensen.

'Even if the FBI do manage to take Abbas alive I doubt they will get much from him. But Christensen is a different matter;

if the evidence against him is strong enough he could be facing the death penalty. When push comes to shove Christensen will talk and I wouldn't mind betting he has a copy of Kransky's video.'

Hazelwood reached for the ornate cigar box and helped himself to a Burma cheroot. 'That could be a mite embarrassing,' he said. 'What do you suggest we do? Dump Jill?'

'You won't have much choice if the FBI get their hands on a copy of *It Happened One Night.*'

Hazelwood struck a match and lit the cheroot. 'I don't believe it's that cut and dried,' he said between puffs. 'It's surprising what dividends a successful counter-intelligence operation can produce.'

'I don't believe I'm hearing this,' Ashton said in a quiet voice. 'What's our line going to be? That Jill participated in a sexual romp involving lesbianism, three in a bed, bondage and sodomy for the sake of Queen and Country?'

'Now you're being ridiculous.'

'We're in the middle of a general election, Victor. Polling day is three weeks this coming Thursday. The opinion polls haven't changed and New Labour is set to win by a landslide. The media has made the Tory Party synonymous with sleaze. You don't think New Labour wants to be tarred with the same brush, do you?'

'If we prevent a major catastrophe the politicians won't care how we did it. The double-cross operation is just beginning to lift off and I'm not prepared to advise my colleagues that we should abandon it on the strength of what you've told me.'

'Would you say this was a textbook operation?'

Hazelwood flicked ash from the cheroot and studied the glowing tip as if he had no recollection of lighting it. 'What's on your mind, Peter?' he asked.

'Several things, all involving Jill. Landon knows about her

star part in a porno movie. When he asked about Kransky, Delacombe sent him to see Mycroft, the Embassy Security Officer, and thereafter Will was on a runaway train. The rest you know.'

'Landon should have got off the damned train when he learned how Kransky made his money.'

'You weren't in his shoes, Victor, neither was I. Will guessed that for us to be interested, Kransky must have something on a high-ranking diplomat or a senior intelligence officer. He came to the conclusion that if he backed away from meeting Christensen, it would create a lot of dangerous speculation. It was a classic case of the adverse effect the need-to-know principle can have when it's carried too far.'

'I see.' Hazelwood glowered at him, then exorcised his anger by crushing the Burma cheroot to pieces in the brass ashtray. 'What other bad news have you been holding from me in these past five weeks?'

'While you were in Arosa I bugged your office and Jill's. I also arranged for her to be kept under surveillance.'

After that disclosure, the rest was comparatively easy. Contrary to what Ashton had anticipated there was no furious outburst from Hazelwood when he told him who had participated in Operation Merlin and what had been learned from it.

'The facts are simple enough,' Ashton said in conclusion. 'On Wednesday, March the fifth Jill was seen by the team leader returning to her house in a tracksuit and pumps. This was at a time when most people were still in the process of getting up to face the day. He thought she had been jogging in Waterlow Park. That afternoon she rang Robin Urquhart and arranged to meet him—'

'I know all about this,' Hazelwood said, cutting him short. 'Jill told me herself. For your information she went to the dead letter box in Highgate Cemetery, which Urquhart subsequently confirmed. What you did was totally reprehensible.'

'And Urquhart told Jill that when the Emiles contacted her again she was to stall them until you returned.'

'Which she did.'

'Wrong. The day you were flying home Jill went to the public library in Highgate and took out a book.'

'You're suggesting the library was used as a dead letter box?'

'I never knew Jill to visit the library in Surbiton when we were living together,' Ashton said.

'Landon represents us at CATO?'

'Yes.'

Hazelwood fell silent for what seemed an eternity. There was an even chance he would decide to remove Landon from the Combined Anti-Terrorist Organisation, which would be seen as a demotion. If this should be his intention, Ashton was determined to fight him all the way.

The necessity didn't arise; instead Ashton was instructed to take Landon aside and warn him of the consequences should he so much as breathe a word of what he had learned in Washington.

'He's to remain a member of CATO,' Hazelwood continued. 'Everything he passes on at the weekly meeting will be vetted by you beforehand. The prime task of your department is to keep after Labur. Do you have any questions?'

'Am I allowed to ask if the Emiles have contacted Jill again?'

'You may and they have. So far Jill hasn't been required to produce anything we can't live with.'

'They're still showing an interest in ancient history?'

'You could say that,' Hazelwood told him.

It was Dilys Crowther's job to record the minutes of the daily staff meeting universally known as morning prayers. The minutes were classified Secret and to an outsider provided an indication of the strategic direction the SIS was taking. The testing time would come when Jill was asked to provide a copy of the minutes.

Shortly after Ashton had returned to his office, Nancy rang to say that in the latest up-date CNN had referred to two police officers who had been shot and killed as they were trying to get in position.

Abbas was sitting on the floor in the den, his back to the internal load-bearing wall. The only window in the room was a narrow oblong slot some four and a half feet wide by five inches high, which was positioned near the ceiling. The glass, reinforced with wire mesh, was, he estimated, slightly thicker than the length of the little finger, and therefore tough enough to take the sting out of a high-velocity bullet. There was, however, little danger of the police opening fire. Standing on a chair, hands tied behind her back was Jassim's wife, Noor, her face from eyebrow to chin framed in the window. Although her back was towards him, Abbas had turned the portable TV on the desk around so that he could see her face on the screen.

It wasn't a good picture because the cameraman had to stand in rear of the police line. The reporter made up for the poor quality of the visual display with an imaginative description of how Noor Jassim was bearing up under the stress of being a hostage. The CNN reporter kept reminding his viewers that the SWAT team had with them a trained negotiator who had established contact with Samir Abbas and had actually spoken to Mrs Jassim on the telephone. He was able to describe her state of mind on the basis of what the negotiator had told him. The great American public was being encouraged to believe the siege would be ended with no further loss of life purely on the basis that Abbas had released the younger child at 8 a.m., followed by the elder one hour and twenty minutes later. According to the anchor man in the studio it was the negotiator who was controlling events, which was laughable. Abbas had released the children at staggered intervals simply to buy time in which to prepare a very nasty surprise.

It had never been his intention to spend over five weeks hiding up in the Jassim household but the good physician was an incompetent doctor. The gash had turned septic and even after the pus had been drained, the wound had continued to throb until Jassim had had to put him on a course of antibiotics. He had also made a bad job of setting his fractured arm and had had to break it and do the job all over again.

Jassim had kept his family under control for the first three weeks, telling the children that their uncle from Canada had been taken ill and would be staying with them until he was better. They hadn't questioned the story; it had been Noor who'd complained, whined and nagged Jassim like a shrew. Abbas had heard her pouring poison into her husband's ear when the children were asleep, telling him he would spend the rest of his life in prison when the police found out he had been sheltering a wanted man. And then what would she and the children do after they had been deported to Iraq?

Abbas couldn't say when she had finally got to him but he could pinpoint the moment Jassim had gone across. Every night before the Jassims retired he disconnected all the phones in the house and took them into his bedroom where he then reconnected the answer machine. This precautionary measure allowed patients to contact the doctor during silent hours but the Jassims were unable to make any outgoing calls except through him. There had been a couple of instances in the last five weeks when Jassim had been called out between the hours of 8 and 11 p.m. and there had been no problems when he was away from the house. But today's call had been different. It had been made at exactly on the hour at 01.00, which had made Abbas suspect it had been prearranged. His usual practice was to stay with Noor Jassim virtually holding a pistol to her head until her husband returned. This morning Abbas had made her dress and tie up both children before doing the same to her. He had then moved all three hostages into the den before turning the house into a minor fortress. From the integral garage he had taken a gallon can of gas belonging to the lawnmower, a quart of paintstripper and a bottle of turpentine, materials he would use to close with Satan's men when the time came. He had surprised them once already by killing two members of the SWAT team as they tried to position themselves either side of the front door; he would do so again. The telephone rang, breaking the long silence. Lifting the receiver, Abbas prepared himself for another session with the negotiator.

From the outskirts of Bosham to Roseland Cottage in Church Lane always seemed the longest part of the journey to Ashton. He had tried to phone Harriet a few minutes after six when he was about to leave the office. Unfortunately he had picked a bad time and had ended up talking to the answer machine in the study, a room Harriet rarely entered. It wouldn't be the end of the world if she hadn't set up the VCR but he would have liked to see the resolution of the hostage situation at Falls Church. On the other hand it was possible the house where Samir Abbas had been lying up was still under siege.

Ashton turned into Church Lane and parked the Volvo down the side of Roseland behind Harriet's Citroën ZX. He let himself into the cottage and moved purposefully down the hall towards the study before calling out he was home. Harriet appeared from the sitting room on his right.

'You don't have to sneak into the study,' she told him, smiling. 'I got your message and acted on it.'

'What makes you think I was trying to sneak past you?'

'Well, your hand is on the door knob.'

'I was looking for you. I called out and when you didn't answer I thought you might be in the study watching TV.'

'Nice try, Peter.'

'I thought so too.' He seized her hands and drew Harriet gently towards him until their knees were touching. She was wearing low heels, which meant she was over six feet and marginally taller than himself. 'How long have we got before dinner?' he asked, and released both hands to clasp her thighs.

'Not long enough for what you have in mind,' Harriet told him.

'That's a pity.'

'Yes it is, but there's always the rest of the evening.' She placed her hands against his chest and straightened both arms, pushing herself away.

'Now go and look at the recording while I see to the casserole.'

Ashton went into the study, switched on the television and found CNN on the satellite dish while the video was rewinding. Falls Church was no longer a news item and he played about with the tape, moving it fast forward until the camera zoomed in on the front door and a woman emerged from the house.

She started running towards the police line as fast as she could with her hands tied behind her back. Abbas appeared to have stuffed a piece of rag into her mouth, which was held in place by a thin leather belt. Then suddenly a tongue of flame raced after her and in the blinking of an eye she became the focal point of a conflagration. Two paramedics carrying blankets raced to smother the flames. In that same instant Abbas came out shooting and cut both men down. There was a fractional pause before every member of the SWAT team opened fire and continued firing until Abbas stopped moving.

Ashton stopped the tape and rewound it. Any hope of establishing a link with Christensen had been snuffed out. It was, he thought, all the encouragement Hazelwood needed to persist with the double-cross game.

Chapter 23

The homes of Eleanor Gadsby and her two co-directors had been raided simultaneously at 03.00 hours on Wednesday, 9 April. All three directors had been detained under the Prevention of Terrorism Act and held in police custody at different stations, Eleanor Gadsby at Paddington Green, and her colleagues at West End Central and Bethnal Green. Exactly four hours later that same morning the offices of Gadstar Promotions in Bruton Place off Berkeley Square had been raided. In the presence of Ms Gadsby's solicitor, every bank statement, invoice, receipted bill, cheque and deposit book had been seized and taken to Scotland Yard, as were the audited accounts for the past seven years, VAT records, computer disks, current files and office diaries.

Landon had been present when the police had arrested Eleanor Gadsby at her flat in Bayswater, and again when they had searched the offices of Gadstar Promotions. At Wales's suggestion he had also sat on the initial interrogation of Eleanor Gadsby. He hadn't contributed anything to the proceedings but then nobody had expected him to. Colin Wales was running CATO and he had been keen to weld the representatives drawn from MI5, the SIS, Defence Intelligence MoD and GCHQ Cheltenham into a cohesive team. Although in the early stages of the investigation Landon's presence had been largely symbolic, he had come into his own once the full extent of Gadstar's business activities had become known and he had been given something to work on.

Eleanor Gadsby had initially been detained for seventy-two hours under the Prevention of Terrorism Act, following which Special Branch had obtained an extension of a further seven days. However, on Thursday, 17 April, eight days after her arrest, Eleanor Gadsby had appeared before the stipendiary magistrate at Horseferry Road charged with four offences under the drug trafficking act of 1994 and had been remanded in custody, the police having opposed bail. Instead of being taken straight from the court to Holloway Prison, she had in fact been returned to Paddington Green where she had spent the night.

The woman who was waiting for Landon in the interview room was a very different person to the one he had met at Orchard's funeral. Gone was the smart business executive; in her place was a dowdy woman who looked her age and a bit more. The dark smudges under her eyes suggested she hadn't been sleeping too well of late.

'Good morning,' Landon said, and sat down facing her across the table with Colin Wales on his left.

'You may think so, I don't.'

'We'll have to see what we can do about that,' Landon said cheerfully. 'You never know, things may not look quite so bad after you've answered some of the questions we have regarding Mercury.'

'Who's he?' Eleanor asked, smirking.

'Don't get smart with me,' Landon told her. 'Mercury is the name of a bucket shop selling airline tickets at discount prices. It's owned by you personally and not Gadstar Promotions. So is Far Away For Less, a travel agency with branches in Acton, Barking, Dagenham, Peckham, Southall and Southwark.'

'Is that such a crime, Mr Landon?'

'It is when you falsify tax returns. The Inland Revenue hasn't got around to hitting you with that yet but they will.'

'I'm not easily frightened, Mr Landon. After all, what's the worst that can happen to me? The tax man doesn't want to send me to prison because I'm no good to him inside,' Eleanor smiled. 'No, he's only interested in collecting what I owe him, plus interest charges, plus a punitive fine. Whatever sum is involved won't be a problem. As a matter of fact I've already instructed my solicitor to settle the tax demand as soon as it's presented.'

'Then he will have to use his own money,' Wales told her.

'What do you mean?'

'I mean your personal current account with the Bayswater branch of Lloyds Bank plc has been frozen, as have the current and deposit accounts of Gadstar Promotions with Natwest. As of this minute all the money you have in the world is in your purse. And that's with the custody officer.'

'Then I'll have to refer the Inland Revenue to you, Mr Wales,' Eleanor said coolly.

'And the World Wide Trading Corporation in the Cayman Islands? Who will you refer them to?'

'Why should I need to refer them to anybody, Mr Landon?'

She had intended to convey astonishment but there had been a nervous edge to her voice and he knew she was rattled. The World Wide Trading Corporation wasn't a client; to all intents and purposes it owned Gadstar Promotions, using the company to launder money earned in the poppy fields of Afghanistan and neighbouring Pakistan. Just who was behind the corporation had yet to be established but for the moment this was immaterial.

'You're a greedy bitch,' Landon said casually, 'that's your trouble. The World Wide Trading Corporation enabled you to set up in business on your own account and continued to reward you for every transaction you effected on their behalf. But you wanted more and misappropriated their money to get it by speculating on the stock market. Trouble was, you picked a lousy set of brokers.'

For a time Charles Yarpole Associates had been coining it in by charging low premiums for high-risk insurance. When the bottom began to fall out of the fire and maritime insurance market, Eleanor Gadsby had been unable to settle her account with the brokers without misappropriating even more money from the World Wide Trading Corporation.

'I don't know exactly when in April nineteen ninety-five Bill Orchard began to have an affair with you,' Landon continued, 'but I can prove exactly when he became your lifeline.'

'You're talking absolute nonsense.'

'You blackmailed Orchard into becoming a name at Lloyd's, then cut a deal with Charles Yarpole Associates, who agreed to pay you a percentage of what they got from him.'

'You can't prove it.'

'I don't have to, Eleanor. I will simply write to the head office of the World Wide Trading Corporation in the Cayman Islands and tell them what you've been up to. I don't think they will be very happy.'

'Go to hell,' she told him without much conviction.

'You must know you are facing a custodial sentence, Eleanor, but don't make the mistake of believing you will be safe in prison. I hope you can take care of yourself because there are women on the inside who will happily kill you for a few ounces of crack.'

Landon expected Eleanor Gadsby to call him every name under the sun; instead she quietly asked what he would be prepared to do for her if she answered his queries regarding Mercury.

'We would tell the judge how helpful you had been.' Landon glanced at Wales. 'Right, Colin?'

'We would certainly do our best to influence whatever sentence the judge may have had in mind.'

It sounded like a ministerial statement prepared by a civil

servant which for all its apparent commitment, lacked real substance. Landon thought they should dangle a bigger carrot in front of Eleanor Gadsby.

'We'll go all out to get you a suspended sentence.'

'That's more like it.'

'But first you have to earn it. You get nothing for free in this world.'

Landon unzipped the thin documents case in black leather and took out a photocopy of a single page torn from a desk diary covering Monday, 24 February and Tuesday, 25th.

'This was taken from your appointment diary,' he said, and handed the photocopy to her. 'You had three appointments on the Monday, at ten fifteen, twelve noon and three thirty. Immediately after the last appointment you made some notes in pencil which were subsequently erased. The indentations left by the pencil were illegible to the naked eye but there's nothing like a spot of ultra-violet for enhancement.'

'Many of the letters still appear to be missing.'

'That's because you were using a unique and personal kind of shorthand,' Landon said. 'In this instance one-one-nine is a British Airways flight number, ISBD stands for Islamabad, Pesh is short for Peshawar. The question mark after it suggests the individual concerned hadn't disclosed how he intended to travel from Islamabad to Peshawar. All I want from you is the name and address of the client and date of departure from Heathrow.'

'How do you expect me to remember some insignificant detail which occurred almost two months ago?'

'Don't give me that,' Landon snapped. 'It's the only entry of its kind in the diary and was so incriminating you attempted to erase it completely. So do yourself a favour and start remembering.'

There was a long silence which led Landon to think Eleanor

Gadsby feared a custodial sentence less than she did the people who had set her up in business. He could not have been more mistaken.

'The client's name was Raja Usman. When the ticket was issued he was living at sixty-one Woodhall Road, Southall. Usman flew to Islamabad on Monday the third of March.'

She hadn't made any arrangements for his onward journey to Peshwar because Usman had been unable to say how long he would be staying in Islamabad.

'Who told you to book the flight to Islamabad?'

'The arms dealer Abdel Mohammed Zubair. He rang my office number from Beirut.'

'Thank you,' Wales said, terminating the interview with a glacial smile. 'We shall have to see how helpful you have been.'

Wales reached under the table and pressed a call button. It was only when a police constable immediately entered the room and beckoned Eleanor Gadsby to follow him that it dawned on her she had been dismissed. Incredulity was replaced by anger; on her way out she leaned over Wales and invited the MI5 officer to go fuck himself.

'You must have been sleeping,' Landon said angrily when they were alone.

'What!'

'When the Director of Humint at Langley was delivering his lecture on Human Intelligence Sources. As I recall, you publicly declared you had benefited from his dissertation.'

'Eleanor Gadsby is a thoroughly unpleasant woman.'

'Nobody said you have to like your informants.'

'And nobody said you have to go overboard when dealing with them,' Wales retorted. 'You offered that woman the sun the moon and the stars above. She was lying in her teeth just now because you practically invited her to do so.'

'Everything fits together. Vladimir Aleksandrovich Labur, the former Director of Chemical Defence Research arrived in

Islamabad on Tuesday, March the fourth, and there's a pretty good chance this Raja Usman went there to meet him.'

'You're jumping to conclusions,' Wales said.

Wales had given Landon Eleanor Gadsby's appointments diary to work on after one of his own officers had examined it. Either his subordinate had failed to spot the indentations below the entries for Monday, the twenty-fourth or had considered them to be of no consequence. Whatever the explanation, they hadn't escaped Landon's notice and with the help of Terry Hicks, he had enhanced the indentations and made sense of them. Now this man Wales seemed to be rejecting his findings out of hand. He recalled what O'Meara had told him concerning a discussion Colin Wales had had with Commander Operations, Special Branch on the line MI5 proposed to take should Porton Down confirm that all eighteen cases of whisky found at forty-four Kimberley Road contained nerve agent.

'Are you trying to tell me we are not going to check Gadsby's information out?' he demanded angrily.

'It's time I was going,' Wales said, and got to his feet. 'There are things to do.'

'You haven't answered my question.'

'We'll be knocking on the door of sixty-one Woodhall Road tomorrow morning three o'clock sharp. You're invited.'

After six weeks and one day in Washington, Manfull was more than ready to go home. Unfortunately when he could or could not return to his wife and family in Harrisburg Pennsylvania, was up to FBI Director Louis Freeh. Manfull had given Director Freeh a verbal progress report every Friday pertaining to the on-going investigation of Christensen; today Manfull intended to submit the definitive version in writing, which summarised everything he had learned about the Deputy Chief of Counter-Intelligence. His appointment with Freeh had been set for 8 a.m. However, when he reported ten minutes early to

Mrs Sharon Lunt, the current PA, he was shown straight into the Director's office.

'Is that a written report you are holding in your left hand?' Freeh asked after they'd shaken hands.

'It is, Director.'

'OK, leave it on my desk, take a seat and tell me all about it.'

'Well, sir, from January the first nineteen ninety-one when Christensen became Deputy Chief of Counter-Intelligence and July the ninth nineteen ninety-six, the date of the last known breach of security, there have been seventeen major leaks of classified information to a foreign power.'

'How have you personally defined a leakage? By quantity or classification?'

'A combination of the two,' Manfull told him. 'The material must be graded Secret and contain more than one page.'

The biggest leak had occurred during Desert Shield, which had started on Wednesday 8 August 1990, when the first planeloads of American troops had landed at a military air base outside Dhahran, to the conclusion of Desert Storm on Friday 1 March 1991 with the total defeat of the Iraqi forces occupying Kuwait. The leaks had begun six weeks after the cessation of hostilities but only one item had passed across Christensen's desk.

'This was a report detailing the many failings of the CIA in the run-up to Desert Storm and afterwards. The agency's evaluation of the Iraqi army was said to have been based on out-of-date information. This was followed by a disjointed psychological profile of Saddam Hussein presented by two CIA analysts, which allowed the reader to draw whatever conclusion he wanted. And finally, the CIA's habitually negative assessment of the damage inflicted on the enemy by the air force, which they fed the President. Personally I reckon the paper is overgraded but I guess the author slapped a Secret classification on the document to mitigate the CIA's embarrassment and limit the paper's circulation.'

'Did Christensen receive a copy?' Freeh asked.

'No, but his initials are on the document and he had plenty of opportunity to photocopy it.'

'Can we prove that?'

'No.'

'What of the other sixteen major leaks? How do they break down?'

'The Defence Intelligence Agency suffered four major lapses of security in the period April 'ninety-one through to February 'ninety-four, all relating to US dispositions in South Korea. The Bureau didn't get a sight of any of those papers, which lets Christensen off the hook. Same applies to seven State Department papers relating to South America and the Caribbean. The remaining six were CIA briefing papers on the Mid-East and North Africa. We were an info addressee in every case. The papers are held in central registry and the records show Christensen signed them out on twenty-three separate occasions in the last six years, which is almost twice as many times as the Head of Counter-Intelligence did. There was no problem about photocopying what he wanted because the machine's in the next-door room and is unguarded. Furthermore, let's not forget that Christensen had constant access to the rogues' gallery.'

Freeh raised an eyebrow. 'You mind explaining what you mean by the rogues' gallery?'

'The profiles we maintain on people like Peter Ashton.'

'At the risk of repeating myself, can we prove that Christensen has been passing information to representatives of a foreign power?'

'The short answer is no.'

It hadn't been for the want of trying. The investigation had been less than a week old when Manfull had decided it was necessary to put Christensen under surveillance. For maximum security he had, with Freeh's prior agreement, summoned four agents from the Harrisburg office. With the permission of the owner, who had been sworn to secrecy, two agents had been installed in a house diagonally across the road from Christensen's property in Alexandria.

'Do you get the impression Christensen has been keeping a low profile since the bombing of the Blue Marlin?'

'Not as far as his social life is concerned. He's been out and about on the town and is running a couple of girlfriends – a navy wife who's separated from her husband and a civilian photo interpreter in the Defence Intelligence Agency. They're strictly for sex.'

'Are you sure of that?'

'Very,' Manfull said.

'I won't ask how you know.'

Freeh picked up the written report Manfull had left on his desk and returned to the summary of recommendations on the end page.

'You're saying we should subject Christensen to a hostile interrogation?'

Manfull nodded. 'I think Christensen should be invited to explain why he had those briefing papers out twenty-three times. Other than sitting around waiting for him to do something stupid, I believe it's the only way ahead. I've also recommended we should turn his place upside down.'

'We have a small, maximum-security interrogation centre out on the Allentown Road. You can use that.'

'Am I to understand you want me to handle the interrogation, Director?'

'With the help of the men you summoned from Harrisburg. Do you have a problem with that?'

'No,' Manfull said, and tried to sound as if he meant it.

'The place hasn't been used in quite a while. If we put a clean-up team in there today we should have it ready by Tuesday morning.' Freeh looked up. 'I'm just thinking aloud.'

'Right.'

'Maybe you and your people had better get off back to Harrisburg and reassemble here on Monday afternoon. I imagine that will suit you?'

Manfull smiled. Damn right it would.

Late afternoon or early evening was never a good time to see Hazelwood, especially on a Friday when he was even more reluctant to go home. Although Victor would never admit to it, Ashton knew the thought of spending the entire weekend with Alice really appalled him and there was nothing he wouldn't do to postpone that inevitable moment for as long as possible. Ashton had spent more time in Victor's company on a Friday evening than the rest of the SIS put together. This was hardly surprising because their relationship went back to the days when Victor had been in charge of the Russian Desk and Ashton had been his gofer.

However, ever since he and Harriet had settled in Bosham, Ashton avoided the Friday night sessions whenever it was possible. Today was one of those occasions when he couldn't slide away. Hazelwood had been on the go all afternoon, shuttling between Vauxhall Cross and the Foreign and Commonwealth Office north of the river. This was the first time he had been available and there were things the DG needed to know before Ashton went home. Since Dilys Crowther had left the office on the dot of five, Ashton simply knocked on the communicating door and walked into the DG's office. Out of politeness he asked Victor if he could spare him a few minutes.

'Take as many as you like,' Hazelwood told him.

'It concerns the final arrangements for the police raid on sixty-one Woodhall Road, Southall.'

'Oh yes.'

'It's been enlarged: Special Branch is now going to lift Mullah Aziz al Bashir, an Islamic Fundamentalist cleric who has a mosque in Ealing. They're also going to interview the manager of the Southall branch of the Far Away For Less travel agency.'

'Good. Anything else?'

'No, that's it.' Ashton had never seen Hazelwood so withdrawn and down in the mouth. 'What's the matter, Victor?' he asked.

Hazelwood opened the ornate cigar box he'd bought in India long ago when on a field trip. He took out a Burma cheroot and tapped one end against the desk as if to firm up the leaves then, abruptly changing his mind, he returned the cheroot to the wooden box. 'We're getting deeper into the mire,' he said in a tired voice. 'What they now want from Jill is a photocopy of every communication we've received from Head of Station, Washington.'

'From when?'

'Since the beginning of nineteen ninety-six.'

'That's a lot of material,' Ashton said. 'Delacombe had a reputation for firing off a cable at the drop of the hat.'

'Is that all you can say?' Hazelwood barked, and struck the desk with a clenched hand.

'No, it isn't,' Ashton told him coolly. 'You have to dump Jill before things get even worse than they are now.'

'I'm afraid we're in too deep for that.'

'Then make sure we don't give the Emiles anything which could damage relations with our friends across the water.'

'What makes you think I haven't already thought of that?'

'Their demand doesn't make sense. They already have a high-ranking source in place.'

'Meaning Christensen?'

'Yeah.' Ashton snapped his fingers. 'It has to be a ruse,' he said. 'They want us to take our eyes off the ball.'

'You want to tell me where the ball is?'

'I wish I could,' Ashton told him.

Chapter 24

When built in the early nineteen-twenties all the houses in Woodhall Road had been identical three bedroom semi-detacheds. The more expensive properties, which sold at nine hundred pounds, had more land and included a garage. There were eight such semi-detacheds in Woodhall Road, which had accurately reflected the number of car owners among the residents before the war. In the fifty-plus years since the end of World War Two, the neighbourhood had changed out of all recognition. Uniformity had disappeared and no two properties were exactly alike. Front gardens had been concreted over to provide hard standings for motor vehicles; rooms had been extended front and back, and lofts developed into studies, playrooms or an extra bedroom. But it wasn't only the bricks and mortar that had changed; of the residents living in Woodhall Road in nineteen thirty-nine not a single one now remained, and English was said to be a minority language.

They travelled in convoy with two police Transits in the lead, followed by Colin Wales and the Detective Chief Superintendent from Special Branch in an unmarked car. Landon was way back in the rear, nursing his ailing Ford Escort, which was getting temperamental in its old age. The leading Transit turned off the High Street and entered Colnbrook Avenue while the rest of the small convoy went on a further forty yards before turning left into Woodhall Road. Despite the home improvements two cars in the family still meant on-street parking both sides of the road. Unable to see the house numbers because of the parked cars, the driver of the Transit slowed right down to a walking pace and swept the houses with a vehicle-mounted spotlight. Even so, he overshot number sixty-one and started to back up until the driver of the unmarked car warned him off with a sharp pap on the horn.

There was no moon, and the stars were hidden by the overcast. At 03.00 hours on such a still, dark morning, the horn sounded loud enough to wake the dead, never mind the living. As Landon got out of the Escort, lights in the upstairs rooms on either side of sixty-one came on. Eight uniformed police officers under an inspector spilled out of the Transit, ran back to Raja Usman's semi and stormed up the front path. A window opened upstairs in number fifty-nine and someone with a high-pitched voice called out in a strange tongue.

'Police,' Wales yelled back, 'don't be alarmed.'

The occupants of number sixty-one had good reason to be alarmed. A police officer wielding a fourteen-pound sledge-hammer smashed the door in, springing the Yale lock from its housing and reducing the panels to kindling. Eight policemen, two of whom were armed, went into the house, twice as many residents came out. Five emerged through the side windows of the downstairs front room. One sat on the windowledge of the front bedroom and pushing himself off, landed awkwardly, breaking an ankle. The Detective Chief Superintendent grabbed two very wiry individuals and tried to keep them at arm's length as they did their best to hack him in the shins with their bare feet. Trouble was, both men were wearing precious little clothing and a cotton vest didn't give the Chief Super much to hang on to. Wales grappled with the largest of the absconding five, announced triumphantly that he'd got him, then gasped for breath and sank down on to his knees as he took a vicious punch in the stomach. As the man drew back a foot to kick Wales in the head, Landon hacked his left leg from under him and elbowed him in the face as he went down.

Landon then assisted the Chief Super to arrest the two would-be runaways he was endeavouring to detain at arm's length.

The jumper from the first-floor bedroom was lying on the patch of lawn nursing his broken ankle, the big man was too busy tending to a bloody nose to think of running off and the two wiry individuals weren't going anywhere. The other escapers from the side window were legging it down the road. It seemed they were not the only ones on the trot, with the hubbub inside the house now abated, Landon could hear the distant sound of raised voices in Colnbrook Avenue.

'This is a bloody shambles,' the Special Branch Superintendent yelled at Wales. 'Any minute we'll have a race riot on our hands.'

'Well, what do you expect me to do about it?' Wales asked plaintively.

The question went unanswered. Kneeling on his prisoner to pin him down, the DCS pulled out his mobile, made a 999 call and asked to be connected with the police operator. After identifying himself and giving his present location, he requested additional officers in riot gear plus dogs with handlers to deal with worsening situations. He also estimated he would need a minimum of two Black Marias, assuming they succeeded in picking up the missing occupants of sixty-one Woodhall Road, who were now running around Southall in their underwear.

It had, Landon reflected, been their intention to arrest one suspected terrorist; instead it looked as though they had disturbed a small host of illegal immigrants. He hoped the other snatch party was having better luck with Mullah Aziz al Bashir. A few minutes later the first milk bottle came sailing out of the dark to shatter on the pavement outside the house.

The Islamic fundamentalists' mosque in West Ealing was a converted restaurant off the Uxbridge Road, the unsuccessful owner of which had tried to recoup his losses from the White

Star Insurance Company. However, thanks to the quick
response of the fire brigade, the property had only been slightly
damaged and instead of the half million he had hoped for, the
owner had been sentenced to eight years imprisonment for
arson. The Muslim community had purchased the damaged
building and had lovingly transformed it into a mosque.
Unfortunately in the last three years the moderate element had
been driven out by Islamic fundamentalists led by Mullah Aziz
al Bashir.

Since the middle of 1996, Special Branch had been keeping
an eye on Aziz al Bashir, a firebrand of a cleric who preached
violence and regularly called for an Islamic jihad against
America. Although his language was generally inflammatory,
he had never openly advocated violence against the British and
up till now had been regarded as something of a blowhard. The
discovery of the VX nerve gas at forty-four Kimberley Road
had heightened interest in Aziz even though there was no
evidence to connect him with the lock-up garage in Harrow
where the lethal agent had been stored.

If ever a man could be said to live over the shop it was Aziz
al Bashir. The mosque was actually a hundred yards south of
the junction of Larkspur Crescent with the Uxbridge Road.
Access to the flats above what was still essentially a shopping
precinct was via an unmade-up lane behind the crescent, which
was used by trucks delivering goods and produce to the
grocery, Muslim butchers and fresh vegetable store. The
snatch party consisted of three Special Branch officers armed
with 9mm P9S Heckler and Koch semi-automatic pistols, and
Richard Neagle, who was travelling independently in his own
vehicle. Their means of entry was considerably more sophisticated than the fourteen-pound sledgehammer favoured by the
uniform branch in Woodhall Road. Aware that the door to Aziz
al Bashir's flat was reinforced with steel plates and dead bolts
top and bottom, they had decided to go in through the kitchen

window. To effect the entry they had brought with them a glass cutter, two suction pads with wooden handles and a pair of metal shears.

They approached the flat from the direction of the Uxbridge Road, both drivers cutting the main beams as they turned into the lane. The flat above the mosque was the fifth one down and they crept towards it in first gear, revving the engine just enough to carry the vehicles forward at a walking pace to the back gate. Copying the Special Branch driver, Neagle switched off the ignition, got out of the car and closed the door silently. The back gate had warped and would have scraped against the concrete yard if they hadn't managed to lift it a fraction as they pushed it open. An iron staircase led to the reinforced kitchen door and the open veranda where a dustbin was positioned near the kitchen window. As was the case with other properties in the shopping precinct, the fire escape was a Jacob's ladder, which hooked into anchor points in the two front rooms overlooking the street. The ladder represented the only escape route for Aziz al Bashir.

The Detective Sergeant in charge of the Special Branch detail placed the suction pads at either end of the windowpane, then cut the glass as close to the frame as possible. Thereafter it was comparatively easy to lift out the sheet of glass and stand it against the outside wall. On the inside, covering the entire length and breadth of the window was a metal grille set into the outside wall at the four corners. It looked a formidable obstacle but in the hands of the Detective Sergeant the metal shears cut through the four securing flanges like a knife going through butter. With the help of one of his subordinates, he turned the grille sideways on and carefully withdrew it through the frame.

The need for stealth was no longer paramount and they went in fast, the Detective Sergeant in the lead. Neagle, being unarmed and far less agile, followed on in the rear at a more leisurely pace. The only occupants of the flat were an old woman in her seventies, who was frightened out of her wits, and a young boy between ten and twelve years old. When the Asian member of the Special Branch team started to question him, it was immediately apparent that English was his first language. His name he told them was Karam, and the old woman was his grandmother in whose charge he had been left while his parents and older brothers had returned to Pakistan two weeks ago to visit family and friends. He did not know why he and his grandmother were living in the flat belonging to Aziz al Bashir when the family home was in nearby Hereford Road.

From the grandmother the Asian Special Branch officer learned that they had moved in nine days ago at the request of Mullah Aziz to look after the flat in his absence. She did not know where he had gone or when he would be back.

Special Branch had come armed with a search warrant and, ignoring the wails of protest from the old woman, they proceeded to take the place apart. Aziz al Bashir received unemployment benefit and supplementary income from the Department of Social Security. In a chest of drawers they found £36,000 in packets of ten-, twenty- and fifty-pound notes.

From the moment the first empty milk bottle had shattered on the pavement outside number sixty-one to the dispersal of the crowd, the riot in Woodham Road lasted seventy-nine minutes. The milk bottles had not remained empty for long; almost within the blinking of an eye, a gang of youths at the High Street end of the road were busy siphoning petrol from the cars parked on both sides of the street. Since Landon's Ford Escort had been nearer the petrol bombers than the police vehicles, it had inevitably become the prime target. Hit by three bombs in rapid succession, it had soon been engulfed in flames.

From the doorway of number 61, Landon had watched the car windows implode one by one in the heat. In what had seemed no time at all there had been an almighty blast as the fuel tank exploded. The boot had been rent asunder and most of the roof had lifted off and landed in somebody's front garden on the opposite side of the road.

By the time the riot squad had begun to arrive piecemeal via Colnbrook Avenue and Cross Street, the unmarked car belonging to Special Branch had been burning nicely. So had the Volkswagen Passat and a Saab 900 owned by two unfortunate householders who had parked their vehicles in the wrong place at the wrong time. Initially the riot squad had numbered only ten officers under an inspector, which had been just enough to form a thin blue line from pavement to pavement. They had then advanced beyond the burned-out Ford Escort and halted, crouching behind their plastic shields while they waited for reinforcements. A little over half an hour later the inspector had sufficient officers under his command to disperse the crowd and effect nine arrests.

After the last of the occupants of 61 Woodhall Road had been carted off to Southall police station in the High Street, Landon went forward to see what was left of his car. It was, he supposed, pretty masochistic of him but there had been a bronze medallion in the glove compartment which he'd won at the South of England Judo Championships and he was curious to know if it had survived the fire. There was, however, no way of finding out; the heat had been such that the glove compartment had been welded in place.

'That's what I call rotten luck,' Wales said joining him. 'Will your insurance cover the loss?'

Landon shrugged. 'I don't know. I'll have to look at the policy and see if there's a let-out clause for damage incurred during a civil disturbance.'

'Well, let's hope you are covered. I want to thank you for saving me from a long spell in hospital. If you hadn't intervened, I would have taken one hell of a kick in the face. I hear you're a judo champion?'

'Losing semi-finalist in a minor competition.' Landon smiled. 'What I did to your assailant had nothing to do with judo. It was street fighting pure and simple.'

'On another matter,' Wales said, changing the subject, 'I'd like you to be present when I interview Raziuddin Jilani.'

'Who's he?'

'Jilani is the manager of the Southall branch of Eleanor Gadsby's travel agency.'

Wales hoped Jilani might have met Raja Usman and could describe him or, better still, pick him out of the identification parade Special Branch would be organising. There was a lot to sort out and Wales doubted if they would be ready before eleven. In the meantime he proposed to send Landon back to his flat in Stanhope Gardens.

'I'll send a car to pick you up from there at ten. That should give you plenty of time for a quick wash and brush-up. OK?'

'That's fine by me.'

Landon took one look at the burned-out cars and the broken glass, stones and half-bricks that littered the street and thought Wales was being hugely optimistic. Woodhall Road had been the scene of a pitched battle, and the incident was going to be the lead story on all the television channels and the press over the weekend. The police would be dealing with a whole army of journalists and the chances of holding an identification parade at eleven o'clock were about zero. But that wasn't his problem.

The 12,000-ton freighter had originally been owned by the Bibby Line when she had been registered as the SS *Clearwater Bay*. Built by Stuicken Sohn, Hamburg and launched in May '71, the *Clearwater Bay* had entered service a year later plying between her home port of Hong Kong to Malaysia, China, Japan, Indonesia and the Philippines. In 1989 she had been sold to Nikos Karavias, a would-be shipping magnate, renamed *Thalia Helene* in honour of his daughter and registered in Panama to avoid taxes. With Piraiévs as her home port, the *Thalia Helene* traded for the most part in the Eastern Mediterranean, calling at Beirut, Port Said, Alexandria and Bari.

As of that Saturday morning the freighter was two days out of Port Said bound for Bari on the Adriatic coast of Italy, where the *Thalia Helene* was due to arrive on Monday 21 April. While hardly a cargo passenger liner, the *Thalia Helene* could accommodate up to eight guests. On this particular voyage there were only four, a Mrs Rita Foss, a widow in her late sixties who was a frequent traveller with the Karavias line, a Mr and Mrs Papadakis from Athens, and a Mr Edward Jaffar, who had boarded the ship at Beirut after presenting bills of lading for a consignment of ceramic rooftiles destined for a builders' merchant in Hertfordshire. The tiles had been manufactured in Baghdad and, in defiance of the sanctions imposed by the United Nations, had been trucked to Beirut via Damascus. From Bari onwards the tiles would be conveyed to England by road transport, as had the previous consignment, which had arrived safely a month ago. A man of many passports, Edward Jaffar's real name was Raja Usman.

Landon reckoned Raziuddin Jilani was no more than five feet six, probably weighed between 120 and 130 pounds, and was small-boned. He was very affable, courteous and had a pleasant manner; he was in fact the sort of man anybody but a member of the British National Party would take to on sight. Instead of summoning Jilani to the police station, Wales and Landon had walked up the High Street to the travel agency, a courtesy that made him even more eager to be helpful when he learned the nature of their enquiries.

'I remember Raja Usman very well.' Jilani smiled, revealing a gold tooth. 'I never met him, of course, but my word, the troubles we had with his plane ticket. Miss Gadsby tells me to get him on the British Airways flight to Islamabad on Monday, the twenty-fourth of February, then four days after I have made the booking, she says it had to be a week later.'

Landon supposed he might have known Eleanor Gadsby would not be entirely honest with him. She had allowed him to believe that the indentations in her appointment diary for Monday the twenty-fourth referred to the instructions she had received that day from the arms dealer Zubair. Why she hadn't bothered to correct this false impression was immaterial; what interested Landon was why the date of departure had been put back a week. He wondered if it had anything to do with Vladimir Aleksandrovich Labur. Maybe the Russian had been forced to postpone his visit to Islamabad and GCHQ hadn't intercepted his message to that effect?

'Do you make out the plane tickets?' Wales asked.

'Oh, no. Like all our competitors we go to a firm specialising in air travel and they issue the ticket and send it on to us. We then inform the client that the ticket is available for collection.'

'And this is what you did for Raja Usman?'

'My goodness, if only it had been that easy. With the first booking, I wrote him a letter—'

'And sent it to sixty-one Woodhall Road?' Wales said, interrupting him.

'Yes indeed. But there was no time to do that when the departure date was changed. Miss Gadsby told me Raja Usman would pick the ticket up from the British Airways desk in Terminal Three. Unfortunately the ticket was already in the post to us and this could not be done.'

Since Raja Usman had refused to collect the ticket from the agency, the only solution had been to send them by courier to Heathrow on the day of departure. The courier, of course, had to know Usman, and vice versa.

'And presumably you also knew the courier by sight?' Landon suggested.

'No, he arrived with a letter of authorisation from Miss Gadsby.'

Miss Eleanor bloody Gadsby had some explaining to do, Landon thought savagely. From the expression on his face it was evident Wales shared his opinion.

'It was very odd,' Jilani continued. 'We had to pay the fare twice because of the late cancellation but we never received a penny from Raja Usman. Perhaps Miss Gadsby was reluctant to charge him.'

That was something else they would be asking the lady in due course.

'This courier,' Landon said, 'could you describe him?'

'Not very well but I might recognise him.'

'We're about to hold an identification parade,' Wales informed him. 'Would you be willing to accompany us to the station?'

'With pleasure,' Jilani said.

The identification parade was held at 14.30 hours. By then, Special Branch had learned that some twenty-one men had been living at sixty-one Woodhall Road, of whom eight were still at large. Those in custody were paraded in two batches; the courier was not among them but Jilani did recognise one man whom he knew quite well. His name was Omar Zenined, a Moroccan who had been employed temporarily by the travel agency during the long vac.

'Are you telling us he is a university student?' Landon said.

'Oh yes, he is doing a postgraduate course at Imperial College of Science and Technology. He is a very clever young man and is sure to get his doctorate in chemistry.'

Chapter 25

'All the business of war, and indeed all the business of life, is to endeavour to find out what you don't know by what you do; that's what I called "guessing what was on the other side of the hill".' When Ashton had been at Nottingham University the training major of the Officers Training Corps had been a huge admirer of Wellington and that particular quotation had been one of several displayed in his office. What the Duke had said all those long years ago was equally true of any intelligence service. Sometimes, however, what you did know was precious little and no help at all when it came to finding out what you didn't know. Listening to Will Landon it seemed to Ashton that five days after the mini riot in Woodhall Road they were still in the business of gazing into a crystal ball.

'Let's see if I've got this straight,' he said after Landon had paused for breath. 'Among all the Asian illegal immigrants who were lodging at sixty-one Woodhall Road, you have this Moroccan graduate student, Omar Zenined. He has been linked to Aziz al Bashir by one of the illegals who claims to have seen them together. Zenined is up for a doctorate in chemistry and making VX by the bucketload would be child's play for him. Correct?'

Landon nodded. 'So far.'

'Then we have Mullah Aziz al Bashir, an Islamic fundamentalist who's skipped the country leaving thirty-six thousand pounds in a chest of drawers. This makes him the paymaster of the terrorist cell. Raja Usman flew to Islamabad in all probability to meet Vladimir Aleksandrovich Labur and is still in Pakistan, as far as we know. The thinking is he could be the mysterious Mr Allum who rented the lock-up garages in Harrow. Correct me if I'm wrong, Will, but isn't this the line MI5 is working on?'

'Well, Colin Wales is pretty cock-a-hoop about the way things are going. He reckons the police can soon go public on the Kimberley Road incident because they have identified the terrorist group and it's just a question of running them down.'

'Any idea which movement the group belongs to?'

'The favourite is Hezbollah, but that's just a guess.'

'Is the courier a member of the cell?'

'They're treating him as such,' Landon said. 'Unfortunately, they don't know his name. Neither, it seems, does Eleanor Gadsby. She maintains that when her secretary presented the authorisation for her signature, she didn't look at the name on the docket. While not a hundred per cent sure, the secretary is pretty certain Ms Gadsby gave her a slip of paper with the courier's name printed on it. Special Branch is going to have another chat with Ms Gadsby. They're confident her memory can be restored.'

'Has Wales thought how this Hezbollah lot might have released the nerve agent given the chance?'

'He thinks they would have favoured the Tokyo solution.'

Ashton vaguely remembered the incident. In March 1995 members of the fanatical Aum Shinrikyo Buddhist Sect had boarded trains on three of Tokyo's subway lines during the morning rush hour. The terrorists had been carrying lunch boxes and soft drink containers and had released the agent by puncturing the containers with a sharp implement before leaving the train. Eleven people had been killed and some five and a half thousand had needed hospital treatment.

'There's a full report of the Tokyo incident in the reference library,' Ashton said thoughtfully.

'I know, I've signed it out.' Landon paused, then said, 'Actually there were two attacks and the agent they used was sarin.'

'And that makes a difference?'

'Well, it's nonpersistent, which makes it easier to deal with. Of course, it's still lethal but the sarin produced by the Aum was pretty low-grade stuff compared with Russian munitions, or the Iraqi weapons for that matter.'

'There's something else we should bear in mind,' Ashton said. 'As far as I know only the Iraqi armed forces have used chemical weapons in earnest. They resorted to nerve agents in the war with Iran and subsequently to crush the Kurds in northern Iraq. Question is, what do we do now?'

'Colin Wales is acting as if the threat of a chemical attack is history.'

'And what's your opinion, Will?'

Landon shrugged. 'I guess I've got an open mind.'

'Good. An open mind is a prerequisite in our line of business.'

What the SIS tried to do was make sense of a mass of information from various sources, many of which were unreliable. It was like completing a jigsaw puzzle without knowing what the subject was.

'Occasionally when some of the pieces interlock you begin to think you know what it's all about. And that's when you are in trouble because when a piece doesn't fit, you're apt to hammer it into place.'

'Thanks for the tip.'

'Don't mention it,' Ashton said. 'Just keep me posted.'

Right from the moment he had walked into Christensen's office in the FBI Building, Manfull had sensed the Deputy Chief of Counter-Intelligence was going to be a tough nut to crack. The drive out to the interrogation centre on the Allentown Road hadn't fazed him one bit; if anything Christensen had given the impression he was on a high. The interrogation centre was a forbidding place in the middle of nowhere, a small compound enclosed by a metal fence ten feet high, which over the previous weekend had been topped with razor wire.

When not being questioned for hours on end, Christensen was incarcerated in a cell designed for maximum discomfort. The only two items of furniture were a bucket for use as a lavatory and a bed board resting on four concrete blocks that raised it six inches above the floor. There was no window and the cell could be made pitch-black at the touch of a switch. Flick the switch the other way and a powerful light out of reach in the ceiling made sleep impossible. There were absolutely no creature comforts for Christensen: his food was intentionally disgusting and the only facilities accorded him was a bowl of cold water first thing in the morning. After just two days in custody he was already beginning to smell.

But the harsh treatment hadn't undermined Christensen yet. He remained unfailingly cheerful and was eager to co-operate because, hey guys, they had made a big mistake and he was just as eager as they were to straighten things out. He had turned over all his bank statements, told his broker to answer any questions they might have, and had happily disclosed the entry code to his personal data base. Financially he had come out squeaky clean: there were no offshore bank accounts and Christensen's lifestyle was in keeping with his salary. Above all, there was nothing to suggest he was in receipt of cash injections from a dubious source. Nothing had been found in his house in Alexandria, which had been searched from top to bottom. When challenged to explain why he had signed out the six CIA briefing papers on the Mid-East and North Africa on twenty-three separate occasions, Christensen had claimed he'd needed time to check the information his source in the Jordanian Embassy had given him.

The only blemish on his character that Manfull could find was a failed marriage when Christensen had been in his twenties. There were no signs of homosexual tendencies, there were no items of women's clothing anywhere in the house that would label him a transvestite and while he might play the field and bed other men's wives, he didn't appear vulnerable to blackmail. A gut feeling that Christensen would sell his own mother for the sheer thrill of it was the only reason Manfull had to press on with the interrogation until hell froze over. It was the conviction that Christensen was a traitorous son of a bitch that had brought Manfull back to the house in Alexandria in the hope of finding something incriminating.

So far he hadn't found a damn thing. He had been through every room in the house, as well as the garage and the workshop in the back yard, knowing all the time the search team had done a thoroughly professional job the first time around. Back in the family room once more, Manfull flopped into an armchair and gazed blankly round the room: music centre, bookcase, TV, video recorder and a stack of videos in a purpose-build cabinet. He left his chair to have a closer look at the cabinet, curious to learn something of Christensen's tastes. There were a number of old favourites that he'd bought, movies like *A Few Good Men, Sleepless in Seattle* and *Witness*; others were ones Christensen had recorded himself, ranging from documentaries to educational programmes, all neatly labelled and boxed.

Manfull ran a finger along the titles and on a whim plucked *American Wildlife Part I* from the top shelf. Switching the TV on, he inserted the cassette into the video and set it running. 'A Thomas Kransky Production' appeared on the screen, followed by, in Gothic script, '*It Happened One Night* starring Sara Gay and Dan Swordsman'. The names of the stars dissolved and the words 'Introducing Jill Sheridan' appeared in blood-red letters.

'Jesus Christ,' Manfull breathed, 'it can't be.'

The opening scene had been shot in a sleazy-looking bedroom and showed an ash-blonde flouncing around in high heels and stockings while making lewd conversation with a buck-naked hunk of a man whose pectoral muscles had been burnished with oil. Then a second woman appeared in high-heeled sandals, hands shackled behind her back, a large brown paper bag over her head. Presently the ash-blonde moved behind her and removed the hood to reveal Jill Sheridan full frontal, with a black leather collar two inches wide around her neck.

Manfull stopped the video and rewound it. He had studied the rogues gallery, as he had called it, and knew beyond a shadow of a doubt that the woman he'd just been looking at was the same Jill Sheridan who was Deputy Director General of the Brits' Secret Intelligence Service. Even if his fingerprints weren't on the cassette he still had Christensen behind the eight ball and there was no way the Deputy Chief of Counter-Intelligence could explain what the porno movie was doing in his possession. What he had to do now was get the video over to the Bureau and let the fingerprint experts see what they could lift. Chances were *American Wildlife Part II* was a duplicate copy of *It Happened One Night*, and would therefore require careful handling.

The video would loosen Christensen's tongue because it implicated him in four homicides and he would want to cut the best deal he could for himself. Manfull knew that sooner rather than later, the Deputy Chief of Counter Intelligence would tell him which Mid East terrorist organisation he had been working for and how he had been recruited. It was possible that way back in time he had been passing low grade information to the Russians who had sold him on to the financial backers of Hezbollah, Hamas, Islamic Jihad or whatever terrorist group Abbas had been connected with.

There remained the problem of what to do about the Brits. They would hardly have left Ms Sheridan in place if they knew about the porno movie. Did he tip them off at his level or did he leave it to the Director to pass on the good news? Manfull flipped a coin to answer the question, then ignored the result and decided to phone Ashton anyway.

The truck was a thirty-eight-ton juggernaut owned and driven by the brothers Umberto and Gianfranco Varvesi. At the back of the cab behind a curtain was a comfortable bunk bed, which the brothers used alternately to catch a few hours' sleep while the other drove. This, coupled with the occasional judicious adjustment to the tachometer, enabled the Varvesis to cover up to six hundred miles in any twenty-four-hour period, including time spent loading and unloading freight.

The *Thalia Helene* had docked at Bari on Monday, 21 April at 07.30 and had begun to discharge her cargo, a task that had been completed twenty-four hours later. The brothers had left the port at nine o'clock on Tuesday morning and headed north on the A14 Autostrada Bologna, a distance of 422 miles, where they had picked up a further load. From Bologna their route took them to Calais via Chambéry, Lyon, and Paris, a further 890 miles.

The Varvesis had hoped to make the midday sailing to Dover on Thursday but a lightning strike by SeaFrance had led to a long jam at the ferry terminal. Directed to a waiting area, the brothers had been informed that with any luck they might get away on the 08.00 sailing the following day. After advising the various consignees of the delay, they had adjourned to the nearest *estaminet*.

In the event they got away an hour earlier than they had been led to believe. They had passed through Dover many times and knew a number of the customs officers by sight. On every other occasion they had been waved through but this time they were directed to an inspection bay. Both Umberto and Gianfranco were more annoyed than they were alarmed.

When the BT phone rang Ashton simply lifted the receiver, grunted hello, and continued reading the latest intelligence summary on known Mid-East terrorist groups. Then Landon told him he was about to receive a phone call from Leroy Manfull and he was all ears.

'How do you know?' he demanded, and mentally kicked himself for asking a damned fool question.

'I inherited your office, remember?'

'And my old extension.'

'Yeah. Manfull hasn't got your new one; he still has you down for 0028. That's why he came through to me.' Landon heard the distinctive note of the Mozart as it began to ring. 'That'll be him now,' he said, and hung up.

Ashton did the same, then picked up the secure speech handset. 'So how are you, old friend?' he asked after the FBI agent had identified himself.

'I'm doing great, how about you?'

'The same,' Ashton told him. 'Now that we've got that out of the way, what can I do for you?'

'You ever seen a movie called *It Happened One Night*?'

'Which one? The classic starring Claudette Colbert and Clark Gable, or the porno of the same name?'

'Do you know the producer?'

'I've heard of the late Tom Kransky but I never met him.'

'Then I guess Eric Christensen is also a familiar name?'

'Will Landon did mention him,' Ashton said carefully.

'Let's stop pussyfooting around with each other,' Manfull told him sharply. 'Christensen is a goddamned spy, and I've just found two copies of that porno movie in his house. Now what have you guys done about Jill Sheridan?'

'She's still in post.'

'Jesus H. Christ. What's with you people?'

'She's a key player in a double-cross operation. Right now three men calling themselves Emile think they are controlling her.'

'And she has been supplying them with false information?'

'You wish,' Ashton said, then told Manfull exactly what was going on and what the SIS hoped to achieve. When he finished there was a long silence, as if somehow they had lost the satellite link. 'Are you still there?' he asked.

'Yeah. I'm thinking.' There was another break, but much shorter this time. 'Are you asking me to hold back, Peter?'

'Absolutely not. You and I are not going out on a limb for this one. Soon as we've finished this conversation, I'm going to brief my Director General and tell him that if he wants you guys to hold off he will have to sell the idea to your boss and the CIA. Meantime you do what you have to do and don't wait a second.'

'Thanks, that's what I hoped you'd say.'

Ashton put the phone down and left the office, locking the door behind him. Dilys Crowther tried to dissuade him from confronting the DG unannounced and pointed to the red light above the door but to no avail. Hazelwood wasn't best pleased to see him; neither was Jill Sheridan.

'Come back later,' Hazelwood said testily. 'Can't you see I'm busy?'

'It's over,' Ashton told him, and related the conversation he'd had with Manfull word for word.

'Did you tell him America is under threat?' Jill asked, tight-lipped with anger.

'That's a big assumption, Jill.'

'Did you tell him?' she snarled.

'No I didn't. Who around here has been telling the CIA what's going on?' He turned to Hazelwood. 'You know what I've said to Manfull, the rest is up to you, Victor.'

'Thank you for pointing that out to me.'

Ashton walked out, leaving them to it. A harbinger of bad news was never likely to win a popularity contest but a neutral observer listening to Hazelwood and Jill Sheridan might conclude they believed he had deliberately sabotaged the double-cross operation. Outside in the corridor, Landon was waiting for him.

'Not more bad news?' Ashton said wearily.

'Depends how you look at it. I've just taken a call from Max Brabazon. Seems customs at Dover have impounded a thirty-eight-ton juggernaut which was carrying long-range multiple rocket launchers and chemical munitions. Max said the chemical munitions certainly weren't produced by a sixth former working for his A level in chemistry.'

'Do we know which country supplied this military hardware?'

'Not yet.'

'What about Customs – were they tipped off?'

Landon shook his head. 'It was just a spot check. Then one of the customs officers heard a tapping noise and when the trailer was opened there were twenty-odd illegal immigrants in the back who were trying to sneak into the country. Naturally the Varvesi brothers, who own the truck, are under arrest.'

'Good. Now get on to Customs, Will, and find out if the brothers have passed through Dover before and, if so, did the officer who stopped them know the Varvesis by sight. If you have any problems getting the information, go see Brian Thomas in Security Vetting and Technical Services. He has any number of acquaintances in the upper reaches of Scotland Yard who owe him a favour or two.'

'Right.'

'Soon as you've done that, get the ops room set up. Chances are it will be our home for the next few days.'

Ashton unlocked the door to his office and went inside. In

rapid order he made three phone calls. The first was to Max Brabazon, who informed him the rocket launcher had been identified as a Russian-made 122mm BM-21 (40 round) Multiple Rocket System, which had a maximum range in excess of twelve miles. The second was to Colin Wales, who knew all about the incident at Dover and was endeavouring to find out the name and address of the consignee. Last of all, Ashton rang the long-suffering Harriet to warn her he wouldn't be coming home that night or the next few either.

Raja Usman had returned to England travelling on a British passport under the name of Syed Haroon. From Bari he had gone by train to Rome, where he had caught an Alitalia flight to Berlin. Twenty-four hours later he had taken the shuttle to Düsseldorf, transferred to Lufthansa Flight LH4110 and had arrived at Heathrow Terminal 2 at 14.10 hours on Wednesday the twenty-third. He was clean-shaven, wore a single-breasted blue pinstripe and carried an executive briefcase. Mrs Rita Foss and Mr and Mrs Papadakis from Athens, his fellow passengers on the *Thalia Helene*, would never have recognised him. Immigration hadn't even spared him a glance; neither had Customs as he went through the green channel.

The courier, Ibrahim Ali, who had delivered the plane ticket to Islamabad seven weeks ago, had been there to meet him near the bureau de change as they'd arranged. After collecting the Citroën XM from the short-stay car park where Ali had left it, they had driven across London and had picked up the A10 via the North Circular.

The dilapidated farmhouse Usman had purchased at the beginning of the year was on the outskirts of Deep Hollow, a tiny hamlet eighteen miles north of London between Ware and Sawbridgeworth. During the war a searchlight detachment manned by ATS girls of Anti-Aircraft Command had been based on the six-acre plot of land attached to the property. All that now remained to mark their presence was a Nissen hut with one end open to the elements. Eight miles due east of Deep Hollow was a wartime airfield that had been constructed for the American Eighth Air Force. With the control tower, dispersal aprons, and concrete runways still in place, what had once been prime farmland was now only fit for grazing sheep. Purely for camouflage Usman rented a few acres and had a small flock of sheep, which were looked after for a small consideration by a farmer who lived nearby.

On and off, Usman had spent most of the day there since 10 a.m. waiting for the Varvesi brothers to deliver the second consignment of multiple rocket launchers and munitions. He knew for a fact that they had caught the 07.00 sailing because they had phoned him soon after embarking. The time was now five minutes to six and there was no point waiting any longer because it was quite evident they weren't going to show.

Cold with anger, Usman switched on the ignition, started the engine and drove the flatbed truck back to the farm outside Deep Hollow.

Chapter 26

Normally the SIS Threat Assessment Team would have been chaired by the Deputy DG but there was very little that was normal about Jill Sheridan's situation and she had ruled herself out before Hazelwood did. Roy Kelso was the senior Assistant Director; however, he had always been admin and therefore had little practical experience to contribute. Although the most junior Assistant Director, Ashton had had operational experience in Belfast, the Falklands and South West Africa. He had also been a member of the Combined Anti-Terrorist Organisation since its inception, which in Hazelwood's opinion made him the ideal choice.

In addition to Heads of Departments, the first meeting of the Threat Assessment Team was also attended by Will Landon, and Chris Neighbour from the Russian Desk, the in-house authority on Russian-made weaponry and chemical munitions. After making a brief opening statement, Hazelwood turned the proceedings over to Ashton and withdrew to attend an emergency session of the Joint Intelligence Committee under the chairmanship of the Cabinet Secretary.

'You've all heard what Victor said. We have to assume the weaponry intercepted at Dover wasn't the first consignment.' Ashton looked round the table. 'Anyone disagree with that assumption?' he asked.

Nobody did. They were already aware the ceramic tiles had been destined for the A to Z Builders' Merchant, Coney Road, Sawbridgeworth. At the request of Customs and Excise the

Hertfordshire constabulary had checked out the address and reported that no such firm existed.

Ashton turned to Neighbour. 'All right, Chris, tell them what you know about the 122mm BM-21 multiple rocket launcher.'

'The system had been around for a long time,' Neighbour said, and cleared his throat. 'It first appeared on a parade in Moscow in November nineteen sixty-four. Currently it's in service with Afghanistan, Egypt, Iran, Iraq, India, Pakistan, Libya and other countries in North Africa and the Far East.'

The 122mm BM-21 had a range slightly in excess of twelve miles, took ten minutes to reload and was normally mounted on a Zil 151 6x6 truck chassis. VX was a persistent nerve agent that in summer would last for three days after release.

'Death by inhalation or absorption through the skin is almost instantaneous unless the casualty is wearing protective clothing as well as a respirator and has been issued with an individual decontamination kit.'

'So we are looking for a Zil truck with six-wheel drive?' Garfield drawled.

Neighbour shook his head. 'Any flat-bed truck with a capacity in excess of three tons will do.'

'Does anyone disagree that London will be the prime target?' Ashton asked.

'Not if you intend to kill as many people as possible,' Calthorpe said. 'The question is, where and when can you guarantee such a target? At some major sporting event like the cup final?'

'They don't need a major sporting event,' Landon said quietly. 'The morning rush hour will do. King's Cross, St Pancras and Euston mainline stations are less than half a mile apart. Then you've got another concentration in Waterloo, Charing Cross and Victoria. Throw in all the Underground stations within those two areas and you've got one hell of a target. During the three-hour morning peak, thirty-four thousand people enter Victoria, London's busiest tube station.'

'How do you know that, Will?'

'Nancy Wilkins got it from the Internet half an hour ago. It was her idea to see what if anything they had on London's transport.'

'Smart girl,' Ashton said, and meant it. 'Any other points, Will?'

'Yes. We're busy putting a range of one-inch-to-one-mile Ordnance Survey maps together covering an area twelve miles out from the centre of London.'

'North, south, east or west?' Garfield interjected.

'North,' Landon told him. 'The area is more sparsely populated and it's easier to hole up. Also the rocket launchers and munitions were consigned to that part of the world.'

'The false address could be part of the deception plan,' Garfield observed loftily.

'We go with what we've got,' Ashton said.

'With respect, it's not your decision,' Garfield told him.

'It's my recommendation, Rowan. We can't sit back waiting for the Varvesi brothers to tell us where they delivered the last lot. When they do, we'll have to think again if it proves necessary.'

There were other recommendations Ashton proposed to make. There were to be no obvious signs of activity by the security forces, which meant no helicopters buzzing around like demented bees whose hive had been overturned. The area to be covered should be divided into sectors, and each sector control headquarters should have adequate response teams on immediate standby.

'They will have missed the rush hour tonight,' Ashton said in conclusion. 'The next prime time is Monday morning; let's get them before the weekend is over.'

'Surely there must be some way we can deter them and gain a little breathing space,' Garfield said, and looked hard at

Landon to make sure he included his remark in the minutes of
the meeting.

Ashton sighed. 'You must read the newspapers, Rowan.
There's no way you can deter these people. Hezbollah, Hamas
or Islamic Jihad – at this stage of the operation they consider
themselves already dead.'

Ashton left the conference room and rang the Cabinet Office
on the secure speech facility in his office. After identifying
himself, he told the Deputy Secretary who took the call that the
SIS Threat Assessment Team had a number of recommendations to make and he would therefore be grateful if Sir Victor
would get in touch with him when an opportunity arose. Five
minutes later Hazelwood was on the line.

Raja Usman picked up the remote and put the TV set on
standby. Thanks to the six thirty evening news on ITV there
was no need to wonder what had happened to the Varvesi
brothers now. They had been paid the equivalent of £18,000
in US dollars for the first consignment. But they had proved
themselves to be greedy men and they had taken money to
smuggle asylum seekers into England.

By their actions they had forewarned the enemy but nothing
could stop Islamic Jihad. He looked at his companions, Ibrahim
Ali and the two cousins, Mohammed Jadan and Hamad Nasif,
whom the harlot Sheridan knew as Emile. He could rely on
them to see it through but with so few men it would take longer
to assemble the launcher and load the missiles into the tubes.
And they would take much more than ten minutes to reload
after the initial salvo because they would be handling the new
improved version of the long rocket, which increased the range
from twelve miles to over twenty and was therefore heavier. No
matter, they would start their preparations earlier and he would
put out a sentry armed with a Kalashnikov AK-47 to hold off
the enemy.

Meantime, stealth must be the watchword. He would phone the other members of his group and order them to disperse, that especially applied to the third member of the Emile team. He had collected the information the harlot had left in the public library and had been most at risk and was perhaps being followed. Unless Emile was warned off there was a danger he might lead the enemy to Deep Hollow. The deception plan Emile had masterminded had been destroyed by events outside Usman's control. The chemical strike against London was to have been the first of many all over the UK and the harlot Sheridan had been suborned because it was essential to know what counter measures British Intelligence had put in place to make further attacks extremely hazardous. Unfortunately the discovery of a quantity of VX agent in Kimberley Road, the stupidity of Mullah Aziz al Bashir and the greed of the Varvesi brothers had ensured there could only be this one strike.

Usman went over the points he wished to make in his mind, then addressed his companions. He was the sort of leader men would follow anywhere and he had their undivided attention.

The Threat Assessment Team assembled again at 19.30 hours, immediately after Hazelwood returned from the emergency session of the Joint Intelligence Committee under the chairmanship of the Cabinet Secretary. The Government, he informed them, had approved their recommendation following a series of telephone conversations with ministers who were out and about stomping the hustings in what was the final run-up to polling day.

'Five will be running the operation with Special Branch. This means Colin Wales will exercise command jointly with the Deputy Assistant Commissioner responsible for Special Branch. We are to provide two observation parties, each consisting of a leader, driver and one relief. They are to operate within the sector we've been given, which is just north of the M25 between Waltham Abbey and Potters Bar.' Hazelwood turned to Ashton. 'Do you have any problems with that, Peter?' he asked.

'No. One party will be led by Will Landon, the other by Chris Neighbour.'

'Then you won't be surprised to hear that you will be in charge of our sector; Richard Neagle will be your liaison officer from MI5. Everybody is to be in position and operational by 06.00 hours.'

The observation parties were to be armed purely for self-defence; when the terrorists were located it was to be clearly understood that the police would deal with them. The ops room was to be manned by Hugo Calthorpe until 08.00, when Rowan Garfield would take over for the next twelve hours. This shift system was to be carried out by the other heads of departments until 20.00 hours on the Sunday, when Roy Kelso was to hold the fort until two hours before first light on Monday.

'I'm afraid that's when you come on again, Hugo,' Hazelwood said. 'If the terrorists are still at large by then, the politicians are going to be very unhappy, which is why Jill and I must be free to answer their distress calls.' He paused, then said, 'If there are no questions, that's it, everybody.'

Ashton assumed Victor had included Jill because people like Garfield and Kelso were bound to question why she had been left off the roster.

As he was about to follow the others out of the conference room, Hazelwood signalled him to remain behind.

'What's the latest on the Varvesi brothers? he asked when they were alone.

'They're still claiming they know nothing about a previous consignment. When asked what they would have done when they discovered there was no A to Z Builders' Merchant they said they had the consignees' phone number.'

'And?'

The number they gave the police is genuine but they can't raise the owner. British Telecom has given them a name but the mobile is one of those pay-as-you-go options and the address doesn't check out.'

Each rocket weighed 170 pounds and was 10 feet 7 inches in length. One salvo of 40 rockets totalled 7 tons, and with one man out on sentry, it was clearly impossible for the other three to collect the 122mm rocket from the various farm buildings and reload the tubes in ten minutes. Usman had therefore decided to position the second salvo within easy reach of the fire position he had selected.

As soon as it was dark, Raja Usman led his group into what had once been the kitchen garden but was now overgrown with couch grass and weeds. In addition to the two duvets that had been taken off the beds, they had a couple of spades and a small coal shovel between them. Usman took one of the spades and marked out the pit he wanted dug and then set them to work.

They cut the turf into sods approximately six inches deep and carefully stacked them on one side. Thereafter the soil they dug out was tipped on to a duvet. When it was half full, two men picked up the duvet and carried the earth over to the hedgerow separating the kitchen garden from the six-acre field beyond. Using the coal scuttle the earth was carefully distributed under the hedge where it wouldn't be seen from the air. Meanwhile the two diggers dumped the soil they were excavating into the second duvet.

There was no let-up. Nobody took a rest, spoke a word, smoked a cigarette. By 02.00 hours the pit had been completed to Usman's specifications and was 20 feet long by 11 feet wide by 2 feet deep. That done, they filled the pit two deep with forty rockets and replaced the sod. First light was breaking when they trooped back indoors totally exhausted.

The relief man on Landon's team was Staff Sergeant Lomas of the Royal Marines, who was the weapons and close-quarter combat instructor at Amberley Lodge, the SIS Training School outside Petersfield. His driver happened to be Eric Daniels, the former sergeant in the Military Police, who knew a thing or two about clandestine operations. One man could put twelve rounds into a playing card at fifty yards with a 9mm Browning semi-automatic pistol, while the other could reverse a Ford Granada into a space only marginally wider than the car with his foot hard down on the accelerator. Landon consoled himself that he was pretty good at reading the ground from a map.

The subsector he'd been given lay between Potters Bar and Cheshunt, both of which were urban areas. South of a line drawn between two locations there was a narrow strip of open, flat countryside that stretched as far as the M25. There was, however, precious little cover in which to hide a vehicle-mounted rocket launcher and eighty missiles for any length of time. Ideally you needed a largish house with outbuildings on the edge of a hamlet populated with people who kept themselves to themselves. The only place that remotely measured up to this requirement was Goff's Oak. From there Euston, St Pancras and King's Cross were just out of range from the BM-21 rocket system.

Landon chose to keep Goff's Oak under observation because he had begun to wonder if he hadn't exaggerated the terrorists' intentions. How many deaths constituted a national disaster? Put a salvo down anywhere in North London when people were on their way to work and you were bound to kill several hundred.

Even from the map Landon could see getting into position was going to be a nightmare; on the ground it would look even worse. In the end he abandoned the shift system and sent Lomas to watch Goff's Oak from the north while he stayed south of the hamlet. He dispatched Daniels to Potters Bar itself with instructions to find somewhere inconspicuous where he could lie up until needed. To keep in touch with one another they would use their own mobile telephones, which were not affected by range as was the transceiver Landon had drawn from the stores. Whether Ashton fully understood when he reported how they were deployed on the ground was questionable; operating at extreme range Landon had to repeat everything twice because the transmission kept breaking up.

It started raining at ten past nine and kept it up on and off all day.

Ashton unwrapped a piece of chewing gum and popped it into his mouth. Waiting for something to happen was always the worst part and he had done plenty of waiting in his time. Boredom wasn't the only thing to take the edge off vigilance; it was amazing how tired you became just sitting still doing nothing. He listened to the rain drumming on the roof of the car and pictured Will Landon out there lying under a hedgerow, getting soaked to the skin. He and Richard Neagle didn't know when they were well off: they had a roof over their heads, and were parked next to the Wheat Sheaf. Beer and sandwiches on tap; his eyes began to droop.

'What brings Colin here?' Neagle said.

The adrenaline started pumping and jerked Ashton back from the edge of sleep.

'We'll know soon enough,' he grunted.

A Rover 600 made a wide sweeping turn in the near-deserted car park and drew up on their right, allowing Wales to transfer to their Ford Mondeo without getting soaked in the process.

'Stealth is out of favour,' Wales told them enigmatically. 'Noise is now top of the pops with the politicians.'

'Can we have that in plain English?' Ashton asked.

'It means there will be lots of helicopters buzzing around all day tomorrow under the guise of a military exercise.'

The troops would be based on the garrison town of Colchester. Lynx and Gazelle helicopters would carry out reconnaissance missions to locate the terrorists' hideout. Three assault teams from 22 SAS would be at two minutes' notice to be air-lifted in by Pumas. To maintain the illusion that it was purely a military exercise, TV news programmes would show elements of 6 Airborne Brigade landing on the Thetford training area.

'This means we will pull out after dark tonight,' Wales continued. 'But the show won't be over for us because we'll be staying at the Roman Road barracks in Colchester. If the terrorists haven't been found by six o'clock on Sunday evening, we are back in business. Any questions?'

'Yes. What are the administrative arrangements?'

'No need to worry on that score, Peter. The army will be looking after us.'

Wales started to get out of the car, then had a last-minute thought. 'Where did your chap get the idea that the maximum range of the BM-21 was a fraction over twelve miles?'

'From the handbook on armour and artillery,' Ashton said.

'He must have been looking at an out-of-date version then. Experts from the School of Artillery have just finished inspecting the missiles and they say the munitions are an uprated version with a range in excess of twenty miles.'

Raja Usman got to his feet, rolled up the prayer mat and left it on the chair by the bed together with a copy of the Koran, then went downstairs. He ached in every limb and had slept badly for no other reason than that he, like the others, had been overtired. Today he could afford to let them rest because they were ready. They had worked through the night using the small vehicle-mounted crane to lift the launcher on to the flat-bed truck and bolt it down in the correct position. They had then collected the forty rockets that had been hidden under sacking in the wartime Nissen hut, and loaded them into the tubes.

The truck with its lethal cargo was tucked away inside the barn, which the previous owner of the farmhouse had kept in a reasonable condition, unlike the other outbuildings. All they had to do on Monday was open the barn doors, drive the truck into the kitchen garden and position the launcher over the small metal spike he'd planted in the grass. The launcher would then be traversed manually through 140 degrees and elevated from 0 to 45 degrees. The salvo would be fired electrically by remote control. The blast effect would, of course, shatter every pane of glass in the house and do the same for the truck, but this was of no consequence.

He heard the noise of the helicopter in the distance and judged it to be heading in their direction. Reacting instinctively, Usman ran into the hall and called to the others upstairs to keep away from the windows.

'We have no reason to suppose the infidels are looking for us,' he yelled. 'All they will see is a car parked outside a farm-house.'

The helicopter passed overhead, then continued on its way, the noise of the rotor gradually fading into the distance until it was inaudible. It was the first of many helicopters they heard that day but the noise no longer alarmed them. Listening to the radio, Usman learned that a big military exercise was going on in the area. By early evening all the TV channels were showing pictures of paratroopers roping down from large troop carriers.

Although Daniels was the only member of the team who hadn't been soaked through to the skin on Saturday, Landon was prepared to forgive him. First thing in the morning Daniels had taken him back to his flat in Stanhope Gardens and waited outside until he had showered and changed into clean clothes. Lomas, being a marine, had, of course, packed a change of clothing, which he'd left in the boot of the Ford Granada.

It was getting on for two o'clock in the afternoon when Landon and Daniels returned to Roman Road barracks in Colchester. There had been one development in their absence. The Varvesi brothers had been persuaded that it was no use pretending they hadn't delivered a previous consignment to the A to Z Builders' Merchant. Faced with a long term of imprisonment, they had caved in.

'The first consignment was delivered to a wartime airfield two miles east of Sawbridgeworth,' Ashton told them. 'The place has been visited but nothing was there apart from a lot of sheep. If there is no result by 18.00 hours Wales will deploy his people on a line from Bishop's Stortford southeast to Basildon. We get the interesting bit from Ware to Sawbridgeworth.'

'Interesting?' Landon queried. 'What does he mean by that?'

'It means the area has been overflown many times today. Colin doesn't believe anything is there.' Ashton gave him a map template. 'This is your area, Will.'

'And where will you be?'

'I'm setting up shop in Sawbridgeworth. As you will see from the map we have extended the operational area northwards by eight miles to take into account the increased range of upgraded missiles.'

'I had noticed,' Landon said quietly.

'I might have guessed you would. The SAS assault teams will be at a lesser degree of notice tonight but they will be back on two minutes at dawn.'

There was nothing they could do now except wait. At six o'clock they were given the go-ahead and Landon headed out of Colchester on the A12, then switched to the A120 at Marks

Tey and motored on through Bishop's Stortford. Three miles further on, he left the trunk route and headed south. While it was still daylight, Landon quartered his sector in the Ford Granada. It was hard to believe they were only a few miles from London; the undulating countryside was crisscrossed with sunken lanes and tall hedgerows. In winter, when the trees were bare and nightfall came early, the land would look forbidding.

The place Landon was seeking would be a largish house with outbuildings on the edge of a small hamlet; he believed he had found it at Deep Hollow.

Leaving the immediate area they headed north and managed to find a big enough passing space in the narrow sunken lane where they could leave the car, then waited until it was dark before returning to Deep Hollow on foot.

Raja Usman arose just before dawn. He washed, put on clean clothes and prepared to lead his fellow believers in prayers. It would be better done by a mullah – even Aziz al Bashir would be welcome, except he would make such a noise he would rouse half the countryside. Aziz was a danger to himself and others. There had been no harm in him while he concerned himself with finding soldiers for Islam amongst the indigenous population and sending them off to training camps in Libya and Afghanistan. He had become dangerous to know when he became ambitious and decided to form his own group. Recruiting that chemistry graduate to produce low-grade VX, inveigling Islamic fundamentalists in Lancashire to steal whisky bottles from a factory yard to hold the liquid agent, and renting a lock-up garage in which to store the stuff; then having no idea what to do with the gas! Folly, pure folly.

Usman put all thought of Aziz al Bashir out of his mind and called the others to prayer. At five forty-five, he put Ibrahim Ali out on sentry to watch the sunken road that ran past the farmhouse. Then, ordering Jadan and Nasif to load their

Kalashnikovs, he led them over the barn. On his signal they opened the doors; completely unruffled Usman walked into the barn, climbed inside the cab and switched on the ignition. He paused for just a moment to offer another prayer in his mind, then cranked the engine into life.

Up on the high ground above the farmhouse, Landon heard an engine start up and was suddenly wide awake, his pulse racing. They had split the night into three shifts and he should never have dozed off because less than three hours had passed since he had relieved Daniels on watch. The trouble was, his brain hadn't allowed him to sleep a wink when he had been off duty. One question had haunted Landon all night long: what if he had got it wrong? He was the man who'd identified the probable target and had convinced the SIS Threat Assessment Team he was right. He had also persuaded his superiors that the multiple rocket launcher was almost certainly located to the north of London within a twelve-to-twenty-mile radius of the target area. What if he had picked the wrong target and the missile system was somewhere else on the periphery of London?

As he watched, a flat-bed truck nosed its way out of the barn below to his left and headed towards the overgrown garden behind the farmhouse. In that same instant all the niggling doubts that had plagued him were stilled; directly behind the driver's cab were forty missile tubes locked in the horizontal or travelling position. Still keeping the vehicle under observation, Landon grabbed the two-way radio he'd placed within reach and drew it towards him. Pressing the transmit button, he said, 'Zero, this is one. Target, target, target. Farmhouse edge of Deep Hollow grid reference 941823. Over.'

A lifetime seemed to pass before Ashton came up on the air and acknowledged his call. By that time the flat-bed had stopped moving and was facing the farmhouse. Two men armed with Kalashnikov AK-47s left the barn and ran across the open ground towards the vehicle. As they did so, the driver jumped down from the cab and, opening a box attached to the base of the launcher, began to extend a cable.

'That must be a remote control.'

Landon glanced to his left and saw that Daniels and Lomas had joined him. The two men who had come from the barn had already elevated the missile tubes and were now traversing the launcher manually.

'That man who's paying out the cable,' Landon said quietly, 'how far away do you reckon he is, Staff?'

'Sixty yards minimum,' Lomas told him.

'Try and put him down, Staff. Looks to me as if they don't intend to wait for the rush hour to peak.'

Lomas thumbed the hammer back on the Browning 9mm, pushed the safety catch to fire, then raised himself up on both elbows and taking aim, squeezed off three shots in quick succession. The two men on the launcher unshouldered their Kalashnikovs and raked the high ground with automatic fire, forcing Landon's team to duck below the crest.

'Did you get him, Staff?' Landon yelled.

'I don't know.'

The two men continued firing even though they had nothing to aim at. Short bursts of five to six rounds furrowed the crest-line and knocked small lumps of earth into the air. Every now and again a bullet would clip a stone just beneath the surface and ricochet, making an angry whine as it was deflected.

Daniels said, 'I think they're coming for us. Break to your right.'

Landon didn't argue with him. There was virtually no interval between the thump of a Kalashnikov being discharged and the crack made by a bullet passing low overhead, which meant the terrorists were too damned close for comfort. Backing away from the crest, Landon got to his feet and, like a crab, scuttled sideways as fast as he could while keeping his eyes on the skyline. He was almost opposite the farmhouse when one of the terrorists appeared head and shoulders above the crest. It was the first time Landon had been involved in a fire fight and it was an inbred instinct for survival rather than any training he'd received that triggered his reaction. He pulled the slide back to chamber a round, thumbed the safety catch to fire and, holding the Browning 9mm semi-automatic pistol in a double-handed grip, fired a shot after shot at the terrorist. From a range of no more than twenty feet he could hardly miss. Hit in the chest, throat, mouth and right eye, the gunman was lifted off his feet by the combined impact and sent tumbling backwards down the slope.

The battle was still a long way from over. Responding to a nudge from Daniels, Landon glanced to his left in time to see Lomas bob up like a jack-in-the-box and take a snap shot at the second terrorist. Before fire could be returned, he went to ground again and rolled a couple of yards or so to his right. Moments later Lomas popped up again, squeezed off another shot, then went down and rolled over and over to the left until he was beyond his initial fire position.

'Sooner or later Lomas is going to run out of luck,' Daniels said.

'Then we'd better outflank that bastard on the forward slope before he does.' Landon applied the safety catch on the Browning, then pointed to the crest. 'Straight up and over. Right?'

'Do what I do,' Daniels told him. 'Go fast, dive over the crest and start rolling.'

Using his left arm as a support, Landon raised himself up and got into position like a sprinter getting set for the 100 metre dash. He took off, body leaning forward, legs pumping like pistons. Five strides brought him within a yard of the crest. Still keeping low, he dived head first over the brow, hit the ground the other side and started rolling. Earth and sky kept changing places and somehow in the process, Landon managed to poke himself in the face with his pistol. When he stopped rolling, blood was pouring from his nose. He had fetched up close to the sidewall of the farmhouse. Daniels was to his left, halfway down the forward slope and roughly ten yards from where he was. The second gunman had started to retreat towards the farmhouse when he and Daniels opened fire on him. As the terrorist swung round to face them, Lomas stood bolt upright and nailed the man with a single shot to the head.

Landon got to his feet and, using the side wall as cover, moved forward towards the barn. The multiple rocket launcher was out of sight but he could see the terrorist who had been extending the remote control cable. The man was sitting on the ground trying to apply a crude tournique above a shattered kneecap when Lomas put four more rounds into him.

'It's over,' Lomas shouted triumphantly.

But it wasn't. A fourth terrorist appeared from the other side of the farmhouse and ran towards the remote control behind the launcher, firing burst after burst in a vain attempt to keep their heads down. He was still a good ten yards from the remote control when Lomas and Daniels cut him down.

It is over now, Landon thought, and slumped down utterly spent, his back resting against the outside wall. Away in the distance he could hear a helicopter.

Chapter 27

The polling booths had been open a good two hours when Ashton turned into Bisham Gardens and parked the Mini he'd borrowed outside Jill Sheridan's house. A preconceived idea of the sort of reception he would get lived up to his expectations when she came to the door.

'I wonder you've got the nerve to show your face,' Jill snarled. 'Why don't you crawl back under the stone you came from?'

'Aren't you going to invite me in?' he asked quietly.

'Go to hell,' she told him, and would have closed the door in his face if he hadn't stuck a foot in the jamb.

'Listen, I don't like this any more than you do but it has to be done.'

'And you volunteered for the job.'

'As matter of fact I did.'

'You bastard.'

'Just back off and let me into the hall. Or would you prefer to see Roy Kelso on your doorstep because it is his job? And you know how much he would love to humiliate you.'

Jill turned her back on him and walked away. Stepping inside the hall, he closed the door and followed her into the drawing room.

'Let's get this over as quickly as possible,' Jill said. 'I don't want to spend a minute longer in your company than is strictly necessary.'

'Whatever you wish.' Ashton unzipped the thin black leather briefcase he was holding, and took out some papers. 'This is your letter of resignation on the grounds of ill health. Sign it and you will receive a year's salary tax free plus a modified pension. You are also required to sign two copies of the Official Secrets Acts.'

'Like hell I will.'

'You've no option,' Ashton said, and offered her a Biro.

'You're loving this, aren't you?' Snatching the pen from him, she signed the letter of resignation and both official forms. 'Really loving it.'

'You're wrong.'

'Balls. You're the man who pulled the plug on me.'

'You did that to yourself and I'm not referring to the porn movie, though it scarcely helped your career. Naked ambition was the root cause of your fall from grace. There wasn't anything you wouldn't do to promote yourself. With a little more patience you would have gone right to the top and succeeded Victor when he finally retired. You had the ability and the time was ripe for you . . .'

'And now you think I'm finished.'

Ashton picked up the papers he needed and slipped them in the briefcase. He was tempted to remind Jill that she was, as far as the SIS was concerned, but he held his tongue. Instead he wished her good luck and offered his hand but she wouldn't take it.

'You think I'm finished,' Jill repeated as she followed him into the hall. 'Well, let me tell you something, Ashton. You haven't heard the last of me.'

'I'm sure we haven't,' he said, and walked out of the house.